KU-493-391

A Letter from America

993785213 7

A Letter from America

Geraldine O'Neill

W F HOWES LTD

This large print edition published in 2016 by
W F Howes Ltd
Unit 5, St George's House, Rearsby Business Park,
Gaddesby Lane, Rearsby, Leicester LE7 4YH

1 3 5 7 9 10 8 6 4 2

First published in the United Kingdom in 2015
by Poolbeg Press Ltd

Copyright © Geraldine O'Neill, 2015

The right of Geraldine O'Neill to be identified as
the author of this work has been asserted by her
in accordance with the Copyright, Designs and
Patents Act, 1988.

All rights reserved

A CIP catalogue record for this book is available
from the British Library

ISBN 978 1 51003 451 8

Typeset by Palimpsest Book Production Limited,
Falkirk, Stirlingshire

Printed and bound in Great Britain
by TJ International Ltd, Padstow, Cornwall

MIX
Paper from
responsible sources
FSC
www.fsc.org   FSC® C013056

A Letter From America
is dedicated
in loving memory
of my dear friend,
MARGARET LAFFERTY

In our letters we are recollecting
And conversing with the soul,
Through both our friends
And ourselves.

~ THOMAS MOORE ~

CHAPTER 1

Tullamore, County Offaly

October 1968

Fiona Tracey stood beside the walnut kidney-shaped dressing-table situated in the bedroom window, her eyes following the postman on the other side of Crow Street. He leant his bike up against the wall of Dr Lafferty's house and then pushed a bundle of brown and white envelopes through the polished brass letterbox. He came back to his bike and postbag and continued onwards along the street, stopping at a solicitor's office and then the bookshop, pausing to push more post in doors and speak to anyone who came in his path. She watched, knowing that he would go on another forty yards or so, and then he would cross over and come down their side of the street.

She wasn't expecting anything in the post for herself, as she had already received her weekly letter from her friend Elizabeth McCormack in New York so there would be nothing more until next week. Elizabeth had promised, when she'd left Tullamore the previous year to take up a position in the kitchen of a big apartment in Park Avenue, that she would write every week. She had kept her promise. Sometimes it was a big long rambling letter telling Fiona about the latest dance she had been to, or the latest frock she had bought, and other times it was just a postcard.

On Monday an unusual red postcard had arrived with a picture of the Brooklyn Bridge and the Empire State Building, and a caption which said, *New York, The Wonder City*. On the back were a quick few lines – *Been very busy, as we're getting ready to go to the family's big holiday house in The Hamptons for a week. Will write a long letter with all the news from there next week. God bless, Elizabeth x*

Still in her dressing-gown, Fiona went out into the corridor to go the bathroom and clean her teeth. She caught the smell of the morning bacon cooking downstairs and could hear her mother and Mrs Mooney, the housekeeper, talking in the kitchen, and then she heard her father coming in the back door. The rattling of iron told her he had carried in a basket of turf and was now raking the huge range in the kitchen. She would go downstairs in a few minutes when she knew the fire had livened up and the breakfast was ready to go on the table.

When she came back into her bedroom, she lifted the two pillows from the bed and laid them on the chair in front of the dressing-table, then she straightened the white sheets and the grey Foxford woollen blankets. She replaced the pillows and pulled the lace counterpane up over them. Then she went around the bed, smoothing the top cover with her hands, making sure there were no wrinkles or small bumps.

Mornings had settled back into the usual routine now her two younger sisters – Angela aged twenty-two and Bridget seventeen – had gone back to their respective places in Dublin and near Athlone. Outside the holiday periods there was only herself and her parents left in the family Georgian house on the edge of Tullamore town in the Irish Midlands. It was a busy household which centred on running Tracey's bar and grocery shop just a few minutes' walk away. The start of the day was marked by the arrival of their widowed house-keeper, Mary Ellen Mooney, around eight o'clock, and from then on, Fiona and her parents – Seán and Nance – went between the shop and the bar and the house as they were needed.

Fiona was not unhappy about this. She got on well with her parents and their barman. At one point after leaving school she had considered options such as working in an office or bank, but decided that working for her father allowed her the flexibility that another employer would never have allowed. Living at home saved money and enabled her to run her grey Austin Mini, which gave her the independence to take off to places like Galway or Dublin with her friends.

But the main thing that kept her going with the

predictable daily routine was that she knew it was not going to last forever. She had other plans for the future.

She moved over to sit at the dressing-table and brush her wavy brown hair. Then she heard the clang of the wrought-iron gate. Footsteps echoed from downstairs going across the hall floor, and she knew by the lively tapping of the heels that it was her mother. The steps came back to the bottom of the stairs.

'An airmail letter for you, Fiona!' her mother called.

'I'm coming!' she replied, already moving towards the bedroom door.

She went down the stairs quickly.

Her mother handed the letter over with a smile. 'I knew that would get you moving.'

Fiona was more than surprised to see that the handwriting was Elizabeth's. The New York postmark was dated only two days after the one on the postcard.

'I don't know how Elizabeth has so much time on her hands,' her mother remarked, 'to write all these long letters to you. Does she write to many others in the town?'

Fiona shrugged, still examining the envelope, and putting off the actual opening of it until she was on her own. 'I suppose she writes home to her family regularly.'

'There are sausages and rashers cooked and in the oven, if you're planning to have breakfast in your dressing-gown?'

'Great,' Fiona said. 'I'm ready for it now. I'll get dressed after eating as I want to have a quick bath.'

This was a small bone of contention with her mother who always arrived downstairs washed and dressed in the mornings. Nance Tracey was ready for the shop in her maroon twinset and black skirt, with a long string of polished black beads. Just turned fifty, small and slim, she always looked well for her age. Her brunette hair was set twice-weekly by the local hairdresser into a fashionable shoulder-length flicked-out style and then lacquered in place. Her pink-painted oval nails were maintained by always wearing rubber gloves for rough work at home and in the bar and shop.

As they were growing up, Nance had tried to ingrain in her three daughters just how much their appearance counted but, to her disappointment, only Angela had taken her advice seriously so far. Fiona was rather a hit and a miss, making the effort chiefly for the weekends and going out. The rest of the time she preferred to have her long wavy brown hair tied back for work, and wore the minimum of face cream and make-up.

'Well, don't take too long over things,' her mother said, heading back down the hallway to the kitchen. 'We have all the sweets and bars still in boxes and the hardware delivery should be arriving around ten o'clock. We need to get it all priced.'

Fiona stood in the hallway for a few moments,

pondering what might be inside the letter, and then she carefully opened it. She quickly started to read down.

Park Avenue
New York
12th October

Dear Fiona,

You won't believe it! Mrs Davis has just told me that you can have the nanny's job! She also said you can live in one of the staff rooms here beside me. It's exactly what I was praying for, and I can't believe it's actually happened!

The nanny is leaving after Christmas as she is expecting a baby, and Mrs Davis says she is going to write an official letter to you this week with all the information, so I thought I would write today to let you know, and get the letter away in the post this afternoon. It means you will have the news that bit sooner so you can start making arrangements.

I know it's nearly three months away but, believe me, the time flies when you have to sort out passports and all the official things. It will be far easier for you as you will have a job and an address to come to, as it's the first thing the immigration people ask you about.

I know you said you would be happy to

work in a shop or an office and get a room in a boarding-house, but living in the apartment here in Park Avenue with the family is the best situation you will ever get. It's a dream come true! I know how lucky I am from talking to other Irish girls I meet up with at the cathedral and at the dances. Some of them are in awful places with landladies who are very strict, and not nice to them.

As I've told you before, Mrs Davis is a lovely woman, and she has a great fondness for Irish girls. The children – Tommy, who is nearly one, and Page, who is three – are good and you will find them easy to look after.

I'm so delighted you will be coming to live beside me in New York. I keep smiling to myself every time I think of it, since Mrs Davis told me the news. It will be great to have a friend from home who knows everyone I know, and will know what I'm talking about. I love living in America, and I love my American boyfriend, but there are still times when I get homesick for Ireland. Having you here will change everything for the better. I won't say any more about the apartment, because you will see it with your own eyes soon. I will just say that you will love it.

Write back as soon as you can and let me know what you think of the news!

Love,

Elizabeth xx

CHAPTER 2

January 1969

Fiona stood on a chair and stretched up to the bar ceiling to reach the piece of Sellotape which held one end of a Christmas decoration, featuring a string of rainbow-coloured, honeycomb bells, made from tissue paper. She had just let the cardboard end fall concertina-like to the floor when the pub door opened and Patrick Trimm came in, followed by his father's plodding old Labrador, Sandy.

Patrick was the dependable barman, who had worked in the bar since he was a teenager with Seán Tracey. Heading towards forty now and still a bachelor, the stocky, auburn-haired Patrick lived in one of the bigger rooms above the pub, while the other three were rented out on a bed-and-breakfast basis to tourists and people visiting relatives in the town. Patrick's elderly parents lived in a cottage on the Arden Road in Tullamore, and he usually went out to stay with them on his day off.

'You should have waited for me to come in

and I'd have got that,' Patrick said now, coming over to Fiona. Sandy went slowly in the opposite direction, across the stone floor to lie down in his usual place in front of the fire. 'I can reach the decorations more easily and not have you stretching for them.'

'I'm grand,' Fiona said, climbing down. 'I don't mind doing it – we're quiet in the shop and my mother is there for the next hour before she and my father head up to Dublin. I think they're leaving just after lunch as he has a hospital check-up. He's up at the house now getting changed.'

Patrick looked at her. 'It's not anything serious – the hospital? I thought he was going up for a meeting with the brewers.'

Fiona shook her head. 'No, he said it's nothing really, just a check-up.' She indicated the decorations. 'Mam's been going on, saying that the tree and the decorations in the shop, the house and the bar have all to be down for tomorrow.'

'Today's the seventh of January,' Patrick said, 'so I suppose it's time to get them down. My mother took hers down last night.'

'There's no time limit on them as long as they don't come down *before* Little Christmas,' Fiona said, 'and that was only yesterday, but you know what my mother's like.' She gestured to the dangling decoration. 'I thought I'd make a start in here before we get busy later. There's a big card game on tonight, isn't there?'

'There is,' Patrick said. 'There's a crowd coming over from Portarlington for it.'

9

He took the chair from her and stood up on it to carefully peel off the Sellotape holding the other end of the decoration. It fluttered down onto the floor. Fiona bent and gathered all the coloured tissue shapes together, neatly folding them back into one thick bell.

She went over and put it on the bar counter. 'If you get the decorations down from the ceiling, I'll dismantle the Christmas tree – if you can call it that.' She lifted the box for the glass baubles and took it over to the imitation tree which stood forlornly by the newly lit fireplace.

'What's it like?' she said, shaking her head and laughing. 'I told Daddy we needed a new tree and new lights and baubles, but he said we'd get another year out of them. He said the same last year – and no doubt will say the same next year. The same old decrepit tree and the same old decrepit ornaments hanging on it. Thank God I won't be here to see it again.'

She started lifting the baubles off one by one and placing them in the box.

Patrick brought a chain of paper lanterns over to the counter. 'How long is it now until you go?'

'Eleven days – Saturday the eighteenth.'

'Are you all packed yet?' he asked.

'More or less,' she said.

'It's a big step, mind you, New York.' He observed her closely. 'No second thoughts?'

Fiona shook her head and smiled. 'None. I'm

really excited about going. Obviously I'll miss everybody – you and Mrs Mooney included.'

Patrick's face reddened. 'Ah, you'll be grand – you'll be too busy to miss anyone.'

'Well, I'll have Elizabeth out there so at least I won't be too homesick. And I'll be writing home regularly, keeping in touch with everyone.' She lifted a green ball sprinkled in hard, silvery snow and put it in the box.

'I'd say they'll still miss you. Sure, they probably miss Bridget and Angela when they go back after a break at home.'

Everyone who came into the shop was telling Fiona how much her parents would miss her, but she really did not want to hear it. She didn't want to picture her parents sad about her going.

'They're busy with here and the shop. When I'm all settled in a year or two they might even come out to visit me. It will give them something to look forward to.'

'I suppose that's a good way of looking at things,' he said. 'And travelling is a great thing.'

'You go over to England every year, don't you?'

'I do,' he said. 'I usually go to over to Manchester for a fortnight to see my brothers and I always enjoy it. And then they come home in the summer themselves to see my mother and father.'

'And do you think any of them might come back home to live?'

He shook his head. 'Ah, I'd doubt that now.

They're all married over there to Englishwomen and have kids and everything.'

It was just on the tip of her tongue to ask whether he had ever thought of getting married himself, when one of the coloured glass baubles slipped out of her grasp and tumbled down through the sparse branches of the tree. A second later it smashed on the stone floor, sending fragments of glass all over the place.

'Damn it!' she said, throwing her hands in the air in exasperation. 'That's another one gone. There's a few already missing out of this box.'

'I'll get the brush and shovel,' Patrick told her, heading towards the back of the bar.

By the time he came back Fiona thought that the glass decoration falling had in fact been a good thing, as it had stopped her making the comment about him not being married. Although he was easy-going, behind it all Patrick was a shy sort of fellow and she thought that quizzing him about his personal life would only embarrass him. He wasn't the sort to pry into other people's business. She had been grateful when he made no comment about her breaking off her romance with Paul Moore recently. He had just nodded and said that she knew her own mind, even though Paul had been a regular customer in the bar and Patrick had often stood chatting with him. Other people – her friends and customers – had been more curious, and it had been uncomfortable explaining that the opportunity to go to New York was more alluring than any romance at this time in her life.

She was just packing away the two sets of lights when her mother came in wearing her heavy blue woollen coat and matching hat, and carrying her black leather handbag and gloves.

Nance Tracey put her bag down on a high stool and then looked around the bar, nodding in approval when she saw the packed boxes containing the Christmas stuff.

'Thank God it's all down for another year and we can get back to normal. Though there's still the parlour to be done.' She turned to Patrick. 'They can go back upstairs when you get a minute. Seán already took the tree from the shop window and the other bits and pieces up this morning so it's all clear in there too.'

'Do you want them back in the same cupboard they came out of, at the top of the stairs?' he asked.

'Yes, that's the best place for them.' Nance turned back to her daughter. 'I'm heading home now, Fiona, to get a quick bite of lunch with your father before we leave. I'll ask Mary Ellen to keep a plate warm for you. She cooked a good-sized ham with roast potatoes and there's plenty if you would like some too, Patrick.'

'Thanks, Mrs Tracey, but I'm grand,' he said. 'The mother will have something ready for me up the road.' He went over to the bar and started checking which of the Christmas boxes he would first take upstairs.

Nance pulled on her black suede gloves, then lifted her handbag from the high stool. 'Right, I'll be off.'

'What time will you be back this evening, Mam?' Fiona checked.

'I'm not sure.' She looked towards the door, slightly distracted. 'I think we're calling out to your Aunt Catherine after the hospital, but we won't stay too long.'

Fiona raised her eyebrows at this news, but said nothing since Patrick was still there. She was surprised to hear that her mother was going to see her Aunt Catherine, as they hadn't seen much of each other recently, even over Christmas. 'Are you seeing Angela, too?'

'Yes.' She gave a small sigh. 'She would be upset if we were up in Dublin and didn't go out to her.'

A look of weariness crossed her mother's face, and Fiona thought she seemed almost over-whelmed by the thought of having to see both her sister and daughter. She had seen that look on her mother's face a lot recently when her Aunt Catherine's name was mentioned. She guessed there was some kind of disagreement between the two sisters but, so far, her mother had said nothing about it. But that wasn't unusual – her mother was a very close person.

She wondered if her mother was embarrassed because Aunt Catherine's English husband had deserted her and their adopted son, Joseph, a few years before. Fiona and her sisters didn't know any details about when and how it had happened. It seemed that Uncle Kenneth had just one day disappeared back to England and not come back. It had been kept very quiet, and her mother didn't like the subject being raised.

She wasn't surprised at her mother's reticence about visiting Angela. They seemed to be on opposing sides about even the most trivial issue, and at times it caused an atmosphere when Angela was home. Fiona wondered why they clashed so much, because underneath it all they were actually very similar. They were both fussy about their appearance, their hair and clothes, and having everything just right.

At times, Fiona found it hard to fathom Angela herself. She knew of course it hadn't been easy for her sister spending half her life in hospitals in Dublin, and missing out on large chunks of their family life – but, as her mother said, nobody was to blame for that. Nobody could help what had happened to her. It was just the way life had turned out.

Nance Tracey checked her watch now. 'I rang Angela to say we were coming up and that we'd call to Leeson Street to see her on our way out to your Aunt Catherine's. We'll only stay for a quick cup of tea. She probably won't be too bothered as she only saw us last week, but it's best to keep the peace.'

'Well, tell her I'll write to her as soon as I'm settled in New York,' Fiona said. 'And tell Aunt

Catherine and Joseph that I'm asking for them too, and that I'll write to them as well.'

'I will,' her mother said. She paused. 'Oh, Fiona, I just thought . . .'

'What?'

'If you get time later, would you make a start on the Christmas tree in the parlour, please? Just the baubles and things – your father will carry the tree out to the back of the house when we get home.'

Fiona's heart sank at the thought of dismantling another Christmas tree.

'I doubt if I'll have the energy to do it by the time we get back home from Dublin,' her mother said. 'Dublin always takes it out of me – and I don't like to ask Mary Ellen. She's not able to stand on chairs to be reaching for things. I'd be terrified she'd have a fall. You're young and fit.' She looked straight at Fiona now and smiled. 'You've made such a great job clearing here, you'll do it in no time.'

Fiona decided it wasn't worth arguing over. 'Fine,' she said in a resigned voice. 'I'll have it all done when you get back.'

She shook her head in despair when the bell sounded as her mother closed the door behind her. Then, out of the corner of her eye, she saw Patrick smiling. She turned towards him. 'Don't dare say a thing.'

'You'll miss all this when you go away,' he said. 'You'll wish you were back here sweeping up all the broken Christmas decorations and gathering up the empty beer bottles. What girl wouldn't miss it?' He turned away, quietly humming 'Jingle Bells'.

She started to laugh in spite of herself.

CHAPTER 3

Angela put her key in the white-painted door of the Georgian house in Leeson Street and then slowly walked along the dimly lit hallway to the first door. In daylight, it was bright with the sun streaming through the fanlight above the door, but on a cold, early January evening with only one small ceiling lamp, it was dark and gloomy. She unlocked her room door and went inside. The room was chilly, with no one home all day to keep a fire going.

She went over to put her handbag and shopping bag down on one of the armchairs by the fireplace. Then she took off her coat and hat, her scarf and gloves. Her leg was painful and she needed to rest it now and take a couple of aspirins for the pain, but she had a few things to do first, before her mother and father arrived.

Resting her arm on the back of the chair for support, she looked around her large bedroom – or bedsit, as some of the other girls referred to it – checking that everything was as it should be. Her brown eyes moved over the mahogany wardrobe and dressing-table, the iron-framed bed draped with the white lace cover her aunt had given her, to the window with the heavy green satin curtains tied back with silk tassels. The fire was already set from that morning – a layer of rolled-up newspaper, firelighters placed carefully over that, then small pieces of wood topped by lumps of coal.

Her gaze moved across the room to the barley-twist, gate-leg, oak table where she ate her meals. Although it was small when folded up and standing against the wall, when extended it seated four. She kept two of the matching chairs at either side of the table, one near her wardrobe and the other for sitting at her dressing-table. On top of the table she had an old silver fruit bowl which was now filled with half a dozen hyacinth bulbs that were beginning to bloom. Looking at them made her smile as she thought of Georgie, the hospital gardener, who had dropped them into her office the day before. He had planted them in an old seed box and, as soon as Angela had got back home, she'd found the silver bowl and transferred them into it.

Everything else in the room looked presentable, and she was satisfied that it would pass her mother's scrutiny. As far as she was concerned, the room was as good as any of the bedrooms back home in Tullamore – and in some ways even better. Since she'd moved into the room in Leeson Street, she had constantly improved it, adding things like cushions and lace covers for the arms of the faded chairs and delicate lacework on the dressing-table. Before her parents arrived, she would freshen up her make-up and make sure her hair was perfect.

She went across the room to light the fire. She picked up the matches from behind the clock on the mantelpiece. As she bent down to touch the flame to a corner of the newspaper, she winced in pain. Her leg was sore today and she now regretted not having used her calliper when she was shopping. The usual vanity – not wanting to look conspicuous. It was the same when she was back home in Tullamore. She hated wearing it as it only drew attention to the difference between her and her two perfect sisters.

Her parents were due in just over an hour's time. It was a quick visit as she had seen them at home only the previous week, but they never came up to Dublin without seeing her. Not after the argument last year when she discovered her mother had come up for a day's shopping with her friend, Nora, and had not bothered to tell her. She had happened to be in Clery's department store in her lunch hour with a friend, when she bumped into the two women. Her mother had made light of it, but later that night Angela had gone out to the phone box at the end of the road and told her mother exactly how she felt about it.

'You could have the decency to let me know when you're coming up to Dublin instead of me bumping into you in the middle of Clery's. I'm sure there aren't many mothers from Tullamore who would come all the way up to Dublin without seeing their daughter, especially if they haven't seen her for over a month.'

'But I didn't know I was coming until last night and I had no way of letting you know,' her mother had said in a high, defensive voice.

'What was to stop you ringing the office and telling me this morning?'

'It was too early before I left to meet Nora and then we caught the train up to Dublin.'

'Well, you could have rung me from the phone box in the station when you arrived in Dublin,' Angela had argued. 'I'm quite sure if it had been Fiona or Bridget you would have made the effort to see them. I'm obviously not worth the effort.'

'Now that's absolute nonsense,' her mother had said. 'We go from term to term without seeing Bridget, and you know that. We see more of you than we do of her.'

'Daddy always makes the effort to see me when he's up in Dublin at the brewery meetings. He'd never come up to Dublin without seeing me.'

'Oh, Angela, you take things too personally!'

Her mother always said that.

'Okay,' Angela had said in a strained tone. 'Okay. I've said what I wanted to say. Let's leave it at that.'

Her mother had obviously listened, and since then been more careful about hurting her feelings, to the point of wariness.

The fire lit now, she hung her coat and scarf up

in the wardrobe, and put her hat on a shelf. She glanced in the wardrobe mirror and decided that the blue twinset, pearl necklace and navy skirt that she had worn to work were fine for this evening. She lifted her shopping bag over to the table and took out a bottle of fresh milk, a fruit loaf and a selection of four cakes which she knew her parents would like.

She then went back out along the corridor to the communal kitchen to make herself a cup of tea, to have with the aspirins. If she took them now, she reckoned, her leg wouldn't be so bad by the time they arrived. She could hear the sound of girls' voices and occasional laughter from upstairs, but when she reached the kitchen there was no one else around. She was relieved, as she preferred her own company for a while after being with people all day in work. The large kettle had recently been boiled, so she turned the electric ring on again and placed it back on top.

She lifted the smallest teapot and found it still had the old tea leaves inside it. No matter how many times this sort of thing was brought up at the meetings about housekeeping rules, there was always one of the girls who would leave their mess behind. She went to the bin to empty the tea leaves and then back to the sink to rinse the teapot.

How long, she thought, until she could have a normal house to live in? A place that was not a hospital or a hostel or a shared house. A place that was nothing to do with her own family, where she could come and go without everyone knowing her business.

A place that had nothing to do with polio.

She had contracted the disease when she was ten, and the episode had left her with a shorter, weaker and thinner left leg and a noticeable limp. Over the years she'd had a series of operations, and for months after each one she had to wear an iron calliper to strengthen and support the leg, along with specially made, awful-looking shoes. Between the operations, physiotherapy and the calliper, her leg had improved, but she had accepted that it would never be right. She knew she would always have trouble with it. She had managed without the calliper recently, but if her leg was still bad in the morning, she would have to wear the calliper to work. It was the only thing that really helped and yet she hated it.

She had too many memories of wearing it when she was a young girl, conscious of the noise the metal made as she walked along. Noticing that people turned to see where the noise was coming from, then quickly looked away when she came limping towards them. She often heard them whispering about her, saying how sad it was to see such a lovely-looking girl crippled.

It was only when she was with the other children from the hospital that she could forget about her damaged leg. After years of being in and out of hospital together, they no longer noticed how their withered arms or legs looked, seeing only the individual personalities. They shared the sadness of being separated from their families – isolated in the early stages of the illness, behind protective glass doors and windows. Not allowed a touch or a kiss from their families, for fear of spreading the deadly germ.

Her visitors were few, mainly her father, Aunt Catherine and Joseph – and occasionally her sisters or other relatives made a rare trip up to Dublin. There were often times when Angela felt disappointment in aunts and uncles who were too busy to think of their niece locked away in a ward in a hospital in Dublin, and in family friends who promised to come and never arrived. Usually, her disappointment was forgotten within hours of visiting time being over. But there was one visitor in particular that she always looked for . . . and whose absence she found harder and harder to forgive.

Her own mother.

As she grew older and understood more about her condition, she realised how lucky she was to have escaped so lightly, especially when she heard of other children and little babies who had actually died from polio when their breathing muscles were affected. She knew that whilst her leg would always be problematic, the operations and the physiotherapy had made a substantial difference to it. The leg had grown stronger and her walking had improved.

Angela had attended school with her sisters before her illness, and had advanced well beyond most of the others in her class in reading and writing and Irish. In hospital, she attended classes when she was well enough, and whilst the education wasn't the same or as consistent as being in a normal school, she managed to pick things up. During those years, she developed a love for reading, and so passed away the long hours confined in bed or sitting in corridors waiting to be seen by doctors or physiotherapists.

It was in hospital that some of the other children received their only education, made their First Communions. Some learned to sing and to play musical instruments – and those with good enough legs even learned Irish dancing. But the biggest lesson they learned was how to be independent and manage without the support of a family.

In between operations she went home. *Going home* was always the goal for most of the children. Every Christmas, Easter and summer, she looked forward to her father driving up to the hospital with her two sisters to collect her and take her back to her home in Tullamore. She would chat and laugh with the girls in the car, and they would tell her about things that had happened in school or about people she knew in the town.

But after a few years she noticed that she didn't know or remember some of the friends the girls were talking about – especially Fiona, who being older was in secondary school – and she didn't know the names of certain teachers in school that Bridget referred to.

Her father would always tell her funny stories about things that had happened in the shop or in the pub. But Angela noticed that he often repeated the same old stories that he thought would make her laugh. Especially the one about the customer who carried home half a stone of potatoes not noticing she had a hole in the bag, and only realising something was amiss when she got back to the house with an empty bag. Another story he repeated was about an elderly neighbour who had recently bought a car, and who, after starting up the engine, would jump out of the car and go to the middle of the road to check if there were any vehicles coming, then get back in again and drive off a minute or two later without looking again.

Angela didn't mind hearing the old stories again, because they reminded her of family life back at home, and she knew her father was being kind to her and trying to include her. She always felt relaxed on the journey home, as she and her sisters pointed things out from the car window, and passed bags of boiled sweets back and forth between them.

It was only as they reached Tullamore that she began to feel apprehensive. She never really knew why, but it always happened. Her stomach would churn and the palms of her hands would grow damp and clammy. Then, when she got out of the car in front of the house, there was the sound of the calliper as it hit the stone pavement. And, as she walked up the path to the house, she would try to remember what her mother looked like and how her voice sounded, so she was prepared when they met once again.

When she reached fifteen or sixteen, one of the teachers brought an electric typewriter into the hospital classroom. Angela was interested as they had an ancient manual typewriter on a desk at the turn of the stairs at home and she had often sat at it, painstakingly copying sentences from her books. The new modern typewriter looked lighter and much easier to use.

The older children were all given a go on it whilst the others gathered around watching from their wheelchairs. They took turns to move into the chair at the desk, laughing and mildly jeering each other as they searched for the letters which seemed to be scattered around the keyboard in no particular order. The teacher showed them how to hold down the key for capital letters and use the return button to move to a new line. She then asked them to try typing their own names, which took most of them three or four goes to get it right. After that, she set them the task of typing out the first verse of WB Yeats's poem *The Lake Isle of Innisfree*.

Angela was delighted as it was a poem she had in one of her poetry collections and had learned it off by heart. She said nothing when the teacher gave each of them a sheet with a copy of the poem. Then they all gathered around the chair as the first person sat down to have a go at typing it out, looking at her sheet and reading down through it before beginning to type.

I will arise and go now, and go to Innisfree,
And a small cabin build there, of clay and
wattles made; Nine bean rows will I have there,
a hive for the honey–bee, And live alone in the
bee-loud glade.

As the others took their turns at typing, Angela joined in with the encouraging comments, but her mind was still on the verse of poetry and the image that it conjured up. She loved the idea of the quiet and solitude in what she imagined was a beautiful setting, and she wondered then, as one of the girls banged away at the typewriter, if she would ever find a peaceful place in the future to call her own.

Within minutes the novelty of the typewriter and the exercise had worn off. Most of the boys had abandoned the task halfway through the verse – bored already – and some of the girls. The others plodded on with it but, by the end of the session, only Angela and another girl had shown any great interest in it.

It was only when the teacher showed surprise at Angela's aptitude for typing and her speed at finding the keys, that she confessed to already knowing the poem and having the old typewriter at home.

'It's still good,' the teacher said. 'It's not an easy skill to pick up.'

Later that afternoon, the typewriter disappeared along with the teacher, but months later another older woman who worked in the Polio Fellowship Office came in to talk to the current group in the hospital classroom about future careers. After she gave the general talk, which included information about training courses in areas that might suit some of the group, the woman spoke to individuals about particular courses they were interested in. When Angela approached her she gave her information about a course in shorthand and typing, saying she had heard from one of the teachers that she was a perfect candidate for the course.

A number of things had started to move quickly in Angela's life around that time. It had become apparent that the last operation on her leg and foot had made a good difference and had more or less finished all the treatment the hospital had to offer. She was seventeen now, and was mobile enough to become completely independent.

Her parents had made it plain that there was a home and work for her back in Tullamore. Her father had told her repeatedly that they would love her to work in the shop or bar, but going back to Tullamore was the last thing that Angela wanted. She had a good group of friends from her hospital days and she also had her Aunt Catherine and Joseph nearby.

All things considered, she preferred life in Dublin. She was used to the city, and couldn't imagine settling back down in a country town she had no real ties with, apart from her family. But, even at that young age, she knew that the decision she made now was going to have a big impact on her life.

Going home to Tullamore would be easier in many ways as everything would be organised for her. It would simply be a case of packing up her bags and moving back into the room she had used on her visits back home. She would not have to worry about the financial things that some of the other girls leaving the hospital were anxious about like lodgings, household bills and travel costs. Her parents would cover all that for her as they had done in all the years she had gone back and forth between Tullamore and Dublin.

If she went back she knew she would eventually get over the self-conscious feelings, and would settle into work in the shop and life in Offaly. She didn't know the people as well as her sisters, but she knew they were decent and would welcome her home. She took her time and gave the decision great thought, talking it over with one of the nuns who nursed in the hospital and whom she had known and trusted for a number of years. Then, one Monday morning she made her decision. In many ways she felt it was inevitable. Regardless of how difficult it was, she was going to stay in Dublin.

Within a few weeks it was organised that on her discharge from hospital she would move into a boarding house for young working women in

Leeson Street, and would attend a college in the city centre that ran the required courses.

It was only later, when she phoned home to tell her mother that she was leaving the hospital and moving to a new address, that she realised she had done all this without consulting her parents. It just had not occurred to her that she should.

Her parents were both shocked at her decision, and tried to get her to change her mind. Her father in particular tried to persuade her to come home and work in the shop, but she told him she had already accepted a place at college and that working in a city office was really all that she wanted to do. The phone calls home over the next few weeks were strained but gradually Angela realised that her decision had been accepted.

The shared house in Leeson Street had been fine and had helped her on the road to independence – and she had made good friends with some of the other girls – but she was hoping for a move to a better place sometime soon.

After she had washed and dried the teapot and spoon she had used, and put the milk jug back in the fridge, she came back down to her room with her mug of hot tea. She placed it on the small table beside her deep armchair and then went over to the shelf where she kept a biscuit tin, and took a digestive out of it. The tin – oval-shaped, with a picture of Victorian carol singers carrying lamps in the snow – had been given to her as a present from her Aunt Catherine when she was in hospital some years ago. She had received lots of gifts over the years at birthdays and Christmases, numerous biscuit and sweet tins which she hadn't bothered keeping. But something about this particular tin, the cosy, olde-worlde cover perhaps, had made her reluctant to throw it away.

She liked the fact that she was reminded of her Aunt Catherine every time she lifted the biscuit tin. She visited her aunt and her cousin Joseph out in Lucan every few weeks. She had always been closer to them than to the rest of the family, because her aunt had been so good to her during her hospital years.

Recently, she had become aware that there was a growing distance between her aunt and her mother. It was rare that Angela heard her aunt complain about anyone – especially their mother – but before Christmas her aunt had said that in the last year her sister wasn't phoning or ringing as often, and she was upset about it.

Angela said she had no idea why her mother wasn't keeping in touch, but she told her aunt that if she got the opportunity, she would tactfully broach the subject next time she was home.

Her Aunt Catherine had suddenly looked worried. 'No, Angela, it might be best if you don't say anything to your mother about it.'

'I won't say anything directly,' Angela had said. 'I won't say that we were talking about it. I was just going to say that I'd noticed she hadn't been in touch with you as much as before.'

'She'll guess we've been talking. She knows you visit me and Joseph regularly, and she'll put two and two together. She'll think I'm trying to come between you, and I don't want that.' She shook her head. 'No, Angela. It might make things worse. I know your mother, and I know how her mind works. She would never forgive me if she thought I'd tried to get you on my side, and I can understand it. I wouldn't like anyone to come between me and Joseph.'

Angela sat down in her chair now with her mug of tea, grateful for the ease to her leg and hip. The fire had caught on and the room was warming up. She swallowed down the aspirins and then sipped at the tea, thinking of the things she still had to do.

A short while later, she went over to get her cake-stand from the cupboard. Then she opened the fruit loaf and cut four slices from it and buttered them. She put the slices on the lower part of the cake-stand and then opened the box of fresh cream cakes: two meringues which her father liked, a chocolate éclair for her mother and a vanilla slice in case they fancied a change.

She began to move around the room more easily now, feeling the benefit of the tablets. She put more coal on the fire and brushed up any stray ashes, and then ran a damp cloth over the mantelpiece and generally tidied around. Then, as she viewed the perfect, warm room she felt herself beginning to relax.

She went over to the dressing-table mirror and

spent a few minutes brushing out her dark hair, and then powdering her face and refreshing her lipstick. She decided she looked okay, and then she thought how much warmer she was now. She unbuttoned the blue cardigan and took it off, then pulled the short-sleeved sweater over her head. She put them on a hanger and hung them in the wardrobe. They were fresh on this morning and she would get another wear out of them for work.

She then lifted another hanger out with a pale-yellow blouse with three-quarter sleeves and a loose tie-bow at the neck. She put it on and re-arranged her hair, then walked down the hallway to the kitchen to put the kettle on to boil and sort cups and saucers on a tray. She could hear voices and, when she got to the door, she saw two of the other girls who lodged in the house – Jeanette and Maureen, both of whom worked in The Bank of Ireland head office. They were chatting whilst heating up a pan of soup.

'Hi, Angela,' Maureen said. 'We were thinking of going to the cinema tomorrow night, if you fancy coming.'

Angela thought for a moment. She had nothing planned. 'What are you going to see?'

'*Madame X*,' Jeanette told her. 'We saw it before but it's brilliant. Have you seen it?'

'Yes,' Angela said, 'but it's worth seeing again. What time are you going?'

'It's on at eight, so if we leave around half seven?'

'Great,' she said. 'Give me a knock when you're

passing the door.' She went over to the cupboard. 'I'm just sorting a tray now as my mother and father are due shortly and I want to be ready for them.'

Jeanette rolled her eyes. 'Sure, you're always ready, Angela. You must be the best-organised person I know.'

'You can't know too many people then,' Angela laughed.

She put the cooled-down kettle back on to boil again, then got the tea caddie and spooned tea leaves into an empty pot and put it to the side.

'If anyone comes in,' she told the girls, 'tell them not to touch that.'

Maureen glanced out into the hallway. 'You'd be better to hide it in the cupboard,' she said in a low voice. 'That one in room five will use anything that's left out. She took Jeanette's last KitKat the other night.'

'A KitKat!' Jeanette said, shaking her head and laughing.

'It doesn't matter what it was,' Maureen said. 'She shouldn't have touched it. She denied it of course, but she was seen walking along the corridor eating it. It's the last time I leave expensive chocolate biscuits in the kitchen.'

Angela rolled her eyes. Petty things like that happened in the house, and it was one of the reasons she wished she had her own place. She chatted to the girls for a few minutes while she sorted the tea things on the tray and then took them back to her room.

Everything ready and waiting, she went to stand

by the window, watching for her father's car to pull up outside so she could get out of her room and out to the main door to let them in. As soon as she saw the car, she moved as quickly as she could.

When she opened the front door, her mother was standing there, holding a cakebox double the size of the one that Angela had brought back from the shop, and she had a bag with magazines dangling from her arm. She put the cardboard box up on the arm carrying the magazines, put the other around Angela's shoulder and gave her a peck on the cheek.

'We're a bit later than we thought – the traffic was busy on the quays,' she said. She gave a shiver. 'And it's freezing out as well. I wouldn't be a bit surprised if it snowed.'

'As long as you got here safe and sound,' Angela said. She held the heavy outside door open. 'I've got a good fire on so the room is nice and warm.'

Her mother came into the hallway first. 'You should get back inside, and put a cardigan on. You're only wearing a light blouse – you'll catch your death of cold.'

'I'm fine,' Angela said. 'I took my cardigan and sweater off because it was too warm in the room.'

'Now, you don't need to be worrying about anything because we won't be staying long.'

Angela heard a strained note in her mother's voice which made her shoulders tense.

'We have your Aunt Catherine to see as well. Just a cup of tea will be fine . . .'

Angela took a deep breath. There was no point in getting annoyed or upset about her saying they wouldn't be staying long. Making it sound as though the visit was an ordeal. She always said that – every single time they came up to see her. This was how her mother was – half the time she didn't even realise what she was saying. It was stupid to expect anything different from her.

Then, she found herself smiling when she saw her father following behind with a huge box of groceries.

'Oh, Daddy, you shouldn't have,' she said, although she was delighted. 'You gave me loads of stuff when you dropped me last week.'

'Will you stop! Wouldn't it be nice if I came with one hand as long as the other?' he said, laughing. 'We're making sure you get the best of Tullamore food. You couldn't be sure what you were eating up here in Dublin – they could give you any oul' shite at all.'

'Seán!' her mother said. 'The language of you! It's your daughter you're talking to, not one of the boys in the shop.'

Seán winked at Angela. 'As I say, Angela, at least you know the beef and the lamb is coming from the butcher just down the road from us.'

They all went down the hallway and Angela opened the door to let them into her room.

'Oh, it is nice and warm,' her mother said, looking around her approvingly. 'And you have the place looking lovely too.'

Angela wondered how she managed to make a compliment sound like a criticism.

'You wouldn't think you could fit so much into one room . . . a bed and a wardrobe and the table and armchairs and everything . . .' She paused as though she'd been about to say something then changed her mind. She handed Angela the cake box and the bag with the magazines. 'I thought I'd bring something to have with the tea, but I can see you've already bought some cakes . . .'

'It doesn't matter,' Angela said. 'I wanted to have something for you anyway. If there's too many you can always take some of them with you to Aunt Catherine.'

Nance Tracey nodded her head, although her eyes looked distracted.

'Or I can take some into the office in the morning – they won't go to waste.'

Her father put the grocery box down on the table then came over to give her a big hug.

'You're looking great, Angela,' he said, stepping back to look at her. 'I don't know where you got the good looks from.'

Her mother laughed now. 'Well, that's a nice thing to be saying!'

'Go on!' he said, throwing an arm about his wife's shoulders. 'You know perfectly well you're like two peas in a pod.' He beamed at Angela. 'How many times have I said it? You're just like your mother was at your age. The spit of her. Fiona and Bridget are a mix of the two of us, but there's no denying who you take after. You were the lucky one taking your mother's looks.'

Angela smiled back at him and shook her head. 'You better not let the others hear you saying that.'

'Pay no heed to him.' Her mother wriggled out from under her father's arm, rolling her eyes and making an exasperated sound. 'He's talking nonsense. He's forever telling Fiona and Bridget how good-looking they are too. Nobody pays a bit of attention to him.' She went over and sat down in one of the armchairs, glancing around her.

'That's nice,' Seán Tracey said, in mock indignation. 'A poor man trying to give his wife and his daughter a compliment and he gets told he's talking nonsense.' He went over to stand by the fireplace. 'A fine room, Angela. And in a fine old house.'

'Well, sit down now in front of the fire,' she said. 'The kettle is boiled and I'll have the tea ready in a few minutes.'

Her mother started to get up from the chair. 'I'll give you a hand.'

'I'm fine, thanks. I only have the teapot to bring down from the kitchen – everything else is already here.'

'Would you be better with your cardigan on? That big hallway is bound to be cold now.'

'I'm fine,' Angela repeated. 'If you wouldn't mind putting some of your cakes on the cake-stand, that would be great.'

'Are you sure there's nothing else I can do?'

'Nothing, thanks. It's all done.'

As she closed the door behind her, she heard her mother sighing and then saying in a low voice, 'I don't know why she never lets me help – why she's always got to be so independent.'

Angela could feel tears stinging her eyes as she limped back down to the kitchen. What else could she have done other than become independent? All the years of being left amongst strangers in a hospital in Dublin, miles away from her parents and her sisters. What was she supposed to have done? Curl up in the bed with the covers over her head and wait until it was time to go home again?

And going home was not the answer she always hoped it would be. Year after year of travelling back to Tullamore at Christmas and Easter and the summer, hoping that during one of the visits she would feel closer to her mother – as close to her as Fiona and Bridget obviously felt. Waiting for her mother to say something nice and under-standing, that would change the way things were between them. Make up for all that had been lacking. But it never happened.

Her mother still didn't know what to say. Her mother didn't even know that there was something she should have said.

CHAPTER 4

Fiona knew there was something wrong when her parents returned from Dublin just after seven o'clock that night. Her mother was pale and quiet as she took her hat and coat off and hung them in the hallway. Her father didn't seem right either. His face had a tight, reddish look about it, and Fiona thought that he seemed sort of agitated, which was unlike him. She also noticed that they didn't seem to look at each other when they spoke. She almost asked them if there was anything wrong and then thought better of it. They had obviously had a row and, from the way they were acting, they thought it had nothing to do with her.

They went into the parlour to sit in armchairs opposite each other by the fire which again was unusual, as they usually sat in the kitchen where the television and radio was. Although Mary Ellen kept a fire on in it every day to keep it from going damp, the parlour was mainly used for visitors or for quiet things like reading or writing letters. The fact that they were sitting in the parlour informed Fiona that they wanted to talk in private.

She followed them in, trying to act as though all was normal. 'Do you want anything to eat?' she asked. As she looked from one to the other, she noticed that they both looked tired and somehow older than they had over the few weeks of Christmas. She wondered if the change in them might be anything to do with her going to New York – if they both had suddenly realised that they would now be living on their own, with all their children gone. A little knot came into her chest. They had never given any indication that they were very upset about her going. They had of course said they would miss her, but they had been encouraging in their own ways. If their sombre mood was anything to do with her departure, it was too late.

'There's some of the cooked ham there and some cold potatoes I could fry,' she said. 'I was going to make something for myself so it's no trouble.'

Her mother shook her head. 'No thanks – just see to yourself.'

Her father didn't even look up at her. 'I couldn't eat a bite,' he said.

Fiona couldn't remember the last time he had said that. He was almost always in good humour, and his appetite rarely wavered unless he was sick.

'Well, I'll make you a cup of tea then,' she said. 'You're bound to be tired after the driving up and down to Dublin. An early night might do both of you good.'

Her father looked up at Fiona. 'I'm going to walk down to the bar.'

Nance Tracey's eyes widened. 'But you were to have the night off—'

'I'm grand,' Seán said. 'I've been sitting around for hours, so it'll do me good to be on my feet for a bit.'

'Please yourself.' Her tone was curt.

'I'll go and make the tea,' Fiona said, quietly closing the door.

When she came back along the hallway with the tray she could hear their voices raised and tense, although she couldn't hear what they were talking or arguing about. She put the tray with her mother's china cup and saucer and her father's mug down on the hall table and stood waiting for things to quieten before going in.

Then, she suddenly heard her father's raised voice quite clearly saying, 'I've told you what to do about Catherine and Joseph, but you won't listen! You have the chance now to right things, and I think you should for everyone's sake.'

'You know well it's not that simple.' Her mother's voice was strained and angry. 'Catherine suited herself all those years ago and didn't take my feelings into account. It was her decision to cut us out, and we don't know how things could turn out if we get involved—'

'It's going to be taken out of our hands if we don't do something,' Seán Tracey said. 'And it's not Catherine's fault and it's not Joseph's fault.'

'It's *my* fault,' her mother said. 'That's what you're saying. You're saying it's all my fault.'

43

'I've never said that,' her father replied. 'Never once have I blamed you for anything. It's just the way things have turned out, and we need to make the best of it.' He paused. 'If it is anyone's fault, it's that *amadán* of a husband of Catherine's – Kenneth Fox – the stupid bastard. He's the one who stirred things up before he went off back to England.'

Fiona's throat tightened. She now knew the argument wasn't anything to do with her, but the small sense of relief was overshadowed by the animosity between her parents. She had rarely heard her father curse in anger, and it was an even rarer occurrence in her mother's presence. He only used bad language when he was watching a match or when he was reporting a funny story where the cursing was part of it.

'There's nothing can be done about Kenneth Fox now. It's Catherine's attitude that I'm more concerned about—'

'Well, just let it rest for tonight, Nance.' Seán's voice was low and weary now. 'That's all I'm asking. The whole thing is giving me a pain in my chest.'

'Well, it's giving us both pains,' Fiona heard her mother counter. 'I've had a pain in my head the whole evening.'

Their voices became too low for Fiona to hear anything more, which she was thankful for. This was not something that she wanted to overhear. It was very different from the snatches of conversations that would drift along the hallway or spiral upstairs to her bedroom at this time of night. Usually, it was relaxed chat and occasional laughter about their day in the shop and bar. Mundane talk about familiar, trivial issues that made her somehow feel safe.

She had no idea what had brought about the change in atmosphere tonight. But, it was clear that there was a serious disagreement between her mother and father, and that her Aunt Catherine and Uncle Kenneth had something to do with it.

She did not want to know what it was about – she just wanted it all to go away. For her parents to sort it out quietly between themselves without involving her. She had enough of her own problems to think about, what with going away. She still felt awkward being asked by friends and customers how Paul Moore felt about her leaving. She wanted to be gone now and living and working in an exciting and anonymous place where nobody knew her.

She carried the tray back to the kitchen, and emptied the tea down the white stone sink. She boiled the kettle again and made fresh tea. From the cupboard she took a packet of her father's favourite Kimberley biscuits, and then put the lot on the tray. Warily, she then went back up the hallway to the parlour again.

She listened as she went along, and then, feeling confident that the major conflict had died down, she knocked on the door and went in.

Neither looked directly at her as she handed them the tea, but they both thanked her and she could tell that things were easier. She felt that a truce had been reached. Exactly how and in what way she did not know, but as long as things had returned to normal before she left for America, she would be relieved.

CHAPTER 5

Angela sat flicking through one of the magazines her mother had brought for her, but she found it hard to concentrate. She had tried knitting too – a cream short-sleeved jumper with a lace panel down the middle – but she could not keep her mind on it and had made several mistakes. She kept wondering how her parents' visit to her aunt had gone.

Just after eight o'clock she decided she would go out to the phone box and give her aunt a quick ring. A heavy frost had settled, so she put on a warm sweater over her blouse and then her coat, hat and gloves. She then went to the little dish on her dressing-table where she saved coins for the phone box, lifted a handful and put them in her pocket. She took her walking stick with her as well, as it served two purposes at night. It helped steady her walk on the slippery footpath, but it was also handy to have with her should she find herself accosted by a drunk or someone who could try to steal any money she might be carrying.

The girls in the house were constantly warned by Sister Gerard Majella – the nun who kept an eye on the house – that these things did on occasion occur in Dublin, and to be vigilant when out at night. Angela had never encountered any serious situations herself, although she had often received unwanted attention from men when she was out with the other girls. She knew her looks attracted them, but when they realised she had a problem with her leg, most would look elsewhere.

But, there were certain types to whom her disability was not a problem, and who felt that she was more likely to be grateful for their attentions. They were also the type who would pester her, but she had grown used to it over the years, both in Dublin and back in Tullamore, and knew she was perfectly capable of handling them with a withering look or a smart remark.

As she walked along the street to the top of the road, she thought it was a lovely bright night even though the air was icy cold. When she reached the phone box she was glad of the shelter, although she hated the musty smell of old cigarettes and the suspicious damp patches on the floor. She took her glove off and dialled her aunt's number. The phone rang a good few times, and she was just about to hang up when the phone was answered.

'Hello, Aunt Catherine. I just thought I'd give a quick ring to see how you and Joseph were getting on.'

'Oh, hello, Angela . . . I wasn't expecting to hear from you tonight.'

She thought her aunt's voice sounded different,

kind of hoarse. 'Are you okay?' she asked. 'Have you a bit of a cold?'

There was a silence. 'I'm sorry, Angela,' her aunt said, 'but I'm afraid you've caught me at a bad time . . .'

'Will I leave it and ring back tomorrow from the office?'

'No, no . . . look, to tell you the truth, I'm a bit upset . . .'

Angela could hear quite clearly now that her aunt was actually crying. 'Are you okay? Has something happened?'

'I don't want to involve you, it's not fair . . .'

'Was it the visit? Has my mother said something to upset you?'

'Oh, it's my own stupid fault for thinking they might help Joseph out. I don't know why I bothered asking, I should have known.'

'What is it?' Angela said. 'You might feel better talking to somebody about it, and I promise I won't say a word to my mother or anyone else at home. If it would help, I could walk up and catch the bus out to Lucan. I could be there with you in half an hour.'

'Not at all. It's too late and too dark for you to be travelling about on buses. And I wouldn't dream of bringing you out here on a freezing cold night like this.' She halted. 'Look, I'll tell you, because I know you'll only worry, but make sure you don't breathe a word to anyone . . .'

'I'm listening,' Angela said, 'and I've plenty of

coins on me, so don't worry if the pips start to go.'

'Do you remember me saying that Joseph left the showband he was playing with and had moved to one of these rock bands?'

'Yes,' Angela said, 'he told me about it himself.' Joseph had told her they were getting very popular and had even been the opening act for a recent Rory Gallagher concert.

'Well, however popular they are, they're not doing him any good,' her aunt said, 'and he's landed himself in trouble at work. He's been out too late at night practising and drinking, and he already had a couple of warnings in the shop for coming in late and missing odd days.'

Joseph worked in the men's clothing department of a big store in Grafton Street.

'I didn't know that,' Angela said. 'But I suppose these musical things go on late at night, especially in Dublin.'

'Well, he's had one too many late nights and they've sacked him.'

'Oh, God. I didn't realise it was that serious. What's he going to do?'

'That's the trouble, he doesn't know what he wants to do. The other thing is that the band has just broken up this weekend.' Her aunt's voice dropped now. 'Seemingly, the main lad in the band – the singer – has got into trouble with the Guards and he's skipped off to England.'

'What did he do?'

'Oh, Angela, it's worrying me sick . . . it was *drugs*.'

Angela's mouth opened in shock and she was glad her aunt could not see her reaction. Drugs were the last thing any family wanted to be involved with.

'It seems,' her aunt said, 'that some other lads were bringing these drugs over from London and selling them at the concerts. Don't ask me what kind they were or anything, but it must be serious if the Guards were involved and he's skipped off.'

'It certainly sounds serious,' Angela said.

'Joseph has promised me that he would never take drugs, that he's happy enough with a few pints, but how do I know that he won't be dragged into it? You read about it in the papers, and hear it on the news.' She started to cry again. 'I'm not up to dealing with this on my own, Angela. I'm worried sick about him.'

'Don't get yourself into a state about it,' Angela said. 'Joseph isn't stupid. It's the music he likes, he always has. And up until now, he's been a great worker. They were talking about sending him on a management course. It's obviously the mixture of late nights and early mornings that's causing him a problem. Now that the band is broken up he might look for something else.'

The pips suddenly sounded on the phone.

'Hold on,' Angela said, 'I won't be a minute . . .' She quickly dipped into her pocket for another coin to push into the slot. 'Are you still there?'

'I am,' her aunt said. 'I was just saying that I think Dublin is not the place for him at the minute. I think that, as long as he's here, he's going to be mixing with that same crowd and God knows where it might lead. I know he's not a bad fellow in any way, everyone says what a cheery fellow he is, and he's got a big heart when it comes to helping anyone else.'

'We all know that,' Angela said.

Her aunt sighed. 'But, you know, since his father left last year, he's gone into himself . . . it really hit him. You would think at nearly twenty-seven years old it wouldn't bother him, but it does. He took it very bad.' She halted. 'That's what makes me worry about him drinking too much, or being around people that are taking drugs. It had been on my mind all day today, worrying about him finding work. So, when your mother and father were here this evening, I asked your father if he might take him on down in the pub in Tullamore for a few months. Just to get him away from here. I thought he might learn the pub trade and it would give him experience for another job.'

'What did Daddy say?'

'Oh, he was all for it,' Aunt Catherine said. 'He said he was very fond of Joseph and that he thought he had the right personality and everything to make a good barman.'

'He has. Joseph would liven up the place, and I bet there would be a few more female faces in the snug if he was working in it.' Tracey's bar had a small secluded side-room – known as a 'snug' – which had its own access to the bar. It was particularly popular with patrons who preferred not to be seen in the public bar, especially ladies who felt their presence would be frowned upon.

'Well, it's not going to happen, Angela, because the minute she heard it, your mother stood up and said they had to go. I could tell by her face she wasn't a bit happy, so I asked her what she thought about Joseph working in the pub and she said they would need to think about it. She was putting her coat and gloves on at this point, so I said I would be grateful if they would think about it, as Joseph is her only nephew.'

'And did Daddy say any more?' Angela asked.

'Not really, but I could see by your father's face he didn't agree with her, and I heard them arguing as they went out to the car.'

'Well, don't take it personally. My mother can be very awkward.' Angela said. 'And there has always been a cold streak in her. I'm not saying she hasn't got a good side to her as well, because she has – but there are times when she just isn't the nicest. There's nobody knows that more than me.'

'Oh, Angela, I don't want to cause any kind of friction between you and your mother. I'm sure she thinks the world of you . . .' She halted. 'I know you've had your own difficulties with her but, believe you me, there's no point in looking back. It doesn't do you any good.'

'Most of the time I don't look back,' Angela said, 'but there are times when it's very hard not to.'

'Your mother and I have had our ups and downs too as sisters – but it's all a long time ago and I think you have to put arguments behind you. Forgive and forget. Your mother needs to think of that when I'm asking for help for Joseph for the very first time.'

'They might come back once they've had time to think about it. If Fiona or anyone mentions it to me, I'll certainly put in a good word for him.'

'You're very good, Angela,' her aunt said. 'I feel better about it all after talking to you, and I've started a Novena to St Joseph. I read in a holy book somewhere that he's the saint you should pray to about jobs and, since Joseph has the same name, I thought he might be the best one to go to.'

'I'll say a prayer for him too,' Angela promised. 'And next time I'm in church I'll light a candle.'

'You're a great girl,' Aunt Catherine said. 'I wish I had a daughter like you myself.'

'I'll see you at the weekend – give my love to Joseph.'

After she hung up, Angela stood in the musty phone box for a few minutes, mulling things over. What was wrong with her mother, she wondered, that she could be so hard and cold with her own family? She felt it, and so did her sister and nephew.

Fiona and Bridget, she thought, obviously had

no big problems with their mam. Of course they laughed and joked behind her back about her fussiness over things like good manners, good clothes and making a good impression – and her disapproval of women she deemed 'forward' and men who used bad language in the bar. But underneath it, Angela felt the girls had a close relationship with their mother, because she had always been there for them when she was needed.

CHAPTER 6

After her father left to go down to the bar, Fiona could tell that her mother did not want to talk about or even refer to the incident. Nance came down into the kitchen, and put the radio on while she tidied around, and then checked what was in the fridge for Mrs Mooney to use for dinner the following day. After that, she told Fiona she was going upstairs to have a bath.

Fiona turned the television on and watched a film for a while, but it had an over-elaborate plot which needed full concentration – which she did not have tonight. Her mind kept flitting back to the row, and she wondered how her sisters would have reacted had they been at home and heard it. She would say nothing about it. As the eldest she had always felt she should keep Angela and Bridget away from things that might upset them. But at times like this it was hard – she would have liked to talk it over with someone who would not think she was being disloyal.

Just after ten o'clock she went up to her bedroom thinking she would check her suitcase again, and to read over some of Elizabeth's letters which gave details about the apartment in Park Avenue. Her own bedroom was the first one at the top of the stairs. She noticed that the bathroom, which was next to her room, was now empty. She looked down towards the end of the hallway, to her parents' room, and could see a light shining from under the door. Her mother must have gone straight to bed. Fiona decided she would go to bed too. By the time her father came in from the pub, both of them would be asleep.

She hoped the row would be all forgotten in the morning. She only wanted to think about good, positive things now before leaving. Things like making sure she had all her clothes packed in a certain order, and had smaller items like her new stockings, tights, brassieres and toiletries packed in the little compartments of her case.

She went into the bathroom, had an all-over wash and brushed her teeth. Then she came back to her bedroom. It was chilly as the fire had died down in the grate, so she got undressed quickly and into her warm striped pyjamas. She took Elizabeth's recent letters down from the mantel-piece and put them on the bed, then went over to her record player and plugged it in. She padded across the floor to the open pine cupboard and flicked through the stack of LP and single records that she had lined up on the shelves.

She lifted out two single records, 'Strangers in the Night' by Frank Sinatra and 'Ain't No Mountain

High Enough' by Marvin Gaye & Tammi Terrell –
two songs she loved and knew would help lift her
mood. Elizabeth had mentioned the singles to
her in her letters and, when they became available
to buy in Ireland, Fiona had asked Angela to go
into one of the big shops in Dublin and get them
for her. She put them on the turntable now, one
on top of the other.

As she listened to the romantic music, her
thoughts drifted to Paul Moore. As always, she
felt bad knowing that she had hurt him by
choosing a new life in New York over their relationship. She thought he had understood, but then
he had asked if they could meet up to talk a few
days later. She thought it was just to talk and part
as friends, and had been unprepared when he
asked her not to go to America. She had been
even more unprepared when he told her he loved
her and that, if she stayed, he wanted them to
become engaged.

As kindly as she could, she explained that she
just *had* to go to New York. She told him she
cared for him very much but that if she didn't
go she knew that she would regret it. Later, she
might begin to blame him for holding her back.
He had just looked at her, then nodded and
walked away.

Remembering Paul triggered off other uncomfortable little memories that she had buried
away – things she had dismissed at the time, and
blotted out. She had wanted one last happy

Christmas at home with her family and friends, then for everyone to wave her off, smiling and looking forward to seeing her again when she came back for a holiday.

She wanted them to say that they were going to save and come out to visit her in New York. She wanted to hear them saying what a wonderful time she would have with her friend Elizabeth there, and speculate about the great opportunities that awaited her.

What she hadn't wanted was to feel guilty about breaking off with Paul Moore, or to feel worried about leaving her parents when they weren't getting on.

And there had been another little incident with Angela over Christmas which was also playing on her mind.

It was one night when Bridget had gone to bed just after her parents, leaving Fiona and Angela listening to records in the parlour. The conversation had been light and easy, and they had been laughing about Fiona's description of some of the drunken singers down in the pub earlier on.

'I don't know how you can do it,' Angela had said. 'How you can work in the bar and the shop. Especially the bar. I've always felt very self-conscious in there with all the men.'

'It's something you get used to, and most of them are nice. If they're not, Dad and Patrick see to them.'

'I don't think I would ever get used to it, but then we're very different . . . due to our circumstances.'

A small silence had fallen and they had both lifted their coffees.

'It's a pity we never got the chance to be really close as sisters when we were growing up,' Angela had suddenly said. 'I always felt different from you and Bridget. And of course I was different with my leg and everything – and spending all those years away from everyone in Dublin. That's why I'm no good in the bar and shop, because I was never there long enough to get used to it. And I'm not blaming anyone. It's just the way things were.' She had looked at Fiona with tears in her eyes. 'I would have loved the three of us to become closer now we're all grown up, but now that's never going to happen with you going to New York.'

Fiona had looked at her, not quite knowing what to say. This was something they had never discussed openly before, and she was not prepared for it now. Especially now. She knew that there was something wrong in their family because of Angela being left in Dublin for all those years – but this wasn't the time to talk about it. That time was gone.

Somehow, the subject had drifted on to something else, leaving the uncomfortable, unfinished conversation hanging in the air. And tonight, Fiona didn't want to remember hurting Paul Moore or think about what Angela had said.

She turned the record player up a little bit

more. Then she lifted Elizabeth's letters from the bed and went through them until she found the one that told her all about the outdoor ice-skating in Central Park. This was one of the first things they would do together, Elizabeth had told her, as it was an easy way to meet new people. She said it was a nice walk from the apartment and at weekends the rink was open until eleven o'clock at night.

The music stopped and then the second record dropped down with a soft thud on top of the other. Frank Sinatra's lovely clear voice filled the room. Fiona smiled and held the letter to her chest, her mind flooding with all the possibilities, the exciting opportunities – and that special, exciting romance with an American stranger that just might lie ahead.

As she listened to the words, all the uncomfortable memories faded off in the distance. *This time next year,* she thought, *I'll be listening to music in New York.*

CHAPTER 7

It was almost one o'clock in the morning when Fiona woke with a start. She lay for a few moments listening to the rain pattering on the window, and wondering what had woken her. Then she heard the door knocker banging again. This time she moved quickly, switching on her bedside lamp and leaping out of bed, then rushing across the floor barefoot to the door.

She called along the hallway to her father. 'Dad! Dad! There's someone at the door.'

There was silence, during which the door knocker went again.

Damn! she muttered to herself. As she walked quickly towards her parents' room she suddenly wondered if her father had drunk too much and it had put him into a heavy sleep. Given his mood before he went out, she supposed there was a chance he had.

She rapped on her parents' bedroom door.

'Dad!' she called again, turning the door handle to open it. 'There's somebody at the door.'

Her mother sat up, clearly just having awoken. Her usually perfect hair was flat on one side and bunched up on the other, as though she had been tossing and turning. She looked at the other side of the bed, still not fully awake. 'Your father's not here . . . he's not come home yet.' Her voice was vague. She looked at the clock. 'That must be him now . . .'

'He must have forgotten his key.' Fiona turned back into the corridor, sighing to herself. 'I'd better go down and let him in.'

She felt a sudden shiver run through her and thought for a moment to go back to her bedroom to get her dressing-gown and slippers, but then the knocker sounded again.

'Hang on a minute!' she called, the irritation clear in her voice. 'I'm coming as quick as I can!'

As she went down the staircase barefoot, she hoped again that the argument earlier hadn't set him off drinking. It wasn't often that he did it, but there had been occasions where he had come home the worst for wear. As she walked across the cold tiled floor she thought it would be the dreadful ending she didn't need to what had been a dreadful night.

She opened the door, stepping back into the hallway to make sure she didn't get wet. And then she saw Patrick standing there, and her hands came up to hold her pyjamas tight to her neck.

He had no coat on and his jersey and shirt collar were damp with rain. 'You have to come down,' he told her, pointing towards the bar. 'Your father's not well.'

Her eyes narrowed. 'Is he drunk?'

'God, no! No, it's not that.' He backed away a few steps. 'He suddenly collapsed and we got him up into a chair, and then he collapsed again. We called the doctor, and when he checked him he phoned for an ambulance and the priest. They're all waiting down in the bar. The doctor said to get you and your mother.'

'The priest and the doctor are there?' The situation was beginning to sink in, and her voice was faltering now. 'Do they think it's that serious?'

Patrick nodded. 'Yes . . . the doctor said it could be his heart.'

'Fiona?' Nance's voice called from the staircase. 'What's wrong?'

'Get dressed quick!' Fiona called back to her mother. 'Dad's not well and we need to go down to the bar.'

'What's happened?' her mother called down. 'What's happened?'

Fiona looked at Patrick. 'I'll have to go to my mother and explain. You go back and we'll follow you down as quickly as we can.'

Shortly after they arrived in the bar, damp with rain and shocked and fearful. They were too late. They found that Seán Tracey had just taken his last breath.

That night Fiona felt the hours drag by minute by minute, as they moved from the bar to the hospital and then eventually back home. Back to cry and drink tea and cry again – to try to digest the fact that her father was indeed dead and they would never again see him alive. Back to wonder why such a thing could have happened so suddenly.

But not completely unexpectedly, Fiona discovered. The visit to the hospital in Dublin had not been as routine had her parents had told her. Results from previous tests had shown that her father had problems with several blocked arteries, and the heart specialist had suggested further tests as there might also be problems with a leaking valve.

'He didn't want me to say anything to you or Bridget or Angela,' her mother had explained during a quiet moment in the hospital corridor. 'He said it would only worry you when there wasn't anything really wrong. He didn't tell me half of what the doctors had said to him. He kept saying any pains he got was just the usual angina and that he was fine, that the tablets he got were all working grand.' She shrugged. 'If I'd known it was so serious I'd have made him go to a specialist long ago.'

Around four o'clock in the morning Nance and Fiona made their way back upstairs to bed.

'I'll never sleep,' her mother said when they reached the top of the stairs, 'but we need to try. Even the rest will do us good. We have a lot to face in the morning.'

'We'll have to let Angela and Bridget know first thing.'

'We'll let them both get a good night's sleep,

because they won't get many more over the next few days. After they're up and about we'll ring Angela's office and then later in the morning we'll ring the nuns and say that someone will come and collect Bridget.' She turned to Fiona and took both her hands in her own. 'I can't believe what's happened and that I'll never see your father alive again. I can't believe it. I know we had that stupid argument earlier tonight – but you know it's rare that we disagreed. We got on well most of the time. We were happier than most couples I know.' She squeezed Fiona's hands tightly. 'I don't want us to think of that row again or for either of us to mention it to the other girls or anyone else. Your father was a private man and he wouldn't want us to think about it. He would prefer us to remember all the good times.'

'I know,' Fiona said quietly. 'I wouldn't have mentioned it anyway.'

'Good girl.' Her mother let go of her hands now and turned to walk down the corridor to the bedroom she had shared with her husband for twenty-odd years. Then, just as Fiona opened her bedroom door, she turned again and said, 'Fiona, thank God you were here tonight. I don't know what I would have done without you. I don't know what I would have done if it had happened in a few weeks' time and you were in New York.'

'I'm glad I was here too,' Fiona said. 'I can't imagine how I would have felt being so far away.'

'You've always been a thoughtful girl. You always know to do the right thing. Your father and I have always said that . . .' Her mother stopped, as though she was thinking of something else to say.

Fiona waited to hear her say something about New York and what she should do. But when her mother simply said, 'Goodnight now,' she realised that she was being selfish, thinking only of herself and her plans.

They hadn't even had her father's funeral yet and here she was expecting her mother to cope all on her own.

As she walked into her bedroom and saw the packed suitcase over by the wardrobe, it struck her that her plans for New York seemed much more real than the fact her father had just died. She could not imagine that her father would never walk into this house again, that tomorrow he would not be in the bar chatting to customers while she and her mother were next door in the shop. That he would not be here in the morning with the fire going and the kettle boiled as he did every morning.

She could not envisage the days that would follow this night, where people would come and go in the house, and her father would at some stage be brought back to the house in a coffin. The thought of it brought a dry lump to her throat. She closed the door behind her and went over to sit on the edge of the bed.

From this night on her life was going to change – all their lives were going to change. Before this had happened, everything was all about dates and travel plans and far-off places, but now the future was just a big blank space.

The family would just have to try to get through each day as it came. Maybe, she thought, after some time had passed, they would get into a new routine. Maybe it would become clearer as to how the coming months and years would be in this house and in Tracey's bar without her father.

She lay back in the bed, her eyes closed. It was too soon for any plans.

She would take it one step at a time. Tomorrow afternoon she would phone Mrs Davis in Park Avenue and explain what had happened.

CHAPTER 8

Bridget woke and looked across the silent room to the tall windows. The crack in one of the heavy silk curtains let in a sliver of grey morning light which told her it was around six o'clock. She had another hour and a half before she had to move.

She closed her eyes again and lay for a while, taking in the silence of the great old building that had been home to her and all the other girls for over four years since she had come here at the age of thirteen. At times, in this place with its thick, panelled walls and ornately coved ceilings, silence was all there was. It dominated everything and wrapped itself around her. At first she had found the lack of laughter or any kind of voices strange, but she now found the silence almost reassuring.

She turned over on her side, conscious of the groans from the springs in her single mattress. Someone across the room coughed several times and she listened carefully, trying to work out who it was. She then became aware of the sleeping sounds from the long rows of beds on either side of the dormitory – the light snores, the creaking as bodies turned, moved around, the sighs and the inhale and exhale of breath. After a short while she noticed the rhythmic sound of her own breathing. It was always a sign she was becoming tired again. She closed her eyes and fell back asleep.

At seven thirty she awoke, startled by a hand on her shoulder. By the time she looked up Sister Bernadette had already silently moved on to the next bed. Bridget forced her eyes to stay open, although she did not feel as bright or alert as she had when she wakened earlier. She also had a strange feeling of unease within her.

She lay as the other girls started to move silently around the polished floors of the cavernous room, methodically retrieving their slippers, quilted dressing-gowns and washbags from their bedside lockers. She waited whilst the first half dozen padded down the dormitory then out into the cold tiled corridor to walk towards the toilets. After they had finished, the girls would move back out into the panelled corridor where there were long rows of sinks. They would wash in silence, under the modesty of nightdresses and dressing-gowns, and then brush their teeth.

It was only in silence, the girls understood, that they could hear God's voice.

Bridget sat up now, trying to shake off the heavy, groggy feeling, when remnants of an uncomfortable dream came drifting back to her. It was about her parents, and her aunt had been involved somewhere. When she started to remember more of the dream, she felt her chest tighten. She threw back the sheet and blankets and swung her legs out of bed until her feet touched the cold wooden floor. She bent to retrieve her slippers from the locker and put them on, and then she reached for her dressing-gown. She buttoned it all the way down from her chin to her ankles, and then she paused to use her hands to smooth down her sand-coloured, bobbed hair. It was always tossed around in the morning, flicking out in the wrong direction as opposed to curving under. It had, she often thought, been much easier to manage when it was long and she could just tie it back in a pony-tail. But the long hair had disappeared with any vanity attached to it, as had the things of her old life.

When she had first arrived at the convent school, she had lined up with the other girls until her turn came and then a pretty young nun lopped eight inches off her hair, and told her how much easier it would be to manage. An older girl was already sweeping up the long strands of Bridget's hair as she moved from the chair, eager to see her reflection. But she was to learn the first of many lessons about patience that day. There were no mirrors to hand. And it would be that night before she saw how her shorn hair looked in the small mirror above the sink as she washed for bed.

The smiling young nun, she soon discovered, was wrong about the new style being easier to manage. She had not realised that Bridget Tracey's hair had a stubborn wave which refused to lie flat. From that day on, her flyaway hair would require taming with a wet comb every single morning to make it reasonable-looking. And living with it would become one of the items on her daily list of mortifications. The list which would accompany her on the spiritual path to becoming a nun.

As she walked out of the dormitory and down the pitch-pine staircase with the ever-present Sister Bernadette and the other girls from her class, she felt the more vivid parts of the dream were lodged firmly in her mind. Memories of being somewhere she should not have been, hearing conversations she should never have heard. Conversations that were now beginning to take on meanings she had not considered before.

She walked across the yard to the church, silently reciting prayers to drown out the snatches of dream. But the memory refused to budge as she went through the morning routine of Mass. She tried to concentrate on the priest's voice, the lit candles on the altar, the stained-glass windows and the statue of the Sacred Heart.

As she ate breakfast in silence in the refectory hall, the uncomfortable feelings lingered on and she found she wasn't as hungry as usual. Normally she devoured a large bowl of milky porridge followed by several thick slices of brown bread and butter and jam. This morning, she found it hard to swallow down one slice of bread.

When they left the dining hall and the silent morning period, several girls and Sister Bernadette remarked on how serious she looked and checked if she was feeling alright. Being naturally chatty, Bridget was usually one of the first to break the silence after breakfast, and they had noticed she was unusually quiet.

'If you need to talk about anything private,' the nun whispered, 'we can go into one of the quiet rooms.'

'I'm grand, Sister,' Bridget said. 'I'm just a bit tired. I didn't sleep very well last night and I think I'm still trying to wake up.'

'Do you feel up to doing your chores?'

'Yes,' she said, annoyed with herself for bringing on all this unwanted attention. 'I'll be fine.'

Sister Bernadette looked doubtful. 'Well, if you change your mind later and you want to talk to someone . . .'

Bridget was grateful for the kind nun's concern but she didn't want to talk about anything to anyone. Especially the dream and the memories it had brought flooding back. Things she had never talked about – that she had tried very hard to forget because of the damage it could do to her family.

After breakfast Bridget joined her designated group for chores. This morning she was on the rota for cleaning the sinks upstairs. It was one of the jobs which she liked, because the white, soap-splashed porcelain showed speedy results after a short period of work. She went to the store to collect her apron and cleaning equipment and then silently climbed the wide wooden staircase to begin.

Half an hour later she was back in the dormitory changing into her school uniform: her navy crossover pinafore, her blouse and tie and her grey V-neck sweater. Her black brogues, well polished the previous evening, went on over her knee-length grey socks.

Dressed and sorted, and carrying her leather satchel full of books, she then joined the other girls out in the corridor which was now filled with the scent of fresh beeswax polish. Silently they made their way downstairs, out across the courtyard, and over to the classroom buildings.

Bridget's first class was English and, as always, the fifth years started their mornings off in school with another round of prayers. After that, they settled down to silent reading of an eight-page extract from a novel by Mary Lavin, followed by two pages of questions on it.

The literature class over, the girls then moved across the yard to the maths lesson taught by Sister Frances. Half an hour into the session, Bridget was in the middle of working on an algebra problem when Sister Bernadette knocked on the classroom door. All eyes turned to watch as the two nuns had a whispered conversation, then

Sister Frances came up the aisle towards Bridget, a serious look on her face.

'You can leave that for today, Bridget,' she said quietly. 'You're to go over to the main office.'

'What about my homework?'

'Don't worry about that.'

An ominous feeling building inside her, Bridget closed her books and put them back in her satchel, then, without looking at any of the other girls, she followed Sister Bernadette out of the classroom.

When they were out in the corridor, Bridget looked at the nun. 'Where are we going?'

'You have to go home,' Sister Bernadette told her, 'so you need to go up to the dormitory now and quickly collect your coat and any other belongings you need to take with you.'

'Is there something wrong?'

'Don't be worrying now,' the nun said, her voice calm and soothing. 'Just run upstairs and get your things and then come down into the office.'

As she walked up the wide staircase, Bridget ran over in her mind all the things that could possibly be the reason for her going home. None of them were good. She had heard of girls being sent home because the nuns thought they were more suited to ordinary life outside the convent. She had heard of others leaving because their vocation had over time become lost to them. A girl could be there one day and gone the next, with no explanation. And, if the other girls asked Sister Bernadette or one of the younger nuns what had happened, they were told that it was private information between the Mother Superior and the families.

Bridget did not think she fell into either of those categories. She'd had a meeting only last week with her Spiritual Director, and afterwards she felt they were both happy that all was going well. Her prayer sessions and her connections with God were at the stage they should be for an aspirant nun in fifth year, and when asked if she felt that her vocation was getting stronger, and if she still felt she was prepared to devote her life to God, she had no hesitation in saying, 'Yes'.

She was also fairly certain that the nuns were happy with her both in school and in her general religious life. And, if they had any problems with her, she felt that they would have given her some kind of indication by now. Surely, she thought, they wouldn't just tell her in the middle of a maths class that it had been decided she was no longer suitable material to be a nun?

When she came back down, Sister Bernadette was waiting at the foot of the stairs for her. She had a smile on her face, which struck Bridget as being nervous.

When she spoke, her voice was kind. 'We're just going to the office now, Bridget.'

Bridget felt her heart quicken as they walked down the corridor to Mother Superior's office. There was no point in asking Sister Bernadette anything more – she had obviously been instructed to say nothing.

As they came near to the door, the nun went ahead of her and after knocking she opened it. She held it back to allow Bridget to enter.

The minute Bridget saw Patrick sitting on the straight-backed chair opposite Mother Superior, she realised something was very wrong.

'Sit down, Bridget,' Mother Superior said. 'I'm afraid Mr Trimm has come to collect you on behalf of your family. We have some very sad news for you . . .'

'Is it Angela?' she asked. Angela was always the first one that came into her thoughts if anything was wrong in the family. Angela was the one who had struggled with poor health all her life – having one operation after another on her leg. Everyone else in the family was fine.

'No, my dear – it's your father,' Mother Superior said, an unusually soft and sympathetic look on her face. 'He took ill and died in the early hours of the morning.'

Bridget looked at the elderly nun, in her mind repeating slowly the words she had just heard. 'My father?' she said, her voice incredulous. 'But he was fine when he brought me back here on Sunday . . .' She turned to look at Patrick. 'Are you sure it's my father?'

Patrick nodded then cleared his throat. 'I'm sorry to bring you this sad news, Bridget. We're all in terrible shock about it, especially your poor mother. She asked me to come and collect you.'

Bridget thought of her mother now, and suddenly

realised that she did not want to go home. She wanted to stay here in the safety of the convent and the nuns, within her daily routine of comforting silences and prayers.

Here, she could imagine that all was the same at home as when she had left it. She could imagine that her father was still there, keeping things running at home and in the shop and in the bar.

'We will be saying special prayers for you, Bridget,' Mother Superior said. 'And you will be in our thoughts until you come back.'

Patrick stood up and went over to lift Bridget's bag. 'The car is outside,' he told her.

Bridget looked at the two nuns and felt she was going to cry. She did not want to leave the convent, and she did not want to go home if her father was not there.

CHAPTER 9

When Fiona looked out of her bedroom window the following morning, she thought it was as bleak as the night before, the greyness and the rain echoing the shock and sadness in the house.

Her mother was already downstairs with Mrs Mooney. After the fire was revived and the kettle boiled, the three women sat and drank tea and went over the events of the previous night in minute-by-minute detail, and then they cried.

After a while the housekeeper took up residence in the kitchen and started to make the first of the plates of sandwiches that would be needed for the next few days. Fiona and her mother forced themselves to make phone calls and answer the door to people – and then come back to make more tea, make more calls and meet more people.

Earlier in the morning, Patrick had put the regulatory signs up on the doors of the pub and the shop, to inform customers that they were closed until further notice due to sudden bereavement.

The time began to quicken as Angela and Bridget returned home, Angela brought down from

Dublin in a car by the manager of the office she worked in, and Bridget collected from the convent by Patrick.

As Fiona expected, both her sisters were shocked and upset, and she and her mother had to put their own sadness aside to comfort them. Angela and Bridget had to be told about the hospital visit all over again in great detail, and how their father himself had not realised how serious his condition was.

'He seemed in great form yesterday evening in Dublin,' Angela said. 'When I think of him carrying in the box of groceries, laughing and joking with me . . .' She looked at her mother now, remembering what her aunt had told her on the phone. 'Was he okay out at Aunt Catherine's later on?'

Her mother shifted her gaze to stare out the window. 'He was the same as always. He didn't mention having any unusual aches or pains.'

'I just can't believe it,' Angela said, her eyes filling with tears again. 'I just can't believe I won't see him again.'

Bridget went over and put her arm around her sister. 'The one consolation is that we know what a good person Daddy was, and he will have his reward for that soon. He wouldn't do any harm to anyone, and would always help whenever he could.'

'He always did his best,' Nance echoed. 'He hadn't a bad bone in his body.'

Angela closed her eyes now, trying not to look

at her mother, trying not to think about the things her aunt had told her in the phone call about the argument.

'He will be in heaven looking down on us all,' Bridget said. 'And we can pray to him and talk to him in the same way we always did.'

'Yes, we can all pray to him,' Nance echoed. 'That's the only comfort we have.'

Fiona looked at her mother, her eyes hollow and ringed with dark shadows. 'But that's acting as if things haven't changed,' she said. 'That's just pretending. He's dead – gone forever. Praying and talking to him as if he's alive, when we can't see him or feel him around. It's just not the same thing at all.'

'Don't be talking like that,' their mother said distractedly.

'I agree with Fiona,' Angela said. 'Praying to him or talking to him is not giving me any comfort at the moment either. I just wish we could turn the clock back and none of this had happened.' Her face crumpled now as she thought how different life would be without her father.

Bridget tightened her arm around her sister. 'Everybody has their own way,' she said, her voice soft and comforting, 'but I've found that praying always makes me feel better when anything is wrong. Even when something as devastating as this happens.'

'Well, we're all devastated, no doubt about it,' Nance said. 'None of us expected this to happen.

Not in a million years. But it has happened, and now we have to pull together, girls. We need to get through the next few days – the wake and the funeral and everything.'

Fiona shook her head. 'Just the thought of it all . . .'

'We have things that need to be done,' her mother said. 'The same that all families have to do when they get bad news like this.'

Then, all three girls listened as their mother outlined what she thought would happen with the funeral arrangements and over the next few days, and what they all had to do.

Seán Tracey's three living brothers and three sisters had been informed of the sad news. The brother and two sisters who lived in Tullamore soon arrived at the house. His brother, Jimmy, was stony-faced and silent, while the two sisters cried and said how shocked they were because Seán always looked so fit and well. Their tears set the family's raw grief off again and Fiona had to lead her mother and Bridget upstairs to their bedrooms to comfort them and leave them for a while to compose themselves in private.

Angela helped Mrs Mooney to make tea for the visitors, and after a while they stopped talking about Seán and the terrible shock of his unexpected death, and they began to discuss how they would accommodate the others who were travelling over from England and from Cork and Dublin.

It was decided that the families from England

would stay at Jimmy's house and the two sisters' houses in Tullamore, and Frank from Cork who was coming with his wife and son and daughter could stay in the rooms above the bar. Patrick, it was arranged, would see to the fires in the room and make sure there was hot water for them, and Mrs Mooney would make sure the beds were all in order and that they were well fed. If necessary, Patrick's sister-in-law would also be on hand to give any extra help needed.

In the middle of the afternoon, a black hearse rolled slowly up the street and came to a halt in front of the house, bringing Seán Tracey's body home to rest. The undertakers in their formal black suits and hats came in to offer their sympathies and find the place where the family wanted the coffin to reside.

'The dining-room,' Nance told them. 'In the centre of the room.'

Then, the women retreated to the kitchen, leaving Patrick and Seán Tracey's brother and brothers-in-law to deal with the practicalities of bringing the coffin in.

A short while later the dining-room door was opened and Nance and her daughters came into the room which was unusually and beautifully lit with large candles, to view the waxen lifeless figure that had once been a husband and father. They blinked back tears as they stared wordlessly down into the coffin at Seán, dressed in his good suit, each noting familiar details like his tie, his wedding ring and the brown rosary beads which were wound around his fingers.

Catherine arrived with her son Joseph who had driven them down from Dublin. Fiona greeted them at the door, and she could tell by her aunt's face how upset she was. Joseph, his dark hair much longer than she remembered, was courteous as he always was, sad about his uncle and full of sympathy for the family. But she felt there was a wariness in him, and it crossed her mind that it might be because he knew about the row that had taken place between his mother and her parents.

As they stood in the hallway, she felt a knot of anxiety about her mother meeting up with Aunt Catherine again, and was relieved when Nance came out of the kitchen towards them and allowed both Catherine and Joseph to give her a hug.

'I can't believe it,' Aunt Catherine said, her voice choked with tears. 'Seán looked fine when we saw him yesterday – he looked so well.'

'Everyone says that. Everyone says he looked fine,' Nance said in a flat, dull voice, 'but it obviously wasn't the case.'

'If there is anything we can do?' Joseph said. 'Anything at all?'

'Thank you, you're both very good – but I think we have all the help we need.'

Fiona noticed that her mother didn't look directly at her sister or Joseph – when she was speaking to them, her gaze was directed over their heads.

'If you go into the parlour,' Nance said, indicating towards the door, 'there's a good fire on and I'll get Bridget or Angela to bring you in some tea and sandwiches. There are some of Seán's relatives and some neighbours in there too, and Fiona will introduce you to anyone you don't know.'

And then her mother was gone, her heels tapping down the hallway.

'She's not herself,' Fiona said. 'I don't think it has hit her yet really. It's all been so sudden.'

'It was certainly sudden for us,' Aunt Catherine said, 'so it must be a hundred times worse for her.'

Fiona brought them into the parlour and introduced them to anyone who they might not know. Most people were standing drinking tea and talking in low voices, while there were others seated by the fire and at different areas in the room. She had just found chairs for them in the corner by the window when Angela came in, and made her way through the groups of mourners to her aunt and cousin. She put her arms around both of them and then she brought a spare wooden stool from the fireside, so she could sit down beside them.

Fiona stood near them for a few minutes, thinking how easy all three looked together even under these strained circumstances. As she listened to them talking, she felt a tinge of envy that her sister had such a nice, easy relationship with their aunt and cousin. She wished now she had someone – a grandmother or an aunt she was particularly close to – or anyone that she could confide in.

Their grandparents had all died when they were young, and most of their relations lived too far away. Her father's family, who lived locally, were nice, but they weren't the sort you could talk personally with. It was just one of those things.

She supposed Mrs Mooney was the closest she had to a confidante, as she understood their mother's moods and ways. But it wasn't the same as being close with a family member, and although they were comfortable with each other, it tended to be more of a practical relationship based on running the house and the business. Maybe, she thought, it was probably just as well that she didn't have too many people who she might miss when she eventually went to New York.

She knew it couldn't possibly be next week now. She couldn't leave her mother so soon after burying their father – and she didn't want to. She hadn't had time to think it all through, to grasp what had really happened in the last twenty-four hours. But, somewhere at the back of her mind, she knew the true enormity of it was waiting to hit her mother, herself and her sisters. Since this morning everyone was just working on automatic pilot. Doing what needed to be done, seeing to the funeral business, seeing to the constant stream of mourners. And then, at different times, each one quietly retreating upstairs to their room and their own thoughts.

*　　*　　*

The next two cold days that followed passed in a blur as more family and more people from Tullamore and beyond came to say the Rosary with the family and to pay their respects. Then, the night before the funeral, Seán's remains were brought from the house to reside in the church overnight.

Fiona drove herself and Bridget down through the town in her car, whilst her mother and Angela went with one of Seán's brothers who had a bigger car that was easier for them to get in and out of. When they all arrived outside the church, Fiona linked her mother's arm on one side, while Angela and Bridget were on the other.

As they made their way up the aisle she saw her Aunt Catherine and Joseph waiting in a pew at the front of the church, and wondered why they hadn't come to the house beforehand as most of the other relatives had done. Fiona noticed her mother's body stiffen when she passed by their pew, but she just kept walking, her head bent, without acknowledging them.

Angela had mentioned that her aunt and cousin had booked into Bolger's hotel in town for the night before the funeral, to save them driving back and forth to Dublin as they had done the previous nights.

After the service all the people filed towards the front of the church to shake hands with Nance, the girls and Seán's brothers and sisters. Catherine and Joseph sat behind, and spoke to anyone who approached them. When there was only the family left in the church, they came to the front row to her mother, and Aunt Catherine once again asked if there was anything they could do to help.

Fiona felt awkward and embarrassed as her mother shook her head and said, 'Thank you, but everything is organised for the morning, and we're just going to go back home now and have an early night.'

'We won't come back to the house tonight,' Aunt Catherine said. 'We'll just go straight back to the hotel now, and give you all a bit of peace.'

Fiona and Angela both looked at their mother, waiting for her to insist her sister and nephew should come back for a cup of tea or a drink. But she said nothing. Instead, she bent down to pick up her handbag and then search inside it for a handkerchief.

Fiona thought of the plates of sandwiches that were already made up and covered in tinfoil, awaiting the mourners who would call in after church. Mrs Mooney had sliced fruit cakes and sponges that neighbours had kindly handed in, and Patrick had brought up extra sherry and whisky glasses for those who would like a drink. But it seemed that none of that hospitality was being extended to Nance's only sister and nephew.

Angela reached across and touched her aunt's arm. 'Come back to the house,' she said. 'You don't need to rush back to the hotel yet.' She looked pointedly at her mother. 'They've travelled all the way down from Dublin.'

Nance tilted her chin and said in a stiff voice, 'They're welcome to do whatever they feel is best.'

'No,' Catherine said. 'We won't come back to the house. You're all tired . . . we'll leave you to it and see you in the morning.' She passed in front of her sister now to clasp Bridget's hands in hers, and then she moved along and did the same to both Angela and Fiona. Then, she put her arm through Joseph's, and they walked down the aisle and out of the church.

Fiona avoided looking at Angela as she knew she was incensed at their mother's rudeness. She was upset about it herself, but the last thing they needed was a confrontation and a big row the night before the funeral. The situation was saved when the priest came out of the vestry, and came over to speak to them about arrangements for the funeral service in the morning.

When they got outside the church, there were more people waiting to offer their sympathies to the family. They stood for a while talking, and when they finally started to make their way back home, Fiona angled it so she and Angela walked behind their mother, Bridget and Mrs Mooney.

'I'm absolutely mortified at our mother's attitude,' Angela said in a low voice. 'Half the town will be back at the house and she can't ask her own sister and nephew.'

'Please don't say anything.' Fiona put her arm through Angela's to draw her to a halt. 'Wait – I don't want anyone else hearing.' She took a deep breath. 'Look, I promised Mam I wouldn't mention it, but she and Daddy had a bit of a row when they came back from Dublin. Well, it was actually a big row. It must have been on her mind, because the day after Daddy died, she asked me not to mention it to anyone else. She says she'd rather we remembered all the good times, and how they always got on well. I wouldn't have broken my promise to her, but otherwise you wouldn't understand why she's like this.'

'Of course I won't mention it,' Angela said. They started walking again now there was a reasonable distance between them and the others. 'I'm the last one that wants any trouble – but a row between her and Daddy doesn't give her the right to be so bloody awful to Aunt Catherine and Joseph. I know she's awkward with her at the best of times, but to do it so publicly at Daddy's funeral was not nice at all.'

'Well, the row between them was actually about Aunt Catherine and Joseph,' Fiona explained. 'From what I heard, they had a row when they were at her house the night Daddy collapsed. After they got home, I heard Mam and Daddy arguing in the parlour. I tried not to listen, but the louder bits I couldn't help overhearing were about Aunt Catherine.'

'Actually, I know all about it,' Angela said. There was no point in staying silent. It was betraying her aunt, but it wasn't fair on Fiona, when she had been so honest. 'I rang Aunt Catherine the night it happened and she was upset and ended up telling me all about it.' She raised her eyes to the heavens. 'Mam is raging because Aunt Catherine asked Daddy if Joseph could come down to Tullamore to work in the bar when you went to New York.'

Fiona looked at her in surprise. 'Mam never mentioned a word about it to me. But isn't Joseph working in a shop in Dublin – one of the department stores?'

'He was let go,' Angela said.

Fiona looked at her for a few moments, turning the information over in her mind. 'I think Joseph working in the bar is a great idea. What did Daddy say?'

'He thought it was great, too – and that's what caused the row.'

'But what's Mam's problem?' Fiona said. 'They would have to get someone after I go anyway. Mam couldn't be in the shop all the time, and Joseph is part of the family. He's a lovely, cheery guy – he would be brilliant in the shop and bar. We'd have all the young ones in the town queuing up to be served by him.' She put her hand over her mouth. 'That's doesn't sound right, but you know what I mean.'

Angela's frown deepened. 'In fairness to Mam, that's not the full story.' She sighed. 'You do know Joseph was in a band?'

'I knew he was in a showband for a while, but then I heard him saying to someone at the house that he had moved to a rock band. I was busy going in and out with sandwiches at the time so I couldn't really listen.'

Angela then went on to relate the information her aunt had told her.

'*Drugs?*' Fiona's hand came up to her mouth. 'Oh, God!'

'Joseph wasn't involved,' Angela said quickly, 'but she said he's come home late at night the worst for wear for drink. She said it would do him good to get out of Dublin for a while and away from that crowd.'

'She's right,' Fiona said. 'I wouldn't be too worried about the drinking bit – a lot of single lads his age go to the pubs at the weekend, and have a few too many. Sure, we see it in the bar all the time. It's the drugs that I'd be worried about. Thank God he's not involved with them himself, but I can see how Aunt Catherine wouldn't want him mixing with a lad who is.'

'And there's more likelihood of drugs in these rock bands – you only have to read the papers. Look at The Rolling Stones and all the trouble they've been in over drugs.' She shook her head. 'I don't think Joseph is the type to do anything like that, but if he's around people who're taking drugs, you just never know when he could be tempted.'

'You would think that Mam would want to help her sister out,' Fiona said. 'You'd think she could at least give him a chance.'

'Aunt Catherine told me that Daddy wanted Joseph to move down and help in the bar, but then Mam put a spoke in the wheel. I'm not a bit surprised.' Angela's voice was flat.

'There's nothing we can do about it now,' Fiona said. 'Everyone is too upset about Daddy. And whatever she says, Mam must feel terrible that they had such a bad argument hours before he died. We'll just have to hope that nothing else awkward happens with Aunt Catherine. We'll leave it until everything has calmed down after the funeral.'

'Okay,' Angela said. 'You know best. You're the one that is the closest to Mam – living at home and working with her every day.'

'I don't know if any of us are that close to her, really,' Fiona said. 'There are times I can't fathom her at all. I don't know why she's so angry with Aunt Catherine, especially now when we have so much going on.'

'Forget it for now. Hopefully it will all sort out.' Angela looked at her. 'What's going to happen when you go away? Has Mam said anything about it?'

'It's unlikely now that I'll be going to New York.'

'I know you're not going *now*. I know you have to postpone the trip. It wouldn't be the best start for you going so soon. I meant when you go away *later*, when you feel more up to it.'

'Everything has changed so much I don't know

what's going to happen. I don't know how Mam's going to be. For all I know I might never go to New York. The nanny's job might go to somebody else. When I rang Mrs Davis she said she would do her best to manage until I let her know what's happening. I'll just have to wait and see.'

CHAPTER 10

On the Friday morning Nance and her three daughters gathered together in the house dressed in black or navy coats and hats, ready to leave for the funeral.

When they stepped outside, it struck Fiona what a still, colourless day it was. Just as still and colourless as the house now seemed without the cheery presence of their father.

The next hour and a half passed in a haze as they repeated similar rituals to the night before, receiving condolences and sympathy and shaking more hands on their way into the church. And then sitting through the funeral Mass, and shedding more tears as they listened to the words the elderly priest had to say about one of their most valued parishioners.

And then they were back out into the freezing crowded churchyard, with more people speaking to them and shaking their hands. Three of the nuns from Bridget's school came over to offer their condolences and Nance Tracey thanked them for coming and told them they were welcome to come back to the bar for a meal later on.

At one point Fiona felt a hand on her shoulder and when she turned around she found herself face to face with Paul Moore.

'I'm sorry for your trouble, Fiona,' he said. His voice was low and serious. 'Your father was a lovely man. Everyone said so.'

'Thanks, Paul,' she heard herself say. 'And thanks for coming to the funeral.' She had dreaded seeing him, but amazingly she felt no awkwardness now, apart from gratitude for his kindness.

He smiled at her, and then he turned back towards her mother and her sisters to offer his sympathies to them as well.

And then, as though emerging from a dream, Fiona somehow found herself walking behind the shiny black hearse on the long road to the cemetery, as flakes of snow started to fall.

'This is all we need,' Nance said, her voice filled with hopelessness.

'It's nicer than rain,' Fiona said. 'And it's only a light shower.'

'It's nice to look at,' her mother replied. 'As long as no one slips and falls on it.' She looked at Angela. 'Are you okay? Are you managing?'

Angela looked back at her mother, her face pale and serious. 'Yes, thanks,' she said. 'I'm managing fine.' She had brought her calliper with her, but so far had managed without it. She was wearing black leather Mary-Jane shoes she had got made for special occasions. At a quick glance they looked like ordinary shoes, but the shoe for her bad foot was a smaller size – it was narrower and had a reinforced sole and a broader heel. Both shoes, the specialist cobbler had reassured her, had been finished with a good grip for weather like this.

'Be careful anyway,' her mother said, closing her eyes and sighing. 'We don't want anything else happening.'

Angela looked away. For once – especially today – she wished her mother could speak to her in a way that was motherly and caring, instead of making her feel like the family casualty.

By the time they turned into the gates of the cemetery, there was a light covering of snow over all the graves and the grass surrounding them. And the snow was still falling, although the flakes had become smaller and lighter.

It struck Fiona, as they slowly walked along, that the scene around her looked like something from a painting. In a strange way, it was almost beautiful. And she was glad for her father that it was, because it made her feel a tiny bit better about what was happening.

But then, as they walked up the avenue towards the grave, where her father's body would soon be buried, a dark feeling descended on her. All that was left of the man they had loved and lived with was now dressed in his best suit and shirt and nailed down in the mahogany coffin in the back of the hearse in front of them.

How could it be that she would never see him again? Never speak to him, never feel his hand on her shoulder when he came into the shop or when she went into the bar. She could not conceive of the fact that he was gone – and gone forever.

All he would be from now on was a place to visit in a cold cemetery, with his name and birth-date on a grey headstone, amidst a sea of hundreds of other headstones.

The thought brought a feeling of panic in her chest, and she felt tears flooding into her eyes once again. Her arm tightened on her mother's, looking for some sort of comfort or reassurance, but her mother did not respond – her mam was just staring ahead to where the men who had dug the grave were standing in attendance beside the priest, waiting for the family to arrive.

Fiona blinked furiously now, then looked over at Angela and Bridget. Their eyes were cast downwards, and she guessed they were thinking the same morbid thoughts as herself. She suddenly felt that if she didn't distract herself she was going to start crying in a way that she would not be able to stop. Her legs felt weak and she imagined she might even fall.

'I'm glad everything is white,' she suddenly heard herself say. 'Daddy always loved the snow.' She leaned forward to look at Angela and Bridget, smiling brightly now – too bright and forced. 'Do you remember how he used to wake us up every winter the first morning when it had snowed?'

'Yes.' Bridget smiled back at her. 'And do you remember us going sledging on the small hill behind the house? I used to love it when he pulled us along and pretended he was going to let us go.'

'There was one morning,' their mother said, 'when he got up early and built a snowman in the front garden for you. And then he laughed because I gave out hell to him when I saw he had used a cashmere scarf I had bought him out of Switzer's for tying around the neck.'

Their quiet laughter mingled with tears.

'He was a good husband and father,' Nance said. 'He adored all three of you.'

They walked along, trying to find more remembered little incidents to give them comfort as they got closer to the dark hole that lay ahead. At one point Fiona noticed how quiet Angela was and, when she glanced over at her, she saw the tight look on her sister's face and the guarded look in her eyes. It dawned on her that while she and her mother and Bridget had endless stories about their father and the snow, her middle sister had not joined in because she had not been part of those memories. Although she had been home most Christmases, she probably had missed the first snowfall while still in hospital in Dublin and, of course, Fiona now thought with a little pang, she wouldn't have been able to do things like sliding and sledging. Angela, she realised, had not joined in with reminiscing because she had nothing to say.

Eventually they reached the graveside and the burial rites began.

Then, as the coffin was lowered into the ground, the snow stopped and the winter sun came out.

Afterwards, as they all walked back to the waiting funeral cars, Fiona noticed that everything around her in the cemetery grounds – the trees, the headstones, the shrubs and grass – was covered in a sparkling brilliant white.

She thought it was the most beautiful sight she had ever seen, on the saddest day of her life.

CHAPTER 11

The funeral cars all pulled up in front of Tracey's Bar which was now open for the first time since the landlord had died. Caterers and waitresses had been hired from a local firm to provide the main mourners with hot dinners of chicken and ham, or roast beef, and a variety of vegetables.

As Fiona and her mother and sisters came out of the car and started walking towards the door of the bar, their mother turned to them and said, 'We just have to get through this last bit now. People have been good and everything, but after this we need to all go home to a bit of peace and quiet. I don't think I'm fit to take much more of talking and meeting people.'

Fiona put her arm through her mother's. 'You'll be fine,' she said. 'You had hardly any breakfast – you'll feel much better when you've had something to eat.

Angela suddenly felt she had to say something before she went into the bar. She touched Fiona's elbow. 'Before we go inside,' she said, looking straight at her mother, 'I've asked Aunt Catherine and Joseph.'

Her mother's face stiffened and she turned her head as though staring down the street, without speaking.

Angela turned towards Fiona and Bridget. 'I'd like to think they will be made as welcome as any of the other relatives and neighbours.'

All three girls looked at their mother.

Eventually, Nance angled her body towards them, although she did not meet their gaze. She shrugged. 'That's fine.' Her voice sounded hoarse. 'We wouldn't expect anyone to come all the way from Dublin and not have something to eat.'

Angela felt her heart starting to pound. She often did what she wanted without any discussion, but this time it was not about her, and she was determined that the right thing should be done. 'I think they should sit with us,' she said, sounding determined. 'She's our only close relative on your side.'

Nance took a deep breath and then pursed her mouth tightly as though trying to prevent her thoughts from forming into words.

'Whatever differences there are between you,' Angela said, 'it's got nothing to do with the rest of us. I'm speaking for myself, but I think Fiona and Bridget feel the same. We all like her and Joseph and we don't want them to think we're taking sides against them. Aunt Catherine has always been good to me, and spoken fondly about everyone, and whatever is behind all this, I'm certainly not prepared to snub her and Joseph today of all days.'

Her mother's eyes suddenly flashed. 'Well, you've certainly made your point, Angela. And I'm not one bit surprised you would take your aunt's side. I know you see her regularly in Dublin and no doubt you have a great time talking about me there, running me down.'

Fiona's throat tightened. This was the last thing they needed the day of the funeral. She looked at her sister and her mother, wondering if she should step in now. Angela was of course in the right, she thought, but their mother didn't look as though she was going to be able to cope if any more was said. If things escalated any further she might refuse to come in to the reception, and that would be a total disaster.

'This is not the time or the place,' Angela said quietly, 'for us to talk like this. All I will say is that if you ever came with me to Aunt Catherine's house, you would see that we don't sit there running anybody down. She's not that sort of person. She's kind and nice. Any differences you have with her are nothing to do with me. But, I do think that it's time you talked to her and sorted it all out.'

Tears suddenly came into her mother's eyes. 'There are things you don't know about Catherine . . .' She went into her coat pocket for a hanky. 'Things that none of you know about . . .'

'I think it's obvious there's a lot we don't know,' Angela stated quietly. 'And I'm not saying you need to sort those things out today. I'm just saying that I'm not prepared to see her and Joseph being snubbed again.'

Bridget came forward now and put a hand on her mother's shoulder and the other hand on Angela's. 'Look, the priest and everyone are going to be waiting for us. Let's go in now and leave all this business behind.' She looked from one face to the other. 'And when we go inside now, I'm sure nobody is going to be snubbed. Daddy wouldn't have wanted anything like that. It wouldn't have been his way at all.'

'We're all in agreement,' Fiona said in a low voice. 'Aunt Catherine and Joseph will be made welcome the same as anyone else, and the rest of the afternoon will go the way it should.'

'That's all we want,' Nance said. 'We want your father to have the same dignified send-off he gave to everyone else.' There was a pause. 'And you can all be assured that this afternoon I'll be civil to anyone who is civil to me.'

Then, one by one, they all gathered themselves together and walked into the bar. Patrick and Mrs Mooney were just inside the door waiting for them and, before they got a chance to say anything, the housekeeper led them to a table over by the fire set for six people.

As they made their way through the crowds, acknowledging people and having a quick word as they went, Fiona noticed that all the tables had white damask cloths on them and small vases with pink carnations.

'I didn't know who you might want to sit next to you,' Mrs Mooney said, 'but I have your sister and Seán's brothers and sisters already seated at a table behind you, and have their dinner orders taken.'

'That's good of you,' Nance Tracey said. 'It all looks very well.'

Mrs Mooney leaned over the table and spoke quietly. 'Father McEvoy and the curate are in the snug now chatting to the other priests, maybe you might like them to sit here beside you?'

Nance looked at her daughters and held her hands out, leaving the decision to them.

Angela turned to Fiona and Bridget. 'That might be best if the priests sit with us,' she said. 'Nobody else is going to mind.' She had already glanced around the room and noticed that her aunt and Joseph were just a few tables away from them and looked to be well settled and in a deep conversation with Jimmy Tracey.

No one said anything, but Fiona felt that there was a sense of relief.

'Everything looks very nice,' Fiona said, as they sat down. Her gaze wandered round the tables and the groups of people who were still to be seated, and eventually she saw where her aunt and Joseph were and gave them a wave and a smile.

'It does look well,' Nance said, 'it must be the caterers who have sorted it, because I didn't order flowers or anything.'

Fiona could tell her mother was really making an effort to sound normal, and she felt a small wave of sympathy for her. She just knew that her mother was seeing the bar through different eyes now that their father was gone. Fiona understood this, because she could feel it herself. Everything was changed.

Patrick and the others who were helping him behind the bar seemed to all be managing perfectly well. Everything was running as it should, the food, the service. People were mixing, beginning to relax and chat more now that the most serious business of the church and burial was over. But, there was no denying that the atmosphere in the bar was different without Seán Tracey. On funeral days his presence added something more to the occasion – something Fiona found difficult to describe. It was as if the master at the helm of the ship had gone and everything now seemed mildly afloat.

Mrs Mooney went into the snug and informed the parish priest and the curate that their meal would be served with the Traceys', and the priests came to join them. Father McEvoy, having had several whiskeys to warm him up after the cold cemetery, was talkative and told Nance and the girls how glad he was to have been available to conduct the funeral. Had it been the following week, he explained, he would have been away on a week's holiday to Scotland. He reassured them that the more serious and abstemious curate, Father Fahy, would have done a fine job with the Mass in his absence, but he said that Seán Tracey was one parishioner whose funeral he would not have liked to miss. A few more exchanges were made between the priests and Nance about the unexpected nature of Seán's passing and how much the town would miss him.

Just then Patrick came with a bottle of red wine and glasses for the table. The wine had been a prior arrangement made by Nance the night before for all the clergy in attendance at the funeral.

Father McEvoy poured himself and Nance a glass, then he looked over at the curate. 'Will you break out and have a glass of wine with your meal?'

'No, thank you,' Father Fahy replied, giving a small smile. 'I'm fine with water.'

Father McEvoy held the bottle aloft looking around at the girls, to see if anyone else would like to indulge. Fiona, aware of her mother's disapproval of young people drinking, and Bridget, who had no interest in alcohol, both said they were happy with a mineral. But, to Fiona's surprise, Angela held her glass out.

'Good girl!' the priest said. His voice was a mixture of surprise and approval. He leaned across the table and poured her a glass. 'It's Angela, isn't it?'

'It is, Father,' Angela said, used to people not being sure of her name.

Fiona's saw her mother's eyebrows rise at the thought of Angela drinking alcohol in front of the priest, but she said nothing.

'How is life treating you in Dublin?' Father McEvoy asked.

'Fine,' Angela said. 'I like the city.'

'And you're working and everything?'

'I am,' she said. 'In an office in the city centre, near Leeson Street.'

'You're a great example,' he said. 'Getting out there and on with your life. There are people I know, perfectly able-bodied, who wouldn't have half the go you have. You're to be admired – you've never let the affliction with your leg hold you back. And you always dress well, better than many a girl in the town. All praise to you now.'

Angela lifted her wineglass and took a drink from it, then she turned away to look in the direction of the snug as though the priest had never spoken.

Fiona's heart had missed a beat at the patronising comment. She saw a slight shifting in their seats from her mother and Bridget, and wondered if they were uncomfortable with it too. In the following silence, the curate lifted his glass of water and took a sip from it.

Fiona watched then as her mother bent down to lift her handbag from the floor, then open it and rummage inside as though searching through lots of things for something important buried at the bottom. Her handbags, unlike Fiona's own casual bags, were always very organised. Mam only believed in carrying the essentials, her lipstick and powder, purse and a hanky or tissues. The gesture made her realise that her mother too felt awkward at the tactless remarks, and rather than saying anything was just trying to look distracted as though she hadn't really heard.

Fiona turned to Angela then, to raise her eyes to the ceiling to indicate how clumsy and insensitive she thought the priest was, but Angela was not looking in her direction. She had a sudden urge to put her hand on her sister's and give it a little squeeze, but something prevented her from doing it. For one thing, the family rarely showed physical signs of emotion unless it was something very serious and, secondly, she knew the priest was oblivious to the fact that his comment about doing so well in spite of her 'affliction' might be perceived as anything other than a compliment.

There was a silence and Fiona noticed that her mother had taken a hanky from her bag, and was now turning it over between her hands almost like she did with her rosary beads.

Then, as if summoned to fill the awkward gap, a waitress appeared at the table holding two plates with roast beef. Anticipating her question about who had ordered what, Father McEvoy moved his knife and fork further apart to allow her to place one of the plates in front of him. The waitress then looked at Nance, and said, 'Roast beef?' and when Nance nodded she placed the other in front of her. Within seconds, two other waitresses followed with plates for Father Fahy and the girls, and then they were all served and the conversation moved to observations about the meal. How floury the potatoes were, how tender the beef was, and how nice the chicken and stuffing looked.

When everyone was more or less finished eating, Nance, who had only picked at her meal, looked at Father McEvoy and said, 'You said earlier that you were travelling to Scotland next week, Father? Whereabouts will you go?'

Fiona was surprised that under the circumstances her mother might be in any way interested in the priest's plans, and then she thought that she was deliberately bringing the conversation back to a safer subject to prevent any further blunders from the priest.

Father McEvoy took a mouthful of wine, then sat back in his chair, smiling. 'I'm actually going to visit an old seminary friend, who is the parish priest in a small mining village called Cleland,' he told them. 'Nice parishioners, most of them from Irish stock who had worked in the mines over here – the Carlow and Portlaoise areas. Their grandfathers would have left Ireland in the twenties and thirties to work in the Lanarkshire mines. It's a grand little village, and very handy as it has a train station and all, with trains running straight to Edinburgh and Glasgow.'

Bridget sat forward now, her hands clasped in front of her on the table. 'Do you travel much, Father?'

'Whenever I get the chance,' he said. He turned and placed a hand on Father Fahy's shoulder. 'And when I know the parish is well taken care of in my absence.'

Nance smiled and nodded her head in the curate's direction.

'I love to get over to my friend in Scotland at least once a year and down to an uncle of mine who is in a retirement home for clergy in Manchester. And I enjoy travelling out to places like Rome and Malta for the church conferences. If I can plan it, I like to have a few days to tour around the cities, and catch a bit of the sun.' He indicated the curate. 'Father Fahy here is more of a home-bird, aren't you?'

Father Fahy smiled and nodded. 'Flying wouldn't appeal to me at all. I feel it's unnatural. If we were meant to fly we would have wings.'

Fiona noticed how Angela caught Bridget's eye and they both smiled.

'Well, for shorter journeys there's always the boat,' Father McEvoy said, 'unless of course you have a phobia of travel altogether. A psychological problem with it.' When Father Fahy sat back in his chair and said nothing, he continued. 'I think travel broadens the mind. I think it's good to see how people in other countries live.' He looked around the group. 'Don't you agree?'

'Indeed,' Nance said, her tone distracted.

The others around the table nodded in quiet assent.

Then, just as Fiona had dreaded, his gaze settled on her and she could almost predict what he was going to say.

'Ah, Fiona – the last time I spoke to your father, God rest his soul, he told me you were heading off to New York, that you had work all arranged out there.'

Fiona nodded. 'Yes, Father, I did.' Her eyes flickered over to her mother for a second and she saw the tight look on her face.

'Now there's a lively city – New York. I visited a cousin there a few years back. And when were you to go?'

Fiona felt her cheeks flushing. 'Next week,' she said, feeling very uncomfortable. 'But with everything that has happened, I've postponed things for the time being . . .'

His face grew very solemn. 'I'd say you might be needed here at home now, to help look after your mother.' He opened his hands expansively. 'At times like this, families need to pull together, look after each other. Wouldn't you say?'

Fiona became aware of a strange lump in her throat. 'We haven't had time to talk about things yet.' She felt flustered now, and found it hard to get the words out, and she could hear that she sounded as though she had suddenly gone hoarse.

Nance took a deep breath. 'We'll see what happens, Father . . . when we've had time to think things through.'

Angela moved forward and placed her two manicured hands on the table. 'Today is about our family saying goodbye to Daddy, not making big decisions for the future. I'm sure you would agree with that, Father?'

Father McEvoy's eyebrows shot up. 'Of course,' he said. 'The future, as they say, will take care of itself.'

The waitresses reappeared and started to clear the empty plates and check whether people would like hot apple tart and custard or sherry trifle.

When the desserts were finished and more plates cleared, cups of tea were distributed. The finale was a free whiskey or sherry for everyone and, after saying a few words about his brother and how much he would be missed, Jimmy Tracey asked everyone in the bar to raise their glasses in a final toast to him.

Shortly afterwards, as the two priests made their farewells, Father McEvoy bent low to speak quietly in Nance's ear. None of the girls could hear what he said, but it looked to be of some comfort to their mother as she smiled and said a tearful 'Thank you' to him.

The priests left, then more people started to move around the room. The men fond of a drink began gravitating towards the bar, whilst others made their way over to Nance and her daughters to repeat their condolences and say a few more kind words about Seán before making their way home.

At one point, Angela got to her feet, giving a little gasp as she did so.

'Are you okay?' Fiona asked.

'I'm fine. My leg is a bit sore from all the walking,' she said. 'I'm just going to ask Aunt Catherine to join us for a while now. People are starting to go and I don't want to miss them.'

Fiona put her hand over her sister's. 'I'll go over to them. It will save you getting up. I was just waiting until everyone had finished to go over to them myself.'

Angela thanked her and then she sat back down.

Nance leaned across to Bridget. 'I've just been looking around. I haven't seen any of the nuns . . . I did say to them outside the church that they were welcome to come back here for something to eat.'

'I was thinking that earlier myself, but I don't suppose they would come into a pub,' Bridget said. 'They probably had to go back to the school anyway.'

'It was good of them to come. It's a fairly long drive from Athlone.'

'It was nice of them,' Bridget agreed. She turned to the table behind, where there were a couple of free chairs. 'I'll pull some extra chairs over to let people sit down beside us if they want to.'

Fiona came back to the table with her aunt, carrying her coat and hat and handbag. Joseph came behind, carrying his mother's sherry glass and another glass with lager.

Angela moved her chair to let her aunt sit beside her, while Joseph sat down between his aunt and his mother. Fiona sat at the opposite side of the table with Bridget.

'That was a great turnout,' Joseph said quietly to his aunt. 'A huge crowd in the church.'

Nance turned towards him, although she did not look directly at him. 'It was,' she said, nodding her head. 'Seán was highly thought of.'

Bridget smiled over at her cousin now. 'He did the same for so many others. When you think of all the wakes he attended, and the funeral receptions that were held in the bar here.' Tears suddenly appeared at the corners of her eyes.

Aunt Catherine noticed, and she leaned over and put her hand over Bridget's. 'The Mass was very nice too. The priest said some lovely things about him.'

'He did,' Nance said. 'He couldn't have been nicer.'

Fiona watched her mother closely, checking how she reacted to her sister and nephew, and so far she felt relieved that all seemed fine.

Catherine leaned forward in her chair to speak directly to her sister. 'I thought Seán's brother Jimmy spoke very well there at the end.' She turned to Joseph. 'Would you mind changing places with me? I feel I'm being bad-mannered talking across you to Nance. It would be easier if you sat next to Angela and I'll move up beside Nance.'

While they were moving seats, Fiona looked

across at Angela and caught her eye. Angela raised her eyebrows and smiled and Fiona smiled back at her, thinking things were working out better than they had expected.

She could hear her Aunt Catherine enquiring after some of Seán's other relatives she knew, and the two sisters sat talking in what Fiona thought was almost an easy way with each other.

Patrick came to the table to see if anyone would like a drink.

Bridget said, 'I'll have a glass of red lemonade, please, Patrick.'

He looked at Joseph. 'Would you like a pint?'

'I would, thanks. I'll have a pint of lager.'

Patrick looked at Fiona. 'Would any of the ladies like a drink?'

There was a silence then Angela said, 'I'll have a Babycham, please, Patrick.' She looked down at her mother and her aunt. 'Will you have the same?'

'Go on,' her aunt said, 'you've twisted my arm.' She looked at Nance. 'You'll have one too, won't you?'

Nance thought for a moment, then she looked at the barman. 'I might as well. It might help me to sleep tonight.'

Fiona waited a few seconds until her mother was talking again, then she turned to Patrick and said in a low voice, 'I'll have a Babycham as well.'

He nodded and winked at her, knowing that Fiona didn't want to draw attention to her having a drink in front of her mother.

The local National School headmaster and his wife came over to shake hands with all the family, and to speak to Nance for a few minutes. As they moved away, some local neighbours came to sit down at the other side of Nance, so she had to turn away from her sister and nephew to give the people her full attention.

Bridget looked across at her cousin. 'Are you still playing music?'

'I am,' he said, 'but I'm taking a break from playing with bands at the minute. I was in a rock band for a while, playing guitar, but the lead singer had to leave and it wasn't the same without him. At the minute, I'm actually trying to write some music.'

Fiona raised her eyebrows, impressed at the news. 'I don't think I've ever met anyone who writes songs before,' she said. 'Is it the music you write or the words of the songs?' It had been so long since she had had a proper conversation with her cousin that she had almost forgotten what a really nice fellow he was. In a way he reminded her a little of Patrick. He had the same soft and kindly manner, although he was much younger than the barman and chattier. And of course he was also better looking, and had fashionable hair and clothes which made a huge difference.

'I'm interested in writing music and lyrics,' he said. 'I did a short course a couple of years ago, and I really enjoyed it and picked up the basics.' He shrugged. 'I've been out of work for a few weeks, and it's a bad time of the year to find anything new, so I'm making the best of the time I have off.' He smiled and held his hands up. 'Look, who knows if I'll get anywhere with writing stuff, but I'm enjoying it which is the main thing.'

'I think it's brilliant,' Angela said. 'You never know where it might lead.'

Catherine turned around now to join in the conversation, her face flushing. 'He's never had time off work since he left school. It's the first time he's been out of work, so I'm sure he'll find something soon.'

Fiona could tell her aunt was embarrassed about Joseph being out of work.

'I don't care what I do,' Joseph said. 'As long as I get something to tide me over, and I can do my songwriting in my time off.'

Some more of Seán's relatives came over to talk to Nance and the girls, and they sat talking for a while and gradually the bar began to empty.

'I think we had better be moving,' Catherine said, lifting her coat. She looked over to Nance now, who was talking to an elderly man who was a regular customer.

'Will you come back to the house for a while?' Fiona asked.

'No, we won't, thanks,' her aunt replied. 'We have to get back up to Dublin and it's snowing again. You never know what the roads could be like. And the house will be cold with us gone since yesterday. By the time we get the fires going and everything it will be dark.'

'Well, we're heading back up to the house now,' Angela said, 'so we'll walk you out to the car.'

Catherine glanced over at her sister, who seemed to be listening intently to the old man. 'You go on ahead, girls,' she said. 'I'll wait to have a few words with your mother.'

Everyone started putting on coats and scarves and hats, and pulling on gloves. Joseph buttoned his heavy dark woollen coat up to the neck and put a checked scarf on over it, then he went to stand by Angela's chair, holding his arm out for her to take it. Angela sorted her hat and gloves and put her handbag strap up on her shoulder and then she slipped her arm through her cousin's.

As she walked with Bridget towards the door, Fiona again noticed the way Angela and Joseph walked together and chatted so naturally, and it struck her that Angela seemed easier with him than she did with her sisters.

In a few days' time, she thought, Angela would be back in Dublin and Bridget back at the convent, leaving her home on her own with her mother. How different it was all going to be without her father in the house and in the shop and bar. Nothing would seem the same. Tears rushed into her eyes as realisation dawned once again that her beloved father was gone forever.

CHAPTER 12

The footpath had a dusting of snow over it. Walking carefully, Angela and Joseph reached the car, which was parked halfway between the bar and the house. When they came to a halt Fiona looked back and saw there was no sign of either her mother or her aunt.

'I'll just put the engine on to warm the car,' Joseph said. He looked at Angela. 'You'd be safer standing in against the wall.' He guided her over to the side and Angela unhooked her arm from his. Then, he opened the door and put the key in the ignition to switch it on. He leaned into the back seat and took out a snow-scraper, and came out to clear the front windscreen and then the back.

'I don't know where Mam's got to,' Bridget said, clapping her gloved hands together to warm them. 'It's far too cold to wait outside for her.'

'Why don't you sit in the car for a few minutes?' Joseph suggested. 'It heats up quickly.'

'You all get in and I'll walk down to the bar and tell them to get a move on,' Fiona said. She went over to where Angela was standing and said quietly,

'It's a good sign they're not back yet – it means they're getting on better, thank God.'

'I was just thinking the very same thing,' Angela said in a low voice. 'Although I think Aunt Catherine is a saint for being so nice to Mam after the way she's treated her.'

Fiona felt a ripple of irritation. It was okay for Angela to complain, she wasn't the one who was going to be left with Mam. In a few days' time she would be heading back up to her own life in Dublin.

Angela gave a weary smile. 'I shouldn't be moaning about Mam – it's probably just because my leg is sore and I've a bit of a headache. I'm sure none of us feel at our best with all that's happened over the last few days.' She halted. 'It's good that they're getting on better, especially at a time like this. It's better to look forward than look back, isn't it? That's what Daddy would have said.'

'It is,' Fiona said. 'And you're right, we all feel the same.'

She put her arm out the way that Joseph had done, and was pleased when Angela took it and they carefully walked over the snowy pavement to the car where Bridget and Joseph were busy chatting away. When Angela was safely inside, Fiona told them she would be back in a few minutes.

She went back to the bar as quickly as she could on the slippery path. She reached the main entrance and was about to go inside to the bar when she thought she heard someone in the shop.

Then she heard her mother's voice. The tone of it made her freeze.

'I don't want to hear anything more about Joseph coming down here again. This idea you have of him coming down to work here in the bar is ludicrous. We don't need any more help. Patrick and Fiona and myself will manage perfectly well.'

Her throat tightened in apprehension. It was clear her mother was talking to her Aunt Catherine.

'But what if Fiona decides to go to New York in a few months?' her aunt asked.

'Fiona has told me that she has no plans to go now, and I don't think she'll want to go at all after what has happened. And if by any chance she does decide to go, we'll cross that bridge when we come to it. But if I decide to take on more staff, that will be my decision and nobody else's.'

'But you know that Seán wanted Joseph to work in the bar. As soon as I mentioned that he had lost his job, he offered to help.'

'Don't bring Seán into this. And I don't know how you can stand there and talk about that night.'

'Nance, you know I'm speaking the truth. And I wasn't going to bring this up today of all days, but you're leaving me with no option. Seán suggested this a while back. He dropped in at the house on his way home from Dublin, and we got talking about Joseph and he asked me what I thought about him coming down to work for him.'

'You'd like me to believe that, wouldn't you?'

Her mother's tone was low, but full of vitriol and anger. 'You can say anything about Seán now he's gone. He was a good, kind man and I know he would have done anything to help anyone – but you're not going to use him to force me into having Joseph down here to work beside us and no doubt live with us as well.'

'I don't understand how you can treat Joseph as if he's a black stranger to you. You, my only sister.'

'You know why,' her mother said. 'You know perfectly well why I don't want him down here. When I wanted to see him – to see you both – you told me that I couldn't. You even moved back over to England to get away from me – you did everything to put as much distance between us as you could. Well, you should have been satisfied when your plans all worked – I left you both alone – isn't that what you wanted? Isn't that what you told me?'

Fiona listened now as her aunt started to cry. 'Oh, Nance,' she said, 'you've twisted everything. You know why I had to do that. At the time you weren't well.'

'And you know *why* I wasn't well,' her mother said. 'It was the situation with you and Joseph that brought it all on. I got over it all – I had no option – and I got on with my life with Seán and the girls. That's what you wanted, and it suited you for years not to have anything to do with me, didn't it?' There was a strained silence. 'Admit that, at least, Catherine. You've painted me as the bad one all these years. Give me the courtesy of admitting the truth over that, and don't make out I'm mad and imagined it all.'

Fiona held her breath, still listening, and trying to work out what it was all about.

'Yes,' her aunt said, 'I did ask you to leave us alone, and yes, we did move over to England – but that was because of Kenneth's work. I had no choice at the time. I didn't move there to stop you seeing Joseph. You know that Kenneth made all those decisions, not me.'

'Well, you went along with him. It suited you.'

'It didn't. I would have rather stayed in Dublin and that we had worked this thing out between us.'

'You could have refused to go.'

'I couldn't. You know what Kenneth was like. And I was young, Nance – we were both young. It wasn't easy for me starting all over again in England with a toddler.'

'Don't expect me to feel sorry for you about that now, Catherine. I remember when it all happened. You just upped and left and I was left for weeks not even knowing where you'd gone.'

'Kenneth wouldn't let me write. He was afraid you would follow us.'

'Well, he must have been happy that I didn't. I picked myself up and got on with my own life, with no help from you. And by the time you moved back to Dublin, and decided you wanted to see me again, I had my own life and family.'

'I tried to see you, I did everything I could. I

kept hoping I'd see you up at the hospital visiting Angela, but you never came.'

'Don't you dare!' Her mother's voice was louder now and vicious. 'Don't you dare bring Angela into this!'

Fiona flattened her back against the wall now, shocked at her mother's reaction. There was much more going on between her mother and her aunt than anyone had envisaged.

'Look, Nance,' her aunt said, her voice shaky and uncertain, 'I came here today to honour Seán's memory and to support you and the girls. I thought the world of him, he was a lovely man. I know things weren't easy for you earlier on, but you had a great marriage and a great family together.'

'I know all that,' her mother said, 'and if things hadn't happened, we might still have him. If he hadn't got all worked up after we had been to your house, then he might never have had the heart attack. He might still be alive.'

Fiona put her hands over her mouth and closed her eyes. Mam had actually said it. She had more or less accused her aunt of causing her father's heart attack.

'Oh, Nance,' Aunt Catherine said, 'that's the most hurtful thing you've ever said to me. And you've said a lot of very hurtful things over the years.'

'It's the truth! He was fine that day after we came back from the hospital. He was fine when

125

we were visiting Angela, and he was fine at your house until you brought up all the stuff about Joseph working for us.'

'But Nance, you know that Seán thought it was a good idea.' Catherine's voice was high and frustrated now. 'I didn't cause Seán to get angry that evening. He was fine with me – the argument was between you and him.'

'You knew I wasn't happy about Joseph coming down here to work – and you knew why. Well, you will be happy to know that we argued all the way home and when we got back to the house. And Fiona heard us arguing which has made it all worse.'

'Oh no!' There was a pause. 'What did she hear?'

'Enough to know there was a problem, but she didn't know what it was about. We spoke about it the morning after her father died. Thank God she knows how well we got on – that the argument was a rare one.'

There was a silence, during which Fiona heard the main door of the building open. She glanced around, but didn't see anyone. She heard footsteps and then Joseph suddenly appeared in front of her.

'I wondered if everything was okay?' he said. 'The girls are still waiting in the car to say goodbye to Mam.'

Before Fiona had a chance to say anything, or make up an excuse to get him away from the door, she heard her mother's raised voice again. The words clear and unmistakable.

'I'm telling you now, the same as I told you

before,' Nance said, 'I don't want Joseph moving down here to Tullamore and I don't need him working in the bar. I'm sure a young man of his age who is used to living in Dublin isn't going to be interested in living in a country town. Just because he's got into a bit of trouble you think you can palm him off on me now when it suits you.'

'God almighty!' Joseph gasped, his face white with shock. 'What are they saying about me?'

'It's nothing,' Fiona said, trying to reassure him. 'They're just having a bit of a discussion . . .'

'A discussion? From what I've just heard, I think it's a bit more than that. And I think I need to sort this out now.'

Fiona moved back to allow him to go into the shop. As he pushed the door open, the bell rang and suddenly everything was silent. She quietly went in behind him, and stood at the door.

'I was outside,' Joseph said in a low but clear tone, 'and I heard what was said about me looking for work in the bar, and I heard Aunt Nance's response.'

'Oh, dear God,' his mother said. She looked over at her sister. 'I'm so sorry . . . we had no idea we could be heard.'

'Well, Mam, I'm very glad I did hear,' he said, 'because now I know what's going on. Did you ask Aunt Nance to give me a job?'

His mother stepped backwards to lean against the shop counter. 'Yes,' she said, 'I did ask.'

'You had no business doing that,' he said quietly.

'But I told you that I would ask around . . .'

'But you didn't say you were going to ask Aunt Nance.' He looked over at his aunt. 'I'm sorry Mam put you in such an embarrassing position, especially on the day of your husband's funeral. And I'm sorry if it's caused any trouble between the two of you.'

Fiona moved forward now. 'You don't need to apologise for anything, Joseph. Not one thing. There's something going on here between my mother and yours – and it's not just today, it's been going on for ages. And whatever it is, I don't think you are the cause of it.'

'Oh, Fiona!' Her mother's face was now drained of colour. 'This is exactly why I didn't want Catherine and me to be near each other. Not today. I knew something like this would happen.'

Joseph looked at his aunt. 'I don't want to be disrespectful to Uncle Seán, but I think I have to tell the truth. I would not come to work in the bar here if it was the last job on earth – and you are the last person I would want to work for.'

Nance's eyes widened. 'Well, there's no need for—'

'Let me speak!' Joseph held his hand up. 'If I'd been asked to work for Uncle Seán that would have been a different matter. He's always been a gentleman to us. But from the way you've treated my mother and ignored me for the last number of years, I know exactly what you think of us. What I heard now just confirms it.'

'You don't understand,' Nance said. 'It has

nothing to do with you. I would never have done anything to hurt you – not ever.'

Fiona stood silent. Her mother had behaved badly and was doing nothing to make things better.

Catherine lifted her bag. 'Come on, Joseph, let's get into the car and go home.'

'Hold on. I've one last thing to say before we go,' he said. 'I was going to leave it for the next few days, until the funeral and everything was all over, but I might as well say it now. I don't need the job here because I already have one. I've been offered a job over in England.'

'England?' his mother repeated in a high voice. 'Where in England? And when did you hear about it?'

'Yesterday morning,' he said. 'When I spoke to my father.'

'Oh, no . . . please, God . . . don't tell me you're going over to him?'

'I have a job in a hotel near him, as a trainee manager for the bar and restaurant.'

'But, Joseph, you know he's not reliable. He'll promise you the moon and stars and then he'll let you down.'

'I know what he's like and I won't be depending on him. I won't be living with him or anything like that. The hotel is giving me accommodation. I've spoken to the manager and it's all sorted.'

Catherine looked at her sister. 'I hope you're satisfied,' she said. 'I hope you've got what you wanted now.'

CHAPTER 13

On a Thursday morning in April, Fiona sat down at the dining table with a Biro and Basildon Bond blue notepad, and scripted letters in her distinctive, clear handwriting to Bridget and Angela. She knew that the fact the letters weren't addressed in their mother's handwriting would cause some concern for both her sisters. The envelopes would immediately tell them that Mam still wasn't well, and had not yet recovered from the severe case of shingles that had hit her within a month of the funeral. It would also tell them that things, as yet, had not returned to normal at home.

As she wrote, Fiona thought that if her mother had been watching, she would have sighed and made her usual remark that an educated young lady should always use a proper fountain pen and ink. Angela and Bridget would not care what kind of pen she used. Bridget would just smile and roll her eyes at their mother's endless comments about ladylike things. She would just be delighted to receive a letter from home.

Angela's feelings about their mother's writing

preferences and her other strong opinions, Fiona could only guess at. She never really commented on things like that, just smiling and occasionally shaking her head in a non-committal way. But, Fiona conceded, she never complained about much either. Angela's communication with everyone in the family was polite and to the point. If she needed something, she asked for it, and if she didn't want to do something or to go somewhere, she said it quietly but in such a way that she was not forced into it.

Writing the weekly letters was a ritual her mother took seriously. Her first letters would be to the girls, and the others to her sisters and cousins in England and America. She would pick a quiet time and sit at the dining-room table – as Fiona was doing now – with a cup of tea and write in silence for an hour or more, giving each person her undivided attention and a letter tailored to the things she thought would be of interest to them.

Fiona had neither the time nor the inclination to write in such detail to her sisters. The same letter, she thought, would do for both, apart from odd little changes she would make at the end enquiring about Bridget's life in the convent school and how Angela was faring in Dublin.

In the first few lines she gave a brief comment about her mother, explaining that she hadn't really made much progress since they had left home a few weeks ago. She didn't go into too many details in case it upset them, but neither did she play down the truth about her mother still languishing in bed day after day.

As the oldest, she had always felt a certain responsibility for her two younger sisters, but lately there was a part of her that had begun to envy their independence. Their freedom from all responsibility of their mother and the family business. Without any discussion, it had just fallen on her shoulders. And the subject of her going to New York had never been mentioned since their father's death. Even before she became ill, their mother had steered any conversations away from America. It was, Fiona thought, as if she had never made any plans. And yet, both Bridget and Angela were off living their own lives exactly as they wanted to, and at an earlier age than she could have dreamed of.

Bridget decided she wanted to enter a convent school to be a nun, and within months she was doing just that. Angela's independence, Fiona knew, was a different case. She had no choice about spending her early years in Dublin but, now she was older, there was no real necessity for her to continue living there. She could easily come back home. There were offices in Tullamore if she wanted to work. But better still, Fiona thought, she could spend a few months here at home with their mother or helping out in the shop or bar.

Although it had never been openly discussed,

she knew that Angela would not want to work in the business. Being away from home for so many years, she didn't know the local people as well as the rest of the family. She was also quieter and more reserved than the others, and although she dropped into the shop and pub when she was home, she had always been treated as delicate and never expected to do any work. In many ways, Fiona now thought, Angela had been lucky and escaped all family responsibility over the years. Now she was older and fitter, it was only fair that she did her bit to help when it was needed. She read back over what she had written to Angela now, and added another line restating how hard it was for one person to deal with everything.

There was no point in labouring the situation with Bridget. There was nothing she could do to help until she was back home for the school holidays. And Fiona knew from hearing of the daily convent regime that Bridget had a hard enough life in her own way, what with prayers from early morning until night, and schoolwork and fairly heavy household chores. And going by the nuns in the school she had attended, they were not always easy to live with.

Angela, she reckoned was her only hope of escape. Her only hope of ever having her own life again.

She spent another while on the letters and, when she had written the names on both the envelopes, she heaved a sigh of relief. Then, she sat back in her chair and contemplated the walk to the post office and the day ahead going between the shop and the bar.

CHAPTER 14

On a Saturday afternoon, Angela, seated at her dressing-table, looked at her reflection in the mirror. Her long dark hair was piled on top of her head with a few loose tendrils escaping at the back. Her newly cut fringe was parted in the middle, framing her face. 'It's really different . . .'

'Well, what do you think?' Maureen, her house-mate, asked. 'Have I got it right?'

'You have.'

Maureen lifted the magazine that she was copying the style from, and put it flat on the dressing-table. 'Well, I think it's fabulous on you. The long fringe suits you and it's more modern than the tight buns you wear to work. I think you look exactly like a brunette Brigitte Bardot.'

Angela started to laugh. 'A few weeks ago you said I looked like Elizabeth Taylor, and they're not a bit like each other!'

'Listen, Madam,' Maureen said jokingly, 'there are plenty of girls who would love a compliment like that. You should be grateful you're so good-looking.'

'Oh, go away with you!' Angela said with a laugh. 'No, seriously . . . do you think the fringe suits me? I haven't had one since I was about ten. I'm not sure if I can get away with it . . .'

'You look amazing.'

The door opened and Jeanette came in, carrying a tray with three mugs of tea and an envelope.

'What's the verdict?' Maureen asked.

'Oh, Angela,' she said, putting the tray down on the coffee-table, 'it's fantastic. It really suits you.'

'Do you think so?' Angela asked.

'I do. Maureen's done a great job on it. You would think she was a real hairdresser.'

'Go away, will you?' Maureen laughed. 'It was only cutting a bit of a fringe and pinning it up.' She passed the magazine over to Jeanette. 'Isn't she the spit of Brigitte, only dark?'

Jeanette nodded her head, staring at the magazine and then back at Angela. 'You just need to do your eyes up a bit more, make the eyeliner more winged, and wear a paler lipstick.'

'You're not sure, are you?' Maureen said, looking at Angela.

'I do like it – and I think you've made a great job of it, Maureen. I definitely like the fringe. But I just don't know . . .' Angela bit her lip. 'I think it's a fabulous hairstyle, but I'm just not sure if it's really me.' She stared back at herself in the mirror. In one way she loved it – she had never imagined herself looking as modern and casual as this – but, in another way, she felt it was looking at a different person. The sort of person she was not really sure she would like to be.

'Well, I think you look stunning,' Maureen said. 'It's all the rage at the minute, and it's an easy style to copy. It's just like doing your usual bun, but making it looser and pulling strands of hair out.'

'I know what you mean,' Jeanette said to Angela. 'I'm like that when I'm trying anything new. When I had my hair cut really short, I hated it at first. But sometimes you need to give it a bit of time to get used to it.'

'You could do with being a bit more modern and daring, Angela,' Maureen said.

Angela laughed. 'I don't know if I'm the modern and daring type. That's all miniskirts and stretchy white plastic boots. And I don't exactly have the leg for miniskirts.'

'Ah, Angela – the rest of you more than makes up for your leg, and you can still wear the new modern tops and things.'

'Now,' Jeanette said, lifting up the magazine, 'talking about your leg, I was just thinking that you should try wearing slacks more. We rarely see you in slacks.' She went back to the feature on Brigitte Bardot and flicked to the next page. She held the magazine up to Angela. 'Look at this outfit – wouldn't that be gorgeous on you?'

Angela studied the page for a few moments. The famous actress was wearing a long black fitted sweater over a pair of slim-fitting slacks with daisies on a black background. 'I like the style, the sweater and trousers – it's really lovely, but could you imagine what my clumpy shoes would look like with the ankle-length slacks?'

'You could wear them with longer, wider legs then,' Maureen suggested. 'You could get a nice flowery tunic and wear it over trousers.'

'Maybe . . .' Angela said. 'I'll think about it the next time I go shopping for clothes.' She turned to Maureen. 'Thanks a lot for doing my hair. Would you give it a good spray with lacquer, please, as I'm going out to visit my aunt in Lucan later.'

Maureen lifted the can of lacquer and then carefully sprayed the sides and the back of Angela's hair. 'That should hold it in for the rest of the day,' she said. She put the can back down. 'We were thinking of going into town for a wander round. Would you not rather come with us?'

Angela shook her head. 'No, thanks, I rang her last night and she asked me to come out.'

Jeanette went back to the tray now to get Angela's mug of tea. 'Oh, I nearly forgot, there was a letter on the table outside for you and I brought it in.' She gave her the mug and the envelope.

'Thanks,' Angela said, taking both off her. It was from Fiona. Her brow creased. 'There's no post this morning, and I never saw it there last night when I came in from work.'

Jeanette shrugged. 'There was a parcel for somebody yesterday, maybe the letter was underneath it. Or maybe it fell down the back of the table and somebody saw it and put it back on top. I had that happen to me with a birthday card from my brother in England. I was waiting on it for ages and I began to think he was just codding me about having sent it. I felt terrible when I eventually got it, and I went straight to the phone to let him know.'

Maureen started to laugh. 'Maybe that one from upstairs who keeps stealing the biscuits took it on you, and then got cold feet and put it back.'

They all laughed.

Maureen took a sip of her tea. 'Any biscuits, Angela?'

'Yes,' Angela said, 'there's a packet of ginger nuts on the shelf near the table.'

'Ginger nuts?' Maureen laughed. 'Where are all the chocolate ones you usually have from the shop at home? The ones that come in the big boxes full of goodies?'

There was a small silence, then Angela said, 'I haven't had a box of groceries from home since Daddy died. My mother's not up to travelling to Dublin yet. She's not been well for a while.'

'Oh, Angela, I'm sorry . . . I forgot it was your father who used to bring them. Me and my big mouth.'

'Don't be daft,' Angela said. 'I know you didn't mean any harm. You can't remember everything.' She shrugged. 'I'm still trying to get used to it all myself.'

Angela went over and got the biscuits and then they sat for a while chatting.

After the girls had finished their tea, they left to get ready to go into town. Angela was just going to clear away the mugs when she remembered her letter.

She opened the envelope, and then began to read Fiona's news telling her all about their mother who was still sick in bed with shingles, and how worrying it was that she wasn't recovering as well as expected. Both their own doctor and a 'quack' from outside Tullamore who had visited her had said that they were concerned that her condition was not improving. But, Fiona stressed, both knew of cases like this when the after-effects of shingles took a long time to shake off.

All they could do was hope and pray that it soon passed out of her system. It went without saying, Fiona wrote, that it was the worst time for it to happen when the family were still mourning the loss of their father. His cheery presence was sorely missed both at home and in the pub and shop. Everything had changed entirely now that he was gone. But, it had to be endured, as nothing could bring him back. The house seemed very big and very lonely with just the two of them, and Fiona said she didn't meant to grumble, but that she was sure that Angela and Bridget would understand that it was very hard for one person alone to try to keep both the business running and their mother's spirits up at the same time.

She asked that both Angela and Bridget might do Novenas or light candles with their mother's health in mind. And they might also say a prayer for Fiona herself. She did not indicate exactly what she needed their prayers for, but reading between the lines she was finding their mother and the situation at home difficult to deal with.

A heavy weight descended on Angela as she read the three pages. The message was quite clear – even though Fiona had recounted some light-hearted stories of characters who frequented the pub – that her sister was feeling the burden of being the one with the sole responsibility for their mother.

As she pondered it, she thought that in fairness Fiona hadn't made any mention of her cancelled plans for New York. And she could imagine how difficult it was for her sister being there on her own with their mother. Of course, Fiona was the closest to her, working in the shop and still living at home, but she had after all planned to move out to America to work with her friend. At the funeral it looked as though it was just postponed until Nance was back on her feet. But so far, that hadn't happened – and it didn't look as though it was going to happen any time soon.

And then it suddenly occurred to her that, when their mother recovered, perhaps Fiona was hoping that she might come home to live with Mam and let her go on with her plans to emigrate. After years of being an embarrassment and almost a stranger to her mother, maybe the time had come when they had found a need for her.

Angela could picture it. There would now be a place for her behind the shop counter or the family bar. There would be a place for her now to help care for the mother who had abandoned her all those years ago. The mother who had left her with strangers – doctors and nurses and nuns – not knowing or caring how she was treated or coping with the situation. Never asking how she felt about it all. The mother who had visited her once a year and who she was brought home to the odd Christmas when she was fit to travel.

No, Angela thought. That was not going to happen.

CHAPTER 15

It was a beautiful warm evening – the first real good day in spring. Angela got off the bus in the centre of Lucan and went into a nearby flower shop and bought a bunch of red and yellow tulips, then she started off on the half-mile walk to her aunt's house.

She was wearing her calliper today, as it would allow her to enjoy the walk in the sun. Walking any great distance without it, she knew, and she would pay dearly for it later.

Her aunt was waiting for her, salad and cold ham and brown bread on the table. She was delighted with the flowers, and told Angela how lovely her new hairstyle looked.

Angela carefully patted her piled-up hair with her hands. After the girls had left, she had put a few more pins in it and tidied it up, so that it looked a little more like her usual style. 'You don't think it's too big a change? The fringe and everything?'

'It's lovely. It really suits you. Give you a bit of a lift.'

Angela wasn't quite sure as to why she needed

'a bit of a lift' but she took it as a compliment. Her aunt also surprised her by having a bottle of Blue Nun white wine on the table.

'I thought you might enjoy a glass with the salad,' Catherine said. 'A little treat for us. We might as well enjoy ourselves. Somebody gave it to me as a present a few weeks ago. I wouldn't open it just for myself, and I haven't had anybody here to enjoy it with.'

They sat chatting over the meal and two glasses of wine, her aunt talking about the weather and what she was doing in the garden, and about her new part-time job in a local gift shop. They had, her aunt said, the most beautiful crystal ornaments and clocks and things. The sort of things you would see in upper-class houses in the posher parts of Dublin.

Angela in turn told her all about the girls doing her hair, their suggestion about her wearing trousers – which Aunt Catherine wholly agreed with.

'Sure, everyone is wearing them now, Angela, and you can get them in all styles. I saw lovely wide ones in the new summer catalogue that one of my friends has. I think they're called bellbottoms after the sailor style of trousers. They would be great for hiding the calliper.'

'I'll think about it,' Angela said.

'Are you still thinking of making a move from the office?' her aunt asked.

'Yes, I am,' Angela said. 'Maybe later in the

summer. There's nothing wrong with the office I'm in – I just feel I could do with a change.'

And then, the talk eventually came around to her mother. She told Catherine about the letter.

'So, she's still no better?' her aunt asked. 'I'm sorry to hear it. Shingles is a terrible thing, and it can go on for ages, especially with older people. Not that I'm saying your mother's that old, but she's no spring chicken either. Neither of us are.'

'Well, Fiona sounded pretty worried. I think she's finding it a bit of a struggle trying to keep everything going.'

Her aunt gave a sigh. 'Didn't we know this would happen? We knew it would be too much without your father there, but with your mother not able to work now as well . . .'

There was a short silence.

'Any news from Joseph?'

A shadow passed over her aunt's face. 'I spoke to him on the phone on Wednesday. I rang because I knew it was his night off from the hotel. It costs me a fortune ringing, but it's worth it every now and again just to hear his voice.'

'And how is he doing?'

'He's getting on great at work, he's been on some course about wine – what to serve with what kind of meat, and that sort of thing. He said it was really interesting, and that he's learned a lot.'

'That sounds great,' Angela said. She thought her aunt sounded more positive now – proud of what Joseph was doing – and she tried to think of something else to keep that note in the conversation. 'And how about his music? Is he getting a chance to do that?'

'He's still doing it in his spare time. There's another fellow who he works with, a chef, and he's great on the piano, so they're working on songs together. They try to get the same days off.'

'That all sounds great,' Angela said. 'You must be relieved he's settled in so well. It's a big change from Dublin.'

'Oh, I am, but it still worries me he's so near to his father. I wouldn't want Kenneth's unreliable ways rubbing off on him, or to see him turning into a ladies' man like he was.'

Angela's eyebrows shot up. 'Was he really?'

'Well, he would like to think he was one. As far as I know he never went off with anyone, but he always had an eye for the ladies. You know, chatting them up, looking at them when he thought you might not notice.'

Angela hadn't been aware of that side of her Uncle Ken. It made her feel uncomfortable now, but she said nothing to her aunt as she had enough on her plate at the moment.

'I don't think Joseph is like that at all,' Angela said. 'He is always very respectful when he's around girls. And he's already had a few serious girlfriends without anything like that cropping up, hasn't he? Didn't you tell me that he broke off with the last one because he felt they weren't really suited, and he didn't think it was fair to string her along?'

Catherine nodded thoughtfully. 'You're right, Angela. He was decent about it.' She took a drink of her wine. 'He actually has a new girlfriend over in England. He's been going out with her for the last couple of months. She's a music teacher.'

'Well, they'll have a lot in common.'

'That's what he was saying on the phone. He sounds fairly keen on her.'

'That's good, isn't it?'

'I'm not too sure about it . . .'

Angela stared at her aunt. 'What do you mean?'

Tears welled up in Catherine's eyes. 'If he settles down with somebody in England then he might never come home again.' She shook her head. 'If that happens, Angela, I will never, ever forgive your mother for what she's done.'

CHAPTER 16

Fiona walked slowly down the wide staircase from her mother's bedroom, thinking how different her life would have been if she had gone to New York at the start of the year. How different everyone's lives would have been if her father hadn't suddenly dropped dead.

It was now May, and she would now be well settled in the enormous apartment in Park Avenue, working alongside her friend Elizabeth. She would be well used to the big, busy streets, the tall buildings and the yellow cabs that her friend described in great detail in her letters. She would be wearing glamorous summer dresses and sandals every day for months on end, enjoying soda parlours and shopping in Macy's department store, and going to Mass in St Patrick's Cathedral. Instead of only reading about all that.

And, by now she would surely have found an American boyfriend. If Elizabeth could meet a fellow from Brooklyn at a dance, Fiona knew she could have easily done the same. She wasn't being vain – it was a simple fact that she had always been one of the first girls asked onto the dance floor in Tullamore. It was the same with her sister Bridget. When Fiona brought her to a dance last Christmas, the boys had been falling over themselves to dance with her too. Not that Bridget had any interest in them, of course. And it would have been the same with boys and dances for Angela, if it hadn't been for the problem with her leg.

Fiona crossed the hallway now to pick up the white and brown envelopes scattered on the Victorian tiled floor. The postman had delivered them when she was upstairs sorting her mother out. She sifted through them, noticing nothing of great interest amongst the bills and invoices apart from the weekly letter from Bridget. Her chatty news would be something, at least, to lift her mother's spirits.

She sighed and stopped for a minute to put the mail on the mirrored hallstand while she adjusted the irritating strap of her sling-back shoes which kept slipping down on her heel. She slipped the shoe off, and then moved the strap along to a tighter hole which she hoped would make it more secure, then manoeuvred it back on again. She tutted: it was now too tight. Hopefully it would stretch a little as the day wore on.

She glanced at the mirror to check her lipstick, eye make-up and hair before she walked the few streets to the family pub and shop where she now worked every day since her father died.

As Fiona stared at her reflection now, and adjusted a strand of her wavy brown hair, she wondered if the effort she put into her appearance for work was worth it. Her mother always advised her that single women should look their best at all times, especially a young woman in Fiona's position where she was in the public eye all day in the shop and bar. Who knew who might call into the shop? So she always wore a nice dress or a blouse and skirt with her pearls. Recently, she had started to wear slacks more often, and was wearing a tan pair today with a cream twinset. Not only were the slacks more modern, but she found them practical when she used the stepladder to reach items on the higher shelves.

It was unlikely anyone other than locals would call into the shop or bar at lunchtime, but they had two commercial travellers booked into the rooms upstairs later in the afternoon whose names she had not come across before. Most of the businessmen stayed in Bolger's Hotel, as they got special rates and the hotel kept a special section of the dining-room especially for them, where they could all catch up on the latest news about businesses in the towns they visited. If the hotel was especially busy, then they sent the men to Hayes Hotel or the pubs with rooms like Traceys'. Most of the travellers tended to be older men who had been company representatives for years, moving around the country but, as her mother pointed out, 'They might have a son or younger brother who they could introduce to you.'

'I'm not that desperate,' Fiona continually told her, but it fell on deaf ears.

When she had brought her mother's breakfast of boiled egg and brown bread up to her room just this morning, Nance had mentioned the fact that the more refined men preferred to see women in skirts as opposed to trousers.

'The way you're talking you'd think we were the family out of *Pride and Prejudice,* and that the whole family would become homeless or bankrupt if I don't find an eligible man with money to prop us all up.' It was rare she was impatient, but her mother was becoming obsessed with finding a suitable match for her. Her mother had always felt that marriage was the safe haven for women, and was especially fearful on her eldest daughter's behalf now that the only male in the family had been taken from them.

'Oh, Fiona, I only want what's best for you!' Her mother was hurt now. 'Don't forget I'm the one now with all the family responsibility since your father died. I never thought about these things before. He was the kind of man who sorted everything, paid for everything. I just want to know if anything happened to me that you'll all be looked after. I don't want to think of any of you being lonely in your old age. That's the saddest thing that can happen to anyone.'

Fiona knew her mother was referring to herself now. 'We'll all be grand,' she said briskly, 'and if I meet the right man, he won't care whether I'm wearing a skirt or slacks. And if I don't meet anyone, I'll do just fine. I have plenty in my life with the shop and my friends, and now that I have the car I can go to Dublin or Galway when I have the time.'

Her mother had sighed and lifted her teacup and Fiona knew that she should not have mentioned Dublin.

'I hope Angela is okay,' said her mother. 'I worry about her up there. I wish she would come back home.'

'She seems to be doing fine. We'd know if she wasn't.'

'I don't know what the big attraction up in Dublin is.'

Fiona shrugged. 'You know she likes Dublin. She's used to it after going up and down to it all these years. She's more used to it than Tullamore.'

'She's still going back and forward to your Aunt Catherine. She sees a lot more of her than she does of us.'

'She has friends there as well,' Fiona said. She shrugged. 'Angela goes her own way. She always has.'

There was a small silence. 'Do you think she might ever meet a nice fellow? Do you think anyone would take her?'

'Of course,' Fiona said. 'She's only twenty and very attractive. She's already got her typing qualifications and she's great with her hands. I know she doesn't tell us much, but I know she's already been out on dates.'

'She never tells me anything . . . I wonder what kind of a fellow she's been out with?'

'You'd never know with Angela,' Fiona said. 'But one thing I do know – for all you're worrying about her, Angela will always be grand – with or without a man.'

'Well, she always looks lovely, in spite of things. She makes the best of herself.'

Fiona went over now and kissed her mother on the forehead. 'You should stop worrying about things and concentrate on getting better.'

'I can't help it – I worry about you all.'

'The doctor said that worrying only makes shingles worse – and you've had a very bad case of it. You were lucky the rash didn't meet in the middle – they say that's a very bad sign. It was nearly as bad as it could have been.'

'I know, I know . . .' Her mother was on the verge of tears now. Lately, she was always on the verge of tears. 'But I can't help worrying. What if anything happened to me now, what would you all do? I'm so exhausted all the time I can hardly get out of bed.'

'I know it's awful and it's taken a lot out of you, but shingles won't kill you. The doctor said that. He said it's only dangerous for very old people or somebody who has been ill. It might take a while before you feel well again, but he said you will eventually get back to your old self. You've got to rest until your system is back to normal.'

'I'd just feel happier if you and Angela had someone to look after you. Especially Angela . . .'

Fiona patted her mother's hand. 'Stop worrying. We'll be grand.'

'At least I don't have to worry about Bridget getting married. She'll be well looked after where she is in the convent. God will look after her.'

'Hopefully,' Fiona replied, smiling now. 'Hopefully God will look after us all.'

As she went into the big old kitchen now and saw the note on the table asking her to order the meat for the coming week for the house, and a list of cleaning things their housekeeper needed, Fiona wondered how she had suddenly come to be responsible for everything. Responsible for the running of the family business. Responsible for the family home and responsible for her two younger sisters.

She had not expected things to get straight back to normal after her father's death. She knew her mother would need time to grieve and to adjust – but she hadn't reckoned on her mother completely falling apart.

New York, along with Paul Moore, was now in the dim and distant past.

CHAPTER 17

On Saturday morning, after the usual morning washing ritual, Bridget and the other girls in the dormitory got dressed in their outdoor gardening clothes and aprons.

They went silently down to Mass then afterwards over to the refectory to have breakfast.

Even though they weren't allowed to talk, Bridget could always detect a more relaxed atmosphere on a Saturday as they had no formal schooling. As they ate their eggs and sausages and buttered brown bread, one of the older girls read aloud to them from a book about the life of Saint Thérèse of Lisieux.

Bridget listened carefully as she ate and drank her tea, as it was one of the books she really enjoyed. She liked hearing about the young French girl, known as The Little Flower, who had overcome various obstacles in her life – such as serious illness and losing her mother at an early age – to become a nun.

When breakfast was over and they had said Grace, Sister Marie Claire led them in a prayer of thanks for the beautiful sunny morning, which made their gardening chores so much easier. The girls went outside to the yard and over to one of the outbuildings where all the garden tools and implements were kept. Sister Bernadette gave each girl a pair of gloves, then she dispensed the rakes and the hoes to the girls who were working on clearing the leaves from the lawns, and the trowels, small forks and kneeling pads for the ones who were weeding the flowerbeds. After three quarters of an hour, they would change over tasks.

Bridget was with the group of girls who were clearing the leaves, which she felt happy enough to do on such a lovely morning. There had been plenty of mornings in the winter when they'd had to do tasks around the farm in the rain and the wind and they were told to offer up their discomfort for the Holy Souls in Purgatory.

They were allowed to choose their own patches to rake, so she decided to start over at the far corner of the top garden which overlooked the gardens below and the small, manmade lake surrounded by tall, swaying pine trees.

Bridget always had a feeling of contentment when she paused to look at the beautiful scene in front of her. At certain times it reminded her of the days her father had come to visit or collect her, and they had walked around these gardens together. It was one of the few times she'd had her father to herself. They would walk and talk about everything and anything, but eventually, he would get around to asking her if she was happy in the convent and if she was still sure she was doing the right thing by becoming a nun. He always made it plain to her that, if she was at all unhappy with her choice of being in the religious order, she would be welcomed home with open arms.

'I had an aunt,' he told her, 'who was a great nun altogether – and very happy being a nun. She occasionally came home on holidays, and I can remember one time that I overheard her telling my mother about some of the poor nuns who had been made to go into the convent from a very young age. She said they were not the same as the nuns who had a vocation – that the poor girls were never truly happy. And yet, they went ahead and sacrificed their chances of getting married and having a family, because they were so terrified of their parents' disapproval if they left. They lived their whole life to please a family they hardly ever saw.'

Bridget could picture him now, taking both her hands in his and saying, 'If you ever feel like that, promise me you'll come back home?'

'I promise I will,' she had told him. 'But I can honestly say that my vocation is getting stronger the older I'm getting. I'm very happy in the convent school, and I'm looking forward to being a postulant and then entering the novitiate.'

As she moved around her patch of the lawn now, stretching the rake out to catch more leaves, she was still firm in her beliefs. Nothing had changed since she told her father her views about carrying on in the convent last year – apart from her now understanding more about her religion and feeling even closer to God.

She was reciting a decade of the Rosary in her head for her father when she became aware of some giggling on the level below her. She moved forward and could see two girls from her year down by the wall – Carmel and Veronica. She wasn't surprised it was them – they were a giddy pair who she always tried her best to avoid. Recently they had been in trouble on several occasions. It was nothing serious, just silly things like going back up to the dormitory when they weren't supposed to, or, when they were given partners to work with in science or PE, swapping their allocated partners over so they could be together. Both girls were from Galway, and they were always in a huddle with some of the other girls after holidays, discussing all that had happened while they were away.

This morning they were supposed to be part of the group raking the leaves, but there was no sign of any rakes near them. Bridget saw them both looking around as if to check if anyone was watching, so she quickly moved backwards out of sight. Then, when she stepped forward to look down again, she saw Veronica tucking something into a gap in the wall, and then they both disappeared. She was mildly curious as to what they were up to, but decided it was best to ignore it and went back to her raking.

There had been occasions when she had wondered what both girls – Veronica, in particular – were doing at the convent school, because they just seemed the wrong types to train as nuns. Veronica had suddenly arrived in the middle of third year, which occasionally happened, as some girls didn't develop an interest in becoming a nun until later.

Bridget remembered Veronica's first day, because everything about it had been unusual. She had arrived wearing a short blue dress with white daisies on it, fashionable white tights and kitten-heeled shoes, and her dark hair had been caught up at the back in a big white bow. She had been accompanied by a serious-looking priest, who turned out to be her uncle. Bridget and the other girls had watched, mesmerised, from the Maths classroom window, as this very pretty fourteen-year-old had been shown around the convent grounds.

From the day she arrived, it was apparent that Veronica came from a well-off family. She constantly alluded to their big house and servants, and the places she had been to abroad. It made Bridget wonder how, with all the advantages she appeared to have in life, she rarely had a smile on her face. She constantly complained about things like the lovely food they were served, and having to sleep in a dormitory with a nun supervising their every move, even at night.

By the following year, Veronica was still showing no real signs of a vocation, even though she seemed to spend a lot of time with her Spiritual Director. Bridget began to suspect that there might be another reason she had suddenly been brought to the convent. Then when they all came back from the summer break, she heard rumours amongst some of the other girls that Veronica had been going up and down to Cork to visit her father, as he no longer lived with the family in Galway. This news had immediately made Bridget feel more understanding and sympathetic towards the girl, because she knew it must have created a terrible scandal where they lived. She knew how embarrassed their own mother was about Aunt Catherine's husband having deserted her and Joseph. She had kept it quiet even from Bridget and her sisters, until Angela had eventually been told by their aunt herself. And even then, Mam had warned all the girls to say nothing to any of the local people about it. 'Your aunt lives in Dublin, so who is to know? Why make people as wise as yourself?'

Bridget wondered if maybe there had been problems going on for a while with Veronica's parents and, if so, perhaps that had been the reason behind her being brought to the convent the previous year. The family might feel that even if she didn't have a vocation, she might develop one if she was in a school surrounded by other girls who did. And the nuns would be kind to her and she would be away from all the upset at home. Bridget thought coming back to the school after her father had died had definitely helped her. The routine, the

Masses and prayers were a comfort to her every day, and the nuns always made time to talk to her if she needed that. Even though Veronica made out she hated being in the convent, Bridget thought that underneath her giddy façade she probably thought that it was a good place to be when life at home was difficult.

Bridget worked away, raking the leaves into small piles and then gathering them all together into a bigger pile, stopping every now and again to catch her breath and look down over the lake and trees.

When it came time to change the groups over, Sister Bernadette gathered the class together and got the girls to swap tools and kneeling pads. She sent the raking group off to start, and then she looked at the others. 'You're to work on your own weeding,' she said. 'I don't want to see any girls chatting as some of you did when you were supposed to be raking. Less talk means more work and more time for private prayers.' She then looked straight at Carmel. 'You go off to the flowerbed on the left-hand side of the Our Lady's statue.' Then she turned to Veronica and, pointing in the opposite direction, said, 'You can work on the flowerbed down to the right of the statue, and Bridget will work on the one in the middle.' She had looked sternly at them as she spoke. 'And remember, girls, you're here to work and to pray. You are not here to *play*.'

As she and the two other girls went off in the direction of the statue, Bridget heard Veronica whisper to Carmel, 'Sister Bernadette would drive you mad – she has eyes in the back of her head.'

Bridget pretended she hadn't heard anything and kept walking until she got to the flowerbed. 'I suppose we'd better spread out,' she said, smiling at the two girls, but neither of the girls smiled back.

'I don't feel like doing this weeding,' Veronica said. 'I think my period is coming and my stomach hurts if I bend down.'

'Why don't you tell Sister Bernadette?' Bridget said. 'She'll let you do something easier or go and sit down inside.' She knew how she felt herself the day before her period arrived, and could understand that bending and kneeling down would not help one little bit.

Veronica shook her head. 'No, she won't believe me.'

'I'm sure she will,' Bridget said. 'But do you want me to tell her?'

Veronica looked at Bridget for a few moments, as though thinking something, then she said, 'No, I'll probably be all right.'

They all settled down on their kneeling mats and began to attack the little weeds. After Bridget finished weeding one area, she moved her mat to the left or right to start on a new patch. After a while, her thoughts drifted off to an assignment she had to do over the weekend about the missions in Africa.

It was just coming to the end of the session when

Bridget stood up to stretch her back and legs, and to wonder what they would have for lunch. She hoped it was Shepherd's Pie, which they often had on a Saturday, followed by something like apple crumble and custard. The food was one of the highlights in the convent, and there were very few dishes that the nuns made that she didn't like.

She looked first at Carmel and then at Veronica. 'It must be nearly time to finish,' she said. 'It should be lunchtime shortly.'

'Thank God,' Carmel said. 'It would nearly kill you doing this.'

'It's slave labour,' Veronica said, sitting back on her heels. 'My mother wouldn't ask me to do this at home. She wouldn't do it herself – that's why we have a gardener.'

Bridget got back down on her knees. This was the sort of conversation she tried to avoid getting into, because she knew it only encouraged the wrong attitude. She thought how Sister Bernadette would handle it.

'Well,' she said, 'I suppose if Sister Bernadette heard us complaining she would tell us we should be grateful we're not in some poor place in Africa where they don't have schools like this with nice gardens, and the girls have to walk miles just to have water to drink.'

'You'll make a great nun, Bridget,' Carmel said. 'You sound just like Sister Bernadette.'

Veronica made a little snorting sound and then both girls started giggling.

'Very funny,' Bridget said. She was taking it in good humour, which she had discovered was often the best way to handle things with these two girls.

She stretched over to the wall to pull out a long trail of bindweed she had just noticed. She moved around, pulling out any others she spotted as the roots came out easily. Then she started pulling at a clump of dock leaves, which was an entirely different matter. She got most of the leaves, but the roots stayed firm. She lifted her trowel and was digging deep around the plant to lift it out in one go when she heard a noise from behind.

She turned around to look and saw Veronica sitting in a slumped position on top of the flowerbed.

A feeling of alarm ran through her. 'Are you okay?' she asked, getting to her feet.

'No,' Veronica said, 'I don't feel well . . . everything is spinning around.' Then, she slowly fell forward in a dead faint.

Bridget threw her trowel on the grass and got to her feet. 'Carmel!' she called to the girl on the other side of her. 'Run quick and get Sister Bernadette or one of the other nuns and tell them that Veronica has fainted.' She pulled her gloves off as she rushed over to kneel by her classmate.

By the time Sister Bernadette arrived, Veronica was starting to come around.

'Did she say anything before it happened?' the nun asked Bridget.

'She just said that she didn't feel well,' Bridget

said, trying to recall, 'and that she had a spinning kind of feeling.'

Sister Bernadette gathered her habit up in a bunch with one hand, and then knelt beside Veronica on the grass, telling her she would be all right and not to worry. Two other nuns arrived now, and helped Sister Bernadette get Veronica into a sitting position. One of them then told Carmel to go down to the kitchen and get a glass of water.

Bridget, standing at the side, suddenly remembered. 'She said earlier that her stomach was sore and she thought it was . . .' she hesitated, embarrassed, 'her time of the month.'

'Ah,' Sister Bernadette said, 'that could explain it.'

A few minutes later Carmel came back with the water. Veronica took a few sips and after a while she said she felt well enough to stand up. Slowly, the nuns walked her back to the main house with Bridget and Carmel trailing silently behind.

The two older nuns took Veronica off to lie down in the sick bay downstairs, where they had two single rooms. Sister Bernadette and the girls went back out to the yard and the sheds. When they went in, everyone was cleaning the small tools in the sink and Bridget suddenly remembered the trowels and other things they had left up at the statue when Veronica fainted. She quickly explained to Sister Bernadette and the nun told her to go back up and collect them, and then give them a quick clean before going to join the others at lunch.

She was walking back carrying the tools, thinking about Veronica, when she remembered seeing her and Carmel over by the wall. Curiosity overcame her and when she reached the steps, she dropped the tools on the ground and went quickly down to the lower garden towards the stone wall. She went to where she had seen the girls hide something. It took her a few minutes to find it, but eventually she spotted something white which was pushed between two large flat stones. She lifted out a folded white envelope, and when she opened it out she could see a name and address neatly printed in ink on the front.

It was a boy's or a man's name – James Toner – and the address was an auctioneers' office in Galway.

She turned the envelope over and saw it was sealed. She stood for a minute wondering what to do with it, and then she spotted one of the younger farmhands walking towards the far end of the garden wall. The farm, to the right of the gardens, was owned by the convent, and several of the older nuns worked there fulltime, driving tractors and herding the cattle. But, at certain times of the year, they hired in extra help, and for the last few weeks there had been a middle-aged farmworker and two younger lads.

She thought quickly. If she took the envelope and gave it back to Veronica and Carmel, then they would think she had been spying on them. They would also think she was acting as if she was in a position of authority and felt she had some right to advise them and tell them they were doing wrong. Both points of view, she thought, would make things very difficult for all three of them in the future. But by keeping their secret – by knowing she had found an unauthorised letter and not told the nuns – she would in some way become an accomplice.

Another alternative was to give the letter to Sister Bernadette and let her deal with it. The girls knew perfectly well that letters written by any of the aspirants were not allowed to go out of the convent without the nuns reading them first.

But did she really want to put herself in the position of a tattle-tale with the nuns? If she handed this letter over, and the contents were read, it might cause all sorts of trouble for the girls. And even if Sister Bernadette told her the girls wouldn't find out who had given them the letter, she would have to live with knowing it was her. And if by any chance they got an inkling it was her, and asked her straight out – she would be lying if she denied it. And that, Bridget knew, was going against all the words and prayers she read every day.

As she saw the farmhand coming in her direction, she made her decision: she quickly folded the letter and put it back where she found it.

She went back up the steps to gather up the tools and then head over to the refectory for lunch. She had walked halfway along the garden when something made her stop, and when she turned around she could see the young farmhand down at the wall where she had just been. She stopped and watched, her hand covering her mouth. Then she quietly moved to a positon where she could watch him without being seen, and after a minute or so, she saw him go straight to the part of the wall where the envelope was concealed.

She watched as he took the envelope out and put it in his pocket. It struck her that the girls must have left it there, by some prior agreement, for him to find. If that was the case, it was yet another cardinal rule of the convent that had been broken. The girls were not allowed to talk to any of the workmen unless under supervision.

She walked quickly back to the outhouse where the tools were kept, gave them a perfunctory rub over with a damp cloth and put them back on the shelves. She went to the sink, washed her hands and dried them, then rushed out to join the others in the refectory.

As she went along, she said a silent prayer for guidance over what she should do about the situation. For the time being, she would do nothing. She would wait until some Divine Inspiration came upon her and then she would know what to do.

CHAPTER 18

'I don't want to pressurise you, Mam,' Fiona said, 'but I think a day out of bed would do you good. A little sit in the garden while the weather is still reasonable.'

There was silence from the bed.

'Once you are on your feet we could go for a run in the car.' Fiona was trying to think of somewhere that might encourage her mother to move out of the bed and out of the room. She knew there was little chance of her mother agreeing to go anywhere, but she thought if the idea was planted, she might just aim towards being well enough to try going out at some point. 'We could take a drive out to the lakes in Mullingar or maybe even down to Galway.'

'Fiona, do you not realise that I'm not up to going out in the car or going anywhere?'

'But the doctor says you need to get some fresh air. The rash has gone now, there's not even a mark on your back or shoulders—'

'It might look as though it's gone,' her mother cut in, her voice slightly muffled by the bedclothes, 'but the whole area where it was is still painful. And I still feel very tired.'

'I know,' Fiona said.

'My head hurts, and at times I find it hard to concentrate on the television or radio, or even read a magazine or book. I'm still not well, even though no one wants to believe me. I find even coming downstairs takes it out of me.'

Fiona sighed and went to sit on the side of the bed. 'Of course we believe you. *I* believe you. I know you wouldn't want to lie in here all day if you were fit to be out and about.' She halted. 'I just thought if we could get you bathed and dressed and down into the fresh air you might feel a little bit better.'

Her mother turned towards her now, the bedsprings creaking. 'If I felt well enough, do you not think that's what I would be doing? Do you think I like lying here day in, day out? Even after having a bath I feel exhausted. And yesterday when I was up for the short time when Mary Ellen was changing the bed, I felt worse after it. My head was dizzy and my legs felt weak.' She turned back towards the wall, and pulled the covers up over her. 'I appreciate your concern, but for the time being I'm better being left alone where I am.'

'Okay,' Fiona conceded. 'If there's nothing I can get you, I'll go back down to the shop and leave you to have another little sleep.'

Fiona had just opened the shop door and put her handbag down, when she realised she had forgotten to bring her clean shop coat. It was still lying on the worktop in the kitchen, ironed and carefully folded by Mrs Mooney. She would have to go back. She pulled the door closed behind her and walked quickly back up the street towards the house.

She put the key in the side door that opened into the kitchen and, as she stepped inside, she heard a voice coming from somewhere in the downstairs part of the house. She thought at first it was Mary Ellen but then as she walked out into the hallway the voice drifted towards her again – clearer this time – and it dawned on her that it was not the housekeeper, and that the voice in fact belonged to her mother. She was quite taken aback, considering her mother's earlier refusal to move from the bed.

She was about to call to her mother when she heard her say, 'I don't need anything from you!'

Something in those few words – in the tone they were spoken – halted her. Her voice sounded sharp, even argumentative. Fiona wondered who on earth she could be speaking to. Who would be likely to be in the house with her at this hour of the day?

It couldn't be Mrs Mooney, as Fiona couldn't imagine her mother speaking to her in such a way. She went quietly along the hallway, so as not to disturb them, but listening for the other person's voice to give her an indication as to what kind of situation she might be walking into. When she heard no other voice, it suddenly dawned on her that her mother was on the phone.

She stood for a few moments, listening, her eyes narrowed in concentration. But she could hear nothing now. She took a few quiet steps nearer to the sitting-room door then came to a halt as she heard her mother's voice again.

'How many times do I have to tell you that I don't want to see you? I'm not up to it.'

Fiona held her breath, shocked by the cold determination in her mother's voice.

After a pause Nance spoke again. 'I disagree. I don't think it can be sorted out. Seán has gone, and it's all water under the bridge – and I want to leave it like that, Catherine. I can't handle anything more now. I'm sorry.'

Fiona waited until she heard the phone click back in place. She moved a few steps to go into the sitting-room but, when she caught a glimpse of her mother – saw her with her head in her hands – something made her halt. All the bitterness seemed to have drained out of Nance, and she just looked weary and sad. Fiona decided it was not the time for confrontations. Instead, she tiptoed her way back out to the kitchen to hover around the back door and give the impression she had just arrived home if her mother looked in.

A few minutes later she heard her mother come out of the sitting-room and go straight to the staircase. Fiona listened carefully, noting that the footsteps were heavy and laden – the slow tread of a woman who was still not back to good health. She heard the weary sigh and then a sound that might have been a small sob.

Her mother was most certainly upset by the conversation between herself and her sister. Things were certainly not being resolved between them. And this row sounded serious. Serious enough to make one sister drive the other away, at a time when any family needed all the help and support there was.

CHAPTER 19

When Fiona arrived into the bar around twelve o'clock, all was quiet with only a handful of regulars propped up on stools. She had a few words with Patrick about the previous night's takings and then she went into the shop. She looked around and decided that the shelves which displayed the tins of cooked ham, John West Salmon, Bachelor Peas and Heinz Beans needed a good wash down.

Fiona put on her brown shop coat, carefully turning up the sleeves. Then, with a small sigh, she turned on the geyser and half-filled a bucket with hot water. The shop bell suddenly sounded, so she set the bucket down on the stone floor and went back through to find the glamorous local hairdresser, Maggie MacConnell, waiting on her.

'Well, Fiona,' Maggie said smiling, showing her even white teeth, 'how are things? Any news? How's your mother keeping?'

Fiona shrugged. 'No news, Maggie. Well, none that I've heard. And my mother's more or less the same. Still not great.'

Maggie nodded understandingly. 'Tell her I'm

asking for her. And when she's up to having her hair done, tell her I'll come over to the house and do it there for her.' She smiled. 'It's surprising how having your hair done can give you a bit of a lift.'

'That's very good of you, and I'll let her know.' Fiona paused, not wishing to get into further discussions about her mother. 'What can I get you?'

'I need a few things, I should have written a list . . .' Maggie bent down to look into the cold cabinet at the joints of cooked ham and beef, and the pork and chops separated by sprigs of parsley which Fiona replaced every few days. 'I'll have six slices of cooked ham, thick-cut, please, Fiona. I have a friend, Anne, coming up from Galway tonight and I thought I'd do a nice salad for us. She's a hairdresser in one of the big salons in the middle of the city. We trained together up in Dublin and have kept up our friendship ever since.'

'That's lovely,' Fiona said. 'You'll be looking forward to seeing her.'

'Oh, I am indeed. We'll have a great chat and a laugh together.' Maggie raised her eyebrows and smiled. 'We might go mad and drop over to the snug for a drink later on. We usually go out for the evening when I visit her.'

'I suppose your friend is used to the bigger places in Galway and Dublin. There's not much here in Tullamore.'

'She won't mind what we do. She's a great character, always on the go.'

Maggie was always doing something herself, Fiona thought with a tinge of envy as she carried the ham joint over to the meat-slicer. She was a single woman in her early thirties, small and curvy. She was a good advert for her shop as her dark hair was always in the latest fashion. At the moment it was cut up short at the back with longer wings at the front. She lived in the house above the hair salon, and rented out the other room to one of the local librarians. She had a great life and was always talking about going off around places in Ireland, or going on holidays abroad with her various single friends.

Fiona wished her own local friends were as adventurous as that. Of her three closest friends, one was married with a baby, one engaged to be married within the next few months, and the third didn't like travelling far from home. And, unlike some of the others, she had no sisters at home to go anywhere with either. She fleetingly thought of Angela who was in the busiest city in Ireland, and who was out and about with her friends. Whilst it was great she was leading such an independent and busy life, how ironic it was that the sister who had always been at a disadvantage should now have the better social life.

Maggie was bubbly and confident, and it seemed to be of no concern to her that she wasn't married or even engaged. She seemed to have no trouble getting boyfriends, as she was always going on dates not only in Tullamore but in further-flung places like Birr and Portlaoise. She also played golf regularly, and at times made being single seem a better option than pushing a pram around the town or struggling with young children like most of her contemporaries.

When Fiona placed the carefully wrapped ham on the counter, Maggie pointed back down to the cold cabinet. 'I'll have half a pound of white cheddar too,' she said, 'and three tomatoes and a bottle of salad cream, and a bottle of Camp coffee.'

Fiona lifted the large piece of cheddar and put it on the cutting board, then she moved the wire cheese-cutter above it, checking it was about the right size for the weight. When she popped it on the scales, she could see she was almost spot on. She wrapped the cheese in greaseproof paper and put it down on the counter, then she moved around the shelves picking up the other requested items. Then, just as she was putting the tomatoes into a brown paper bag and calculating the total bill, Maggie moved to the covered cake stand, which held an array of buns and pastries.

'I know I shouldn't because Anne is always watching her weight – but I'll have a couple of meringues.' She paused, deliberating for a few moments. 'And two jam doughnuts. We might fancy them with our coffee later tonight.' She laughed. 'Well, *I* might fancy them. And if they don't get eaten tonight, I'll have the doughnuts for my breakfast in the morning!'

Fiona laughed along with her. 'As long as they get eaten and don't go to waste.'

'But that's the problem,' Maggie said, opening her coat and, over her pink sweater, pinching a small fold of flesh. 'They go straight to my waist! How on earth do you keep so slim when you have all these lovely things in front of you every day? I only have to look at cakes and I put on a couple of pounds.'

'I'm so used to them I hardly see them now,' Fiona confessed, knowing it wasn't a good advert for the shop that she could take or leave the fancies they sold. 'And to be honest, I've never really had a sweet tooth.'

'Not even for chocolate?'

'Now and again.'

'Lucky you,' Maggie said, rolling her eyes. 'If I open a box of chocolates I'm not happy until the last one is gone. I've got up out of bed to eat them. It's one of the good things about not having a husband, at least I don't need to worry about him catching me in the kitchen, standing up on a stool in my shift!'

'But why,' Fiona asked, 'would you be standing on a stool?'

'Because I keep the chocolate in the highest shelf in the kitchen – out of temptation's way, so it's not too handy for me.'

'That's priceless, Maggie! I could never imagine doing that in a million years.'

Maggie winked at her, then said in a low voice.

'Now, don't go telling Patrick about my night-time habits or it might spoil my chances with him.'

'Patrick?' Fiona's voice was high with laughter now. She covered her mouth with her hand and shook her head. 'I don't believe it!' Maggie, she deduced, was obviously joking. Patrick was so quiet and kind of old-fashioned that she couldn't imagine any woman having their eye on him – and definitely not someone as bubbly and modern as the hairdresser.

'Oh, some would say there's a lot worse around than Patrick. An awful lot worse . . .'

Her tone made Fiona suddenly feel unsure as to whether she was joking or not. Rather than risk saying the wrong thing, she double-checked the cakes that Maggie had picked then busied herself making up a small cardboard box. When it was assembled she picked up a pair of food tongs and carefully lifted the cakes into it, folded the lid down and secured it with two pieces of Sellotape. She then totted up the bill, and rang it up on the till as Maggie put the items into her flowery canvas shopping bag

Just as Maggie lifted her bag, the door opened and the two young Grattan sisters came in. Doloreen was around ten or eleven and the younger one, Helen, was around six. Fiona knew they lived in one of the little cottages out near Charleville Castle. Their mother often called in for shopping on her way home from town, as it was the nearest shop on the way home for carrying potatoes and flour.

179

Doloreen rushed to hold the door open for Maggie.

'You're a great girl,' Maggie said. 'Tell your mother I was asking for her.'

The girl came back to the counter, handing over the shopping bag to Fiona. 'Can we have a bottle of red lemonade, a bottle of white lemonade, and a packet of Kimberley biscuits and a pound of mixed broken biscuits, please?'

'You can indeed, girls,' she said, smiling at them. 'Are you having a bit of a party or something?'

Helen, the younger one, giggled. 'No, not a party, but our granny is coming over from Portarlington tonight, and Kimberleys are her favourites.'

'Well, that's lovely,' Fiona said. 'She'll be delighted you're making such a fuss of her.'

'My mammy has baked an apple tart too,' Doloreen said, her face more solemn than her sister's.

The little one stood on her tip-toes to rest her chin on the counter. 'And my daddy bought half a bottle of brandy because he says Granny likes a sup and it puts her in good humour.'

The older sister looked at her with an open mouth, then she grabbed her sister roughly by the shoulder. 'Be quiet, you! Daddy never said such a thing – and Granny doesn't like brandy. She says she only takes it for medicine, to help the rheumatism in her legs.'

'Well, it must have helped her legs,' Helen said, 'cos it made her laugh and dance around at Christmas.'

Doloreen's face was now flushed. 'You're always

talking nonsense. And Mammy will give out to you when she hears what you've been saying!'

The six-year-old shook her sister off and went over to stand by the door with her arms folded and her bottom lip stuck out.

Doloreen looked up at Fiona now, embarrassment stamped on her face. 'She's always saying stupid things like that. Mammy will kill her if she hears her.'

Fiona smiled at her. 'Sure, she's only young – nobody will pay any attention. There's no need to go annoying your mammy about it.'

She took the green plastic scoop they used for the broken biscuits and one of the big brown paper bags and went over to the container to fill it. Silently, Helen moved over beside her sister again, and then both girls moved along the counter to watch which biscuits were put in the bag. Fiona filled it up to what she reckoned was a pound weight, and then dropped it gently on the scales. It was just over. She turned to look at them. 'What's your favourites, girls?'

'Coconut,' Doloreen said, then a moment later her sister said, 'Kimberleys.'

Fiona went back to search in the biscuit container with the scoop until she found two of each.

'They're extra just for you,' she told them, then she gave them one each and put the other two in the bag.

'Oh, thanks!' Helen said, clapping her hands together, her earlier bad humour now forgotten.

Doloreen looked up at Fiona. 'That's very good of you.' Her voice was quiet, but her face had brightened up.

They stood eating the biscuits and smiling at each other as Fiona packed the bottles and packages into their bag. She came around the counter to them then, suggesting they take a handle each as the bottles were heavy.

'Now,' Doloreen warned her sister, 'make sure to keep a good grip on it. Not like the last time when you let all the potatoes fall out.'

Helen's brows came down as though she might answer back. Then, having thought better of clashing with her sister again, she started humming loudly to herself and took the handle as directed.

'Good girl,' Doloreen told her. 'That's how to do it.'

Fiona smiled to herself as she saw them out the door, and she stood for a minute watching them as they went along swinging the bag. How easy it would be, she thought, if all family problems were solved so quickly and easily.

The bar was quiet during the afternoon opening hours, but Fiona was kept fairly busy in the shop. She had several periods when she had three or four people queuing, and after five she had seven people at one stage, coming off the train and on their way home for work. In between serving she continued wiping down shelves and washing the meat-slicer, and later sticking price-tickets on mops and brushes and scrubbing boards that had been delivered from the hardware company.

Patrick closed the bar around three and went upstairs to his bedroom to collect his jacket, and then, as he did every day, he headed out for the half-mile walk to his elderly parents' house where there would be a meal waiting for him.

At six o'clock he returned to re-open the bar just as Fiona was closing up the shop. 'Are you okay for later this evening?' he asked.

'Fine,' Fiona said. 'I'll just have a couple of hours at home with my mother and I'll be back.'

Mary Ellen, dressed as usual in her apron, was in the kitchen when Fiona arrived home, and had a plate with two lamb chops, boiled potatoes and peas waiting for her over a pan of hot water. When their father was alive, they had always eaten their main meal around one o'clock, but lately they had taken to having it in the evening, in the hope that Nance's appetite might be better at a later time.

'I took the same up to your mother,' Mary Ellen said, as she stood washing up at the sink, 'and she managed one of the chops and three small potatoes. She had a small glass of milk too. It's not a lot, but it's better than she's been eating recently.'

'It's good that she's managing more,' Fiona said. 'And thanks for encouraging her to eat.' She looked at the solitary place the housekeeper had set for her at the wooden kitchen table, and for a few moments she remembered her father and how he used to sit at the top of the table every evening with her mother on one side and herself on the other. She thought back to the way her mother was this time last year – fit, well and happy enough around the house. How different things were now.

The housekeeper finished drying the colander she had used for draining the vegetables. She put it back in the cupboard where it was kept, and then she turned around. 'Are you all right, Fiona?'

'I'm grand,' she said quietly. 'And thanks again, Mrs Mooney, for everything. I don't know what we'd do without you.'

'Doesn't it give me something to do?' Mary Ellen said, smiling. 'Sure, I'd only be up there on me own looking at the four walls and worrying about the family, how they're all getting on over in England and up in Dublin. Am I not better keeping busy?' She took her coat from the back of the door. 'Keeping busy is what keeps us going whether we're young or old. You're lucky you have the shop and the bar down there. It would be hard for you being stuck here in the house all day the way things are . . .'

Fiona looked at her. 'It is,' she admitted. 'I never expected Mam to go down sick so soon after Daddy died.'

'It's the shock,' Mrs Mooney said. 'I've seen it happen to countless people over the years when they've lost someone. And shingles is one of the worst things, it's treacherous – it can hang on for a long time after the rash goes. A brother of mine

184

had it and it lasted for over two years. He was washed out and tired all the time.'

'Oh, God!' Fiona gasped. 'Two years? That long?'

Mrs Mooney's hand came up to her mouth. 'I'm sorry now, Fiona, I shouldn't have said that. I didn't mean to frighten you. It usually goes in a few months, but it depends on the person's system.' She lifted the tea towel now and began to dry cutlery. 'Your mother is very low, Fiona, because she's still grieving for your father. And I'd say she's feeling depressed, because her whole life has suddenly changed. She's finding everything hard without your father there. He was a man you could rely on to see to things and sort situations out. He did everything so quietly and so nicely that you didn't realise half of what he did.' She looked directly at Fiona now. 'And she's not just missing him for all the practical things in the house and the shop and bar – she's missing him as her husband too. The one person she could talk to about things. The person she went to sleep with and the person she woke up with for twenty-odd years. It's a lot to lose.'

Mrs Mooney's words cut through all the muddled feelings Fiona had about her mother. She looked at the housekeeper through tear-filled eyes. 'I'll try harder to be more understanding.'

'You're doing as well as anyone can do under the circumstances. And don't think I don't know that you've lost a lot yourself – a father you were very close to, and now you've lost your own independence.' She halted. 'But it will all sort out eventually. Your mother will get well again and life will get back to normal.'

'Do you think so?'

'Yes, things have a way of working themselves out.' The housekeeper put her hand on Fiona's shoulder. 'Don't be hard on yourself, Fiona. People around here admire the way you and Patrick have kept things running between the shop and the pub.' Then, she went over to the cooker. 'Now, I've left some rice in a pot there that you might heat up for your mother later before you go back out. She likes it with a couple of spoonfuls of strawberry jam. There's enough there for you as well.'

'That's great,' Fiona said. 'When I've finished my own meal I'll take it up to her.'

'You know I'm not in tomorrow morning?' Mrs Mooney reminded her. 'I have a hospital appointment in Dublin, but I'll be back in the afternoon to get the tea ready.'

'That's fine.' Fiona looked at her. 'I hope it's nothing serious?'

'No, no – just a bit of women's trouble that the doctor wants checking out.'

'Good luck with it anyway.'

The older woman smiled and shook her head. 'A waste of time queuing in a hospital when there's nothing wrong with me.' She lifted her coat and scarf. 'I'll see you tomorrow afternoon, so.'

She went out and closed the door behind her.

Fiona finished her meal and then sat for a while at the kitchen table looking through an American magazine which Elizabeth had sent her every month since she went out to New York. She loved looking at the clothes and the advertisements for the big shops, although she no longer allowed herself to imagine being out there and actually going into the shops that her friend had described. There was an article about a florist who did flowers for the White House, and it showed photographs of her displays in one of the big hotels in Park Avenue, which Fiona knew must be close to the big apartment where Elizabeth worked.

She sat back in her chair thinking and wondering, and then eventually she looked at the clock and moved to warm the rice to take up to her mother.

CHAPTER 20

Fiona was surprised how busy the bar was when she came back down at eight o'clock that evening. Through the greyish-blue haze of pipe and cigarette smoke she could see that it was filled not only with local people, but a lot of the commercial travellers who stopped off in the town, plus a few strangers. It was an unusual mix of young and older – most formally dressed. The sort of mix of men her mother would have approved of.

She caught Patrick's eye and gestured that she was hanging her jacket up in the kitchen, and a few minutes later she stepped in behind the bar to help out. It was so busy she didn't have a chance to talk to the barman as an impatient-looking Dublin man pushed forward and gave her an order for four pints of Guinness. She smiled and took his money and after she had rung it up, gave him his change.

As she was waiting for the pints to settle, she moved over to Patrick. 'What on earth is on tonight?' she asked, feeling guilty that he had been left on his own with such a crowd. 'If I'd known I would have been down earlier.'

'I think there's a farmers' meeting in Hayes Hotel but there's a big funeral in the morning as well,' he said quietly. 'I didn't know him myself. It's some commercial traveller fellow from Dublin who was living somewhere out the Clara Road the last ten years. Seemingly he was married to a woman from the town. He was only in his early forties.'

'Oh God, I'm sorry to hear that.' Fiona did not ask what had happened to the man and, whether he knew it or not, Patrick offered no explanation. The memory of her father dying was still too close for both of them. 'You should have phoned down for me earlier. You must have been run off your feet here on your own.'

'Ah, it's been okay. They're a grand crowd. They just waited their turn.'

The door opened and another group came in, so they both went straight to them to take their orders, and it was nearly twenty minutes later before the bar quietened down and Patrick got a chance to tell her that two of the bedrooms were taken for the night.

'Two of the travellers asked me about an hour ago, and I said as far as I knew it would be all right and that I'd check with you as soon as you came in.'

'That's perfect.' Her father had always been delighted to let the room, as it was always great to get a few more pounds in, especially midweek. 'The rooms are fine, aren't they? Mary Ellen changed the beds yesterday.' Her eyes narrowed. 'I'm sure she'll probably have done everything, but I'll go upstairs and check the bathrooms for towels and soap when I get a minute.'

When she came back down, happy that the housekeeper had left everything in order, Patrick came towards her, a serious look on his face.

'God, Fiona,' he said, looking worried, 'I've just remembered that Mary Ellen said she had an appointment at the hospital in the morning, so she won't be around to do the breakfast.'

'That's okay, I can do it.'

'Are you sure?'

'It's no trouble. We have fresh sausages and rashers that were delivered to the shop this morning. And there's plenty of black and white pudding in the fridge. I can fry them some of yesterday's soda bread as well, so we'll be grand.'

'What about your mother?'

'I can see to her before I leave.' She shrugged. 'She only has tea and toast, so ten minutes will sort that.'

'I'll check what time they want it for,' he said. 'Probably around nine if they're going to the funeral at eleven – that would give them time for the hour fast before Communion.' He indicated the right corner of the bar where around half a dozen men dressed in suits were standing chatting. 'That's the fellows over there. They said there might be another fellow coming down from Dublin tonight, but they couldn't be sure. He might just drive down in the morning. I'll go and have a word with them.'

Fiona looked over to the corner Patrick had made for, and saw him talking to two young men around her own age whom she didn't recognise. She wondered where they were from and how they knew the deceased man, and then she wondered whether they were single. She caught herself. God, she thought, I'm getting as bad as my mother. Then, the main door at the side of the bar opened and she moved her gaze towards it to check if it was someone who might be coming back from the Gents or someone who might want to be served.

The figure stopped at the side of the bar, just inside the door. It was the one quiet space as the rest of the bar was occupied by people sitting on high stools or leaning against it.

'Hello, Fiona, are you well? I haven't seen you in a while.' Paul Moore's voice was low and his face serious.

Fiona felt her face flush. 'Hello, Paul. I'm grand, thanks. And yourself?' He looked well, she thought, and smartly dressed.

'Oh, I'm ticking over,' he replied, tapping his fingertips on the bar. 'I said I'd meet a few lads I know from Kildare after the church tonight. They're here for the funeral in the morning.'

Patrick came back behind the bar now, carrying a tray of empty glasses and beer bottles. When he saw who Fiona was chatting to, he nodded to

Paul and then diplomatically went to the far end of the bar.

'Did you know the poor man?' Fiona asked now. It was a safe and normal question under the circumstances.

'I did. He was one of my insurance customers. His family have a farm out near Durrow. He was a nice man, and very young to go so soon.' His face changed, and he moved in closer to the bar and closer to her. 'How are all the family doing since your own loss?'

Fiona felt a pang at the sudden reminder. Her gaze moved to the curtained window behind him. 'It's been hard on everyone,' she said, 'especially my mother.'

'I would imagine that,' he said. 'I've heard when something like that happens suddenly, it makes it all the harder. I hope as time goes on that it gets easier for you all.'

'Thank you,' she said.

'It's a pity that all your travel plans have gone by the wayside. You were serious about going to New York, weren't you?'

Her head jerked up now, and she looked at him. Something about his tone made her think he was questioning whether she had really planned to go there – or whether she had just said it as an excuse to break the romance off with him. His face gave nothing away.

'Well,' she said, 'it was serious enough for me to have organised a job and somewhere to live, but then everything suddenly changed at home when my father died and I was needed.' Most Irishmen knew the responsibilities that death could bequeath to certain family members.

'Of course . . . of course . . .' His voice was lower and softer. 'And it's all credit to you that you did the decent thing in spite of all your plans.' He paused. 'No doubt it was a bad situation for you, Fiona – the timing and everything. I suppose it would have been worse if you had just gone and then had to come back home.'

'It would.'

A silence fell between them which made her feel awkward, and she wondered what was going through his head. Was he genuinely sorry for what had happened to her or was he gloating – thinking he was now better suited to Claire Ryan than he had been to her?

She lifted a bar towel, trying to look busy. 'Can I get you anything?'

His face creased in thought, as though he had not considered what he might drink. 'I suppose I'll have a pint of Guinness, please.'

She turned to the beer pump and took a clean glass from the gantry.

She had never imagined him just turning up in the bar like this. She had not spoken to him since the morning of the funeral when he came up to offer his condolences to her and her mother and her sisters. And afterwards, during all the weeks and months since they buried her father, she had only seen him from a distance – once at Mass in Tullamore church when he went to Communion, and on a few occasions she had seen him drive past the shop in his car. He had never been a regular in Tracey's bar, and had only come in to see her when she was working and to stand chatting to her with a pint at the bar. She had not been to any dances or the local cinema where she might see him since it happened. It was too soon after a death in the family.

In the meantime, he had got in with Claire Ryan and, from what she had heard, he might be ready to settle down with her. Thankfully, she had never met them together, but her friends kept her up to date on sightings of them. So much so, that recently she had made a point of saying that she had no interest in hearing what Paul Moore got up to and who he was with. He was a chapter in her life that was over and done with.

'If I had really been keen on him,' she had told them, 'I would never have thought of going to New York.'

But, at close quarters with him now, she was not quite so certain how she felt about him, and was glad none of her friends were there to witness them meeting up.

As she stood behind the pump filling his glass, she looked at the commercial travellers in the corner – and compared Paul to the two she knew would be staying overnight. Looks-wise, he had the advantage; the other two were average-looking at best. She also knew his good points whereas she knew nothing of the well-dressed strangers. He was local and from a good family, a steady worker. He had not been mean – which would have been a major drawback. She had grown up with a generous father who dropped off potatoes and meat to families in need and, on occasion, quietly handed over bottles of beer that he knew would never be paid for.

Paul, she felt, would have those same kind qualities. The only real concern she had about him was that he was inclined to be serious and predictable in his ways. On the occasions when they had ventured out of Tullamore on the train to Galway and Dublin, it was she who had suggested it. He had seemed to enjoy wandering around the cities with her arm through his – around Stephen's Green in Dublin and around the small streets in Galway when they walked down to Spanish Arch. But she would have enjoyed it more if he had been a bit more adventurous and occasionally came up with an idea for them.

When she mentioned her reservations about this to her parents one evening, her father had laughed and said that the man she was looking for didn't exist in Ireland. Her mother had said that there was a lot to be said for a safe and steady man.

Shortly after this, she began receiving letters from Elizabeth telling her about the different kinds of people she had met in New York. The thought occurred that her father might just have hit the nail on the head. That she might be casting her net too close to home. She had started to wonder about Paul, and wonder whether she would feel stifled living in a small country town and married to someone who did not mind it. Then, the idea of New York had come up.

As she stood beside him now, it all seemed longer than just last Christmas.

Two customers came to the bar now and she left Paul's pint to settle while she served one and Patrick served the other. She was quick with her order for three glasses of Tullamore Dew whiskey, and when she gave the man his change she turned back to Paul's glass to add the creamy head.

'How are your sisters?' he asked when the bar was quiet again.

'They're grand. They were home just recently and have both gone back.'

'Hard to believe that Bridget will be a nun one of these days,' he said, smiling now. 'She's a lovely girl and has a great way with people, not like some of the nuns we all know. I'd say she will do well out in the community working with people.'

'She will,' Fiona agreed. 'And she's very dedicated to the religious life. She's up for Mass every morning here when she's at home, but at least it's not as early as she has to get up in the convent.'

She hadn't expected him to be so chatty or so personal. She thought that there was a change in him, that he seemed more forthcoming and confident. Then, she wondered if Claire Ryan would be happy if she knew that he had been in the bar, talking so familiarly with his ex-girl-friend. A group of men came to be served and she and Patrick were kept busy again. At one point Paul caught her eye and nodded, and she felt relieved when he went off to join a table at the far end of the room.

Apart from feeling awkward about Paul, she was pleased to see a packed house, the way it often was when her father was alive, though tonight it was a little more subdued than normal because of the funeral.

It was around quarter to ten, when things had quietened off again and she was washing the glasses, that she heard the door to the snug bar opening. When she glanced over, she could see three figures through the frosted glass. She couldn't tell whether they were male or female.

It was unusual to have women in during the week in the evenings, so she thought it might be strangers who had travelled for the funeral. It was surprising who might frequent the smallest and most private part of the public house. In general, it was frowned upon to have ladies in the bar, so the snug was ideal, as it was completely separate from the rest of the pub, with its own door and lock inside. It also had its own bell for customers when they wanted to order a drink, which was then served through the hatch by the barman. The frosted glass on the doors and the hatch gave privacy, which suited people such as priests and members of the local Guards who would often pop in for a quiet pint, and the odd courting couple.

Fiona recognised one of the voices – it was Maggie O'Connell – and then she remembered Maggie saying that she might drop over with her friend. Patrick returned with empty bottles, and made to go straight to the snug end of the bar.

'I'll get them,' Fiona told him. 'I think it's Maggie O'Connell and her friend.'

'Grand,' he said, turning to resume his bottle collection.

It crossed Fiona's mind how lucky they were to have such an efficient, dependable and easy-going barman. What, she wondered, would they have done after their father had died without Patrick? They would have had to take on someone else to manage the pub, and neither she nor her mother would have had the experience to interview and choose someone who could do all the things that Patrick very quietly did. They were lucky that he could just continue with the exact same daily routine he and their father had been used to. The routine that kept both the business and the Tracey family from disintegrating into small pieces.

When she went to the snug end Maggie was there, leaning on the bar chatting to a young man in his late twenties. He had longish fair hair and was dressed casually in a cream fisherman's sweater, a denim shirt inside it, and jeans. He didn't look like their usual sort of customer and, if he had been younger, she would have taken him for a student. Her gaze shifted to the red-haired woman who was seated at the table behind, and who Fiona guessed was Maggie's friend from Galway. She wondered if he was her boyfriend.

'What can I get you?' she said, smiling at them.

Maggie turned to the young man. 'This is Fiona, the girl who might be able to help you.'

'Hi there.' He smiled and stretched out his hand. 'I'm Michael O'Sullivan.'

His name was Irish, but his accent was not. It was unmistakably American. There was something immediately likeable about him.

'I'm pleased to meet you, Michael.'

He took her hand in a warm and firm handshake.

Maggie looked back at her friend. 'Fiona, this is my friend, Anne, who I was telling you about earlier on in the shop.'

Fiona looked over at the attractive woman with the lovely flowing red hair, and said hello. Both hairdressers, she thought, were good adverts for their trade.

'Well, it's been a day of surprises,' Maggie said. 'We met Michael as we were coming up the street. He's been to Hayes Hotel and Bolger's looking for a room for the night, but they're both packed. I said you often let the rooms and it was worth giving you a try. I'd no idea it was so busy in the town tonight.' She lowered her voice. 'What on earth is going on with all these well-dressed men in Tullamore?'

'A funeral and apparently there's a big farmers' meeting in Hayes Hotel as well.'

'Ah!' Maggie said. 'That explains all the strangers, and why there are no rooms anywhere.'

'I'm not sure how we're placed. We might have one of the rooms free, but I'll have to check with Patrick. He said something about a fellow coming down from Dublin.' She looked over to the table where he was chatting to some locals. When she caught his eye she waved and a few moments later he came back to the bar.

'Do you know if that third room is needed tonight?' she asked.

'It is – I meant to say it to you earlier. There's another man on his way over from Kildare, so we have a full house.'

Fiona felt a dart of disappointment, and it must have shown on her face.

'Is there someone else looking for a room?' he asked.

Fiona thumbed towards the snug. 'Maggie met an American fellow outside who has been round a few places and can't get anywhere to stay.'

He raised his eyebrows. 'An American?' He thought for a few moments. 'I could stay up at the family house tonight and let him have my room.'

'Not at all,' Fiona said. 'We can't put you out of your own room for a stranger!'

'I've often done it on fair days,' he said. 'And the mother and father are always delighted to have a bit of company for the night.'

Fiona shook her head. 'It's too much trouble.'

'Look,' he said, 'the poor fella's probably been travelling for hours, and you can imagine how it must feel landing in a strange country, and not having a bed for the night.' He paused, thinking. 'I'll nip upstairs and move any bits I have lying around the room, then I'll go on up to the parents' house and let them know I'll be home for the night.' He smiled. 'Sure they'll be only delighted to have the company. They'll sit up until I finish – they sit up late at night anyway – and I'll bring a couple of bottles of stout for the old lad and a drop of whiskey to make a toddy for my mother, and they'll be as happy as Larry.'

'Are you sure?'

'Go and tell the Yank he can have my bed. It was only changed the other day, but if he's a fussy type there are clean sheets and pillow covers in the wardrobe. Mary Ellen always leaves a clean set in case anyone comes unexpected.' He glanced around the bar now. 'There's a few gone now, so it's quieter. Can you manage on your own for a while?

'Of course I can. On you go.'

She went back to the snug. 'I've checked with Patrick,' she said, 'and there's a spare room for you.'

'Oh, that's wonderful,' Michael O'Sullivan said.

Fiona thought she should explain. 'It's actually the room Patrick uses himself when he's staying overnight, but he's sorted it out for you. He's happy staying up at his parents' house. He occasionally does that if we're very busy.'

'Are you sure?' Michael O'Sullivan looked slightly alarmed. 'I don't want to put anyone out.'

'I've checked with him and it's really no problem. As I said, it's not the first time, and he does stay at the family house on his days off.'

He relaxed again. 'Well, that's very good of him, and I appreciate it.' He gestured towards the bar. 'And this is exactly the sort of place I was looking for – a traditional Irish bar. It couldn't be better.' He put his hand on Maggie's shoulder. 'The least I can do is buy you ladies a drink for helping me out. What will you have?'

Maggie looked back at her friend. 'I'll have a Babycham – is that okay for you, Anne?'

'Grand,' Anne said.

He took a five-pound note out of his pocket. 'And I'll have a Tullamore Dew. What will you have, Fiona?'

'Oh, that's okay.' she said. 'I don't drink that much.'

'No, please,' he said, 'I insist. If it wasn't for you, I could have been sleeping in the hired car tonight.'

'Go away out of that!' Maggie said. 'We would have found you a bed somewhere, wouldn't we, girls? I'd have even risked my whiter-than-white reputation and given you the couch for the night.'

She winked and everyone laughed. 'Fiona will have a Babycham the same as us.' And before Fiona could refuse, she said, 'You've been on your feet all day – it will do you the power of good to have a little drink.'

'So,' he said, 'we'll have three Babychams and a glass of Tullamore Dew.'

Fiona rolled her eyes and laughed. 'I don't suppose a Babycham will do me any harm.'

She only had time to serve the drinks and take a quick mouthful of her own, and then she had to help Patrick with the rush for last orders at the bar.

Afterwards, they both went around the room, picking up glasses and bottles. Fiona kept away from the corner where Paul Moore was sitting, in case he thought she was trying to catch his attention.

The crowd in the room began to disperse. Patrick said he had checked his room upstairs and that it looked fine to him. But, since he knew that women had different ideas about what was fine, he didn't mind if Fiona wanted to double-check it for the American guest.

'I wouldn't think he is the fussy sort,' she said. 'He seems decent, and he insisted on buying me a drink.'

Patrick raised his eyebrows. 'Did you get time to drink it?'

'I'll finish it later when I get time. I just want to check the room first.'

He looked up at the clock and then rang the 'drinking-up' bell. 'I'll try to get them moving out of the bar now. When you come back down go into the snug and enjoy your drink. Maggie just bought you a second one, so they're waiting at the table for you.'

As she went upstairs, it occurred to her that tonight had turned out differently than usual with Paul Moore turning up and the friendly American. The fact that there were a number of strangers in the bar was surprising too. For once, her mother was proved right. You never know with a bar who might drop in.

And as she walked along the narrow corridor to Patrick's room at the bottom – past the Sacred Heart picture, lit with a small red bulb – she became aware of a feeling she had not had since her father died. A feeling of hope or perhaps even of anticipation. Something similar to the feelings she had every time she received an airmail letter with the Manhattan postmark. A feeling that there was something more for her out there. Something in the bigger and wider world. Something better.

CHAPTER 21

Fiona changed the sheets and pillowcases on Patrick's bed and straightened the blankets and the top cover. Patrick had moved any personal items into drawers, so she just gave a quick dust around, and straightened the tie-backs on the curtains.

Michael O'Sullivan, she thought, like most men, probably wouldn't notice whether things had been freshly washed and ironed. But, then again, you never knew with Americans. She felt the perfectly ironed creases that Mrs Mooney left on the folded pillowcases gave a good impression of their business. She knew from Elizabeth's letters from New York that their small pub would not live up to the modern standards that Americans were used to – where everything was bigger and better. But there was nothing could be done about that. Everyone knew Ireland was Ireland and America was America – and that they were both worlds apart in every way. She wondered what had brought him over from America, and why he had come on his own. The usual reason was looking up ancestors, and he had an Irish name. She smiled to herself – no doubt Maggie would have got all that kind of information out of him.

As she passed through the bar there were still customers at half a dozen of the tables, who Patrick had not succeeded in moving out as yet. She glanced over to where Paul Moore had been sitting and was relieved to see that he had gone. Their meeting up again had made her feel happier. It now meant that if she came across him and Claire Ryan in the town at the weekend, she wouldn't feel too awkward.

She went through the bar and into the snug where Maggie and Anne and Michael O'Sullivan were sitting chatting together. Anne was telling them about a new restaurant that had opened in Galway. They all looked relaxed, as if they knew each other well. Maggie had a knack for putting people at their ease, something Fiona wished she had herself.

She caught the American's eye, and said, 'Your room is all ready now.' She looked at his rucksack which was lying by the empty fire-grate. 'If you want to put your stuff up now, it's no problem.'

He came over to her, his drink in his hand. 'That's great,' he said. 'I'll carry the rucksack with me when I'm going up later.'

'Whatever suits you,' she said. 'There are clean towels on your bed, and the bathroom is at the bottom of the corridor. The boiler comes on early in the morning, so the water should be good and hot if you want a bath. If there's anything else you need, just let me know.'

Fiona turned and went back into the bar, and he came out behind her, leaving the door slightly ajar.

'It's so good of you people to do this for me, especially at such short notice.'

She paused, smiling at him. 'Oh, we're used to it. We've had phone calls to the house in the middle of the night.'

'Don't you ever have a problem with the unpredictability of it?' He moved over towards a table now and put his glass down on it, then he pulled a chair out for Fiona and one for himself.

She sat down opposite him. 'I don't mind it,' she said, shrugging. 'Most people are decent and you want to do your best to help them out.'

It occurred to her how easy it was to talk with confidence to an attractive man, when you were talking business. When you had to give information or serve someone, no one could accuse you of being forward. People were expected to chat in those circumstances. Her father had told her that the first day she stepped behind the bar. He said communication oiled the wheels of any business in Ireland. Talking was as necessary as the products you were selling.

Michael O'Sullivan smiled warmly at her now. 'I'm truly grateful to you for sorting me out. I guess it was kind of stupid of me to think I could just turn up in town, and find somewhere to stay.'

'Well, normally you could find a place easily,' she said. 'But everywhere in town is busy tonight. We often have a couple of the rooms free. We're only really a stopgap – the hotels have most of the bed and breakfast trade as they have better facilities.'

'Well, I'm sure glad to be here,' he said 'I know it's different to the hotels I usually stay in . . .' He caught the look on her face. 'I mean that it's different in a good way. It gives you a better feel for places when you get to meet the locals.'

There was something nice and easy-going about him, and she liked the tone of his voice. It was soft and warm, and not like some of the louder American accents which she had heard. 'Where are you heading after Tullamore?'

'I'm going to Connemara,' he said. 'I promised my mother I would attend to a few family things on this trip.'

The way he said 'on this trip' made Fiona wonder. 'So, have you been to Ireland before?'

'Yes, we used to come regularly when we were children. We flew over most summers to stay in Connemara.'

Fiona nodded her head slowly, trying not to look surprised. No families she knew flew back and forward from America. Up until recently – certainly her parents' generation – people went to America and never came home again. Things had changed in the last few years. The cost of flights had come down enough to allow people to come home now and again, but those who visited every year were very few and far between.

Elizabeth had told her she was saving money every week from what was left of her wages, as she planned, at some time in the future, to come home for a month. She reckoned it would take about three years to be able to afford the plane fare and the presents she wanted to bring back with her.

Michael O'Sullivan – for all his casual clothes and longish hair – clearly did not come from an ordinary family.

He caught her eye and smiled, then took a drink of his beer. 'I'm hoping to surprise my mother,' he told her. 'I've heard the old family home is up for sale in Clifden – my great-grandparents' house and the house my grandmother was born in. A local guy owns it but it hasn't been lived in for over five years. It's a fisherman's cottage – and my great-grandfather was a fisherman. It's pretty basic, but in a good location just outside the town. When I wrote to him to enquire about it, he got straight back saying he would be very happy to sell it.'

Fiona was interested now – she leaned forward, her elbows on the table. 'And what are you thinking of doing with the house?' she asked.

'Extend it with a couple more bedrooms, put a bathroom in and maybe add a small courtyard. Then, I plan to give the deeds to my mother as a sixtieth birthday present next year. I think she would love to spend her visits in the place she grew up in, rather than having to stay in hotels and bed and breakfasts.' He grinned at her. 'I'm quite excited about it. It will be a lovely project – if it comes off.'

She smiled. 'I'm curious – how would you organise all the work while you're in America?'

'Well, I'm not in any real hurry back home from this visit. I hope to get things started and sort as much as I can while I'm over here.'

She smiled understandingly, as though people told her things like this all the time. As though flying across the Atlantic and the price of flights were of no consequence.

'Well, isn't that great you don't have to rush back? Having the time to travel and suit yourself.'

'I suppose it is.'

There was a small silence. Fiona suddenly felt she was talking too much, asking him too many questions. She started to gather the beer mats that were scattered on the table, and square them up on top of each other.

He took another drink of his beer then looked at her again. 'It will be just fine if it all works out. I'll draw up plans while I'm here and leave them with local builders to do the work.'

'And can you draw plans up yourself? Would you be able to do that?' She was back asking him questions again, as though unable to stop herself. All the days and the weeks of having the same old conversations with her mother and Mrs Mooney and Patrick, made everything Michael O'Sullivan said seem different and exciting.

'Yeah, I reckon so. I've tackled bigger things, so it should be okay.'

'And where did you learn that?'

'University, when I trained as an architect.'

He said it matter of factly as though that's what everyone did, and Fiona suddenly felt childish now, and out of her depth. What did she know about plans for houses and that sort of thing?

'Well, that explains why you would have that kind of interest in houses and buildings, and why doing up a little cottage would be no trouble to you.'

As he had talked, she had formed a picture of the old derelict place in her mind, even though she had never been to Connemara and was not even sure where Clifden was. She wished the cottage was closer to Tullamore, as she thought she would like to see the work starting on it, and then watch it progress.

Fiona suddenly saw Maggie at the door of the snug, smiling over at her and winking and she felt herself blush as though the hairdresser could read her silly thoughts.

Maggie waved. 'Come back in and sit with us,' she said. 'It's cosier in here. There are drinks here for you both, and Patrick is joining us as well.'

Michael smiled at the hairdresser. 'Ah, that's very kind of you.' He picked up his drink and finished it off.

'I'll be there in a few minutes,' Fiona said, pushing her chair back and standing up. 'It's been a busy night and I don't want to leave Patrick doing everything on his own.' She didn't want to look too eager to join Michael O'Sullivan. She made a show of looking over to the bar, where Patrick was lifting the last few glasses and wiping down the tables, having seen the last customers out and locked the door after them.

Maggie came into the bar now. 'We'll all help and it'll be done quicker and then everyone can sit and relax for half an hour.' She turned to call back into the snug to her friend. 'You don't mind picking up a few glasses, do you?'

Fiona tried to protest but Maggie wasn't listening. Anne came into the bar now, and Maggie picked up cloths from the counter, and gave them to her friend and to Michael O'Sullivan and then they went around clearing and wiping the tables that Patrick had not yet done.

Ten minutes later, the bar was clean and tidy and they were all back seated in the snug, Maggie, Anne and Patrick on chairs, and Michael and Fiona on the bench.

'Ye should come every night!' Patrick said, lifting the glass of brandy that Maggie had bought him. 'It would make my job a whole lot easier.' He took a drink and then sat back in his chair.

The little glint in his eye told Fiona that he was pleased with the help and the unexpected turn that the night had taken with the girls in the snug, and then the American suddenly turning up. It struck her that maybe even Patrick liked a change in routine.

As she looked around at the others, chatting and laughing, and then thought back to the crowds earlier, it occurred to her that it was the first night she had enjoyed in the pub since her father died.

When Patrick got into a discussion with Maggie and Annie about a friend who had recently moved to Galway, Michael moved along the bench closer to Fiona.

'I hope I didn't bore you with all that talk about buildings and my plans about renovating?' He smiled. 'I know Americans have a reputation for having big ideas, but I don't want to come across like that. I hope I come across as a more down-to-earth kind of guy.'

'You didn't bore me at all,' she said. 'I enjoyed hearing all your plans, and I really hope you get the cottage. It's a lovely idea to buy it for your mother – it's very thoughtful.'

'Thank you, that means a lot to me.'

She lowered her voice. 'I think people should make plans. Believe it or not, I actually had plans to move to New York myself – not even a year ago. But then everything changed . . .' She halted, catching her breath at the memory of what had happened. 'Well, things changed at home – and it became impossible.'

'Go on,' he said. 'You have me intrigued now.'

Fiona could see him now, smiling at her, waiting

to hear all about it. But she couldn't start telling a complete stranger all about her father's sudden death and then how things had been with her mother since. She couldn't say how disappointed she was that her plans had come to nothing, and how fearful she was of being stuck at home with her mother and becoming a bitter old spinster. Like all the Americans she had met, she guessed he was only interested in hearing about big plans that actually worked out. But, she had started now, and she had to tell him some version of her story.

'Well,' she started, 'I have a good friend called Elizabeth who is working in Park Avenue in New York—'

'Park Avenue – wow! That's a top area. She must be doing good. What does she do?'

She faltered, realising that he thought Elizabeth was some kind of important businesswoman. 'Oh, it's nothing important, she's not a businesswoman or anything like that. She works for a family there, in a big apartment.' She spoke quickly now, making sure he got the true picture. 'She helps with the housekeeping and the general running of the house. We're good friends and she was anxious for me to join her out there because she said it was the sort of life that would really suit me. We both feel we want something different from here.'

'Well, New York is very different from here,' he said, 'and that's for sure—' He halted, as though not wanting to sway her opinion.

She glanced at him and then looked away, suddenly wondering if she sounded naïve. 'Anyway, the family needed someone to help with the children, and she put in a good word for me, and the lady of the house asked me to send out my educational qualifications and references.' She shrugged. 'They were happy with everything, so they offered me the job. I thought it was worth it for the experience. I thought, if it didn't work out, I could always come home.'

He smiled at her. 'I think you would love it. New York is the heart of America, and a great place to start off in. I worked in Manhattan for a couple of years, which is the centre of the city. But recently, I've been working more in Boston.'

'Is that far?' she asked.

He calculated. 'Driving – around four hours.'

'That far?'

He smiled. 'That's not far for America. People travel long distances there. A day's drive isn't unusual.'

'It sounds far enough to me.' She calculated. 'I suppose it's about the same distance as going to Cork. People here would think that's far enough to go for a week's holiday.'

'Well, this is a small country. I suppose it's all relative.' He leaned in towards her. 'Tell me what happened to your plans about New York, if it's not too personal.'

'Well, it's not really that personal now – everyone here knows all about it.' She looked him square in the face. 'I had all my cases packed, my passport sorted and everything organised to go to America when my father suddenly died. It happened only days before I was supposed to go.'

His face became solemn. 'I'm so sorry . . . I had no idea it was something as serious as that.' He held his hand up. 'Please, you don't have to tell me any more if it's too painful to talk about.'

'I'm used to living in a small place where everyone knows your business. The people who come into the shop or bar knew I was going, and why my plans were suddenly changed.'

'It must have been a terrible shock to all your family.'

'It wasn't just losing my father, it was the effect it had on my mother. She became ill shortly afterwards and I just couldn't leave her.'

'Well, family are very important. I think I would feel the same if my own mom was sick. Sometimes you have to make choices you don't want to make – but it's the right thing to do.'

'That's exactly how it was,' she said. And then, because she felt he really understood her situation, she found herself telling him about Angela living her own life in Dublin, and Bridget at the convent training to be a nun.

Patrick interrupted them briefly, when he brought back another round of drinks from the bar. 'I'll sort it with you in the morning,' he told Fiona.

She nodded, knowing that she wouldn't take the

money off him, but pleased that he had offered to pay for the drinks in front of the others.

Maggie beckoned to Fiona and Michael. 'We want to hear all about your plans while you're over in Ireland, Michael. Where you're going and what kind of things you're going to be doing. Anne has just been telling us all about the racing and the sailing down in Galway. Would that be the kind of thing you'd be interested in?'

He grinned at her. 'I am interested in absolutely everything to do with Ireland, and I'll be very happy to listen to any suggestions you have.' Then, he turned to Fiona and quietly said, 'We can finish our talk later, if that's okay?'

The way he looked at her made her neck start to flush. And, as he turned back towards the others, she suddenly realised that she liked him. She liked him a lot. And something made her think that he liked her too. Where, she wondered, could it possibly lead? What was the point of getting involved with someone who she knew was going to be travelling back home in the next few weeks? Someone she would never see again. It could only lead to more unfulfilled wishes and dreams. She'd had enough of those.

She picked up her drink now and took a sip. What harm was there in being friendly with him, she reasoned. If she ever did go out to New York, it might be good to have another contact out there – they might meet up again. Then, she caught herself. There was no point in running ahead of things. She would wait and see what happened.

Almost an hour later, when they had finished the last round of drinks, Fiona reluctantly called a halt to the night. 'If we stay any longer,' she told the two girls, 'I'll never make it up in the morning to make the breakfasts for the men staying upstairs.' She could feel the effects of what she had drunk already and, afraid of making a fool of herself, she had moved from Babycham to lemonade shandy.

Maggie and Annie started to put their coats on.

'If you want to go on with the girls,' Patrick told Fiona, 'I'll turn the lights off and lock up.'

Fiona was disappointed that she hadn't had a chance to say goodnight to Michael on her own. She knew it would look rather obvious that she liked him if she made an excuse to stay on after Maggie and her friend had left.

Her thoughts were correct. As soon as they were outside the bar door, Maggie turned towards her. 'You're mad rushing home, Fiona! That lovely American lad obviously fancies you! You should have stayed on – you should have had another few drinks with him – got to know him a bit better.'

Fiona could now see the effects the drinks had had on Maggie, and was glad she'd been more careful.

'I was watching you,' Maggie went on. 'The way the pair of you were chatting away as though you'd known each other for years. I'd say he'll be very disappointed you've gone off now and he's left there chatting with Patrick.'

Fiona raised her eyebrows as though she didn't know what Maggie was talking about. 'Do you think so? I didn't notice anything.' She knew she shouldn't care what others thought, but she didn't want to be the subject of light-hearted gossip in the hairdresser's the next day.

Maggie looked at her friend. 'What do you think, Anne?'

Anne raised her eyebrows. 'Sure, it was fairly obvious he likes you. No doubts about it.'

They started to slowly walk up the street now.

Maggie laughed. 'God, Fiona, could you not tell by the way he was looking at you? I'd say he's very keen on you. He's a lovely lad, not one of those Yanks who are constantly bragging about how great America is and full of big ideas. He's a nice quiet type, down to earth and I'd say very genuine.'

Fiona guessed that Michael O'Sullivan had not told them anything about his plans to buy the cottage in Connemara – or the fact that he was an architect with fairly big ideas. She wondered what Maggie would have thought if she knew. Would she have thought he was a typical bragging Yank then too? She almost smiled at the thought.

'He does seem genuine,' she said, 'and I do think he's very nice, but it's a bit complicated getting friendly with someone who lives so far away.'

Anne patted Fiona's arm. 'You should live for

the minute. Enjoy your few days with him while he's here. Who knows what could happen?'

'Exactly,' Maggie said. 'You don't want to miss any opportunities. When I look back over the years, I know I've missed plenty, and I'll bet Anne thinks the same.'

Anne rolled her eyes. 'Don't talk. We thought we had all the time in the world, now we're wishing we'd grabbed the best ones first time around. If you hesitate at all they're gone.' She clicked her fingers. 'Just like that. There's always another girl waiting who sees the value in them that you took for granted.'

A picture of Paul Moore suddenly flew into Fiona's mind. She wondered if she would regret not grabbing her chances with him in a few years' time.

'And who knows,' Maggie said, nudging Fiona's elbow, 'in twenty years' time you could be living out in America with half a dozen kids.'

Fiona looked at her incredulously. 'Are you mad? I've only just met him, and I'm sure the poor fellow would die with embarrassment if he heard what you just said.'

'Embarrassment be damned. He didn't look like that when he was gazing into your eyes all evening. You would know just by looking at Michael O'Sullivan that he's not the sort to be embarrassed when he's with women. It's well known that American lads are far more romantic than the Irish.'

'How do you know that?' Fiona asked.

'You can tell it from watching the films. The way they dance, and all those drive-in movies and everything.' She gave a dramatic sigh. 'And the lads wearing those American Army uniforms are only gorgeous!' She dug Anne in the ribs now. 'And don't tell me that the only place their hands go is into the boxes of popcorn.'

Maggie shrieked with laughter and then Annie joined in.

Fiona eyes widened in shock. 'I don't believe you just said that! Imagine if anyone heard you!'

They both kept laughing and giggling and knocking against each other until they had to lean on a wall to support them. They looked so ridiculous and the worst for wear from drink that Fiona found herself laughing too.

The more they laughed, the worse they all three got.

'Come on!' Fiona said in a loud whisper, pulling Maggie by the arm. 'We'll have the neighbours coming out to see what's going on if you make any more noise.'

'You'd better not mention the popcorn,' Anne giggled.

Maggie moved away from the wall and then started back into fits of laughter again.

'Oh, don't! I'm going to wet myself if I don't stop laughing.'

Somehow, Fiona managed to get them moving again, and heaved a sigh of relief when the other two crossed the road towards the hairdressing salon and she walked on home.

Tomorrow, she thought, she would be able to tell her mother that something different had actually happened.

CHAPTER 22

Fiona put her key in the door and opened it as quietly as she could so as not to disturb her mother. She was halfway along the hallway when she noticed something. She paused for a few moments and then it hit her. She could smell cigarette smoke. Her mother didn't smoke and her father had given up a few years ago, so there had been no regular smokers in the house for a long time. Who, she wondered, had been in the house so recently, and so late at night?

Various scenarios started to run through her mind. Had something happened to her mother while she was out, and did a neighbour or someone else who smoked have to be called?

A feeling of alarm came over her. Then she began to reason with herself. If anything had happened to her mother and other people had come to help, someone would have run down to the bar to get her. There was no emergency. Someone had been smoking in the house, and that was all.

She stopped at the foot of the stairs and called out 'Mam? Are you okay?' There was silence. Fiona dropped her handbag and started up the stairs. She was halfway up when she heard a noise from below. She froze, listening, then she heard her mother's voice calling.

'I'm fine! I'm here . . . downstairs in the kitchen!'

She leaned against the staircase, her hand over her thudding heart. She gave herself a few moments to catch her breath and then went back down towards the kitchen. The feeling of relief when she went in to find her mother sitting in the armchair by the fire was replaced by confusion when she saw the cigarette in her mother's hand. She had never seen her mother smoking.

'What's wrong?' her mother asked.

'I got a shock when I smelled the cigarette smoke . . . I thought someone else was in the house.'

'No, it's only me. I thought a cigarette might just give me a bit of a lift. The last time the doctor was in – when he gave me the new tablets – he said to try and do little things I used to enjoy. I tried to read one of your magazines, but I couldn't concentrate. I came down here to try to listen to the radio but there was only rubbish on, so I decided to try a cigarette.'

'But you've never smoked before!'

'Oh, I did – I used to be a demon for them when I was younger. I stopped when I was expecting you.'

'You never mentioned it. Neither did Daddy.'

Her mother shrugged. 'I didn't want to set you all a bad example when you were younger. I thought if I told you, it would only encourage you all to try it out. It's not really a good habit and some people find it hard to stop it once they start.'

'Where did you get them? The cigarettes?'

Nance closed her eyes for a few moments as though deep in thought. 'They were in the pull-down part of the desk in the sitting-room. Someone left nearly a full packet behind during the time of the funeral. They were on the mantelpiece. Mrs Mooney found them and I told her to put them in the desk in case anyone called back for them.'

'Oh,' Fiona said.

She came no further into the room, and instead leaned back against the doorpost as though prepared for a quick departure. She stood watching in silence as her mother took a deep drag on the cigarette. It was like watching a stranger, she thought. The way she pursed her mouth and narrowed her eyes as she casually blew the smoke out – as though she had been practised at it all these years. But, Fiona thought, there was more to the change in her mother than just the smoking. There was a difference about her. She couldn't pin-point what it was exactly – it was something in her manner, in her whole demeanour.

As her mother continued to smoke, unperturbed by the silence between them, Fiona studied her closely. She noticed the greyish pallor from months of being indoors which was echoed by the thin streaks of grey in her hair. This was usually covered by a vibrant brunette rinse at the hairdresser's every six weeks and then carefully styled. Tonight, her hair looked as it had in recent months, the parts that were not grey faded to a nondescript colour and caught back by a tortoiseshell clasp in a loose sort of pony-tail.

Fiona's gaze moved to her mother's dark-ringed eyes now, which were paler than usual and almost vacant-looking. The lines and wrinkles around them looked more pronounced than before. And yet, in a weird way, there was something easier and more relaxed about her tonight than there had been since after the funeral. Was it the cigarettes, she wondered? Surely they couldn't have such an immediate effect on her.

There was a small creak as her mother shifted in the armchair as though trying to get more comfortable. 'You're very quiet, Fiona,' she said. 'Especially after all the laughing and carry-on outside in the street.'

'What do you mean?'

'Maggie MacConnell and her friend – I heard you all coming up the road, and then I saw you from the window. I don't know why you're so surprised. If I heard you all, then half the street probably heard you too.'

'We weren't that bad,' Fiona said, feeling as though she were a teenager being chastised. 'We were only chatting.'

'Well, Maggie and her friend were doing more than only chatting, they were laughing and skitting out loud – and they both looked the worse for drink.' Nance sucked her breath in disapproval. 'Don't tell me they were down drinking in the pub with all the men?'

Fiona straightened her back against the door. 'They were actually in the snug,' she said, a defensive note in her tone. 'And they were quiet enough – they weren't doing any harm.'

Her mother tutted and shook her head. 'I don't mind the farmers' wives waiting in there for the men to bring them home after the market, but it's only the low-class ones that go in at night. I'm surprised at Maggie. I've only ever seen her in there after a funeral or a wedding.'

'She had a friend with her and they came out for the last half an hour.'

'And what was her friend like? Was it somebody from the town?'

'No, she's from Galway. Her name is Anne, and she's a very nice girl.' Fiona was trying to keep her voice even and not rise to her mother's critical tone. 'She trained as a hairdresser with Maggie.'

'No doubt she will be used to a more modern way of life down in Galway,' her mother said disapprovingly. 'The women go in and out of the pubs there quite freely. Well, certain types of women.'

'That's not very nice, Mam – and it's a bit old-fashioned to talk like that. Lots of women go into pubs now, and all the female students in Dublin go into the pubs for the music.'

'That's Dublin, Fiona – not Tullamore. Things are still more dignified down here and people still talk. Anyone with an eye in their head could see those two were drunk.' She held her hand up. 'And before you say anything, I'm not accusing you. I could see you trying to get them moving. I'm not putting you in the same class as them.'

'They were only laughing, Mam,' Fiona said. 'It's not a crime, you know. Just because we haven't had much to laugh about recently doesn't mean the whole world has to stop. Maggie and her friend actually came over to the pub to check on an American tourist who was looking for a room for the night. He couldn't find anywhere else in Tullamore, and the girls directed him up to our place. So you should be thanking them for getting us a bit of business.'

Nance took another puff of her cigarette. 'Well,' she said, 'I suppose that's different.'

There was a pause and Fiona wondered now if her mother was going to ask her all about Michael O'Sullivan, and she decided she did not want to get into a big discussion about him with her mother.

'And are all the rooms full tonight?' her mother asked.

'They are,' Fiona said. She thought of something to change the subject. 'Oh, while I remember, Maggie said if you're still not up to coming over to the salon, she'll come over to the house and do your hair.'

'That's good of her, but I don't think I could

face somebody touching my head just yet.' She paused. 'Maybe in a few weeks.'

Fiona suddenly felt hopeful. Her mother was actually considering a suggestion she had made. It was only a visit to the hairdresser's – a small thing by normal standards – but a big step for her mother. Was this, she wondered, the first sign that the future might return to something that resembled their past life?

'You seem a little bit better, Mam, and it's good to see you up and about.'

'Well, the doctor says I can't stay in the bed much longer, even though it's the only place I feel fit for.' She gave a deep sigh. 'Apart from joining your father . . .'

Fiona felt a cold hand on her heart. Surely their mother couldn't feel that bad about things? 'What do you mean?' she asked now.

'Well, there's not much left for me here without him . . .'

'But there's the shop and the bar and everything – and you're not that old. You're still young enough to enjoy your life.'

'I don't feel young and I certainly don't look it.' Her voice was flat and dry. 'I can't stand looking at myself in the mirror these days.'

A picture flew into Fiona's head. A picture of her mother dressed up – for a wedding last year – in a peach suit, with bows for buttons down the jacket and long white gloves. How different the woman in front of her now looked.

'When you feel better,' Fiona said, 'we can go out for a day shopping. It will do you good. A day in Dublin or maybe Galway.'

'Oh, Fiona! You've been very good and everything, but I'm not stupid.' Her mother spoke now with an ironic amusement, almost as though she was laughing. 'I'm sure the last thing you want is to be tied down with me, taking me shopping and working with me every day in the shop. Especially when you should have been out enjoying your own life in New York.' She took a last drag on the cigarette now, and then moved out of the chair – stiffly, and as if it pained her – to stub it out on the top of the range, and then throw it on top of the turf in the big coir basket.

Fiona was surprised at the turn in the conversation. It was the first time that her mother had mentioned New York in weeks, and it wasn't the way she had imagined they would discuss it. She had imagined her mother being well – back to her confident, capable self, with her hair dyed back to its usual dark colour, and wearing her fashionable clothes. In her mind they would have been in the sitting-room, with the sun streaming in the tall windows, chatting over a cup of tea and a cake that Mrs Mooney had baked.

Tonight was not at all the way things should have been. The woman in the worn dressing-gown in front of her now did not look like the mother she remembered. The way her mother was speaking made her feel guilty – as though, by having stayed at home and done her best, she had only added to the depression by making her mother feel guilty.

'There's no rush about New York,' Fiona said. 'I'm fine in the shop and bar for the time being, and Patrick is happy enough to keep things running. We're doing okay until you're back on your feet.'

'So you say,' Nance's voice was low and sort of frail, 'but that can't last forever, keeping both places running.' She straightened up now, and then just stared straight ahead at the tiled wall over the range. 'No doubt there will have to be changes all round at some point, but I don't feel up to thinking about them just now.'

As she slowly turned around Fiona noticed that her pale eyes had a kind of glazed look. It occurred to her that maybe she had been drinking. But then, she had seen her mother merry a few times before after weddings or Christmas, and she hadn't appeared like this. Her eyes had been sparkly and lively, and she had been more animated and giggly. No, Fiona decided, it wasn't drink. But something was wrong, and she was just not sure what it was.

'You'll be better soon, Mam,' she said.

She wished now that when she came in she had started talking about Michael O'Sullivan and his travel plans. It would have been lighter and far removed from the depressing conversation they had just stumbled into.

'We should both go to bed now,' she said. 'It's late.'

Her mother nodded. 'You should have a lie-in tomorrow.'

'I can't. Mrs Mooney won't be there in the morning – she has a doctor's appointment.'

'So you'll have to get up early to do the breakfasts?'

'I don't mind, it's not often I have to do it. You go on now – I'll see to the fire and the lights. And I'll bring you up a boiled egg and some tea and toast in the morning before I go down to work.'

Her mother went past her and when she got out into the hallway she slowly turned back. 'I'm sorry, Fiona. This isn't how I imagined things would turn out.'

'Things will improve, Mam.'

'I'm not so sure. We can't turn the clock back.'

'Other people recover from things.' Fiona said. She thought of Michael O'Sullivan. 'Life can sometimes surprise us.'

CHAPTER 23

Fiona woke to the sound of something banging into her window. She sat up in bed, startled, and when she realised it was probably the bird, whose nest was under the roof awning, she quickly moved out of bed to pull her curtains and check whether the bird was okay. The September sunshine blinded her for a few moments, then she shielded her eyes with her hand, trying to see if it was lying stunned on the windowsill, but there was no sign of it. Her heart dropped a little – she hoped it hadn't been killed.

She wondered what time it was. It couldn't be that late, she thought, as the alarm, set for half past seven, hadn't gone off yet. She went back over to the bed to check and discovered that it was only ten to seven. She shivered, and then decided to get back into the warm bed for a few minutes, to wake properly and run through all she had to do for the morning.

Before she got around to thinking of her chores, her mind flitted briefly to her mother and the odd feeling she had about her last night. Looking back, at least her mother was moving around the house which was definitely a step forward. And whilst it was strange to see her smoking, it wasn't the worst thing that could happen. Plenty of women smoked – she sold them cigarettes every day in the shop. She decided she would not start the day off worrying about that.

Instead, she closed her eyes and somehow her mind found its way back to the previous night in the bar when she was talking to Michael O'Sullivan. She found herself going over the conversation they had about the cottage he was going to look at in Connemara, and then the conversation they had when he told her about him being an architect. Some things she remembered quite clearly and other things were more difficult to recall and seemed a little blurred. She didn't think she had drunk that much, but she supposed she had drunk more than normal, which might account for it. Their conversation had also been halted at certain times, as she didn't want to be rude to the others, and she supposed they never returned to every point they had been discussing at the time.

There were so many more things she wanted to know about him. She found him intriguing and interesting. She liked his voice, his smile, his hair and she had liked sitting beside him. She liked the warm, almost exciting feeling that she got from being near him.

She had felt something very like it when she was with Paul Moore, but what she felt with this American stranger was much more intense. Now, as she lay in bed, even just the memory of him brought the same tug in the pit of her stomach and a warm glow to her neck and face. She found herself smiling as she remembered the way he had looked at her, and she rolled over and buried her face in the pillow to stop herself from laughing aloud.

She would see him in an hour's time in the snug where they served the guests breakfast, and she wondered whether they would act like polite strangers or whether they would just resume talking in the same easy and relaxed way they had last night. Even the unpredictability of it all, Fiona thought, seemed exciting to her. She needed something different from the boring routine she had lived these last few months. She needed something more.

Later, when she was up and washed, she pulled on a pair of navy slacks and a soft blue sweater which she loved and always felt good in. She went downstairs quietly so as not to wake her mother, and went into the kitchen to rake the ashes in the range until there was only glowing turf embers left. As she gave a final rattle to the iron bars, the noise suddenly reminded her of her father, as it was he who had started the fire off most mornings before the housekeeper came in. He made sure the heavier jobs were done so the women didn't have to do them, like emptying the ashes and lifting in buckets of turf or coal.

The memory sent little waves of sorrow through

her – over and over again. Blinded by tears, she found herself moving away from fire, back towards her father's old chair, where she sat with her head in her hands until the sadness drained away.

If only, she thought, she might go to sleep for a while in the chair and wake up to find it was all a bad dream, and that her father was only upstairs shaving or having his morning wash. Or maybe that he had left the house early to walk down to the shop, to slip an *Irish Independent* out of the big tied bundle left at the shop door, and bring it back to read over his breakfast.

But she knew that it was no dream. Her mother was upstairs in bed and still needed her as much now as when her father died. And the house and the shop and the bar needed her too. There was nothing else to be done but to get moving and get on with things.

She went back to finish raking the ashes and then went out of the kitchen door to empty them in the bin outside. The sky was dark as though it might rain, and there was a growing breeze which made the young silver birch trees her father had planted at the bottom of the garden last autumn sway. Then, as she poured the ash into the bin a stronger gust sent half of them scattering into the air and down around her. She swore out loud, glad her mother wasn't there to hear her. She stood there, sighing and muttering to herself as she brushed the ash off her clothes – and then, as she went to go back inside, she suddenly remembered the bird. Swinging the empty ash can in her hand, she walked around the front of the house to check. There was no sign of it, which meant it had survived. She didn't know why, but for some reason it meant something to her that it had.

Smiling now, she went back inside and finished off cleaning the range and then got the fire blazing again with half a dozen turf briquettes. She boiled the kettle, and then she switched on the radio and heard Joe Dolan's cheery voice singing 'Make Me an Island'. It was a song her father loved, and he always turned the radio up when it came on. She now remembered him laughing and smiling. She remembered him joking and teasing her and her sisters. She stood for a few minutes, remembering those good times, which is what she knew her father would have wanted.

Feeling lighter, she moved around quickly, brushing floors, wiping the top of the range, humming along with the radio as she did the other morning chores that Mary Ellen Mooney would normally see to. Half an hour later she took a boiled egg and toast and a cup of tea up to her mother.

There was no sound as she went along the corridor, and when she reached the door she gave it a firm tap, and said, 'Are you awake, Mam?' Then she went in, and saw her mother was moving to sit up.

'What time is it?' she asked.

'Twenty to eight.'

'You're early. Have you been up long?'

'Nearly an hour.' She went over and put the tray down on the bedside table. 'I wanted to make sure you had something to eat before I go. I told the commercial travellers I would have breakfast ready for around half eight.'

Her mother looked vaguely at her. 'Isn't Mary Ellen doing it?'

'No, she's at the doctor's this morning.' Her brow furrowed. 'Don't you remember? I told you last night, and I'm sure Mary Ellen told you as well.'

Nance nodded her head, and said, 'Oh right . . .' as if just remembering.

When she was sitting up straight in the bed, Fiona lifted the tray onto her lap. 'You'll feel a bit brighter when you've drunk your tea and had something to eat. I'll finish off downstairs and come back up for the tray before I go.'

'What time will Mrs Mooney be back?'

'I think around dinnertime.'

'And will you be back home for a while after cooking the breakfast for the men? You don't need to open the shop before half nine.'

Fiona thought about Michael O'Sullivan. He wouldn't be rushing away like the other men. She wasn't sure what his plans were, but she wasn't going to tie herself into having to come home for a short while.

'Sure, it's not worth coming back up,' she said. 'I'll get something to eat down there, and then just go straight into the shop. There are always people looking for the newspapers.'

The disappointed look on her mother's face told her she was lonely. Fiona supposed it was no wonder, being at home all day.

She paused at the room door on her way out. 'You look tired. Did you sleep okay?'

Her mother stared at her for a few moments, as if she hadn't quite comprehended the simple question. Fiona felt the same little note of alarm she had felt last night when she discovered her smoking.

'Not too bad,' her mother eventually said, 'but I can't really remember. I'm sure I took one of the sleeping tablets, so I should have.' A small frown came between her eyes, and she turned slowly to look at the bedside cabinet. 'It's not on there, so I must have taken it.'

'Do you think you might try to get up this morning?'

Again Fiona noticed the vacant look.

'I'll see . . . I'll see how I feel after this.'

Fiona went downstairs and topped the fire up. Then she went back upstairs to wash her dusty hands and tidy herself for going to work. She gave her jeans and sweater a good brush-down to make sure there were no lingering specks of dust or ashes, then, checking her watch, she quickly put on some mascara and lipstick – which she normally never did in the mornings.

As she closed the front door behind her and started walking down to the shop, Fiona thought that her mother should be showing some signs of getting better at this point. She wondered if she really was still unwell, or whether she had got used to being lethargic and found anything too much effort.

Then, a few heavy splashes of rain hit her and the fear of getting her sweater and jeans wet made her run down the hill towards the shop. As the shop doorway came into view and she saw a tall male figure coming towards her wearing a hooded jacket, she slowed down to a fast walk. She didn't want to meet anyone red-faced and breathless. Then her heart rate moved up again when the man stopped and took the hood down and she realised it was Michael O'Sullivan.

He came to a standstill at the shop door just a few seconds before her. 'Good morning,' he said, smiling at her. 'You look like a woman in a hurry.'

Her heart was now racing faster than it had been when she was running full tilt. 'And you,' she said, trying to catch her breath, 'look like a man who is in a hurry for his breakfast.'

'Do I?'

'I didn't realise anyone would be up so early, so I hope you haven't been waiting long?'

'I'm not waiting at all. A cup of coffee will be just fine.'

She turned to put the key in the shop door. 'Have you been out for a walk?' she asked.

'Yep,' he said, 'and I was lucky. I've been out for half an hour and it's just started raining now.'

She opened the door and he came in behind

her. 'Did you sleep okay?' she asked. 'Was every-thing all right in the room for you?'

'Perfect,' he said, 'but I woke around seven thirty and thought I would take a little walk out to see Tullamore in the daylight.'

She closed the shop door behind them and they stood at the bottom of the staircase, between the shop and the bar. 'I imagine the town was quiet enough. Not much happens until after ten o'clock.'

'It was nice,' he said. 'I walked right down through the town, past . . .' he paused, trying to remember, 'was it The Bridge House?'

'Yes,' she said, nodding.

'Then I carried on until I reached the canal.' He smiled. 'I took a walk down the towpath. Not too far, but enough to see that it's really beautiful around there and very peaceful.'

'It is. We often go for a walk there or out to Charleville Castle. That's another place you should see if you get time. It was built in the late 1700's – if I remember correctly from our history classes in school.'

'Really? That is old. I'd love to see it.'

Fiona had feared there might be an awkwardness between them this morning, that they would go back to the beginning again when they had just met as if last night had not taken place. But the two of them seemed to just pick things up exactly where they had left it.

She lifted the end part of the counter and went in behind. 'The kitchen is through here,' she told him, 'just behind the bar.' She looked up at the clock which hung above the till. 'Breakfast should be ready in about half an hour, and I'll bring it through to the snug. The other men will probably be down soon so I'd better move and get started.'

'Could I help you?' he asked. 'I'm not in any rush for breakfast – I can wait until the other guys are finished.'

She looked at him in surprise. 'Oh, no, I couldn't ask you – you're a paying guest after all.'

'That doesn't matter. I'd like to think we're friends now, and friends help each other.' He shrugged and grinned at her. 'I don't mind setting tables or anything like that. My mother has me pretty well trained.'

Why not? She thought. The idea of the two of them in the kitchen together sounded wonderful to her. She had imagined chatting to him when she brought his breakfast to the table in the snug, politely enquiring about his travel plans while he was in Ireland. But Michael O'Sullivan was asking if he could actually help her, and this was much better than anything she could have imagined.

She knew it was odd to have him in the kitchen as they only ever had family or staff there, but who else would know? It wasn't as if her mother or Mrs Mooney was around. The other men who were staying were strangers to the town, so they wouldn't know who he was and neither, she thought, would they care.

'Okay,' she said, 'if you don't mind you can help me set the tables and then you can make us both a cup of coffee.' She smiled at him. 'I take it that's why you're offering? To hurry me up with the coffee?'

'Darn,' he said, grinning at her. 'You've got me right there.'

'Well, don't get too excited,' she told him, opening the door into the kitchen now, and holding it open for him. 'It's not the kind of coffee you'll be used to in America – it's only instant tinned coffee or bottled coffee.'

'As long as it is some form of coffee it will be just fine.' He followed behind, taking his coat off. 'Don't forget I've been in Ireland before, so I know exactly what the coffee is like.'

'Okay,' she said, filling the electric kettle, 'I'll get this boiling and then you can make yourself a big mug of it.'

'What will I do first?' he asked.

She showed him where the loaf of brown bread was and gave him three white side-plates. Then she asked him to cut six slices and put two on each of the plates. She told him where the cutlery and the blue paper napkins were, and asked him to set three places at different tables in the snug. While he did so, she went over to the fridge and got the sausages and black and white pudding into a frying pan to make a start.

By the time he came back, she was busy separating rashers of bacon to cook in a second pan.

'You look very efficient,' he told her. 'You seem to have everything under control.'

'It's not a very big kitchen,' she said, 'but then it doesn't get that much use. It's just really for the breakfasts and for us making cups of tea during the day.' She put six rashers in the pan and left them to start cooking on a medium heat while she sliced up mushrooms.

He lifted two mugs down from the shelf. 'Is coffee really okay for you? I know most Irish people prefer tea.'

'I like coffee too,' she said, bending down to the cupboard by the oven to get a small pan, 'but I'm going to have mine made with half milk and a spoonful of sugar. How are you having yours?'

'Black,' he said, 'and as strong as I can get it.'

'Well, I hope what we have bears some resemblance to what you're used to,' she said, in a light tone. She put the milk on to boil on one of the rings, and then went to the fridge to get the eggs.

He moved the mugs over to the boiling kettle and filled one to the top and the other almost half full. Then he turned back to the cooker to check if the milk was boiling yet, just as Fiona came back to turn the bacon. They both laughed as they almost collided.

'I told you it was a small kitchen,' she said, weaving her way around him.

His face suddenly grew serious. 'Am I getting in your way? I didn't think. Maybe I'm holding things up here talking?'

'No,' she said, 'you're not . . . I would tell you.'

She turned to glance at him and their eyes locked and held for a few seconds. Then he smiled at her and she smiled back. She thought he was going to say something but, when he just kept looking at her and smiling, she felt silly and embarrassed. She turned back to the cooker, but she was just a few seconds too late as the milk came bubbling up to the edge of the pan. Like a small, foaming white waterfall, it flowed down the sides and onto the top of the cooker.

'Oh, damn!' she said, lifting it up and turning off the heat.

'I'll take that,' he said, taking it out of her hand, 'and let you get on with the cooking.'

She felt suddenly self-conscious now as she lifted the spatula and began turning the bacon, and she realised that she had just caught it before it started to burn. She turned the heat down low, and told herself to concentrate as she turned each piece over. She moved the shrunken rashers closer to the cooler edge of the pan, put another lump of lard in the middle and added the mushrooms.

She then bent down to open the oven and check how the other things were doing. Thankfully, they were fine, and after turning them over she closed the door and gave a little sigh. The commercial travellers' breakfasts were almost ready. She only had the eggs to fry and she would wait until they came down to do that.

When she turned around he was holding a mug out towards her. 'Milk and one sugar, just as you ordered, ma'am!'

She laughed now and took it from him. She took a sip. 'It's lovely.'

'I'm glad,' he said, in a low voice, 'Because you are lovely too. Very lovely.'

She looked at him, shaking her head and smiling, and then she saw his face was serious.

'I mean it,' he said. 'I like you very much, Fiona. I like everything about you that I've seen so far.'

She did not know what to say, because the way he looked made her think that he was going to kiss her, but yet he was making no move to do so. He was just still standing opposite, holding his coffee mug and looking at her.

She thought she should make some light-hearted remark to show that she didn't think he was really serious. But before she could think of anything, footsteps sounded above their head and then could be heard on the stairs.

'That's the men,' she said. 'I better get moving.' She took another sip of her coffee and, as she moved towards the boiling kettle, she felt her legs were shaking.

She made the tea and took it out to the men, along with the butter which she had forgotten to ask him to put at each place. The thought of making more silly mistakes focussed her concentration. She pushed all thoughts of him out of her head, and went back to finish cooking the men's breakfasts to the usual high standard that they expected.

When the businessmen were happily settled with full plates and pots of tea, she went back into the kitchen.

'I warmed your coffee up in the pan,' he said, going over to get it. 'And I think you need to stop and drink it.'

'Thank you,' she said, pushing her hair back from her forehead, 'but straight after that I need to make your breakfast.'

'I'm not in any rush to leave.' He poured her coffee back into her mug and put it down on the worktop. 'Actually, I was thinking . . . have you a room available for tonight? I mean a room apart from Patrick's? I wouldn't want to take his again when it's not an emergency.'

She caught her breath. He was going to stay another night. He wasn't just disappearing. 'Yes,' she said, 'I think so – I'm sure the men are all leaving this morning, and we only have one booked in for tonight.'

'Well,' he said, 'you now have two men booked in. I think I'd like to spend a little more time in Tullamore – maybe see that castle you mentioned. And I'd like to spend a little more time getting to know you.'

She looked straight at him. 'That's nice, because I'd like to get to know you better too.'

He caught her eye and smiled at her, and a feeling of excitement ran through her. She still felt embarrassed, but when he put his coffee mug down on the worktop and came over and put his arms around her, it didn't feel awkward – it felt right.

At first, he held her tentatively – as though checking he wasn't presuming anything – but when she did not move or pull back, his arms tightened around her waist and his breathing deepened. She reached up and put her arms around his neck and then his lips came down on hers. It was like no other kiss she had ever experienced. It awakened something deep inside her which was now slowly spreading to all the little fibres in her body.

It seemed to last for ages, and then he drew back and gently took her face in his hands. 'This is not what I expected to happen, Fiona.'

She thought again how much she loved the sound of his voice, his American accent.

'I didn't come to Ireland to meet someone – to have the feelings that I now have for you. I know it's all very quick . . . but something is telling me that this is meant to happen.'

As she looked up at him, she felt such a wave of emotion that she almost felt like crying. 'I feel the same. I never imagined something like this happening to me.' She smiled, almost laughed. 'Especially not here – not at home. Not where I work and everything.'

'I never thought I could feel so close a connection with someone from such a different world. I couldn't sleep for thinking about you last night. I lay awake for hours trying to figure this thing out.' He stroked her hair. 'And the only conclusion I can come to is that we should make the most of the time we have now – getting to know each other and then see what happens.'

She heard a chair scraping on the stone floor in the snug which meant that one of the men had finished his breakfast. She did not move. She did not care. He pulled her close and kissed her again and she felt the same physical intensity that she had felt earlier. It became stronger when she felt his tongue in her mouth, and made her wish they were in the privacy of a bedroom where she could let the feelings just carry her off. She had heard and read about this sort of physical passion – the feelings that were racing through her – and she now knew exactly what it was. She now understood why it made women take all kinds of risks.

The bell on the shop door loudly sounded and, as footsteps came through the shop towards the kitchen, they moved apart.

Patrick walked in, carrying a large brown envelope. He looked from one to the other.

'Good morning,' Michael said.

Patrick nodded to him and said good morning, a slightly surprised look on his face. He turned to Fiona. 'I thought you might need a hand . . .'

'That's good of you, but I've already served the breakfasts to the men.' She felt her face hot and red. She wondered if he had guessed there was something going on between them. 'I was just going to make a start on Michael's now.' She moved across to the cooker. 'Have you had anything yourself?'

'A cup of tea and a bit of bread,' he said.

She looked at the clock. 'Well, if you keep an eye for anyone coming into the shop, I'll cook the three of us something now.'

Patrick clapped his hands together. 'Sounds good to me.' He handed the brown envelope to Michael. 'That's the book I was telling you about, the one that gives you a bit about the history of Tullamore and Offaly.'

'You remembered?' Michael said. 'It was so late I thought neither of us would remember.'

'Truth be told,' Patrick said, 'I remember saying I would bring the book down to let you have a look at it – but I've actually no idea what I was going to show you in it!'

Michael started laughing. 'Well, that makes two of us.' He slid the book out of the envelope.

'If you two want to go into the snug,' Fiona said, 'I'll bring a pot of tea in to you while you're waiting for the breakfast.' She looked at Michael and in mock exasperation said, 'Do you Yanks drink tea at all – or will I have to make you a coffee?'

She caught the amusement in his eyes. 'Tea would be just lovely,' he said.

Fiona busied herself with cooking again, although

eating was the last thing on her mind. From what she could remember, he had planned to set off to Clifden today, but surely, she thought, he wouldn't have kissed her and said what he did, knowing that he was going to be gone in a few hours? But some men were like that. Even though she had never been let down by a boyfriend herself, she wasn't stupid or naïve enough to think that it couldn't happen to her. She had heard her friends talking about boys they liked, or were actually courting, blowing hot and cold. And there was even more chance of it happening to her, because the fact was, Michael O'Sullivan was an American on holiday. It was temporary. It was something that could never develop into a real romance. But yet, something would not let her give up hope. Something made her feel that what she would gain from knowing him – even for a short time – would be worth it.

She would just have to wait and see.

CHAPTER 24

The morning in the shop had been one of the longest that Fiona could remember. Fridays usually went by quickly because they had several delivery vans calling, but everything seemed painfully, irritatingly slow. The baker took ages to unload the bread and cake boards because he was talking to someone he knew outside, and the hardware delivery fellow parked the van and then came into the shop to ask her about the funeral that morning. He stood there, enquiring as to who had attended it, instead of bringing in the brushes and mops and boxes of nails that the shop was low on.

She found each customer seemed to take an age to say what they wanted, their eyes wandering along the shelves and then down into the cold cabinets as if they had never seen the displays before. Even routine tasks like slicing the joints of cold meat on the machine, or using the wire cheese-cutter seemed more problematic than usual. And everyone just seemed to want to talk, talk, talk, when it was the last thing she felt like doing.

She found she could not concentrate on serving them, and keep track of the conversations at the same time. A few times someone had spoken to her and she found herself staring at them blankly, not sure what they had said or what item they had asked for.

Time was just dragging by when she wanted it to disappear so she could be on her own with Michael again. Somehow, she muddled her way through, and managed to keep herself satisfied by going into the bar every now and again to catch a glimpse of him. He had found a quiet spot there where he was reading a book and slowly drinking a pint of Guinness when it was busy, and chatting to Patrick when it was quiet.

Patrick, she thought, surely must have guessed there was something between them when he came upon them in the kitchen earlier on. Guests never came into the kitchen, and certainly didn't stand there drinking cups of coffee. She knew men were slower to catch on to things like that, but she reckoned that if Maggie and Anne had noticed it last night – before anything had actually happened between them – then Patrick must surely have guessed this morning.

As she had cooked the breakfast for the three of them, she had veered between elation at the memory of being in Michael's arms and him kissing her – to total depression when she thought of him going away.

Then, after breakfast – when Patrick left them

alone in the snug – Michael had reached across the table and taken her hands in his. 'If it's okay with you,' he said, 'I thought I might stay around Tullamore over the weekend. If the rooms here are all taken, then I'm sure I can find somewhere in town.'

Fiona looked at him, feeling weak with relief. 'That's great,' she said, 'and there's no problem about the room. We're usually quieter at the weekends as the commercial travellers go home.' Then, she stopped. 'But what about Clifden? What about your plans to look at the cottage?'

He shrugged. 'I'm not on any schedule. I haven't booked my return flight home or finalised anything yet. I have until next week to decide when I go back. I'll phone the auctioneer this afternoon and tell him I'll be down Monday.'

'That's great if you can change your plans . . .'

He leant towards her and touched her lips gently with his. 'I want to spend all the time I have with you. Whatever time you have spare.' He moved his hands over her hair. 'I know you have a lot of responsibilities with running the shop all on your own, and working in the bar at night – but when do you get time off?'

'It's different every week,' she told him. 'It all depends on what is happening.' All sorts of problems ran through her mind. Tonight was quiet in the bar, but tomorrow night, Saturday, there was a big card game on, and she would be needed. 'I'll sort something out.'

'I don't want to put pressure on you – I do understand about your mom being ill and everything – but I'd love to see some of the local places you mentioned like the old castle, and I wondered if there was any chance you could take a day off so we could go to somewhere like Dublin or Galway together?'

Her brain started to tick over, to work out how she could spend as much time as she could with him. 'I have a half-day Wednesday and a Sunday off as the shop is closed,' she said. 'But there isn't much open on a Sunday anywhere. Most of the shops would be closed.'

'Who needs shops?' he laughed. 'I'm just interested in seeing places and spending time with you. Sunday is good for me, if that's the best day for you.'

'I'm off some evenings,' she said. 'I'm actually off tonight. I'll check with Patrick about tomorrow night, but I doubt if he could manage on his own when they have the card game.'

'You don't have any other staff you can call in for emergencies?' His voice had a note of surprise.

Fiona bit her lip. 'Not really . . . occasionally we've had Patrick's brother working in the bar, and his sister-in-law helping out in the shop. But there's only been me in the shop since my mother has been ill and I wasn't going anywhere further afield, as I couldn't really be too far away from her. I'm okay for the odd half an hour or so if I've something to do at the house, as Patrick can mind both the bar and the shop.' She shook her head. 'It's all changed since Daddy died. Before there was my mother, my father and me, and Patrick. Daddy did both the shop and the bar. They were planning on getting someone else in when I went to New York, but they hadn't sorted it when Daddy died.' Her face tightened. 'And then of course Mam took sick and I've just plodded along with things in the shop on my own.' Listening to herself she knew it sounded a sorry tale.

'You've had a tough time,' he said quietly, 'no doubt about it.'

His concern brought a lump to her throat. 'It'll work out eventually,' she said, but her voice was unconvincing even to her own ears.

'Okay,' he said. 'I want to get a few things, so I'll take a drive out in the afternoon to one of the nearby towns. Patrick said Athlone is interesting, and it isn't too far, so I might head out there.'

She wanted to say 'Don't go, don't leave me' – but she knew she couldn't ask him to sit about in the bar hour after hour waiting for her to steal a few minutes in between customers. He had even come into the shop when it was quiet to lean on the counter to chat to her, but it was not relaxed as they were both conscious that a customer or Patrick might walk in at any minute. And Fiona knew that it would already be talked about that there was a Yank up in Tracey's bar, sitting in the corner with a book of all things. She had told him that, and he had laughed incredulously.

'And I was sitting there quietly, thinking I was almost invisible, and people were watching me all the time. But I can't be the only stranger around – you must get other tourists in the town, right?'

'Yes,' she said, 'and very few go unnoticed.' She shrugged and smiled. 'It's a small place and everyone knows each other. It's just the way it is.'

'I was in a small village in Scotland a few years ago, on a tour of the Highlands with my mother – and it was the same thing – if we went off the main tourist places, people were curious about who we were and what we were doing there.' He grinned. 'I don't know why I'm so surprised, because it's the same in some of the small places in the States. I remember when I was a student and doing a project on bridges, my friend and I drove down to Iowa. They have some really amazing covered bridges that date back to the late 1800's.' He shrugged. 'Which as you probably know, is really old for the United States. We don't have old castles and monasteries dating back to the seventh century or anything like you have here in Ireland.'

Fiona had listened to him with rapt attention, loving his voice, his accent and the way he described places. Hearing him talk made her think back to the places she had seen on the postcards Elizabeth had sent to her. The streets and shops described in the airmail letters she had spent hours reading over and over again, until she almost imagined she had been to those places herself.

257

And when she had to leave him again, to go back to serve newspapers and tobacco, packets of biscuits and tins of scouring powder, she carried the images he described in her mind. Every time she thought of them – whatever mundane task she was doing – she found herself smiling.

She went back to the house at one o'clock to check on the fires, and to heat up the stew and potatoes Mrs Mooney had left for her mother. She went straight upstairs to her mother's room.

'Are you awake, Mam?' she said quietly, and when her mother moved to sit up, she then asked the same question she asked every time she went into the bedroom. 'How are you feeling?'

Nance leaned her head back against the mahogany headboard. 'I thought I was brighter earlier on, but then I felt a bit dizzy when I went to the bathroom. So I came back to bed then and slept for another while.' She ran a hand over her lank hair. 'Is Mary Ellen back from the hospital yet? Has she been in?'

'No – do you not remember us saying she wouldn't be back until later?'

Nance's frown deepened. 'Surely they can't keep her that long? She's been gone all morning and it's only a ten-minute walk from her house up to the hospital.'

'Mam,' Fiona said, a note of exasperation in her voice, 'it's not Tullamore hospital she's gone to. Do you not remember us talking about it last night? She was getting the early train up to Dublin and by the time she's seen and gets the train back down it will be late. She might not even feel like coming up to the house after all the travelling and everything.'

'Oh, yes,' Nance said, nodding her head. 'I remember now, that she said it was Dublin . . .'

Fiona looked at her, and thought she had that same vacant look about her again that she had last night. And there was something else odd too. She was almost out of the door to go back downstairs when it dawned on her. She looked back to her mother's bedside cabinet.

'Mam,' she said, her voice rising, 'have you been smoking up here?'

'I wasn't up to going downstairs.'

'But you shouldn't be smoking when you're in bed,' Fiona said. 'You would never have allowed that when Daddy was alive. I can't believe it – I remember you going mad when Uncle Dermot was over from England and smoked in one of the spare bedrooms. You made Daddy go and tell him that it wasn't allowed.'

'Oh, Fiona, for God's sake stop going on at me,' her mother snapped. 'I have enough to put up with without you starting on at me. I only had the one cigarette – that's all.'

'But that's all it takes, Mam – one spark on the bedclothes and we could have a disaster.' She looked at her mother's glazed eyes. 'If you fell asleep while you were smoking . . .'

'I won't,' Nance said. 'I'm not that stupid.'

'Well, if you're determined to keep smoking,' Fiona said, 'you'll have to come downstairs or do without. It's not as if you're dependent on them, because you've only been back smoking a few days.'

'True,' her mother said, looking towards the widow.

'I'll bring your lunch up now, and you might feel better when you've eaten again.'

Her mother turned back towards her now that the subject had been changed. 'Are you busy down at the shop?'

'Busy enough,' Fiona said. 'I'll bring your stew up in five minutes and then I'll head back to it.'

'You're surely in a hurry – are you not having lunch yourself?'

'No, I had a big breakfast this morning after I served the guests.'

'Did you have guests?'

'The commercial travellers and the American chap. Remember, Mam? We were talking about it last night.'

Nance nodded. 'Yes, of course . . .'

Fiona came back downstairs, wondering what to make of her mother. At times she seemed on a different planet. Whilst she was worried about her, there was a part of her felt almost angry with her for giving in so easily. Maybe if she just shook herself up a bit – pushed a little beyond what she felt like doing, it might gradually get her back into a normal way of living again.

In the meantime, Fiona decided she was not going to waste this time she had with Michael O'Sullivan worrying about her mother. She did what she had to do in the house and took lunch up to her mother.

She was just about to leave the house when the phone rang. As she went quickly along the hallway, she called up to her mother, 'If it's for you, are you well enough to take the call?'

'No – not today!' her mother called back.

Fiona answered the phone and it was her Aunt Catherine.

'Oh, Fiona,' she said, 'I hope you don't mind me ringing.'

'Not at all,' Fiona said. 'It's lovely to hear from you.'

'I'm just checking how your mother is. I've rung a few times but she's not been up to talking. I asked Mrs Mooney to see if I could come down and visit her, but when she asked your mother she said she doesn't want any visitors yet. I must say I'm worried about her, Fiona. You must think I'm terrible that I've not seen her for months, but Angela has told me the same, that she just hasn't the energy for visitors. I don't know what to do . . .'

'Hang on . . . I won't be a second . . .' Fiona went over to close the sitting-room door. It was unlikely that her mother could hear her, but she didn't want to take a chance. 'Sorry,' she said, when she came back, 'I just had to check

261

something.' She paused. 'Mam's still not great, Auntie Catherine. And it's not just you – she doesn't want to see anyone and most of the time she's in bed and not up to answering the phone.'

'Well, will you say I rang again and . . .' Her voice trailed off. 'I'd love to come down and see her, Fiona, but I'm worried it would only make her feel under pressure. I've written to her and sent her a *Get Well* card, as you probably know, but she hasn't replied.'

'She's not written any letters since – since Daddy died. I just don't know what to say. That shingles thing has really knocked her for six. I've never seen her like this before.'

'I've heard it's a terrible thing – that it can go on for a long time.'

'Well, the rash and the terrible pain and everything has gone all right, but it's the tiredness and the awful flat way it's left her. She has no energy or interest in doing anything. It's like she's left with some kind of depression.'

'I can imagine exactly what she must be like,' Catherine said in a strained tone, 'I can remember her being like that before . . .'

The revelation took Fiona by surprise. 'When? I don't remember hearing anything about that.'

'It was a long time ago,' her aunt said, 'but she was very bad then and was in her bed for a good while.'

'Did Daddy know?'

'Oh, it was long before she was married. Before

she met your father. It was when I was first married and living in England. She came to stay with us for a while and then after she went back home to Ireland she was sick for months, and couldn't get out of bed.' Her tone suddenly changed. Fiona thought it sounded almost urgent or panicky. 'Don't mention to your mother that I told you that, Fiona – please! I shouldn't have said anything about it. If you reminded her about that time, it might make her worse.'

'I won't say a word,' Fiona reassured her. 'But can I just ask you – what brought it on before? Especially if she was only young.'

'Oh, God, Fiona – I can't remember,' Aunt Catherine said, sounding vague. 'It was years and years ago . . .'

'Was it after she had been ill? The way she is now after the shingles?'

'I don't know . . . We were living in Manchester so I didn't see much of her. Joseph was only young and people didn't travel as much.' She halted. 'But I think she might have had something like glandular fever around that time. I'm not at all sure but, as I say, it wouldn't help to remind her of that now. And your mother wouldn't like to think we were talking about her. She wouldn't like it one little bit. Promise me you won't say anything.'

Fiona was surprised at the intensity of her aunt's tone. 'Of course I won't say anything.'

'My phone number is in the book, isn't it?'

Catherine checked. 'If you ever feel she's up to seeing me, phone me straight away, won't you?'

'Yes, I will. And thanks for ringing again.'

When she put the receiver back in its cradle, Fiona stood for a few minutes, just having realised something. Aunt Catherine was terrified of offending their mother. How her aunt even bothered with her sister after the funeral, when she was so awful to her and Joseph, she didn't know.

And then it struck her – *everyone* was terrified of offending her.

Something clicked within her and, instead of heading out the front door and straight to the shop, she found herself going back upstairs. She tapped lightly on her mother's bedroom door and went in.

Her mother was sitting up in bed, her head leaning against the pillows and with the tray still on her lap. The spoon was lying on the bedspread as though it had fallen out of her hand, the bowl of stew only half-eaten.

Fiona went over and lifted the tray. 'Mam!' she said in a loud hiss.

Nance's eyes fluttered open. 'What . . . what's wrong?'

'You're asleep with the tray on the bed.'

She looked at her daughter with glazed eyes. 'I didn't realise – I'm just so tired.'

Usually when she saw her mother like this, Fiona felt pity for her, but this afternoon she felt frustrated and fed up. How much longer could this go on?

'That was Aunt Catherine on the phone.' She watched her mother's face darken at the mention of her name. 'As soon as you're up to it, you need to phone her. The poor woman has phoned several times a week since you've been sick, and not once have you phoned her back. She's written to you as well, and sent a nice *Get Well* card you didn't even bother to open.'

'I know all that,' Nance said. 'You don't need to talk to me as though I'm a child.'

'But she's your sister and you act like she's a stranger you can't stand. I don't know what you have against her, but it's . . .' she sighed in frustration, 'well, it's just not normal. You're leaving me and Mrs Mooney to take the phone calls and make excuses. Whatever you think she's done, she must think it's finished, or she wouldn't keep phoning and wasting her time. You need to sort it out with her, Mam. It's not going to kill you making a phone call to her, surely?'

Tears came into her mother's eyes. 'I don't know what's got into you today, Fiona. You wouldn't have spoken to me like this when your father was alive – the other two girls would never speak to me like that.'

'Well, I'm sorry,' Fiona said, 'but they're not here all the time.'

'Do you think I like being this way?' her mother asked in a choked voice. 'How do you think it feels to be like an invalid in bed, day after day? To be like an old woman? Do you not think I'd like to be up and about as I used to be? I'm tired, Fiona, in a way you don't understand. I'm tired deep down inside to my very bones. There are days I feel so tired, I wish that God would just let me go to sleep and never wake up again.' She reached over to the bedside cabinet to lift her embroidered hanky and then bring it up to her eyes.

Nance's response suddenly made Fiona feel guilty. As if she had no compassion or under-standing. As if she had been almost cruel. 'Oh, Mam!' she sighed, 'Don't say things like that.'

'I know I'm a burden on you, Fiona. Don't think I don't know it.'

'You're not a burden – we just need to get you well again.' She halted to choose words carefully now, wary of upsetting her mother further. 'Maybe if we got to the doctor's and saw if there's anything more they can do.'

Nance nodded her head. 'He says I've got to give the new tablets a few weeks. I'll go back after that if things aren't any better.'

Fiona lifted the tray. 'Have another sleep and see how you are when you waken later.'

It was only as she was walking back downstairs that she realised her mother had completely changed the subject, and she had not actually agreed to phone her sister.

CHAPTER 25

Bridget put down her cleaning box on the front pew, then she went to genuflect in front of the small side altar in the church. She stood up, and then moved back a few steps to observe it, and decide where she should start cleaning. There were three tall brass candlesticks at either side of the statue of Our Lady, and two big vases of pink and white lilies at each side. She only had half an hour before her English class began, and she wanted to have the beautiful little altar sparkling

A few moments later she went up the carpeted steps to the white marble altar, and lifted down the two biggest brass candlesticks and set them down on the floor at the side. She repeated this until she had taken all six candlesticks down. She then removed the vases, carefully lifting them one at a time.

She took her damp cloth and wiped over the surface of the altar. There was little dust or anything to clean. The centres had been taken out of the flowers by Sister Magdalene, before being put in the vases. She had done a good job with them, as there was hardly a speck of the orange pollen which the girls complained stained their hands and clothes.

When the marble was dry, she took a dry cloth and buffed it till it shone. She then began replacing each item.

She was just about to start wiping a side table when the sacristy door creaked and Sister Bernadette came in. She came down the main altar and over to where Bridget was working.

'Bridget,' she said, her voice quiet and calm, 'you can leave the cleaning for now. Mother Superior would like to have a word with you in her office.'

Bridget's face froze. 'Is there something wrong at home?' Her mind flashed back to the last time she was called into the office. The day Patrick was waiting on her to take her home.

'No, no – not at all. It's nothing to do with home.' Sister Bernadette put her hand out and touched her cheek. 'I'm sorry if I gave you a fright. It's not actually anything to do with you personally. Mother Superior just wants to have a little chat with all the girls in your class.'

Relieved, Bridget dropped her cloth into her cleaning box, and then stooped to pick the box up. 'Are the other girls there already?' she asked.

Sister Bernadette shook her head. 'No, she wants a little chat with each person individually. You don't need to worry about anything.'

They walked quickly across the yard from the

church to the main building, stopping to put her box back in the cleaning room. As they walked down the corridor, Sister Bernadette said, 'There might be a few nuns here, and do your best to answer any questions as truthfully as you can.'

'Of course,' Bridget said. She presumed she was going to be questioned about her vocation again. It happened on a regular basis with her Spiritual Director and Sister Bernadette. But since they were in their second last year of school now, she supposed Mother Superior was becoming more involved. In just over a year's time she would be moving to another of the order's convents near Limerick, where she would become a postulant nun.

Sister Bernadette knocked on the door, and then she gestured to Bridget to follow her in.

Mother Superior was sitting at her usual place behind her desk, with a nun at either side. All three nuns had notepads in front of them.

'Sit down, Bridget,' Mother Superior said. Her face was serious and when she smiled it did not reach her eyes. 'We are interviewing all the girls in fifth year. We just want to ask you a few questions about two girls in your year. We want you to answer all the questions with complete honesty. Nothing you say will be repeated back to them, and this inquiry will be completely confidential.' She looked Bridget in the eye. 'Do you understand exactly what I am saying?'

Bridget's felt her heart start to thump. Whatever

this was about, she felt it was something serious. The incident with Veronica and Carmel suddenly flew into her mind. 'Yes,' she said, 'I do.'

'The girls in question are Veronica and Carmel. You know who I am talking about?'

Bridget felt her throat run dry, and her legs start to shake. She was right. 'Yes,' she replied.

'You know the rules of the school, don't you?' Mother Superior said. 'You know what the girls are allowed to do, where they are allowed to go?' She paused. 'And you know who they are allowed to speak to?'

'Yes,' Bridget repeated once again. She was filled with dread as to what she might be asked next. She wondered now had someone seen her down at the wall when she found the letter?

'Now, it has come to light that they have been seen in places they shouldn't have been, and involved with males outside the school.'

One of the other nuns cleared her throat and then said, 'We have been informed that this has happened both during school time and outside of it.'

Mother Superior sighed, and it occurred to Bridget that she was tired of repeating these questions. There were over twenty girls in their class, and she was probably saying the same thing, repeating the same questions to each and every one of them.

She looked at Bridget now. 'Have you ever seen either of those girls doing anything they were not allowed to do? Have you seen them speak to anyone they shouldn't?'

Bridget suddenly felt as though she was going to be sick. She had tried to put the memory of the day in the garden with the two girls out of her mind. She had told herself it was something stupid and trivial. It now appeared that it was more serious than she thought. She looked at Mother Superior now, knowing that whatever she said was not going to be the right thing.

If she denied knowing anything, there was a chance it would remain her secret and no one would be any the wiser. The girls had not seen her checking the note hidden in the wall, and the nuns, as far as she knew, had not seen her either. She didn't think the boy working on the farm had seen her. But, there was always the possibility someone had observed her. If that had happened, all the nuns sitting in front of her now would know she was lying. And, if they didn't know, she would have to then live with the fact that she had told an outright lie, and hope that it did not burden her conscience too much.

Her other choice was to tell the truth – now. And although that was right thing to do, she knew she would be in trouble for not telling anyone about what she had seen that particular Saturday, and her suspicions about the girls. She would be in trouble either way.

She looked up now, and saw all the nuns staring intently at her.

Mother Superior put her hands flat on the desk. 'Do you want me to repeat the two questions I just asked you about the girls, Bridget?'

Bridget shook her head. A large lump seemed to have formed in her throat. 'I remember now . . .' She stopped to swallow, but the lump wouldn't budge. 'I did see something, but I didn't think it was important. I didn't really understand.'

The two nuns at either end of the desk bent their heads and started to write in their notebooks.

'Tell us everything,' Mother Superior said, her voice quiet and calm. 'Start at the beginning, Bridget, and tell us every single thing you know about the girls.'

Half an hour later, Sister Bernadette and Bridget walked along the corridor again. Bridget's face was puffy and red from crying.

'You don't need to be so upset,' the nun said. 'You have done nothing wrong.'

'I kept a secret,' Bridget said. 'And Mother Superior said that was a sin. A sin of omission.' She looked up into the kindly nun's face. 'I didn't mean it. I just didn't think – I didn't realise that something serious might be going on. I didn't want the girls to think I was a tittle-tattle.'

'I understand,' Sister Bernadette said. She drew Bridget to a halt. 'You can't go into class like this. We will go down into the kitchen – I think a cup of tea and a biscuit might help you.'

When they got to the kitchen, Sister Bernadette

went to the hot water urn to make the pot of tea, and she told Bridget to get two cups and saucers and then she directed her to the cupboard where the biscuits were kept. When everything was sorted, they came out into the dining area and sat at one of the tables.

Bridget lifted her cup to take a drink of her tea, but her hand was shaking so badly that she had to put it back down on the saucer.

'You seem very upset, Bridget,' Sister Bernadette said. 'You've no need to be. This business has nothing really to do with you. Apart from seeing the girls put the note in the wall, and saying nothing about it – you are not in any way involved.'

Bridget stared down at the cup. 'Mother Superior seemed very angry with me. She said she was surprised that I hadn't told you, at least.' She shook her head. 'I really didn't think it was important, or so serious.' She started to cry. 'And I didn't realise that keeping a secret was a sin. I always try my best to do the right thing . . .' She searched in her skirt pocket for her hanky.

'Is there anything else wrong, Bridget? You don't seem to have been yourself for a while. Is it just this issue with Veronica and Carmel, or is there something else worrying you?'

Bridged dabbed her eyes. 'There's nothing else wrong at school,' she said. 'This is the only thing that has ever happened. The only thing I know about.'

'Is there something worrying you at home? Something you need to talk about?'

Bridget took a long, shuddering breath. 'It's another thing I've kept secret. I thought I was doing the right thing . . . protecting my mother.'

'What is it?'

She closed her eyes and shook her head. 'It was something I overheard between my father and my aunt – just days before he died. Something no one else knows.' She brought her hanky up and pushed it hard against her eyes. 'I need to tell someone, but I'm afraid of what will happen . . . my mother is ill and I don't want her to know.'

'Sit up, dear,' the nun said kindly. 'Take a few deep breaths.' She waited and watched while Bridget took several good long breaths. Then she said. 'Now take a good drink of that tea. It will do you good.'

A few minutes later, having drunk the most of the cup, Bridget felt more composed. She dried her eyes again and looked at Sister Bernadette. 'If I tell you, will you have to tell Mother Superior?'

Sister Bernadette pressed her lips tightly together, thinking. 'It depends on what it is,' she said carefully. 'But, Bridget, you should know that God only judges us on what we do – not what others do. Mother Superior is the same. She's not going to judge you on what other members of your family have done.'

Bridget nodded her head slowly, trying to take in what the nun had said. She thought it meant that Sister Bernadette would probably have to tell the nun in charge. She suddenly had a picture in her mind of Mother Superior talking about sins of omission, and she realised that she could not commit the same sin twice in one hour. How could she even imagine she could be a nun if she could not tell the truth? And yet, she wondered what the nuns would think of her father when she told Sister Bernadette what she had overheard.

'Is it alright if I just say a silent prayer?'

'Take your time,' Sister Bernadette said. 'There's no rush.'

Bridget closed her eyes and then, in her head, said the silent prayer she said every night: *Remember, O most gracious Virgin Mary, that never was it known that anyone who fled to thy protection, implored thy help, or sought thy intercession was left unaided. Inspired with this confidence, I fly to thee, O Virgin of Virgins, my Mother; to thee do I come; before thee I stand, sinful and sorrowful. O Mother of the Word Incarnate, despise not my petition, but in thy mercy hear and answer me. Amen.*

When she finished the prayer she sat for a minute or so, thinking. Then, she opened her eyes and looked at the nun. 'My father has a son who my mother doesn't want anything to do with.'

Sister Bernadette stared at her in shock. 'What do you mean?'

'I heard him say to my aunt, on the phone, that it was time to be honest and tell the girls about their brother. He said he wanted to introduce him but my mother was adamant she wouldn't have anything to do with him. She was going to leave the house and not come back, if he insisted on bringing him home.'

'Are you sure?' the nun said.

Bridget nodded her head. 'That's what I heard him say.' Tears streamed down her face. 'I've thought about it over and over again, and all I can think of is that Daddy has had an illegitimate child with another woman.'

CHAPTER 26

In the afternoon, when Michael O'Sullivan had driven off to Athlone, Fiona was on the small ladder in the shop, stacking packets of flour and porridge oats, when Mrs Mooney came in.

'How did you get on?' Fiona asked her.

'Ah, grand,' she said. 'I had to go on a machine and then get blood tests and get weighed and all that kind of thing – you know what the hospitals are like. It's something to do with the change of life, a lot of women get it. He said it would do me good to do a bit of walking and lose a stone or two in weight. I thought there's not much chance of that happening, but I said nothing to him of course. I'd like to see him striding out along the Charleville Road if he had legs like mine.' She rolled her eyes and waved her hand dismissively. 'All in all, I don't think I'm too bad.'

'Oh, I'm glad.'

'I've been up at the house and I was delighted to see your mother is downstairs. She was sitting by the fire in the kitchen when I went in . . .'

There was a silence and then Fiona looked at her. 'Was she smoking?'

Mrs Mooney nodded her head. 'So you know about it? She told me she just started the other day, but I didn't know what to make of it.'

'She told me she thought it might give her a bit of a lift.'

'A bit of a lift?' The housekeeper's voice was high. 'She didn't look very lifted this afternoon!'

'To be honest, I lost my patience with her when I was up there at lunchtime . . . I was annoyed she won't speak to my Aunt Catherine on the phone.'

Mrs Mooney rolled her eyes. 'I'm not one of the family, so it's not my place to say anything. I'm only saying this to you like. It makes no sense to me at all the way she is with your auntie – you'd think she'd be glad that she has a sister that cares about her.'

Fiona felt her stomach tighten. She touched her hand to her mouth. 'There's something not right with her, Mary Ellen. I know she's still not right from the shingles, but there's something I can't put my finger on. She's slightly better in one way, and I'm certainly delighted she's up and moving around a bit more, but there's something odd about her that's worrying me.'

'I know exactly what you mean – I've noticed it myself. A kind of vagueness about her.'

Just then the door opened and a man they knew, a mechanic from the nearby garage, came in for a packet of cigarettes. After exchanging greetings, Mrs Mooney moved down to the vegetable rack as though she was examining some onions. The man made a remark to her about the wind knocking over his bin that morning, and then, while Fiona sorted his change at the till, they chatted about the good weather forecast for the weekend.

'Sunday especially,' he said, 'is to be fine. And they're saying on the radio it's to last for up to two weeks. An Indian summer they're calling it, whatever that means.'

'You'd imagine they'd have good weather in India all the year round,' Mary Ellen said. 'Those weather people on the radio and television don't know what they're talking about, half the time.'

'True for you, Mrs Mooney,' the man agreed. 'You'd think they were making it up.'

The minute the door closed behind him, Mary Ellen moved back to her earlier position at the counter and the two of them resumed their earlier conversation.

'I told her that smoking wouldn't do her one bit of good,' Mary Ellen said, shaking her head in exasperation. 'I had a brother, Bartie, who smoked sixty a day. He ate cigarettes! When I think back to the state of his chest, the coughing and everything.' Her eyes narrowed. 'He died at fifty-three, and I'd swear it was the smoking that killed him. They said it was his heart, but those cigarettes couldn't have done him any good.' She lowered her voice. 'Not to mention all the money that it cost them, for his wife smoked like a

279

chimney too – but, as the oul' saying goes – *ach sin scéal eile* – that's another story.'

Fiona had heard stories of Bartie and his family before, so was not shocked by this new piece of information about them. Two more men came into the shop, one for tobacco and the other for cigarettes and a packet of Fisherman's Friends.

After the doorbell sounded behind them, Mrs Mooney said to Fiona in a disgusted voice. 'Another one that ates the fags. The Fisherman's Friends will be for his chest, no doubt. A lot of good that'll do him, I'm sure. Don't you think?'

'Exactly,' Fiona said in a distracted tone.

A woman came in then, who had ordered a birthday cake from the baker's for her eight-year-old son and, after paying for it, she gave Fiona a ten-shilling note for the Christmas Club. Fiona got her club book out and noted it down, and gave the woman a carbon copy of the page.

After she left, Fiona said to the housekeeper, 'Mary Ellen, did Mam ever mention to you about getting somebody else to work in the shop?'

'Recently?'

'Well, since . . . you know, since Daddy died. Since she's been sick.'

Mary Ellen thought for a few moments. 'There was a lot of talk about it when you were going to America, but I can't recall her saying anything about it since.'

'Well,' Fiona said, 'if she doesn't get any better soon, we're going to have to think of taking someone on. Can you imagine how we'll be here at Christmas if there's only me serving? I've just started taking payments for the Christmas clubs, and all the orders for bikes and dolls' prams and the big toys are already coming in.' She shrugged, feeling overwhelmed at the thought of it all. 'And come the end of November, we usually have to get the window sorted and all the toys and things displayed. How am I going to do all that on my own?'

'It's early days yet,' Mrs Mooney said. 'We have a few months until Christmas.'

'I suppose so, but I can't see Mam being able for work for a while yet.'

'There's a bit of an improvement in regards her health, but she needs to get out of the bed and start living a normal life again. She's at a bad age for something like this. I've seen people taking to the bed and never getting back out of it again . . .'

Fiona's face dropped. 'Oh, don't say that. I can't imagine what our lives would be like if that happened. She would need looking after for the rest of her life!'

'Now, I'm not saying it will, Fiona, I didn't mean to give you a fright. All I'm saying is she should be doing a bit better at this stage than she is.'

'She's agreed to go to the doctor in a few weeks, if the new tablets haven't started to make a difference.'

'Let's hope they make a good difference and if

there's no improvement you'll just have to start making your own arrangements to get help down here. There's no doubt about it.'

Just then, Fiona noticed the blue hired car pulling up outside the shop and her heart lurched when she saw it was Michael O'Sullivan.

'How are the two girls doing?' the housekeeper asked. When she got no reply, she looked at Fiona then slowly followed her gaze to the window. 'Well, that's a new face I've never seen around here.' She gave a little laugh. 'He's all the fashion with the long hair.'

Fiona turned back around, her face flushing red. 'Actually, he's an American. His name is Michael O'Sullivan and he arrived in Tullamore yesterday.' She spoke quickly, to tell all the relevant information before he came in. 'He stayed in one of the rooms upstairs last night, and he wants to see around the place before going to Connemara, so he's staying until next Monday.' She saw him coming out of the car now, and took a deep breath so as to appear calm. 'He's really nice . . . Maggie O'Connell met him when he was looking for somewhere to stay and she brought him up here as there was nothing else in the town, and Patrick said we would sort him out.' She deliberately mentioned everyone else who had met him, so it didn't look as if it was just her who had instigated things. 'Anyway, we were all chatting after the pub closed last night and then I got chatting to him again this morning . . . and he's asked to take me for a meal tonight.' She lowered her voice now. 'We wouldn't be late or anything. It would be around seven o'clock, so I wondered would you be able to look in on Mam later on? I don't like to leave her on her own unless I'm working. It'll only be for a couple of hours.'

'Well, a date with an American! I'm delighted for you. You deserve a night out.'

Fiona's eyes widened in alarm. '*Shhhhh!* He's coming in now . . .'

'You go and enjoy yourself and forget about—' Then, as the outer door opened, Mary Ellen halted mid-sentence and niftily moved over to the shelves where the fruit was displayed, to look as though she was examining a bunch of bananas.

Fiona turned away as if checking something on the till, and then the shop door opened, and Michael O'Sullivan came in. She swung around as though surprised, 'Oh, hi,' she said. 'You're back . . .'

'Hi,' he said, smiling warmly at her, and then came over to lean on the counter. 'I don't want to disturb you at work or anything . . .' He inclined his head in Mrs Mooney's direction, and then said quietly, 'I thought I'd check how things were for tonight . . . if you can get away for a few hours.'

'It's fine,' she told him. 'I can be ready for about seven, if that's okay?'

He winked at her and said, 'That's great.'

Fiona noticed the housekeeper glancing sideways

to get a better look at him. 'Oh, Michael . . .' she suddenly said, 'I'd like you to meet Mrs Mooney – she helps us up at the house.'

Mary Ellen turned around, with a vague smile on her face, as though she hadn't been aware of anyone else in the shop.

'This is the nice American man I was telling you about,' Fiona said. 'He's staying in the room upstairs.'

Michael stretched his hand out immediately. 'A pleasure to meet you, Mrs Mooney.'

'And the same to you,' she said, holding out her hand and allowing him to take it. 'And how are you finding Tullamore?'

'Very nice,' he said. 'It's a very interesting little town. Patrick, from the bar, loaned me a history book with information about the castle and the canal. I'm hoping to see some of the places over the weekend.'

She looked over at Fiona with raised eyebrows. 'Well, isn't that great? It's good to know that we have some things worth looking at, and I'm sure we've never seen half of the places ourselves.' She paused, thinking. 'What part of America are you from?'

'My family are from Boston,' he told her, 'but I spend a lot of time in New York.'

'I have a first cousin out in a place called Yonkers,' she told him. 'Her name is Teresa O'Rourke. I don't suppose you were ever out that far, were you?'

'I have been there actually, a few years back when I was studying.'

'She's a smallish, thin woman. She's been out there for over thirty years, and she still sends me photos of herself and the family. She married a fella from Limerick called Paddy O'Rourke. Seemingly, they met at a church dance. I don't suppose you ever came across them? He's a tall, well-built fella, and according to Teresa he's a great worker. He has his own garage out there.'

Fiona stood listening, trying not to look as though there was anything amusing about Mrs Mooney asking Michael O'Sullivan if – out of all the millions of people in New York – he knew her cousin.

Michael narrowed his eyes in thought. 'O'Rourke, did you say?'

'Yes, Paddy O'Rourke.'

He shook his head. 'I can't recall seeing a garage by that name, but next time I'm in the Yonkers area, I'll certainly keep a look out for it, and call in and give them your regards.'

Mrs Mooney beamed at him. 'Can you imagine it? If you were to find the place, and to go in and tell Teresa you were speaking to me in Tullamore!' She shook her head. 'Isn't it a small world?'

She then went on to tell him about someone else she knew who was out in Pennsylvania. 'Stella West – lovely name, isn't it? She was a niece of a neighbour of ours,' she explained, 'she was a good five years older than me when she went out there. I used to hear all the news about her through the neighbour after she first went out. Stella was great one for writing letters, but then the old neighbour died and that was that. I never heard a word about her since, and I doubt now if I ever will.' She gave a little sigh. 'Funny enough, I always think of her when I hear Glen Miller playing that tune, "Pennsylvania 6-5000" on the radio.'

'Ah,' Michael said, 'that's one of the old greats. My mother loves Glen Miller.'

A young lad came in looking for a sliced pan and half a pound of butter, and Fiona left them chatting while she served him. As she went out to the fridge for the butter, she thought how kind it was of Michael to indulge the older woman's ideas of how people lived in America.

'He's a lovely, lovely fella,' Mary Ellen said, after Michael left the shop to go in to see Patrick. 'If I had my time over again I wouldn't think twice about going off with a fella like him. Sure, what did we know? We were too young and innocent and knew nothing about life.' She came over to the counter and put her hand over Fiona's. 'You take your chances when you get them. Go out and enjoy yourself tonight, and don't give a thought to anyone else.'

Fiona suddenly felt all emotional. 'Thanks, Mrs Mooney – you're very good.'

Mrs Mooney looked at her. 'Enjoy yourself, but be careful. That's all I'm saying.' She glanced around her in case there was anyone coming into the shop. 'The last thing you want is him gone back to America and you left with a bundle in your arms.'

'God almighty!' Fiona said, blushing furiously now. She wondered if she had heard correctly. She had never heard the housekeeper talking like this before. She knew she could be outspoken, but she had never heard her refer to sex in such a direct manner. 'Surely you don't think – I've only just met him. That would be the last thing on my mind . . .'

The housekeeper gave her a long, knowing look. 'That's what they all say before it happens.' Then she started to laugh. 'Mind you, I wouldn't blame you – he's a fine-looking fella. Well, apart from the straggly hair and the long oul *geansaí*.'

'I like his hair,' Fiona said, 'and those long jumpers are all the go at the minute.'

Talking about him kept Michael O'Sullivan present in her mind, although she hadn't imagined talking about him like this with – of all people – Mary Ellen Mooney.

'Ah, well, I suppose it's the modern way,' the older woman mused. 'The styles and the fashions and that kind of thing. Believe it or not, we had all that kind of thing when we were young too. We didn't have the same money to spend of course, or much choice when it came to shops, but we made the effort with our hair and things.' She halted, thinking. 'Did you say it was Maggie from the hairdresser's that brought him back here looking for a room?'

'Yes, she had a friend from Galway staying for the night, and they bumped into him down the town. He told them Bolger's Hotel was full with the funeral, and he was looking for somewhere else to stay in the town. The girls felt sorry for him because he had driven all the way down from Dublin, and he was going to have to drive on to Birr or Mullingar to find somewhere to stay.'

'Begod, you're lucky she didn't get there first. Maggie is always on the lookout for a man. And she's a good-looking girl with plenty of good chat as well.'

Fiona started to laugh. 'You're gas this evening, Mrs Mooney! Maggie wasn't a bit interested in him – besides he's a few years younger than her.'

'Sure, what difference does age make?' The housekeeper gave Fiona a clap on the back of her hand, before turning towards the door. 'I might even be tempted to go off with him myself!'

'Not tonight,' Fiona laughed. 'I need you to look in on my mother.'

Mary Ellen halted at the door, her face serious now. 'Are you going to tell her about your date?'

'Yes, I will,' Fiona said. 'It wouldn't be fair not to. But it's not as if I'm a teenager and need her permission.'

'Make sure you have a nice time. I'll see to the fires and everything for the night. And I'll be in early in the morning to see to your mother's breakfast, so you can sleep it out without worrying about anything.'

'Thanks,' Fiona told her. 'I feel a lot better than I did when you first came into the shop.'

CHAPTER 27

Fiona looked into her wardrobe, wondering what to wear. She wasn't sure where they were going to go in Mullingar, but she guessed it wouldn't be too fancy. She had a feeling that if Michael changed at all, it would probably be into something casual.

For some reason, he didn't strike her as a typical American. Not the type that Elizabeth described so vividly in her letters. According to her, the young men from New York who went to the dance-halls were confident, snappy dressers with bold-coloured ties and slicked-back hairstyles like Elvis Presley. Some of the more sophisticated ones, Elizabeth wrote, wore cologne. Fiona could not imagine Michael O'Sullivan being like any of the men her friend described. She found it hard to picture him standing on the side of a dance floor with a gaudy tie, and when she thought about it she started to giggle to herself.

It was a mild evening for September, so she decided to wear a blue A-line, sleeveless dress which had a fashionable round white neckline and was hemmed in white. She would wear it with a white cardigan, which she thought she could take off if it was warm inside. She pinned her hair up in a loose bun, and then put a large diamante clasp to hide the pins. She put some light make-up on, and then decided to try a new dark-brown eyeliner she had bought in a chemist the last time she was up in Dublin.

She had only one eye done when she realised she had made a mistake. The liner was too dark and heavy – more like black – and looked ridiculous with her light-brown hair. How, she wondered, did Angela always manage to get it just perfect? The eyeliner she wore for evening was the thinnest line with a tiny flick at the ends, which made her look like a model from one of the magazines. Sighing in exasperation, she reached for her Anne French cleansing cream and cotton wool, rubbed it all off, and then started all over again.

Earlier on, when she came in from work just after six o'clock, her mother had been in bed, but Fiona was pleased to see her propped up on pillows reading a magazine. She was also pleased to notice that there was no sign or smell of cigarettes in the room.

When she explained her plans, her mother had been fine about it, and had also been agreeable when Fiona told her that Mary Ellen would be calling in around nine o'clock. Fiona had explained about Michael – about how he was staying down in the pub over the weekend to see a bit more of Offaly. She emphasised that he was a real gentleman, a qualified architect with an Irish family background, and all the things that her mother put great stock on.

'An architect? Well, that's a good profession,' Nance had said. 'And his mother was from Connemara?' She nodded her head, digesting the details. 'All in all, he sounds very nice . . . but isn't it a pity he's only here on holiday? It would be better even if he was from Dublin or somewhere within reach.'

Fiona had let her breath out in a sigh of impatience. She should have predicted this reaction. 'Well, I'm sorry he's not an Irishman, Mam, but so far I've never come across anyone remotely like him at home. And it's only a meal out, it's not as if I'm getting married to him or anything.'

'Oh, Fiona, there you go again. I didn't mean it like that.' Her voice became softer now. 'I'm actually delighted you're having a night out, and he sounds like a very nice chap.'

Fiona felt the annoyance seeping out of her. In truth, her mother had only touched the raw nerve she herself had been trying to avoid. Of course it would be much better if Michael O'Sullivan was an Irishman – in fact, it would be perfect. It would be the answer to everyone's prayers. But what was the use in even thinking things like that?

'I'm going to get ready,' she said.

Her mother smiled at her now. 'What are you wearing?'

Fiona's face lightened, glad that peace had been

restored between them again. She told her about the blue-and-white dress.

Her mother nodded in approval. 'That sounds lovely. Is he calling to the house for you?'

'No, I've arranged to meet him down the street at his hired car around seven. I didn't ask him up here because I wasn't sure whether you would be downstairs. I didn't want you feeling awkward about being in your dressing gown.'

'I suppose I would feel a bit uncomfortable,' her mother said, 'with my hair not the way it should be and everything – so you did the right thing.' There was a little pause. 'I'm going to come down and have a cup of tea shortly, and see how I feel.'

'That's a good idea,' Fiona said. 'The more you move around, the better you will feel.'

'Come in and see me before you leave,' her mother said. 'I'd like to see you dressed up.'

As she got ready, Fiona thought that, despite the little jarring notes, her mother was in a more positive frame of mind than she had been. She wondered if the row they'd had in the afternoon had perhaps made her think, and make her decide to push herself that little bit further. Neither of them had mentioned her contacting Aunt Catherine, and Fiona decided to leave it for the time being. She would not think about it tonight.

Tonight was all about herself and Michael.

After getting her mother's approval on her outfit and make-up and hair, Fiona took her light raincoat from the hallstand and left the house just on seven o'clock. She walked carefully down the street towards the pub, taking her time as she was wearing a pair of navy patent shoes that had higher heels than she was used to. They had a white bow on the front that matched her dress, and she had bought them for a friend's wedding last year.

As she walked along, she wished she had worn them a few more times since the wedding as they had not been sufficiently broken in to make them comfortable. As she got nearer she could see the blue car and Michael O'Sullivan leaning on it reading a book. She smiled to herself, noticing that he was wearing a blue open-necked shirt with fairly smart black trousers. They would match nicely, she thought, and was glad she had made the effort to dress up herself.

He looked up when he heard her heels on the pavement coming towards him, and waved, and then he reached through the open window to put the book into the back of the car. He walked up to meet her, and then he put his arms around her waist and kissed her lightly on the lips. 'You look absolutely beautiful,' he told her. Then he took her hand in his and they walked to the car.

As they walked the few yards, Fiona saw a neighbour on the opposite side – a woman in her thirties – out walking her dog. She called hello across to Fiona, and smiled and said what a nice evening it was.

Fiona smiled and gave a little wave of acknowledgement, knowing that she and Michael holding hands in the street would be discussed the minute the woman got inside.

Michael held the passenger door open for her. 'Have you decided where you would like us to go? I'm in your hands now.'

'I think Mullingar will be grand. There are a couple of nice restaurants there, and we shouldn't have any trouble getting a table since it's a Thursday night.'

'Sounds good to me,' he said and went around to his own side.

'It's just dawned on me,' Fiona said, as he started the engine up. 'That maybe I should have offered to drive us in my car – it's harder on you driving on the wrong side of the road.'

'Not at all. I'm used to it already.' He grinned. 'I like the challenge, it keeps me alert.'

Fiona rolled her eyes. 'I think I would die if I had to drive on the other side – it just seems complicated and scary to me.'

'I am not going to make sexist comments about women drivers,' he said, laughing, 'because I appreciate the offer. Maybe I'll take you up on it another day.'

'*Sexist?*' she repeated. 'I've never heard that word before.'

'I suppose it's a fairly new term,' he explained. 'It's when you make general assumptions about people because of their sex – as in "women drivers". He shrugged. 'I'm sure there are plenty of sexist remarks you could make about men.'

She laughed now. 'I'm sure there are!'

Fiona directed him out of Tullamore and onto the Kilbeggan Road.

'Beautiful green countryside,' he commented, as they turned down the leafy lanes.

As they drove along, he asked her about the various places, and listened carefully whilst she told him all she knew about the houses or the land or the villages through which the local canal ran.

When they arrived in Mullingar, they found a restaurant in the middle of the town, which Fiona remembered being in with her parents and her sisters a few years ago. Only half the tables were occupied so the waiter had no problem finding one for them in a corner at the back.

They both ordered melon to start with, then Michael ordered steak with an Irish whiskey sauce and she ordered duck in a glazed orange sauce.

'We can have a bottle of wine with the meal, if you can drink most of it,' he said, 'because I wouldn't chance driving on your winding roads when I've been drinking.'

Fiona lifted her eyes to the ceiling as though she were shocked. 'I could not drink three-quarters of a bottle of wine on my own,' she laughed. 'And especially not after last night – after drinking quite a bit more than I usually do.' She decided on a glass of white wine and Michael chose a red.

A few minutes later the waitress brought the drinks to the table.

Michael reached his glass out to hers and they

touched them together. 'To our weekend exploring Offaly!'

She asked him about his architecture work back in America and he told her about projects he had been recently working on in both Boston and New York. They moved from one subject to another easily, with the rise and fall of conversation and occasional laughter from the other diners in the background. When they had finished their main course, Fiona had profiteroles and Michael had homemade trifle. Afterwards, as they sat chatting over coffee, the conversation turned to Fiona's family and how she had found it growing up as part of the family business.

'When you don't know anything different, you just feel it is normal,' she said. 'But looking back, I suppose it was pretty different to the lives most of our friends had. For one thing, our mother worked – she was always going between home and the shop.' She smiled and shrugged. 'Just like I am now, except I'm younger and single. I think it gave us a fuller, busier life in many ways. I enjoyed going up and down to the shop to see Mam, and then helping her when I got older. And I always liked going in and out to Daddy in the bar. It was fine, I have no complaints about it, except I didn't see myself ever doing this long term.'

'What about your sisters?' Michael asked. 'Did they like helping with the business?'

Fiona pursed her lips in thought. 'They never really did,' she said. 'Bridget left for her convent school when she was twelve or thirteen, so she would not have really been old enough to help in the shop. She does help now when she's home, and she gave me a hand at Easter.' She halted. 'And then Angela – well, Angela never really worked in the shop at all because she had a problem with her leg. She wasn't really at home for a lot of the time.'

'This is your second sister?'

'Yes,' Fiona said, 'the one who is two years younger than me.'

'That's the same difference between my brother and me, only he is the oldest. You said Angela had a problem with her leg?'

'Polio.'

'Polio? Wow . . . that's a tough one. Did she have it bad?'

'Yes, when she was younger. She's had a lot of operations on it, and it's improved over the years. She used to have to wear a calliper all the time, but now she only wears it when it's very bad.'

'You said she wasn't at home a lot of the time – why was that?'

'The specialist hospital that dealt with her condition was in Dublin,' she shrugged. 'All the kids who had polio went there . . . Angela was in it for a lot of her childhood.'

'How old was she when she got the polio?'

Her eyes narrowed as she calculated. 'She was at National School, maybe around seven or eight.'

'That must have been a really traumatic time for

your family,' he said. 'Having such a terrible thing happen to her. I have an older cousin, Scott, back in the States who had polio. Both his legs and an arm were affected. He caught it when he was a baby, and he's been in a wheelchair all his life.'

'That sounds really bad, much worse that Angela . . .'

'It certainly was for the family, but everyone rallied round, making sure he had as normal a life as was possible. His older brothers had a soapbox cart – a sort of racing buggy that they'd made out of wood and old bicycle wheels – and Scott used to sit outside in the wheelchair watching them. Then, one weekend the brothers said they had something on, and when they reappeared they had made him a specially adapted cart, which they used pulled him around in.' He shook his head, smiling at the memory. 'The other guys did every-thing they could to include him in things, and he grew up kind of thinking he could do just about anything. In fact, he's a very clever guy – he trained as an accountant, and he has accomplished more than most able-bodied people. The family have a chain of really successful steak houses in Boston, and it's all down to Scott. They had a middle-of-the-road restaurant which wasn't doing well, and he went in and studied the decor, the menus and the order books, and then he spent time in the kitchen watching how they did things. After that, he spent a few weeks going around successful restaurants and diners, asking questions and taking notes, and when he came back to his brothers, he had facts and figures about what was going wrong, and what he thought needed doing to whip things into shape.' Michael shrugged. 'Amazing guy, really.'

'He certainly sounds it,' Fiona agreed. 'It's a brilliant story and great that he was able to succeed regardless of being in a wheelchair. Thank God Angela wasn't that badly affected.' She paused. 'You know, I've never really thought that it could have been much worse.'

'But Scott spent all his time at home – it must have been real tough on your family when she had to go away and for all those years. You must have felt it badly at the time, your young sister suddenly becoming seriously ill and then disappearing from your home and not coming back. And it must have made her feel very estranged from the family. Has it has a long-lasting effect on her?'

Fiona got the same uncomfortable feeling she got any time Angela mentioned being in hospital in Dublin for all those years. 'Angela is a very independent girl,' she said. 'She always has been. I think it didn't affect her the way it might have affected others.'

'Does she talk about it a lot?'

'No,' Fiona said, 'not really . . . I think she prefers to forget it. I think we all do. She has a good job in an office in Dublin and she has a good social life there as well. She's so busy she doesn't come home that often.'

He nodded his head slowly up and down, digesting what she had said. 'Well, it's amazing both she and Scott have made such good lives for themselves after going through all that stuff with polio. They're obviously very strong people.'

The waitress came over to clear their cups and glasses and they ordered two more coffees.

When she came back with their fresh drinks, Michael took a sip from his then leaned his elbows on the table and looked at Fiona, a serious look on his face.

'You've been open about your family,' he said, 'and I think there's something I should tell you now about mine. It's one of the reasons I came over here – why I planned to take an extended break from home. I had a fight with my brother, Greg. A pretty bad fight. Bad enough that if he'd pressed charges I could be in a penitentiary somewhere.'

She was taken aback by the sudden, serious turn in the conversation. 'What happened?'

'It's a long story that goes way back . . .' He shrugged. 'I'm sure he has his own version of growing up with me, but I've always found him bull-headed and competitive. Competitive in every way you could imagine. He's two years older than me, good at sports, good at music and fairly good in school, although he dropped out early because he couldn't take teachers telling him what to do.' He stretched back in his chair and gave a wry smile. 'And as if he didn't have enough going for him already, he's good-looking too, and naturally girls always adored him. He was one of the reasons I decided to go to university in New York, rather than being at home in Boston. Even back then, I knew how he could get my hackles up and how difficult he could be under certain circumstances. I thought it was best if there was a bit of distance between us until we both were mature enough to handle our differences.'

Fiona lifted her spoon and stirred the sugar in her coffee, listening carefully to every word. She knew by his voice and the serious way he looked that what he was saying was important to him.

'I had been back living in Boston and seeing this nice woman – Kim – for almost two years. She was a lovely person and an artist with her own successful craft shop. We had some really good times, going out to music bars and concerts and art events . . . that sort of thing. But then, earlier this year I started travelling to New York again for work and I suppose things weren't working out as easily as before. There were weekends when I didn't come home.' He lifted his coffee and took a drink from it.

Fiona listened, wondering about Kim the artist, whether she had dark or blonde hair – long or short. Imagining what she looked like, and imagining Michael with her at all the exciting music bars and concerts. Glamorous places she had never been to. Places she dreamed of when she thought she was going to New York. As she looked across the table at him now, she wondered if he found this restaurant very tame and boring compared to it. If he found her very tame and boring compared to the artistic – and no doubt, beautiful – Kim.

'I got the feeling there might have been someone else,' he continued, 'another artist guy who she got close to, and I don't blame her as I wasn't around. I think they were also probably more suited to each other than we were. Looking back, we had become more of a habit, but we were good friends as well and neither wanted to pull the plug on things, so we kind of drifted along doing the same old things.'

Fiona put the cup back down in the saucer. The last piece of information about him and his girl-friend only drifting along, and then eventually breaking up, made her feel better. She did not want to be haunted by images of him with another girl, or to feel that she had broken it off with him, and that he had come to Ireland, pining and trying to forget about her.

But, she could tell that there was some fairly serious problem back home that had instigated his travels, and she needed to hear more about it, to work out where exactly she might fit in.

'So,' she asked, 'where does Greg come into all this?'

'Stupidly I thought things had improved between us over the last couple of years,' he said, gesturing with his hands. 'You have this thing because you're brothers, and you feel you should get on. And it seemed to be working out. He had even come to stay with me in New York on a couple of weekends. He got drunk, and we had a few verbal run-ins about politics and stuff – he's a Republican and I'm a Democrat – but nothing major came of it. He's always been unpredictable with drink, and Mom reckoned he went through a phase of dabbling in cocaine as well.' He shrugged. 'He never said anything about it to me, and I never picked up on anything. It's not my kind of thing, but I know people use it.'

As Fiona listened, she remembered what Angela had said about one of Joseph's band members being involved with drugs.

'It was Greg's birthday in August,' Michael continued, 'and Mom decided to invite me and Kim over for a meal since we hadn't all been together in a while, but I ended up going on my own. The night went well, we had a couple of bottles of wine with the meal and then Greg, Dad and I had a couple of beers and we all went and sat outside on the porch. Mom asked about Kim and I said that things were cooling off a little, but that I thought we would work it out.' He sat forward now, his hands joined together on the table. 'Later on, Greg asked me about it, and well, it all seemed so easy and relaxed that foolishly I mentioned about Kim and the artist guy.'

He stopped talking as the waitress came with a jug to check if they would like more coffee and they both said they would. As she filled one cup and then the other, Fiona went over in her head all the things he had said to her about his girl-friend and his brother, trying to work out what might have led to the fight. What could be so bad that he had flown across the Atlantic to get away from it?

As soon as the waitress left, she stretched her hand across the table and touched his arm just above his wrist – the part not covered by the casual rolled-up sleeve. Something quivered deep in her stomach as she felt the unexpected warmth of his skin on her fingertips. She suddenly had the urge to lean right over and kiss him. Instead, she moved her hand and smiled at him and said, 'Finish your story, I really want to hear what happened.'

'Okay,' he said, taking two quick mouthfuls of the coffee as though it might spur him on. 'I know Greg so well, and I knew that night that something was simmering away with him. We talked for a good while and we played a couple of rounds of table tennis with Mom and Dad.' He stopped and laughed. 'I know it's kind of strange, grown adults playing such a game but it's something we've always done since we were little kids, and it's a kind of reminder of the good parts of growing up in the family. Anyway, my parents went off to bed and then Greg and I had another beer on the porch and then he said he had something to tell me about Kim. He said that he didn't want me to work it out with her because he knew she had

305

cheated on me. He wouldn't tell me how he knew, but he just kept saying that she was a cheat. Of course, I couldn't let it go. How could I? So I went back inside and even though it was well after midnight I phoned Kim and I told her what Greg had said about her being a cheat, and I asked her what he was talking about. She started to cry and then it all came out. She said that he had made a pass at her when he was staying at my place one night but she had pushed him off. And then she told me that he turned up at her apartment one weekend when I was in New York. She said they had a few drinks and he had brought some pot and insisted she try it – he said lots of artists used it as it helped their minds become more creative.' He rolled his eyes. 'It was bullshit. Greg hasn't an artistic bone in his body. He said if she tried just one joint then he would leave, so stupidly she did. After it, she said she asked him to leave, and he said it would be best if he stayed to look after her, as the pot sometimes has a bad effect on people who have never used it. They were arguing and then she said she suddenly felt strange.' He gave a huge sigh. 'After that, she said she didn't know what happened, but she woke up the next morning and he was lying in the bed beside her.'

Fiona's face was tight with shock. It was like something out of a gangster film. 'Oh, God,' she said, 'that must have been terrible for her – and terrible for you.'

'When I came back out to the deck after speaking to her, he was just sitting there smiling as if nothing was wrong. I just couldn't stop myself. I punched him and then it went into a big fight, and it finished when we rolled off the deck.'

Fiona's hands were covering her mouth. 'Oh, my God,' she whispered.

'Any time we fought before, when we were teenagers, he usually had the upper hand. But this time I was so fired up, I didn't hold back.' He sighed. 'I'm not proud of myself. Whatever way it happened, he landed awkwardly and ended up with a broken nose, bruised ribs and a broken collarbone.'

'It sounds just awful. How long ago was this? And is he okay?'

'Just over a week ago. I stayed long enough to check there wasn't anything wrong with him that couldn't be fixed, and to check that Kim was okay. And then I just packed up and came over here. I had been planning a trip to Ireland, but it had never been the right time.'

'How was Kim?'

'Pretty shook up with the whole thing. She still wasn't sure what had happened. He denied having touched her and she decided to leave it at that.' He closed his eyes. 'She admitted that he had been openly flirting with her, and she thinks she may have given him the wrong signals because of the pot and everything. But, whichever way you look at it, he should never have gone to her apartment and then encouraged her to take drugs. And the only reason he did it was to get at me – and he certainly achieved that.'

There was a silence then Fiona said, 'What about the artist you thought Kim was seeing?'

He shrugged. 'I didn't even ask. I just needed to know that she was okay and was handling what had happened.'

'And do you still have feelings for her? If this hadn't happened?'

'No, no. She's a good person, but I think we both knew whatever was between us had kind of fizzled out anyway. It wasn't going to go anywhere long-term. She was embarrassed and upset about the incident, and blaming herself for being stupid. I think I talked her out of that, and we left as friends.'

'How were your parents? That must have been awful for them.'

'Of course, they were really shook up with what happened to Greg. They had to take him to hospital, and when the doctors realised his injuries were the result of a fight, they wanted to call the cops in, but Greg refused. He could have done it and, depending on what he said, I could have been in real trouble, but I guess he knew he had crossed a line with us. I did lose my temper and I did hit him on the nose, but the way he fell off the deck caused the ribs and his shoulder injury.' He lifted his eyes to look at her. 'You must be horrified hearing this – and I know what I did was bad, but you have to know it was totally out of character for me. I've never hurt anyone before and I never will again. Greg and I are done with each other.'

She reached over and touched his hand. 'I understand. I think most people would.'

Later, as they left the restaurant to walk back to the car, Fiona looked at her watch. 'It's only ten o'clock. Do you want to go somewhere for a drink . . . or back to the pub?'

He put his arm around her and pulled her close. 'I just want to be with you, so anywhere is fine.'

'To be honest, there's not many bars around that women are really welcome in, unless we go to one of the hotels.' She smiled. 'It must sound a bit old-fashioned to you?'

'Country towns are like that everywhere,' he said.

'Our own bar will be quiet tonight,' Fiona said. 'I suppose we could go into the snug again.' It was not ideal, but she couldn't think of anywhere else.

'Patrick will be there, and we'll end up drinking and chatting to him like I did last night. He's a really nice guy, but it's not what I had in mind.'

Fiona suddenly had a thought. 'There are some lovely lakes around Mullingar – Lough Ennell is actually on our way back home. We could pull in there for a little while if you like.'

'Sounds great.'

'Night is probably not the best time, but it mightn't be too bad – it's a good bright sky.'

'It is.' He dipped his head a little to look through the windscreen glass. 'I think it's a full moon.'

He started the car up and Fiona directed him back out of the town and out towards the lakes. She told him all she knew about Mullingar, about the lakes, little things she knew he would find interesting. Then, after about ten minutes, she pointed to a small laneway on the right, which she said would take them down to the lake.

'It's a bit bumpy,' she warned him, 'so go easy.'

They drove down the laneway then Fiona guided him between rows of trees until they were driving along by the lakeshore. There were two other cars there, which she suspected were other courting couples, so she suggested they drive along a little further until there was a good distance between them.

When the car pulled up Michael moved around, trying to see all that he could from the windows, then he turned back to her. 'This looks amazing, but I think I need to get out to get a better view. Is it too cold for you, or will we take a little walk?'

Walking around in the dark at night would not normally have appealed to her, but everything seemed more interesting and somehow worthwhile when she was with him. He walked slowly with her, while she picked her steps carefully in her high heels. When they came to a stop, he moved to stand behind her with both arms encircling her and his chin resting on her head. Then, they stood in silence, looking out over the moonlit lake.

'This is spectacular,' he said. 'The light on the water, the sky . . . it's the sort of sight that inspires artists and poets and songwriters.'

'You're on the ball,' Fiona laughed, 'Although I'm not sure it's the sort of writing you were thinking about – apparently the lake in front of us inspired *Gulliver's Travels*!'

'Really?'

'Well, Johnathan Swift lived around here some-where, and the story goes that he was in a boat on the lake, and when he looked back and noticed how tiny the people on the land looked at that distance, it gave him the inspiration for *Gulliver's Travels*.'

'That's amazing . . . although I must admit I've only read the children's version.'

'Me too.'

'I was reading somewhere – a couple of years ago – that the original, adult version had a lot of interesting points in it.' He laughed and squeezed her tightly. 'But that didn't inspire me enough to seek it out and read it.'

Fiona put her arms over his and hugged him closer, and her gaze wandered around the nearby trees, the water, and back to the grey-and-red-streaked sky.

'Isn't it all just amazing, to have all this so close to where you live?' he said now. 'But then, that's what Ireland is all about. It's why my family have loved coming back here time after time.'

'The Midlands have nothing to compare with the mountains and all the spectacular scenery in the west – like in Connemara – I don't think many tourists come here for the scenery.'

'I think they should. It has its own beauty – the canals and the bridges and the lovely old castles. I intend to get around and see more of them tomorrow while you're working.' He paused. 'And I think I'd like to come back and see the lakes in daylight, although the experience of being here at night has been wonderful. I don't think I've been anywhere quite so silent.'

'It's funny how it seems totally silent until you start to really listen,' Fiona said, 'and then you can hear all sorts of sounds like the water, the birds and even noise from the trees.'

They stood listening to all the small sounds and after a while Michael gently moved her around to face him. He bent his head and kissed her. 'I hope I haven't frightened you off with all the stuff about me and Greg back home? I know it's early to confess your worst behaviour – I should still be trying to impress you at this stage, not scare you away.' He kissed her again. 'I just want you to be clear that the behaviour I told you about is not any kind of indication of who I am. I'm ashamed I lost my temper and there's no excuse for it.'

'I understand,' she told him. 'I really do. It sounds like you spent years avoiding a clash with your brother, and then he did the most terrible thing to you and your girlfriend, and you reacted instinctively.' She touched his face. 'Some people might say he had it coming. And in your defence, you did take him to hospital and you waited until you knew he was okay.'

'Yes,' he said, 'I suppose I did.'

'And then you left to give you both some breathing space. I think you've handled it as well as anyone could.' She paused, thinking. 'Do your parents know where you are?'

'I told them I was coming to Ireland – I wouldn't worry them by just disappearing. They were actually okay about it, and said it was a good idea to take some time to myself.'

'You said they know what your brother's like, the problems with drink and drugs. They probably think he nearly dragged you down along with him.' She squeezed his hand now. 'You've checked everyone else is okay, which was really decent of you. Everything I've seen of you in Ireland, and what you've just told me, makes me think you're a kind and caring man.'

He looked at her, his face still serious. 'If that's the case, you must know that I am really grateful to be spending this time with you, and would rather be on my own for the whole trip than be with anyone else.'

She smiled at him. 'That's good to hear.'

He pulled her into his arms, and hugged her tightly. 'Talking that thing out with you has put a lot of it in perspective.' He touched his lips to her forehead. 'I feel a weight has been lifted off me. Thank you.'

She could see and feel a difference in him. 'I'm glad you feel it helped. And now,' she said, 'you really do need to forget about what happened back home, and get on with all the plans you have for over here in Ireland.'

'That's exactly what I intend to do,' he replied.

Fiona looked out across the lake again, at the moon reflected in the middle, lighting everything up. 'There's a path that goes around the edge of water – will we have a bit of a wander?'

'I think that would be great.' He took her hand and then he started to break into a run, pulling her playfully behind him.

'I can't!' she said, pulling out of his grip. 'I'm wearing high heels!'

He came back to her and, before she realised it, he had lifted her up in his arms and started walking over to the path carrying her.

She began to laugh, and then as he came to a halt to put her back down, she buried her face in his chest. She laughed and laughed, and then, she suddenly realised she actually felt happy for the first time since her father died.

She also realised that she had never felt this free, uninhibited way with any other boy before – where she felt she could suddenly laugh or sing out loud. It was the elated way she had imagined she would feel when she went to New York and saw all the bright lights and the glamorous dance halls. Where she could be the person she really wanted to be.

And then it occurred to her – she didn't need to go to America to feel like that.

America had come to her.

When they arrived back in Tullamore, Michael slowed down as they came towards Tracey's house.

'Do you mind driving a little bit further down the street, please, so we can't be seen from the windows on either side?' She gave a small laugh. 'I don't want my mother or Maggie O'Connell peering through the curtains at us. My mother is probably dying to know what you look like.'

'That's understandable,' he said. 'My mom will be as curious about you when I tell her about us.'

While he slowly drove another fifty yards or so, Fiona felt something akin to sadness come over her. She did not want this night to be over. She did not want to say goodnight and then have to leave him. It felt all wrong that they should be parted. It hit her with a jolt that she wanted to go back to a room with him and lie down beside him. What would happen next, if she did, she had no idea. All she knew is that she did not want to be parted from him.

He stopped the car at a quiet spot in the road that was midway between the house and the bar. He turned to her. 'I suppose this is where we say goodnight?'

She nodded. 'I suppose it is.'

'What are we going to do? When can we meet again?'

'I'm sorry but tomorrow isn't good,' she told him. 'I'm in the shop all day and then we have a busy night in the bar, so I'll have to give Patrick a hand.'

'Could I help? Even just picking up glasses or something like that?'

She shook her head. 'Thanks, but it wouldn't work . . .' She could just picture the faces on the locals when they realised that the strange fella helping around the bar was a Yank.

'Okay,' he said, 'I'll head off to one of the local towns again in the afternoon. I'll have a look at the book again and work out which place has the most interesting buildings, and then I'll talk it over with you in the morning. I will see you at breakfast again, won't I?'

'Of course,' she said. 'Have you any idea what time you'll be ready for it?'

'If it's the same as this morning, any time from five o'clock . . .' He looked at her and smiled. 'Hopefully, I'll get a little more sleep tonight. Last night my head was too full of you.' He leaned over and kissed her. 'Let's see if we can work out a way to spend more time together in the next few weeks.'

'Well, we have Saturday night and all day Sunday. We could drive to Galway on Sunday.'

'That's great,' he said. 'And maybe we'll think of something for the following weekend.' He looked thoughtful. 'How would you feel if we could organise some time for us to go away for a few days together? Maybe to Galway or Connemara?'

Every reason why she could not do it – and why she *should* not do it – ran through her mind. It was against everything she had been brought up to know as good and decent, and it was against everything a young Catholic woman had been taught. And yet it seemed to her the right thing to do. This year she had done all the right things, giving up her dream and staying at home to look after her mother and the family business.

'I'd love it,' she whispered. 'I'd love us to go away together.'

She had always done the right thing for other people – and now, she decided, she was going to do something for herself.

CHAPTER 28

Angela was typing up a document when the phone rang. She leaned across the desk to pick it up.

'It is Angela, isn't it?'

The voice on the line was one of the directors of the Polio Fellowship, Stephen Hall, a big easy-going man who often called into the office.

'Yes, Mr Hall,' she said, moving the phone to rest between her ear and shoulder while she reached for a memo pad and pen in case he wanted her to take a message.

'Good, good,' he said. 'You're the very person I had hoped to speak to.'

'What can I help you with?'

'I was out with a few of my old friends for lunch at the weekend,' he told her, 'and it came up in conversation that one of them, Major Harrington, is looking for a private secretary.' He paused. 'Someone who can type and deal with household accounts and filing . . . that sort of thing. You get the idea?'

'I do,' Angela said, 'and would you like me to pass that message on to the Office Manager?'

'Well, actually,' Mr Hall said, 'you were the very person who came to mind. I would think a young lady like you might be ready for a bigger challenge in life? What do you say?'

'You're asking me if I would be interested in the position?'

'I am indeed. For some reason you came straight to my mind. Major Harrington needs someone who can organise things for him, mainly his papers and accounts and that sort of thing. And of course the main thing he needs is someone who can type and edit his memoirs. I thought you might be interested as he's offering a live-in position. I know you are out in Leeson Street in a shared house, and I heard that you were looking for a more private accommodation.'

Angela was intrigued now. 'And where does Major Harrington live?' she asked.

'That's a good question,' Mr Hall said, laughing. 'No, really – his Dublin place is out in Ballsbridge – Merrion Road.'

Angela caught her breath. Merrion Road was in one of the most exclusive parts of Dublin.

'A very nice big house,' Mr Hall went on, 'and he has a few staff out there already – a housekeeper and gardener. He plans to spend the next year or two working on his memoirs and family history, and apparently he has a lot of the books and documents in a library there and it would suit him very well if the clerical assistant could live on the premises, so to speak. If I remember correctly, there would also be some travelling involved back and forth to England. The major has another family residence outside Manchester, so he will be doing research there as well, and he will want his secretary to accompany him.'

Angela's mind was ticking over quickly. 'It sounds very different to what I've been doing . . . but very interesting.'

'I hoped you might think so. You've always been highly thought of by the Fellowship – great worker, very efficient and of course, always very well presented. I've mentioned it to one or two of the directors and they would be delighted to recommend you.' He paused. 'You're fairly mobile, aren't you? Getting around wouldn't be a huge problem to you.'

Her face flushed. 'I'm fine, thank you. The last surgery made a good difference.'

'Well, from what I know of him, Major Harrington doesn't live life in the fast lane physically. He tends to take life as it comes to him – and, in any case, you would be driven around so it wouldn't entail any great exertion for you. What I do know is that he is keen to get started with his memoirs, so I think it would be a good idea if you and he were to meet up.'

'For an interview?'

'Yes, I suppose it would be an interview. I'll ring him now, and then I'll get back to you with the details of meeting up. I would say it will be in the next day or two.'

After he hung up, Angela sat for a while going over the unexpected turn of events in her mind. Whilst she had been planning at some stage to move out of the shared house, and also to look for work in a different office, she hadn't expected them both to turn up at the same time. It had never occurred to her that the sort of clerical position that Mr Hall had suggested really existed and had certainly not thought it would be something that would be offered to her. She had always imagined that she would just move to a bigger office – something like Guinness's or maybe a secretarial position in a legal office.

And the idea of moving out to Ballsbridge was something she would never have considered, as it was too expensive and that bit further out of town from where she currently worked. The fact that the position would be live-in, she thought now, put a whole different slant on it. But, she thought, it would all depend on what kind of person this old Major Harrington was. He was obviously of English extraction and a lot of those types tended to be cold and aloof with ordinary people. Whilst she did not expect an employer to be over-familiar or friendly, she did not want to work in a place where she would be made to feel beneath someone. She had endured those feelings with regards to her leg for most of her life. That was something she had no power over, but she could make the decision whether she moved jobs or not.

She had little time to ponder things any further

before the phone rang again and Mr Hall was back on the line. 'Does tomorrow evening suit you after work, Angela? Major Harrington has some business in town and he suggests you could meet up in The Gresham Hotel in O'Connell Street around half past five. How does that sound to you?'

She thought quickly. What did she have to lose? If she didn't like the major or like the sound of the work, then she would just have to think of a reason to turn the position down. But if she didn't give it a chance, she might never know what she could miss. 'That sounds fine to me, Mr Hall,' she said. 'And thank you for thinking of me.'

'As I said earlier, Angela, you're a great worker and I'm happy to recommend you.'

'Thank you,' she said again, delighted to hear what he thought of her work. She suddenly thought. 'Will you tell Major Harrington that I'll be inside, sitting at one of the tables and I'll be wearing a blue outfit.'

'I will pass those details on, Angela.'

It was only after Mr Hall had hung up that Angela realised that she hadn't asked what her prospective employer looked like. She supposed it didn't matter – he was obviously an older man and probably a bit like Mr Hall and the other directors who she had met on numerous occasions over the years.

When Angela walked into the lounge in The Gresham, she spotted an empty table in the corner with a sofa and two chairs, and she walked across to it. She sat down, slipped the long floral scarf from around her neck, carefully folded the silk material, then laid it down on the sofa beside her. She then unbuttoned her pale blue linen coat.

Although it was warm in the lounge, she decided to keep the coat on as it was more formal and suited to an interview. Left opened, it revealed part of the matching, sleeveless dress which had a white bow positioned beneath her breasts. Her outfit was classic without being old-fashioned, and it was not as outrageously short or modern as some of the styles that were now being sported around Dublin. She was surprised that some of the more abstract prints that were now appearing in the windows of Clery's and Switzer's – were beginning to grow on her. But the short styles, she knew, were something that she could never wear.

She reached up to pat the back of her dark, pinned-up hair, checking that no stray wisps had escaped from her neat chignon. She had no hat with her today, as she didn't wear them quite so often as she used to. They were less fashionable these days – and she preferred the freedom of not wearing one.

She sat back in the tapestry-covered sofa, her manicured hands joined in her lap, then she casually looked around the half-filled room. Her slow entrance now would be almost forgotten, and anyone who had stared as she came in would have gone back to their own business. She hated herself for even caring what other people thought, but it was entrenched in her.

A handsome young waiter came towards her now, and she could tell by his confident, almost cocky approach that he had only just spotted her. She could always tell the difference between those who had only seen her sitting down and those who had seen her moving around.

'Good evening, madam,' he said. 'Would you like a menu?'

She glanced down at her gold watch – a gift from her parents for her sixteenth birthday. 'I'm waiting on someone, and we won't actually be eating.'

She lifted her eyes and caught him staring straight at her. His look was so obviously admiring that she had to stop herself from smiling. It was nothing new. Men always stared at her. She could not deny that her face had helped her on many occasions – especially as a child – but there were times when she found it had also been a hindrance.

The waiter bent towards her now. 'Would you like anything to drink while you're waiting, madam?'

She smiled politely at him and said she was fine and would wait until the other person arrived. He went off to attend to people on the other tables and Angela sat back on the sofa and checked her watch again. It was now gone half past five and there was no sign of Major Harrington. She wondered now if she was doing the right thing having agreed to this interview. What if she took an instant dislike to him – and then was offered the job?

And even if she thought he was just okay, it would mean living in the house in very close proximity to him. Perhaps eating with him and possibly travelling around. She realised she would have to think things over very carefully, before deciding.

Several lone men came into the hotel foyer, but none of them glanced around the way people do when they are meeting someone they are not sure of. Then, she saw the young waiter heading towards the door and a few minutes later she saw him walk back in with another man. He was casually holding his tray to his chest whilst chatting with the man who was around average height and of a slim build, dressed smartly in a pinstripe suit. He had greying hair, slightly receding at the temples. He was, Angela thought, not particularly good-looking, but there was something distinguished about him.

Angela wondered if it could be Major Harrington. As they came closer she estimated him to be in his fifties – not much younger than her parents' age – which was younger than she might have imagined someone who was writing their memoirs, and with the title of major, might look. The waiter and the man then stopped dead for several minutes, talking animatedly to each other. Then, the waiter put his tray between his legs to fish out his notepad and pen and write something down. When he had finished the older man said something and they both began laughing quite loudly, causing people to look around at them. Angela wondered if they were friends, but thought it odd that the waiter would behave that way when he was supposed to be working.

Then, the man in the suit consulted his pocket watch and his expression suddenly changed. He said something to the waiter and then both their heads swivelled in her direction. As they came walking towards her, Angela realised that it looked as though this was indeed her intended employer. As her heart started to beat faster, she took a deep breath to steady herself and shifted her gaze to the right-hand side of the foyer as though she hadn't noticed them.

They came to a halt at her table.

'Excuse me, my dear,' the man said, smiling at her, 'am I correct in assuming that you are Miss Tracey?'

She turned towards them now as though surprised. 'Yes,' she said, 'I am indeed.'

'I must apologise,' he said, 'for being late. I met a neighbour outside and we got talking and I quite lost track of time.' He gestured towards the waiter. 'And then Tony and I got into a discussion.' He reached his hand out. 'I'm Edward Harrington. And again – my apologies for keeping you waiting.'

'Oh, there's no need – I haven't been here long,' Angela replied. She went to stand up.

'No, no,' he said, coming round the table towards her. 'Please don't stand up.'

They shook hands and then, still standing, he turned to the waiter. 'I'll have the usual, Tony, and whatever Miss Tracey would like.'

The waiter lifted his notepad and wrote down the order, saying aloud, 'A large gin and tonic.' He looked at Angela and grinned at her. 'I didn't know who you were waiting for. Major Harrington here is a very good customer of ours. I served him the very first day I started.'

'You certainly did,' the major said, 'and very efficient you were.'

Tony winked at Angela, as though they were fellow conspirators. 'We're always delighted to have the major here.'

'Thank you, Tony,' Major Harrington said, smiling, but with a slight tone of dismissal in his voice. 'Now, Miss Tracey – would you like to join me in a gin and tonic or would you prefer a glass of wine or perhaps something else?'

Angela hesitated – she had expected him to order tea or coffee.

He looked from Angela to the waiter and smiled. 'It's Friday after all. Time to relax at the end of the week for those working their way through from a Monday. Don't you agree?'

She looked back at him and something in his eyes made her realise that her answer would carry some weight – and might determine whether she got the job or not. She couldn't say why – but his jollity and openness, and the way he had been with the waiter made her suddenly realise that there was something she already liked about him. Made her realise that she actually wanted this job.

'You're right about it being Friday,' she said, smiling now, 'and I would be very happy to join you in a gin and tonic.' When she saw his face light up, she knew she had made the right choice.

'Splendid, splendid!' he said, clapping his hands and rubbing them together. 'Now, Tony, you can make that two gin and tonics with the usual lemon and ice.'

As the waiter went off with the order, Major Harrington settled himself in the chair opposite her. 'I've heard some very complimentary things about you and your work, Miss Tracey. I believe you have certificates in shorthand and typing and bookkeeping, and are generally very efficient. Would that be correct?'

'Well, I do have certificates, plus general experience in running an office on my own.' She thought for a few moments. 'My typing speed is around seventy words per minute.'

'Seventy words per minute?' he repeated. His eyes narrowed as he considered the information. 'Well, that sounds top notch – excellent. And how are your skills at accounting? I'm afraid mine are rather lacking, and if I'm not careful I tend to get behind with household bills and the like. I really need someone to take over that end of things.'

'Well,' Angela said, 'I have been running the Polio Fellowship office accounts, things like the electricity and heating . . .' She paused to think. 'Paying the coalman, the company that provides the office stationery, the petty cash . . .'

'Excellent,' Major Harrington said. 'Just the sort of thing I was thinking of. We have the tradesmen like the butcher and the coal delivery service and the dry cleaner's. I'm sure you know the sort of thing that makes running a household efficient, and my housekeeper is very good and will help out.'

Angela thought of Mary Ellen Mooney now and the great work she had done over the years for their own family. She organised lists for the butcher shop, the baker's and paid electricity bills for them, dry-cleaning and that sort of thing. It wasn't at all comparable with running a big house in Ballsbridge, but it gave her an idea of what to expect.

'My family have a shop and public bar, and I've helped out there when I've been home.'

'And where exactly would that be?' he enquired.

'Tullamore, in Offaly.'

'Ah . . .' Major Harrington said, 'Offaly indeed.' He pondered it for a few moments, which led Angela to believe it was an area he wasn't too familiar with. Then he suddenly said, 'I have an old chum somewhere outside Birr, haven't seen him in yonks. I wonder how he's doing?'

Angela wasn't sure if he was asking her or talking to himself, so she stayed silent for a while and when he did not elaborate any further, she leaned forward and said, 'I should have mentioned that my shorthand is over one hundred words per minute, and I'm also a qualified audio-typist.'

He looked at her, beaming. 'What can I say? You have a multitude of talents. Exactly what I'm looking for!'

Angela caught her breath, and then waited for him to elaborate on important elements of her new job, and perhaps ask her more questions. It all seemed somehow too easy to her.

'I've just thought of something . . .' His face became animated. 'Isn't Tullamore the town that had half the thatched houses burned down by a hot-air balloon?'

'Yes,' Angela said. 'It is.' She remembered learning about it in her history lessons in school. 'I think over a hundred houses were damaged.'

'Fascinating! Who would think that such an inconsequential place in the Midlands of Ireland would have a hot-air balloon crashing down in the eighteenth century?'

She shrugged and smiled. 'It is surprising, isn't it?'

'Tell me,' he said, 'do you know where the balloon was actually going? And where it had taken off from? After hearing that story I've often wondered about the circumstances.'

Angela regarded him now, thinking that his smiling face and his enthusiasm about the hot-air balloon reminded her of a young boy.

Before anything more was said, Tony appeared at the table with the tray holding the drinks. He set a small frilled white mat on the table and placed what looked like a very large bulbous wineglass on top of it. He then turned to Major Harrington and placed a similar glass in front of him. He then poured Angela's tonic water into her glass, and then started to do the same with the major's until he was halted when the bottle was still half-full when the major held his hand up saying, 'Good man – we won't drown it.'

The waiter immediately did as he was bid and put the bottle back on the table. 'Is that everything?' he asked, looking from one to the other.

'For the time being,' the major said. Then, after Tony had gone to serve another table, he lifted his glass and held it out to Angela. 'Here's to our success as a good working team.'

Angela quickly lifted her glass and touched it against his. 'Does this mean I have the position?' she asked.

He took a gulp of his drink. 'Of course you do!' He said it with some surprise and then he smiled broadly at her. 'I thought that fact was already quite clear. Your credentials are first class and you come highly recommended. And you seem a very personable young lady. The job, my dear, is yours.'

'In that case,' she said, 'I am delighted to accept.' She lifted her glass and took a drink from it. The gin tasted stronger than she had expected, but the lemon and ice made it refreshing. She waited then took another drink and it tasted better. She sat back on the sofa. 'I believe the main reason you need a secretary is that you are writing your memoirs. You must have had an interesting life.'

He nodded. 'I have had a very varied life in many ways – and I would like to get it all down in print for those in the family who follow me. Not my own children, of course . . . I've never been married, you know, and my only brother died young.' He took a long drink from his glass. 'I can't say I didn't have my opportunities, but nothing ever really worked out in the conventional way, as it did for some of my family. I spent twenty years escaping life and responsibility in the army, and that naturally isn't conducive to relationships. And then, when I was discharged, I discovered that I missed the daily routine – was institutionalised, so to speak. Not surprising after years of boarding schools – but that, as they say, is another story.' He smiled at her. 'Of course I found it hard to settle into anything, so to escape that feeling of being displaced, I travelled extensively. I enjoyed most places but there comes a time when you have to come home – wherever home is at that point. Time and years just pass without you really knowing.' He took another drink and then his gaze shifted across the foyer and off into the distance.

Angela sipped her drink, quite startled by the sudden change in her circumstances, and how she had accepted the post without asking for time to think about it or talk it over with someone else. And yet, she had a feeling that had she stalled for more time, she might find the opportunity drifting away from her. When would such a chance come her way again?

It was highly unlikely that it ever would. If she turned it down through fear of change in both her work and living situations, it would undoubtedly become one of those episodes in her life that she would look back on and regret – always wondering what might have been. And while she was much younger than Major Harrington, she could understand what he meant when he had said about time drifting away.

She gave him a sidelong glance now, still trying to work him out. All the years in hospital, often amongst strangers, had taught her about the range of human nature. He was, she had already ascertained, a peculiar sort of man – not just because of his slightly odd looks, or because of his upper-class manner – but odd in himself. And whilst she was intrigued and almost entertained by his forthright ways, she still did not really know what to make of him. She had never met anyone of his age who had been so open about their life so quickly, but she reasoned that was probably because she was going to be privy to all these things when she started typing up his memoirs.

Major Harrington turned back towards her now. 'How soon do you think you can start?'

'How soon would suit you?' she asked.

'I think in the next few weeks. However long it

takes you to detach yourself from the Polio Fellowship office and your lodgings. I know these things can be tiresome, having to wait until someone else is ready to step into your shoes.'

'I don't honestly know how long it will take,' Angela said, 'but I'll let the office manager know on Monday.'

'Splendid! I'll get Mrs Girvin or Eileen to air out your rooms in Moorhill House, and have everything ready for your arrival.' He smiled at her. 'I believe your current accommodation is rather cramped?'

Angela nodded her head. 'Yes, and it can be noisy at times . . .'

He looked at her now – she felt almost studied her.

'You strike me as a young lady who would prefer peace and quiet – and maybe more privacy?'

'Yes,' she said, 'I would.'

'Well, you will have all of that working with me. And time off for yourself. I suppose you go back down the country to visit your family regularly?'

'Mainly at the holiday times,' she said. 'But I have an aunt in Dublin who I visit often.'

'The work you would be doing for me wouldn't require much walking, it would mainly be sedentary. You would be sitting at the desk typing, reading through documents and books for research, using the phone, and of course the household accounting and so forth.'

She presumed he was referring to her bad leg, but she decided not to embarrass him by making an issue of it. 'That all sounds fine,' she said. She was waiting for a suitable opportunity now to bring up the subject of wages. So far nothing had been mentioned, and she was slightly anxious about losing money if her living costs at the house were higher than she was currently paying, and were deducted from her pay.

'Any travel involved for research would be by boat or plane to England, but we can organise that to ensure there's no huge walking involved.'

'The work sounds very interesting,' Angela said, moving the subject away from her leg. She was glad he had brought it up, but did not want them to focus on it more than necessary. 'And I think I would really enjoy the travelling.'

'Have you done much?'

She shook her head. 'No, not outside of Ireland, but I've always wanted to.'

His face brightened, obviously pleased with her response. 'Have you eaten yet, Miss Tracey?'

'I ate at lunchtime,' she told him. She had her usual sandwich, which she had made in the kitchen in her lodgings, sitting at her desk. Today, being Friday, she had tinned salmon and cucumber.

'And then you came here straight from work?'

She told him that was the case and he then asked her if she had any plans for the evening.

'No, nothing in particular . . .'

He waved a hand to catch Tony's attention. The

waiter was wiping a table in readiness for fresh customers. He came quickly over.

'Tony, would you be a good man,' the major said, 'and check if they have a table for two in the restaurant.' He looked at her. 'It would be a pleasure to have your company, and it is of course my treat – but I hope I'm not being presumptuous with your time? You have no other arrangements?'

'No, I'm free and dinner would be lovely.'

The day, she thought, was becoming more and more unexpected. But, it was unexpected in a good way.

The longer she spent with her new employer, the more definite she felt about her decision to take the job. She had not changed her initial views on him being slightly odd, but he was growing on her. She felt there was a kindness about him and that made her feel more relaxed. They still hadn't got around to discussing wages, but she knew if they were eating together she was bound to find the right time to bring it up.

Tony came back and told the major that there was a table for two available whenever they were ready.

'Good man,' the major said, pressing a florin into the waiter's hand. 'I think we'll head in now.' He got to his feet, showing signs of stiffness in his legs as he did so. He then straightened his back and circled his shoulders a few times.

Angela picked up her scarf and put it around

her neck, then stood up. The major moved back to allow her to walk before him. As she did so, she suddenly became conscious of her leg and limp. She straightened her back and then stepped forward, concentrating on keeping her gait as even as possible as they walked across the foyer.

CHAPTER 29

The restaurant was busy, but somehow a table had been found over in a corner. The menu was brought and the major told Angela to choose whatever she fancied.

'I think,' she said, 'it will have to be fish.'

His brow furrowed and then it dawned on him. 'Ah, yes,' he said, his face solemn. 'Of course . . . the Friday fast.' He surveyed her for a few moments. 'You know of course I'm of the other persuasion? The Protestant fraternity – Church of Ireland. That's when I choose to go, of course, which isn't too often these days. High days and holidays. It's just occurred to me now – your family won't have any concerns with you working for me?'

'No,' Angela said. 'I can't see that they would. Besides, I make my own decisions about work and that sort of thing.'

'Excellent,' he said. He halted. 'I hope you don't mind me being personal about another subject?'

She felt a sudden wariness. 'I suppose it depends on what the subject is.'

He lifted his drink now and finished it off. 'Do you mind me asking about your polio condition?'

'No, I don't mind. It's my left leg . . .' For a moment she considered lifting her leg up to show him as she would to a doctor or a nurse in the hospital, but she then thought better of it. It was too personal to show to a stranger.

'Does it give you much trouble?'

'It's improved in the last few years,' she said. 'Since I had the last surgery I don't have to wear the calliper so often. I don't have it on today as I knew I wouldn't be doing much walking.'

'Excellent,' he said. 'I have a young relative in England with polio – a cousin's daughter – affecting both her legs and an arm, so I know how very debilitating it can be. It was because of her experience of it, that I was asked to become involved with the Polio Fellowship.' He paused. 'From my observation of you, your affliction is very little – comparatively, of course – I don't mean to make light of it. You must have had the slightest brush with it.'

Angela felt a sudden surge of gratitude towards this odd, formal man. He had just confirmed her own thoughts about her weak leg – it had indeed improved.

'Thank you,' she said. 'But it is the best it has ever been.' From somewhere inside her now, tears started to appear in the corners of her eyes. She blinked them back. 'I spent long periods of my childhood and teenage years in hospital in Dublin, away from my family, having operations. I think in many ways it has made me more independent.'

'I can see that – and I applaud you for making your way in a very difficult situation.'

Angela smiled and shrugged, feeling embarrassed now at having revealed such a personal thing to someone she hardly knew. She wondered if it might be the gin and tonic.

'Few people are perfect, some are just better at hiding things than others. There are times when I have some difficulty with walking myself. The old back can play up, and at times I suffer from sciatica.' He caught her eye and smiled. 'Bit of an old crock at times – but that's the ageing process for you, while you of course still have youth on your side.'

The waitress came to the table now and she took their orders – Angela choosing cod in breadcrumbs and the major steak in a red wine sauce.

'Would you like anything to drink with your meal?' the waitress asked, holding out a wine menu.

'My thought exactly,' Major Harrington said, taking it from her. He looked at Angela. 'Have you any preference?'

'No,' she said. 'I'm not really a wine drinker.' She had only drunk it on occasions like Christmas or birthdays, and didn't know one wine from another. In truth, she wasn't over-keen on it, but she felt that it was something that most people in Major Harrington's class were used to, and perhaps something that she would have to get to know a bit more about.

He studied the menu. 'I think a white will be

fine,' he said to the waitress. 'Maybe a Reisling?' After she had left, he settled back in his chair, his clasped hands resting on the table and said, 'Tell me about your family, Miss Tracey. Have you any brothers or sisters?'

'I have two sisters, Fiona and Bridget.' After making a mental note not to say anything more that was too personal or too contentious, Angela then proceeded to tell him about Fiona running the bar and shop since her father died, and then she explained about her younger sister's vocation and the convent school where she was an aspirant nun.

'You sound as though you have a very diverse family,' he said. 'I like that. I like hearing about young people who choose their own path in life. You and your sisters sound like independent young ladies.'

Angela thought about Fiona and New York and their mother. 'At the moment,' she said, 'things are not that straightforward.'

The waitress arrived with the wine and an ice-bucket and stand, and the major directed her to pour them a glass each. After she left the bottle reclining in the bucket and went, the major held his glass up again – and repeated the toast from earlier.

'To our working happily together!'

Angela held her glass up too, echoing his words and thinking again how strange a situation she had found herself in tonight. Then as she looked at him, something about his eyes and the way he was gesturing with his hands made her wonder about him. She had seen enough men coming and going from the family bar to recognise the signs. As she watched him lift the glass of wine now and take a good gulp, it occurred to her that not only had Major Harrington probably been drinking all afternoon – but now he actually seemed drunk.

As they ate their meal, the major talking loudly all the way through about a book of old family photographs he hoped to locate in England, Angela was conscious of some of the other diners glancing in their direction. There were two well-dressed women at the next table who kept watching them and, she thought, making comments about them. On several occasions, she noted one of them talking behind her hands, whilst gesturing with her eyes towards Major Harrington. It then dawned on Angela that they were probably speculating as to what the relationship might be between herself and her prospective employer. They probably thought she was his daughter. Their curiosity was so blatant that, when he held the menu out to her to pick a pudding, she deliberately leaned across the table, as though she found every word he said fascinating.

'No,' she said, smiling at him, 'I'm quite happy with what I've eaten, but if it's okay, I'll have a coffee please.'

'Splendid,' he said, beaming at her. 'We'll make that two. The daily puddings aren't always good for the old waistline. I can see, Miss Tracey, you're going to have a good effect on me.'

Angela laughed now, and as she sat back she was conscious of the two gossiping women still watching her. Something about it struck her as funny. She lifted her glass up and took a drink, then she said in a clear voice that could be heard by the next table, 'I'm really looking forward to moving into Moorhill House with you, Major Harrington.'

Then, just as she knew, he held his glass up again in a toast and said, 'And I am happy to have found someone so suitable, so quickly.'

As they were drinking coffee, Angela's thoughts returned to money, and she decided she needed to sort it out before they parted. 'I hope you don't mind,' she said in a low voice, 'but we haven't discussed finance yet.'

His eyes widened and he put his cup back down in the saucer. 'Of course . . . I'm glad you brought it up, I should have mentioned it much earlier. I have already been advised of your current wages, which if I recall correctly was around twelve pounds? I thought if I upped it by say . . . another three pounds a week? Does that sound agreeable to you?' His brow suddenly furrowed. 'Your lodgings and meals would be free of course.'

Angela smiled at him now, delighted. 'That sounds very agreeable,' she said. The pay rise was as good as she had hoped for, and the saving in lodgings and food would make a massive difference.

'Excellent,' he said.

Then, as she watched him go to lift his coffee cup, and then change his mind and lift his wine glass instead, she hoped that he would remember all the promises he had made in the morning.

CHAPTER 30

The following morning Angela woke up feeling nauseous and with a dull pounding in her head. When she turned in the bed she felt dizzy, and wondered what on earth was happening to her, and if she was fit to make it out to the bathroom.

And then it all came flooding back to her. The memory of the night before in The Gresham Hotel with Major Harrington. She closed her eyes and groaned at the memory. How could she have been so stupid as to drink two glasses of wine after a gin and tonic? It wasn't as if she didn't know how it would affect her. When she was younger and new to living in Dublin, she had gone out with a fellow called John, who was an official in the Four Courts who was fond of a drink. After the cinema, they often went to a hotel lounge where he would have a few glasses of beer and she would drink lemonade or shandy or on certain occasions, a Babycham.

On one occasion they met up with friends of John's – two couples – and the men all took turns buying rounds of drinks. One of the men came back with a surprise drink for the women which turned out to be brandy and Babycham. On first sip, Angela wasn't too sure as it didn't seem as sweet as the Babycham on its own. But, as she sipped some more, she got used to it and quite liked it. The other two men followed suit buying the same drinks and by the end of the night, Angela was seeing double. During the night, she had been violently sick, and the following day unfit for work. Since then, she had given strong drink a wide berth – until last night with Major Harrington. What had happened that had made her drop her guard and drink more than she should have, she didn't know. Whatever it was, she thought it was stupid, stupid, stupid of her.

She pushed the stomach-churning thoughts away and concentrated on getting herself into a sitting position in bed, then she swung her legs out and stood up on the cold linoleum floor. She closed her eyes to steady herself, then carefully opened them and made her way over to the deep armchair to sit down and put on her slippers. She then went across to the wardrobe for her dressing-gown and, after putting it on, she lifted her stick which was hanging on the metal door handle. She stretched over to the top of her chest of drawers, for the hand-towel she kept there for her own use, as she did not like using the general towel in the bathroom.

She wasn't too bad after all, she thought when she got out into the hallway. She was slightly fragile and still a bit dizzy, but she knew she was going to be okay. She had, she thought, got off lightly – given that she wasn't used to drinking wine. She used the bathroom, brushed her teeth and washed herself, and then she went back to her room and lay down on the bed. She tried to fall back asleep again but instead she found herself going over the events of the previous night. It had, she remembered, been the oddest interview she had ever been to or heard about. She knew no one who had gone to meet a prospective employer and ended up having dinner with them and drinking far too much.

What, she wondered, had led to things veering off in such a bizarre direction? She then started going over the evening in minute detail – scrutinising things she might have said or done that contributed to it. She went around in circles and each time she reached the conclusion that the way things had turned out had not been because of her. Anything odd that had occurred or been spoken about, had been instigated by Major Harrington. She remembered quite clearly now that she had tried to monitor everything she said, recalled that she had stopped herself from telling him any real personal information. She was quite sure of that. She knew she had told him bits about her family, but nothing more than she had told anyone else who she knew in Dublin. There was, however, one thing that made her squirm with embarrassment when she remembered, and that was when she told him about being in hospital as a child. When she described how she felt on Christmas Day with no immediate family to visit her apart from Aunt Catherine and her husband and son, she knew it had come across as self-pitying.

She was embarrassed even now, thinking about it. Major Harrington had been sympathetic, but looking back she thought he might have felt she was being sorry for herself and resentful towards her parents and sisters, when no family was to blame for the unfortunate circumstances of her catching polio.

She tried to move her thoughts on to something else more constructive, but they kept sliding back to analyse each little scenario. Eventually, she decided that sleep was not going to come so she got up and went out into the kitchen to make a cup of tea. As she was waiting for the kettle to boil, she thought that she might visit her Aunt Catherine over the weekend and tell her about the new job and that she was moving out to Ballsbridge.

She needed to talk to someone about the interview and how she had stayed on to have a meal with her new employer, and maybe confide her fears about working for an older man who she thought drank a lot, probably on a regular basis. She would say nothing to Fiona yet until she had told her employers in the office, and had worked out the actual date she could start out in Moorhill House.

*　*　*

Angela was only in the office on Monday morning half an hour when she received a phone call from Steven Hall congratulating her on her first-class interview and subsequent job offer.

The job was definitely hers! The major had not been so intoxicated that he forgot his promises or changed his mind. Angela sat back in her chair, full of relief, as she listened to Mr Hall elaborate.

'Major Harrington rang me first thing Saturday morning,' he said, 'to tell me how grateful he was that we had suggested you, and how impressed he was with your qualifications and office experience. He thought you were a most efficient and independent young woman. He was also delighted that you showed such an interest in his family research and great understanding of the project.' He paused. 'I believe he offered you the post on the spot?'

'Yes. I have to admit I was surprised,' she said. 'It was all so quick. I thought he might want to interview some other girls or take some time to think it over.'

'Well, as you have probably realised, Major Harrington is not like other men. He has his own views and makes his mind up quite independently.'

'He wants me to start as soon as possible,' Angela said. 'Will that be a problem?'

'Well, we will be sorry to lose you, but we have others waiting in line for promotion, so hopefully it will all work out. I do understand that it's a very quick change in both your work life and living circumstances. Have you any questions or worries about it?'

Angela thought for a moment. 'No, I think it's mainly just organising things here . . .'

'We can sort a van out to move your stuff across the city, so don't worry about things like that.'

'I'm not really worrying,' Angela said. 'I think it's just because everything has been so quick. Hopefully, when I start work it will all work out . . . I suppose it's a little strange going to live with people you don't really know. But I'm sure it will be fine . . .'

'You've nothing to worry about with the major,' he said. 'He is a little eccentric, always has been – but Edward Harrington is a kind man.'

'Oh, I'm sure he is,' Angela said, worried now that she might have given the wrong impression.

'He's very generous too. He has given substantial donations to the Fellowship, and is always there to help out anyone in need.'

'He came across as a very nice man,' she said, 'and the work sounds really interesting. I'm looking forward to it.'

'Any problems at all, you know you can always ring down to the office.'

'I'm sure there won't be any problems,' she said, 'and thanks for the support. I appreciate it very much.' Angela suddenly felt more confident than before. What could go that wrong? The worst thing that could happen was that she didn't like living in Ballsbridge or didn't get on with Major Harrington or like the work. And if that happened – as it could with any job – she just had to leave.

And it wasn't as if she was totally on her own. She had the Fellowship to help out, and if she couldn't find another job, she always had a home back in Tullamore, and there would always be work for her in the shop or bar. She felt a little knot in her chest at the thought. Going home would be a last resort. Especially now that her father was gone. Before that happened she would turn to her Aunt Catherine in Dublin.

There was no point in meeting trouble halfway. She looked around the office now and smiled. She had been happy here for several years, but it was time to move on. Over the coming week she would pack up her bits and pieces in the office and all her stuff in her lodgings. However things turned out, she would give this new opportunity every chance.

On Tuesday evening when she arrived back at her lodgings after work, there were two letters for her. One was from Major Harrington, officially offering her the position of Personal Secretary, and also outlining the terms of her working conditions. She read down, and felt happy when she saw that she only had to give a week's notice should she decide the position was not for her. It also gave the major the same rights with regards to him deciding that she was not suited to the job.

The other letter was from Fiona. She hadn't been expecting to hear from her sister so soon, and felt guilty as it was actually her turn to reply. She had intended to do so over the weekend and post it on Monday, but with the interview and then the visit to her aunt's, and her head being so full of the new job, she hadn't got around to it.

She opened the letter, which was short and to the point. Fiona was asking if Angela could come home the coming weekend to be there with Mam as she had been invited to go to Connemara with a friend. She asked that Angela ring as soon as she knew if she could come, so that she could let her friend know.

On reading it, Angela immediately felt a wave of guilt. She could tell from the tone of the letter that Fiona was desperate for a break, and she knew she needed to reassure her that she would do whatever she could to help. She would ask work tomorrow morning if she could have the day off on Friday and then ring Fiona later. She knew she was owed a few days' holiday, and by rights should use them up before leaving for her new job, so hopefully it wouldn't be too big a problem.

Then, on a sudden impulse, she decided she could not wait another day to reassure her sister. She put her coat and hat back on and walked out to the nearest phone box and dialled the shop number, where she knew Fiona would be at that time of the evening. Patrick answered and, when he realised who it was, said how nice it was to hear from her. Angela asked him how he and his family were keeping, and how things were in the bar and shop.

'Busy enough,' he said. 'We've had a couple of funerals and big matches, which always bring in the crowds.' He told her a few bits of local news and then asked, as he always did, how things were in Dublin and when she told him everything was fine, he asked when they would see her down in Tullamore again.

'I'm hoping to be home this coming weekend.'

'Oh, Fiona didn't mention it,' he said.

'I'm going to talk to her about it now.'

'Well, I'll get her for you now,' he said, 'and I'll look forward to seeing you soon.'

Fiona came on the phone.

'I'm just ringing to let you know that I got your letter,' Angela said. 'And I'm nearly sure I can sort things out at work to get Friday off. They're very busy at the minute, but I am owed some time off, so hopefully it will be okay.'

'Oh, that's great,' Fiona said, the relief obvious in her voice.

'I'll confirm it one hundred per cent tomorrow after I've spoken to the office manager.'

They chatted for a few minutes and then Angela asked how their mother was.

'There are signs of small improvements. She's out of bed nearly every day, but she's still not able to stay up for more than a few hours at a time without feeling tired. Mrs Mooney helps during the day when I'm working, but it's the evenings that are the problem. If I'm working down in the bar, she's on her own for most of the time.'

'Well, I'm sorry she's not getting better quicker,' Angela said, 'but I think you definitely need a break. I was just thinking . . . I've got a half day tomorrow as the rest of the staff are at a big conference. The shop is shut Wednesday afternoon, so why don't you come up to Dublin for a change, and we could have a chat over lunch? I've a few bits of news about work as well, and you can tell me all about your trip to Connemara.'

Fiona thought. 'I suppose I could . . . I just need to sort a few things out with Mam and Mary Ellen, and check I'm not needed in the bar or anything.' She paused. 'To be honest, I haven't been shopping for ages, and I could do with picking a few things up while I'm in Dublin for going to Connemara.' She didn't know what she would tell Angela about going with Michael, but she'd worry about that tomorrow.

'It would be nice for you to get a day away from Tullamore and the responsibility of Mam. Even a day away from the house will make a difference, and you'll have your weekend to look forward to as well.'

Fiona suddenly felt as if a weight had been lifted off her. The thought of a trip to Dublin tomorrow was great. Since Michael had gone away, she was already finding time dragging, and an afternoon out would take her mind off it and give her a bit of a lift.

'Let me check if I can sort things for tomorrow,' she said, 'and I'll ring you back.'

An hour later she rang to say she had organised everything. Mrs Mooney would sort her mother's meal and anything that needed to be done in the house.

Angela had only put the phone down when she received a phone call from Major Harrington enquiring as to when she might be moving out to Moorhill House. She told him that she hoped to be there the week after next, and would ring him as soon as she had an exact date.

CHAPTER 31

Fiona stopped in the doorway of Bewley's Café to take her umbrella down and give it a good shake. She then closed it and secured the press-stud on it. She had an anxious feeling about meeting her sister, in case Angela might not have been allowed the time off work after all. And, she still had to break the news about going away with a man for the weekend.

She had known Michael almost a week now, and in that time she felt she knew him better than any other boyfriend she had ever had. Last weekend they had spent every spare minute she had off from work together, and they had gone to Galway for the day on Sunday. Mary Ellen had come up to the house to cook dinner for Mam and had told Fiona she would spend a few hours with her in the afternoon and in the evening. Michael had stayed another extra night – until Tuesday morning – but then he had to leave as the auctioneer in Clifden was pressing him to come down and see the cottage, before they contacted solicitors and started the searches for deeds and land inventories.

Michael also told her that he would have to phone the airport to book his flight soon. He planned to have about a week in Connemara, to sort out as much business as he could, and then he said he would come back up to Tullamore, to see her before he left.

'To make plans for us to meet again soon,' he told her. 'I don't know how we'll do it, but I know we will.'

Fiona felt something wrench in her stomach every time she thought of him going away, because she could not see a way out of things. He lived in Boston and she lived in Ireland – it was as simple and devastating as that.

'Whatever happens,' she said, 'I'm coming down to see you in Clifden. I don't care how I do it, but I will find a way. I've already written to ask Angela to come home for the weekend, and I'm counting on her to help me out with Ma. We're going to have that weekend together no matter what.'

And so he had gone and Fiona already found herself lost without him. He had promised to ring her either during the day at the shop or in the evenings at home. And he was waiting to hear if her plans to come to join him were working out.

They had to work out, she thought. She could not bear it if Angela let her down the first time she had asked for help. She was trying hard not to feel resentful about the fact that she was in the position where she had to ask for help. That she now found herself wholly responsible for their mother, the shop and the bar was making her feel overwhelmed, and she knew she would have to try not to let it show.

She walked inside, the comforting warmth of the café hitting her along with the exotic smell of freshly brewed coffee. Bewleys Café was like nowhere else that she knew, and in normal circumstances it filled her with a sense of anticipation, of not knowing who she might see or meet or happen to sit beside. They were not the usual clientele she would run into in Tullamore or any of the other cafés or tearooms in Dublin. She loved the old, unusual building and the emphasis being on coffee, although tea was still a strong favourite.

As she walked through the main dining area towards the back where she had arranged to meet her sister, Fiona glanced around her, pushing her fears about the weekend to the back of her mind. This afternoon, she noted, there was a mix of middle-aged married couples and well-dressed female shoppers gathered in groups to chat over coffee and cakes.

There were other tables with men dressed in suits having business discussions plus the usual smattering of single professional males of varying ages who were sitting with a lone cup of coffee, leafing through a newspaper or studying official-looking documents. She passed a girl with curly hair and glasses, whose eyes were fixed on a paperback and who Fiona thought was probably a student. Further along she brushed past a table where a young man who reminded her of Joseph, with long curly hair, sat reading a heavy hardback book and taking notes.

She had just come into the back part of the café when she saw her sister waving to her from a table in the corner. She smiled and waved back and then went towards her. Angela, she thought, looked as lovely as usual. Her dark hair was immaculate, swept up into a loose bun secured with a tortoiseshell clasp at either side of her head. She was wearing a green swing-coat with a black collar and cuffs. She could have stepped out of a fashion magazine, and their mother would have remarked on the outfit using words to describe it such as 'classy' or 'stylish'.

Fiona knew that she looked more like one of the students in comparison to her glamorous sister, but that would not bother either of them. They had long accepted they were different in many ways and that was fine. But, it struck her as she looked at Angela, how very much alike in fashion and attitudes her sister and mother were, and yet how very opposite they seemed in other ways.

'What a day!' Angela said, her brow wrinkled in concern. 'Was it a terrible drive up? I never thought to check the weather forecast before we arranged to meet today. Was the road up from Tullamore very bad?'

Fiona thought her sister's concerned comments about the weather were like something an older woman might say to a younger one.

'It was fine, I took it easy,' she said, taking her raincoat off and putting it on the back of her chair. 'The road was quiet enough, I just had to concentrate on the blooming potholes.'

Angela tutted and shook her head. 'They need to do something about those country roads.'

A young waitress wearing a long black dress and white pinafore and small cap came to stand at the side of their table.

'What do you fancy?' Angela asked. 'Would you like a sandwich or maybe soup?'

Fiona thought. 'A sandwich would be fine for me. What are you having?'

'I think I'll have the same.'

They took a few minutes choosing their sandwiches from the menu and then they both ordered coffee made with hot milk.

After the waitress had gone, Angela leaned forward. 'This is my treat, you've had the expense of travelling up.'

'Not at all,' Fiona said. 'I'll get it.'

Angela said back straight in her chair. 'I insist. You've come up here today because I suggested it, so I'm sorting it.'

Fiona knew there was no point in arguing. 'Okay,' she said, smiling. 'That's very good of you.'

She had warmed up now, so she took her scarf off and settled herself into the chair. She still had the anxious feeling she'd had walking into the café.

'Well,' she said, 'any news?'

Angela looked at her. 'Yes,' she said, smiling. 'I

do actually. I have a few bits of news of my own but first – I've explained the situation to my office manager and she's fine about me having this coming Friday and Monday off, so I'll be able to come down.'

Fiona felt the tension suddenly ease, as if a great weight had been lifted off her. 'Oh, that's great!' she said, nodding her head and smiling. 'I'll let my friend know I can go down to Connemara.' She felt tears of relief at the back of her eyes and had to blink them back.

'I'm sorry I didn't get a chance to reply to your first letter,' Angela said. 'I've been really busy and I was planning to do it when the next one arrived.'

Fiona waved her hand. 'Don't worry, I understand. It's just that I really, really want this weekend away . . .'

'I understand,' Angela said. 'And you deserve it, all the work you do. And it's awful the situation you're in, Fiona – that you have to do all this organising to get a few days away. It must be hard for you, not being able to just go ahead and make your own plans.'

'It is,' Fiona said. 'It's not what I imagined was going to happen. It's not what any of us imagined. This is the first time I've been away since . . . since Daddy died.'

'I know it is, and it will be good for you to have a break in Connemara.' She paused. 'Have you arranged for Patrick's sister to work in the shop on Saturday?'

'Yes, that's all sorted. She'll have someone minding her children for the day. She's one of the few people Mam is happy to have in the shop, but she's not available very often as she has her own family and Patrick's parents to cook for.'

'I'll go down to the shop and check everything is okay, so don't worry. You go and enjoy yourself and don't even think about it.'

There was a silence, during which Fiona waited for Angela to say something else. She realised she needed her sister to say something about New York. She wanted her to at least acknowledge that all her plans for going to New York had been totally wrecked.

'Is it a friend from school?' Angela asked. 'The person you're meeting?'

Fiona was thrown off guard. For some ridiculous reason, she hadn't anticipated that Angela would ask her anything about Michael. Her mind had been so full of organising her mother for the weekend that she hadn't taken time to consider it.

When she got no immediate reply, Angela's face started to flush. 'I didn't mean to ask about your business. I was only chatting. You don't have to tell me if you don't want to. I don't mind . . .'

Fiona shook her head. 'No, I don't mind you asking . . .' She could hear her voice faltering. 'It's just I don't want Mam to know.'

She had planned to tell her mother she was meeting up with an old school friend, because

362

she knew there would be a massive row if her mother thought it was Michael O'Sullivan – or any other man. She didn't want to lie to Angela, but she could not really anticipate what her sister's reaction might be.

She decided to take a chance. 'It's actually a man I've recently met. He's thinking of buying an old cottage in Connemara and he wants me to go down there for the weekend.' When she saw the look of surprise on her sister's face she quickly added. 'I know it must sound terrible, going away with someone I've only met. But he's the nicest, most decent man I've ever met, and we'd be staying in separate rooms . . .'

Angela raised her eyebrows and smiled. 'You don't need to explain anything to me, Fiona. It's your own business. Did you say he's buying a cottage in Connemara?'

'It's a bit of a long story,' Fiona said. 'He's an American.'

'Ah well, I suppose that makes it slightly less surprising. If anyone is going to buy an old Irish cottage, it's more likely to be an American.'

Fiona bit her lip. 'To be honest, I wasn't sure if I was doing the right thing, going to meet him. But then I thought why not? I know it's taking a bit of a chance meeting someone you hardly know away from home, but he's very nice and respectable. He talks a lot about his mother – she was born in Ireland. Everything he says gives the impression that he's from a good family.'

'I'm sure he is. I'm sure you would know whether he was a decent sort or not.'

Fiona was surprised that she felt comfortable telling Angela so much. Just talking about Michael made him feel closer to her. But then, when Angela said nothing for a few moments she wondered if she might have said too much. Then she began to worry that Angela might decide to tell someone else, and it could get to the wrong people. People like her mother or her aunts or uncles who would undoubtedly be scandalised and advise her not to go.

And it wasn't just older people who were easily shocked, there were plenty of the girls at school who would think along the same lines. It might be the Swinging Sixties in London where anything went, but things were still the same old way in Tullamore.

She felt her face flushing now and she glanced up at the calm expression on her sister's face, trying to read what Angela really thought about her going off with a man she had only met. But she could not tell.

'You won't say anything to Mam about it?' Fiona said. 'It's easier if I let her think it's one of the girls from school.'

'I wouldn't dream of saying anything to anyone,' Angela said. 'It's your own business. And he does sound like a lovely man.'

There was a pause then Fiona said, 'He is, but

I suppose it would be better if I could talk to someone who knows him really well.'

'Your own instincts are the best about people. I've found that out over the years, being up in Dublin on my own.'

Fiona felt a little stab of irritation at Angela, for referring to the time she spent in hospital. What, she wondered, had that to do with her telling her about Michael O'Sullivan? It felt as though Angela was just making a point. She wrinkled her brow now as though she didn't quite understand what her sister meant.

'You learn to trust your own instincts, especially when you have to mix with different people—' Then, as if something had just occurred to her, Angela suddenly stopped. She looked at Fiona and smiled. 'So, this American – where did you actually meet him?'

'In the bar at home,' Fiona said, glad the conversation had returned to the main subject. She then went on to relate the story about him meeting Maggie and her friend who suggested that he ask in the pub if they had a spare room. And she explained how they had all sat chatting together with Patrick that first night and how she had cooked Michael breakfast.

'Well,' Angela said, 'Maggie is a nice person and I think that she wouldn't have encouraged him in any way if she didn't feel he was decent.'

'I thought that too,' Fiona agreed.

'And did Patrick have any opinion about him?'

'They seemed to get on very well. Patrick said he thought he seemed a nice, friendly lad. He said he was intelligent and well-educated, but not too intelligent that he couldn't talk to ordinary people.'

'I would put a lot of stock on what Patrick thinks. I know he can be quiet, but he's certainly no fool when it comes to people. He has a good way with the customers – I've seen and heard him manage the most awkward and difficult people in the bar.'

'I don't know what we'd do without him. He's been fantastic since Daddy died. He's there every morning to open the place and is there most nights, even when he's supposed to be off, to lock the place up.'

'He has always been like that,' Angela said. 'He obviously loves his job.' She tilted her head to the side, thinking. 'Although you would wonder at him devoting all his time to his work and to his parents. He seems to have little time for his own life.'

'I suppose so,' Fiona said. 'But I don't know how we would manage without him.' She shrugged. 'We wouldn't – I wouldn't.' Her voice cracked now and then she felt her face crumpling and knew that if she didn't catch herself she was going to dissolve into tears. She turned away now, rummaging in her pockets for a hanky.

Angela leaned towards her. 'Are you okay?' she asked in a concerned voice.

Fiona looked up and tried to smile, but she couldn't, and her gaze moved downwards again.

She suddenly felt upset – a mixture of missing her father again and missing Michael O'Sullivan. And if she was honest, she just felt generally sorry for herself. She cleared her throat and then rubbed the hanky to her nose. 'I'm fine,' she said.

Then, a group of two men and two women came towards them carrying bulging shopping bags and dripping umbrellas. They had to turn sideways to squeeze between the tables and Fiona moved her handbag to the other side of the floor away from them, then stood to pull her chair in further to allow them more space to pass by. They thanked her and one of the men smiled first at her and then at Angela. She noticed, without any feeling, that his eyes lingered for a moment longer on her sister, as men's eyes usually did.

He then laughed and said something along the lines of it being the wettest day he'd seen in a long time – a day so wet that you wouldn't put ducks out in it. She smiled back at him and said she hoped the rain would ease off soon, and then sat back down in her seat, glad as the distraction had shifted her away from the threat of tears. She turned back to lift her handbag and put her hanky away.

Angela reached over and touched her hand. 'Are you sure you're okay?'

'Honestly,' Fiona said, giving a proper smile, 'I'm fine. It's just that occasionally things get on top of me, missing Daddy and then thinking of Mam and what's going to happen.'

'She's a lucky woman that you care so much about her, but you need to look after yourself too. This shingles thing with Mam won't last forever. She'll hopefully be up on her feet soon and able to go back to work.'

Fiona shook her head and sighed. 'I don't see any great improvement in her these last few weeks.'

'Has there been any more talk about getting someone else to work in the shop and the bar?'

'Not at the minute. I keep hoping Mam will suddenly get better and come back to work.'

'What a pity she wouldn't agree to Joseph working there.'

'Don't mention it,' Fiona said, rolling her eyes. 'That was a big mistake, not taking him on, and I'm sure he and Patrick would have got on great.'

'Oh, they would have. They would have been great friends.' She gave a little sigh. 'Anyway, he seems well settled in his new job in England, so thankfully it turned out okay for him.'

Just then the waitress appeared at their table with the tray with their sandwiches and drinks. They sat in silence waiting until she had finished putting everything on the table.

'I'll take the bill, please,' Angela said, holding her hand out.

The waitress gave it to her, saying, 'I'll check again when ye've finished, in case ye want anything else.'

Angela smiled and slipped the girl a coin. 'You're very good,' she said. 'We'll let you know if we want anything else.'

The waitress thanked her and then moved on to another table.

Fiona looked at her sister, wondering at her self-assuredness. It was almost like sitting with her mother, except that Angela had a nicer way with the waitresses. Her mother was polite, but Angela was genuinely friendly with them.

'If you want anything else like a cake or a pudding after you've finished your sandwich,' Angela said to her, 'then let me know and I'll order it.'

'If I manage this I'll be doing well. But thanks anyway,' Fiona said. As she looked down at her substantial sandwich, she thought it was kind of Angela. Her office wages weren't probably that big, but their parents had always given her a monthly allowance to help with the rent of her room and the higher cost of everything in Dublin. It was easy to tell by the style of her clothes that she paid a lot of money for them. Any time people complimented her on a suit or a coat and asked where she bought it, Angela usually told them Clery's or Switzer's in Grafton Street which were the best shops.

Fiona went shopping with her mother to Galway or Dublin before Easter and Christmas every year, and her father had always given both of them money for their new outfits. But her mother never suggested that they meet Angela to go clothes shopping in Dublin. Any time Fiona herself had ever suggested it, her mother had put her off, saying not to mention it to Angela, as she would be working and that a day's shopping would be too hard on her leg. Angela obviously managed to go around the shops by herself or with her friends. Fiona now felt a pang of guilt that she had never pushed the point with her mother, instead of just accepting what she said. She became aware of her sister's gaze on her and she felt awkward, as though Angela had been able to read her thoughts.

Angela picked up a quarter of her sandwich, and took a little bite. 'Just thinking about Mam – she needs to start making some changes. And she needs to realise she's not the only one who misses Dad . . . losing him affected all our lives.'

'She's lonely at times,' Fiona said. 'Her friends have stopped calling because she told them she would ring them when she feels better, but she never has the energy. It's a vicious circle. And she finds the house empty without Daddy.' She looked over at her sister now. 'She's mentioned a few times about you moving back home for a while . . . just to help out until she's back to her old self.'

'I'm quite sure she would like it if I came home to help,' Angela said sharply. 'But that's not going to happen. I am not coming back to stay in Tullamore.' She took a little breath. 'I'll come next weekend while you're away, and I'll try to help out other weekends, whenever I can. But I'm doing it for *you*, Fiona. You need a break away and you deserve it after all you've done for her.' She took a sip of her coffee. 'And when I'm down in Tullamore at the weekend, I'm going to talk very straight to Mam and tell her that she needs to take someone else on. I'm going to point out how good you've been to her, but how she can't depend on you forever. She can't expect you to take Daddy's place.'

'But she'll be completely on her own if I'm not there . . .'

'Well, she'll have to do something about it, because I won't be moving back to Tullamore. I didn't grow up there and I just don't feel as at home there as you do. But that's not the only reason – I've actually just accepted a new job.'

Fiona looked at her. 'When?'

'This morning.'

'Where will the job be?' For a moment, she wondered if the job might be nearer to Tullamore – within travelling distance – somewhere like Mullingar or Portlaoise.

'It's in Ballsbridge.' Angela's voice was even and calm.

'In an office?' Fiona asked, trying to sound as though it was a casual chat. Trying not to sound resentful that her sister could make choices so easily, without having to consider anyone else.

Angela's hand came up to tighten the back of her earring. 'It's a clerical post – personal secretary. It's a live-in position, so I'm going to be moving out to Ballsbridge. I'm going to be working for an army major, typing up his memoirs and helping him with research and his household accounts.'

'It sounds interesting,' Fiona said. 'And you're going to be living in a lovely area too. You've really fallen on your feet!'

'It's a much better salary and I won't be paying any rent, so I'm going to tell Mam that I don't need her help any more – she can use the allowance they've always sent me to pay for full-time help in the shop and pub.' There was a silence, then Angela leaned forward and put her hand on Fiona's. 'Things will change, Fiona. I'm sorry I'm not moving back to Tullamore but it just wouldn't work out. I'm not close to Mam the way you are . . .'

'I disagree with you, Angela,' Fiona said. 'I'm sure she would love you to come home.'

'She's scared, Fiona. She's scared of being on her own and taking responsibility for everything, and she hopes you and I will take over things, the way Daddy did.'

'I can't leave her.'

'When she gets better you have to leave her to lead her own life,' Angela said. 'For your own good and for Mam's. You're not doing either of you any favours. Eventually the time will slip away and so will your plans for New York – or whatever else you want to do.' She paused. 'Are you still as keen on going as you were last Christmas?'

Fiona thought of Elizabeth and the big apartment in Park Avenue. It no longer seemed as real to her. She could not picture all the places Elizabeth had described. She could not picture the children, Page and Tommy, who she was supposed to look after. Nothing came to her mind. It all seemed like a distant dream.

Then she thought of Michael who would be going back to America soon. Tears began to prick at her eyes. 'I don't know – so much has happened, I can't think straight about it anymore.'

Angela put her coffee cup down now and reached her hand across the table. 'Well, we'll get the shop and the bar sorted, and then if you still decide you want to go to New York – even for a year or two – I want you to promise me you'll just go.'

'But the job with Elizabeth will probably be gone!'

'Then you can always get another job.'

Fiona looked at her sister, wondering if any of this was possible. Just six months ago she had been full of hopes and dreams about the future. Full of confidence that they would all come true. And then, they had all come crashing around her in the most unimaginable way.

Was it possible, she wondered, that she could start planning for the future again?

CHAPTER 32

As she drove along the main street in Clifden, watching out for Foyle's hotel, Fiona felt a surge of excitement at the thought of seeing Michael O'Sullivan.

On her journey there she hadn't really known what to expect of Clifden – she just knew it was a town an hour or so outside Galway. The narrow, winding drive out from Galway seemed to take her longer and further into a landscape with a constantly changing patchwork of mountains and colourful fields and lakes. And, although it was a pleasant, sunny evening and she enjoyed the glorious scenery and the purple of the heather and the brilliant pinks of the fuchsia – all she could think of was reaching Clifden and reaching Michael.

It occurred to her several times, especially as she got nearer, that they had not discussed room arrangements. She knew they were staying in Foyle's Hotel, because he had told her during one of their phone calls. She had been in the shop at the time, and was afraid to ask him about the sleeping arrangements in case anyone came in and overheard her, but it had been the uppermost thing she had thought of every time the weekend came into her mind.

Whilst she would have loved to have been brave and share a room with him, the more she thought about it, the more fearful of the whole thing she grew. She had no real sexual experience at all, and she knew he would soon find that out. She had kissed all her previous boyfriends – some more passionately than others – and had gone a little further than kissing with Paul Moore. But although he had been more confident and keen to go further again, he had always been respectful of her and stopped when she became uncomfortable.

She knew Michael was a similar type of person, and would understand that she wasn't ready for such a big step when they had only known each other such a short time.

There were more people around the small town than she expected, and there were quite a few cars parked along the street. But then, she thought, it was Friday evening and she supposed it was likely to be their busiest time. She spotted the hotel sign across the road, and she was just indicating to pull over when she saw him, sitting on a bench outside, reading a newspaper. He was wearing a denim shirt with lighter faded jeans.

A tinge of excitement ran through her when he saw her and waved – and she knew with certainty that he had been sitting there – just passing the time – waiting for her.

When she came out of the car he came straight over to her and swept her up in his arms. 'I have missed you very, very much.'

Fiona felt her heart skip a beat as he bent down to kiss her full on the lips, and she was glad she was in this small town on the edge of the Atlantic – far away from anyone who could possibly know her. She closed her eyes, and she kissed him back.

'I've missed you, too,' she said.

Then, when she drew away, he said, 'Here, I'll carry that for you,' and took her green flowery weekend bag off her shoulder and put it over his.

She shook her head and smiled, pleased with the gentlemanly gesture and amused that he didn't care that he was carrying a woman's bag.

As they walked through the foyer, heading towards the check-in desk, Fiona slowed down, not quite sure how to word the question she needed to ask. 'Do you mind me asking . . .' she could feel herself blushing, 'what you've booked for us?'

'Two rooms,' he said, taking the keys out of his shirt pocket. Then he smiled and winked at her. 'I didn't want to be presumptuous or to tarnish your good reputation. So you will be safe under lock and key if that's what you want.'

'You're very kind, sir,' she said, grateful that he had made light of it. She could feel her face still hot with embarrassment, but she was beginning to feel the anxiety about the sleeping arrangements starting to seep away. 'I have money with me,' she said. 'So let me know what my half costs.'

'It's all sorted,' he said, handing her one of the keys. 'My treat. And I told the lady on the desk that we are down here on business looking at property. Which, I believe, is fairly accurate.'

'Okay . . .' Fiona wrinkled her brow in mock confusion, then she started laughing. 'So are we auctioneers or are we wealthy clients buying loads of houses?'

'Neither,' he replied, leaning in close to her. He gestured to the middle-aged woman behind the desk, who was looking at them over her small glasses. 'I'll tell you all about it when we get upstairs to our rooms.'

The rooms were next door to each other, he told her as they walked upstairs and along the corridor. On the way he told her a few interesting snippets he had learned about the history of the hotel so far, then he pointed out the intricate detailing on the wooden bannister and the coving on the high ceilings.

'And you are a lucky lady,' he told her, 'because you have your own bathroom adjoining your room, while I have to walk down the corridor to a shared one.'

'Oh, no,' she said, stopping to look at him. 'That's not fair. You're the tourist, you should have the best room.'

'Well,' he said, 'I like to think I'm a gentleman first, and the way I've been brought up, women have the first call on these things. I don't think my mother would be too impressed if I took the bigger and better room.'

As they walked along the corridor, Fiona wondered what Michael's mother looked like and what type of person she was – and whether they would like each other if they ever met. From what he had told her, she had a feeling she would.

Then, she fleetingly wondered what Mam would think of him. She honestly didn't know. She would definitely think him a bit too casually dressed, and she wouldn't be too gone on his long hair. But, Fiona thought, she would certainly like his good manners and the fact he was an architect would probably help her see past the denims and hair.

But, Fiona did not dare to speculate on what her mother would think, if she knew she was in a hotel with a man she hardly knew.

'Okay,' he said, coming to a halt outside room number sixteen, 'this is mine, and you're next door at number eighteen.'

She waited, but he didn't move. 'Aren't you going to let me have a look inside your room?' she asked, smiling up at him.

He raised his eyebrows. 'Are you sure?'

She looked to the right along the corridor and then to the left. There was no one else around. 'Go on,' she said. 'I'll risk it.'

He unlocked the door and let her in past him to look. It was an average-sized room with a double bed with a blue-striped bed cover and matching curtains.

'Okay,' she said, 'let's go and look at mine.' She had half expected him to come in behind her and kiss her again, and she felt slightly disappointed that he hadn't.

They went to the next room, and she unlocked the door. She went in a few steps then she turned back and smiled at him. 'I think it's okay if you bring my case in.'

'As long as you don't forget you invited me,' he said light-heartedly.

'Oh!' she said, wandering into the middle of the room. 'It's absolutely gorgeous – and big. Really beautiful.' She turned around, looking at the peaches-and-cream bedspread and curtains, and the feminine cream floral wallpaper. The wardrobe and dressing-table were dark wood with spindly, delicate legs.

'I'm glad you like it,' he said, putting her case down on the stand by the door. 'They had rooms of different sizes, so I asked to have a look at a few of them, and I took a guess that this one would be your taste.'

'I love it,' she said, 'and I'm going to feel really spoiled here.' She turned around to face him and his eyes met hers. Then, all the light banter suddenly faded and they both just stood there looking at each other.

'I missed you,' he said, 'I couldn't stop thinking about you from the minute I left Tullamore.'

'And I missed you,' she said, 'from the minute you left.'

She did not know who moved first, but suddenly they were in each other's arms and he was kissing her face and her hair and then he took her face in both his hands, and gently kissed her lips. The kisses grew harder and deeper and as it went on she felt as though a part of her was leaving herself and, somehow, falling into him.

Eventually, Michael eased away from her, slightly breathless.

As his arms moved to release her, she had to move to steady herself, and then she started to sort her tousled hair back into place.

He cleared his throat. 'We need to call down to reception and let them know what time we want dinner.' He looked at his watch. 'It's six o'clock now – what do you think?'

Something in his eyes drew her back to him, and she found herself wrapping her arms around his neck, stroking his hair and drawing his head down so his lips were on hers again. They kissed for longer this time and this time their bodies came closer, and she shivered when she felt his hands moving up and down her back through the soft cotton of her blouse.

And then, without even realising she was doing it, her hands moved down his back and then she gathered the soft denim shirt in one hand and the other moved upwards to stroke his bare skin. They moved closer to each other and Fiona gave a little gasp as his hands found her hips and he pulled her closer still, until she could feel the hard ridge in the front of his jeans pressing into her. Her insides gave a little jump as she realised what it was.

She knew she should retreat now, not encourage him any further, but instead she wondered then how it would feel if the layers of clothes separating them were gone, and they could hold and touch each other. The thought made her suddenly quiver and when he felt it he stopped and held her tightly to him.

'Are you okay?' he whispered, kissing the side of her head.

She could not speak, so she just nodded and buried her face in his chest.

'Shall I go downstairs and let them know about dinner, and leave you to get settled here?' he asked. He hands moved down along her hair, but he now seemed a little different, slightly distant from her, and she instinctively knew he was afraid of things moving too quickly – going too far.

He was taking responsibility for them both, which was decent and good, and doing all the right things she had wanted him to do. She had wanted them to be sensible and careful. And yet – there was another part of her that was becoming stronger – that did not want him to stop any of the things he had been doing – the kissing and the touching.

A part of her that wanted him to go on and on, until they reached something or somewhere she was not even sure existed.

She stood leaning against him for a few more minutes, feeling his heart beating beneath the denim and the warmth of his tanned skin. Breathing in the faint, clean scent of him.

And as he shifted and loosened his hold on her, she wanted to tell him not to leave this lovely hotel room, which he had chosen with care, in case it broke the spell of whatever was now between them.

Instead, she looked at him and said, 'I suppose we should get moving.'

He moved towards the door, smoothing down his shirt, his jeans, his hair. Making himself look presentable for the woman in the glasses at the desk downstairs. 'What time?' he asked.

She shrugged. Food was the last thing on her mind just now 'Seven?' she said. 'Is that too early? Half past seven?'

'I'll see what she says.' He put his hand on the door, and then he looked back at her. 'Do you think,' he said, 'that it's possible for people to fall in love in such a short time?

Fiona looked at him. 'I think it might well be possible.'

They were sitting in the dining room later when Fiona remembered the conversation from before. 'Okay,' she said, smiling at him. 'You were going to tell me something about us not being auctioneers or millionaires – so what are we?'

'This is according to the lady on the desk.' He started to laugh. 'Let me think. . . I can't remember the exact words . . . it was something like – we are the "typical Americans who come looking up old family properties – like John Wayne in *The Quiet Man*".'

'*What?*' she said. 'Have you actually seen the film?'

'Of course,' he said. 'I told you my mother's family are Irish. Everybody in America who is Irish has seen *The Quiet Man*.'

'So you're Seán Thornton then?'

He nodded. 'And you must be Mary Kate.'

They both started to shake with quiet laughter.

'She didn't even see the insult in it,' Michael said. 'She said it with a big, friendly smile.'

'She probably thinks you're a millionaire.'

'I wish I was, but unfortunately there is a limit on it.' He reached over and put his hand on hers. 'We'll go out to the cottage tomorrow and have a look and you can tell me what you think.'

Later, as they sat across from each other at small table in the lounge, she looked over at him. 'Did you sort out your plane ticket back to America yet?'

'Yes,' he said. 'Things with the cottage are going slower than I thought – the solicitor is still having trouble locating the deeds. I rang the airport and, if I pay a bit extra, I can have it extended for another week or two.' He caught her eye, and she saw the serious look on his face – which told her he had thought this out carefully. 'It's not just the cottage – I thought it would give us some more time as well, to work things out.'

She looked back at him, holding his gaze for a while without speaking. She turned things over in her mind, thought about what this meant for them both. 'I'm glad,' she said, 'because what you said upstairs earlier about wondering if a week is long enough to know about your feelings . . . well, this gives us time to be sure.'

'You've got it,' he said.

'Can I ask you something? It's about money. All this must be costing you a fortune.' She gestured around the lovely big room – the flowing curtains edged with tassels, the marble fireplace, the antique tables and carefully selected pieces of furniture. 'Not to mention changing your plane ticket. I don't want you going bankrupt because of me.'

He shook his head. 'As I said earlier about the cottage, money isn't unlimited, but it's not a huge problem. I more or less work for myself, and if I'm prepared to work between Boston and New York I can pick up work easily.' He smiled. 'And I do have savings and—' he leaned forward, talking low, 'I received a legacy from my grandfather a few years back. He left me the house I live in, in Boston, and another small one between me and Greg. We rent it out, so we have a monthly income from that as well, so I suppose I'm pretty okay.' He grinned. 'I'm not exactly a Yank with millions, but I guess I'm lucky enough compared to others. It gives me choices.'

'That's great,' she said. 'I was worrying that it might be a problem.' She halted. 'But you must let me pay something towards this weekend. I can afford it. I don't have the same money as you, but I have more than enough to get by for holidays and things.'

'Okay,' he said, 'you can buy us dinner tomorrow night. How does that sound?'

'It's a start,' she said, smiling back at him.

An older German couple came to the next table with a map, and after a few minutes they asked, in fairly good English, if Fiona or Michael could tell them the best route to Cork. They got chatting and the man told them that he worked for one of the wine companies in the Rhineland. Michael was really interested, saying it was one of the places he had read about and that he hoped in the future to do a tour of Europe – especially, France, Spain, Italy and Germany. He also wanted to visit Czechoslovakia, as he had heard about the beautiful old buildings in Prague.

'If you like old architecture, you must come to the Rhineland,' the man said, 'and see our famous castles – some of them go back to the twelfth century. They are the romantic castles that are described in . . .' He put his head to his hand, thinking.

'Fairy tales!' his wife said, smiling.

'I've seen pictures of them,' Michael said, voice full of enthusiasm. 'They are beautiful delicate works of art.'

Fiona listened as they talked, and she pictured the life she might have with him if this romance of theirs worked out. He would want to travel to places she had hardly thought of, and he would want to keep learning about things. It was all she had hoped for when she imagined meeting someone out in New York. In fact, she thought, it was much better.

Another month would make a big difference as well. If they spent a lot of that time together, they would get to know each other quicker than most ordinary couples. Surely, she reasoned – another month would tell them whether or not this was going to work?

They already knew a lot about each other – he had spent days with her, hanging around the shop and bar. He had got on well with Patrick and Mrs Mooney. His family were Irish Catholic. She didn't know if he went to church regularly or not – she hadn't thought of it – but that wouldn't be a problem. She knew, without having to ask, that he would do whatever she wanted while he was in Ireland that would make things easier for her.

He was not only unbelievably attractive and clever – he was also kind and thoughtful. He had taken nothing for granted; he had booked and paid for two rooms so she would not feel under pressure. And he had understood about small-town curiosity in Ireland, and had made sure everything was discreet to protect her reputation – both in Tullamore and now here in Clifden.

They would have this time together until Monday. After he had sorted out the business of the cottage, he could come back up to Tullamore and stay in one of the rooms above the bar for the next few weeks. Bridget would be home at the end of the month for the summer, and he could meet her. She could take him up to Dublin to meet Angela. Her mother hopefully would get better too, and she would bring him back to the house to meet her properly.

She would explain how it was between them with Mam – omitting this weekend in Clifden, of course – and say they were going to take things slowly, keep in touch. She would say that Michael would be coming back again if the cottage worked out. Mam would be most impressed when she explained more about his work and the houses he owned back in Boston.

She could see it all unfolding in front of her now – how it just might all work out.

The German man went to the bar and came back smiling broadly, with a waiter behind him carrying a tray with four glasses of Riesling wine. They sat together and they told Michael and Fiona about all the places they had visited in Ireland, and about a recent trip to Paris.

Afterwards, Michael ordered four Irish coffees, which the Germans had never heard of, and they sat talking and drinking for the next couple of hours. Michael told them about the cottage and they were very interested in it, and the man asked him about the price of property in Ireland generally.

It was heading to midnight when Michael looked across at her and gestured with his eyes that maybe it was time they headed upstairs. When she nodded, he finished his drink and then stood up.

'We'll wish you nice people a goodnight now,' he said, shaking hands with them both. 'And hopefully we'll see you tomorrow and hear more stories of your travels.'

They walked upstairs together, his arm around her shoulders, and along the corridor to her room.

He kissed her lightly on the lips and said, 'It's late now, and we're up in the morning to go out to the cottage, so I'll say goodnight.' He moved back to look into her eyes. 'I've had the most wonderful night with you, and I'm so happy we're going to have longer.'

She put her arms around his neck and drew him closer to her again. 'The night isn't over yet,' she said quietly. She kissed him, and then she took the room key from her handbag. She unlocked the door, then – without checking whether anyone else was around – she took his hand and brought him in behind her.

She locked the door and drew him into the middle of the room. Then she turned back to face him. 'I want you to stay with me here tonight. I want us to sleep in the same bed.'

His eyes searched hers. 'Are you sure?' he said. 'I wasn't expecting this . . . I don't want you to feel you have to.'

'I don't feel I have to do anything,' she said. 'I'm asking you to stay, because it's what I want. I feel as certain about this as I've felt about anything important in my life.' She touched his cheek. 'Whatever happens to us in the future, tonight is going to be one of the most beautiful memories I will ever have. And, I know you staying with me is going to make it even more beautiful.'

'Are you sure?' he repeated.

'I'm not going to say I'm not nervous,' her gaze shifting downwards now, 'because it's my first time being with a man . . .'

There was a small pause and then he said, 'Well, I'm deeply honoured that you've chosen me. You have no idea how much that means to me.'

She instinctively knew that he had more experience, had probably slept with the girl he had mentioned – Kim. And maybe others. But she didn't want him to have to explain. He was a little older and had led a different life. What mattered now was what they had between them.

'I just know that if you go back to your own room now,' she whispered, 'I will only lie awake here all night, on my own, regretting that I wasn't brave enough to do this – and I don't want to feel that regret. I would much rather feel the happiness I feel with you instead.'

He pulled her close to him and kissed her again. 'I'll do everything I can to make sure you never have any regrets about us.' He touched her cheek. 'I love you, Fiona, and I would never do anything to hurt you.'

She hugged him tightly, and then she took his hand again, and led him towards the bed.

CHAPTER 33

Angela travelled down on the train to Tullamore on Friday evening as arranged. Patrick was waiting at the station to drive her the short distance home.

'I could have walked,' she said, 'instead of putting you out.'

'I know,' he said, smiling at her. 'But I knew you were bound to have a bag or a case, and I thought it would save you carrying it.'

'Ah, you know me too well, Patrick,' she laughed, handing him the heavy weekend case and the bulging bag she had over her shoulder, secretly relieved she wouldn't have to carry them.

'It's a lovely sunny evening,' he remarked, 'and the weather forecast is giving it good for the whole weekend.'

As they drove along, he told her that Fiona had already left in her grey mini for Clifden a few hours earlier. 'The break will do her good,' he said, 'and it will be nice for her to see her friends. It's supposed to be sunny down in Connemara as well.'

Angela agreed, realising that Fiona had given the impression she was meeting girlfriends for the weekend to him, as well as Mam. It was just as well, she thought, to say the same thing to everyone. It was no one else's business.

When she arrived in the house, her mother was downstairs in the kitchen with Mary Ellen Mooney waiting for her. It had been a good few weeks since she had been home, and she thought her mother looked slightly better than the previous visit, but she was still in her dressing-gown and Angela was taken aback at how much older her greying hair made her look.

'You're looking great, Angela,' Mary Ellen told her. 'But you always do.' She had gone over to the oven. 'There's a nice dish of cod and parsley sauce there for you both, and some lovely floury mashed potatoes and vegetables.' She put her hat and coat on. 'I'll be in early in the morning to do the fires and the washing and all the usual things.' She paused. 'Are you down in the shop tomorrow?'

'No,' Angela said. 'Patrick's sister is helping out, but I'll probably drop down to see that everything is okay.'

'Well,' the housekeeper said, 'if there is anything else, you can let me know.'

After Mary Ellen had left, they sat down immediately to eat.

'You do look well, Angela,' her mother said, 'and that's a lovely twinset you have on.'

'Thanks,' Angela said. She noticed her mother didn't actually look at her as she was speaking, and her voice sounded a little strange, as though

391

she had a slight slur in it. She lifted her glass of water and took a sip. 'Are you still not up to going to the hairdresser's, Mam?'

Nance shook her head. 'No,' she said, 'Just the thought of anyone touching my head . . .'

'What does the doctor say?'

'He just said shingles can take a long time to go.' She halted. 'That reminds me, I need to take my tablets. I keep forgetting about them.' She put her hand in her dressing-gown pocket and felt around, and came out with three different pills. She put them in her mouth and swallowed them down.

Angela noticed her mother's nails were bare of polish, and were almost grey-looking. She couldn't remember the last time she had seen her with unkempt hair and without nail varnish.

The next morning Angela woke to sunshine and she was surprised when she looked at her watch to see it was half past nine. She heard a noise downstairs and listened, and realised it was Mrs Mooney rattling around at the range. Then she caught the smell of bacon frying and realised that the housekeeper was probably waiting for her to come down and eat with her.

When she came downstairs, the housekeeper was sitting drinking a cup of tea. She had another cup and saucer set on the table, and she immediately poured one out for Angela.

'I have some bacon and sausages in the oven for

us,' she said, 'and a bit of black and white pudding. It will be ready in another five minutes.'

'You're very good,' Angela said. 'That's one of the things I look forward to when I come to Tullamore.' She lifted her cup and took a drink of the lovely hot tea. No one, she thought, made a cup of tea as well as Mary Ellen Mooney.

'Have you any notion of coming home to live in Tullamore again?'

Angela shook her head. Mrs Mooney had been asking her that same question for years. 'No,' she said. 'I'm too used to Dublin now.'

Mary Ellen nodded her head. 'I suppose you are.'

Angela knew the housekeeper was fond of her, and always had been. There was no agenda behind her question, it was simply that she liked her and wanted to see her more often. For a moment, she thought she would tell her about the new job, but she stopped herself.

Mary Ellen leaned forward. 'When you've finished your tea – would you mind going up and having a look at your mother. I was up earlier on and I'm not too happy with how she is.'

'What's wrong?' Angela asked. She lifted her cup and took a few quick mouthfuls to finish it, then got to her feet. 'I'll go up right now.'

'I'm sorry now, making you go up the stairs again with your leg. But I don't feel she's just right. I'll turn the oven down now, and I'll come up with you.'

They went up the stairs, and down the corridor to her mother's room. Angela tapped on the door but there was no sound.

'Just go in,' Mary Ellen said. 'She was the very same earlier on. She takes a minute to come round.'

Angela opened the door and went across the room to the bed. Her mother was lying very still on her side, facing the wall. She touched her on the shoulder, and when she didn't move, she then gave her a small shake. She had to do it three times before her mother responded with a small moan.

'Mam?' she said. 'Are you all right?'

Eventually, Nance opened her eyes. They were dull and glazed. 'What is it?' she said.

'I'm just checking you are all right. You don't seem very well.'

'I think if we get her up and on her feet it might help,' the housekeeper said. 'I've seen her a bit like this before – certainly not as bad as this – but maybe if we get her moving.'

Angela leaned forward and put her arms under her mother's to prop her up. When she was in a sitting positon, she gently pulled her towards her. 'Come on, Mam,' she said, 'let's get you up now. You could do with going to the bathroom. A little wash might help you to wake up.'

Between them, they got Nance sitting on the edge of the bed, then they went on either side of her and eased her into a standing positon. Then, she moved with them, one slow step at a time until they were out in the hallway.

Angela noticed that her mother had not really spoken, and still seemed half-asleep.

'Good girl, you're doing fine,' Mary Ellen said, as though she were praising a child. They went towards the bathroom door. 'Can you stand on your own now, Nance? Will we see if you can manage on your own?' The housekeeper looked at Angela now, and gestured with her eyes that they should let her go.

They stood back, and watched as Nance took a few steps, swaying as she went along. And then, as she reached the bathroom door, she seemed to go to one side and then suddenly her legs went from underneath her and she crumpled with a thud on the floor.

Angela and Mary Ellen had rushed forward to catch her, but she was already down before they could.

Angela knelt beside her, talking to her and trying to bring her round, while the housekeeper ran the cold tap on a face flannel which she then pressed to Nance's forehead.

Eventually, Nance's eyes fluttered open again. She stared at Angela, and then she closed her eyes, and it dawned on Angela that she did not recognise her. The vague look in her eyes gave the impression that she did not recognise anything around her.

Somehow, between them, they got Nance up

again and Mary Ellen suggested they get her sitting on the toilet.

'She's not fit to know if she needs to go or not,' she said to Angela. 'You go on, and I'll wait with her. I'm used to it with all the children I've looked after.'

Afterwards, when they walked her back to the bedroom, she had difficulty putting one foot down.

'I think she twisted that foot when she went down,' Mary Ellen whispered. 'That's all she needs.'

They settled her back in bed, then Angela gestured to Mrs Mooney that they should leave the room. When they got outside she said, 'I'm going to call the doctor. I know it's a Saturday and you're only supposed to ring in emergencies, but there's something seriously wrong. I think how she is qualifies as an emergency.'

'I think you're right. This is worse than anything I've seen.'

Angela rang and the doctor's wife said he was out on a call, but she would tell him the minute he arrived back at the surgery. Mary Ellen put their breakfasts out while they were waiting for him to come, but they only picked at it, listening for any sounds upstairs. As they sat, Angela thought of all the breakfasts she had eaten with her father at this table, listening to his cheery banter. Those mornings, she thought, were her happiest memories of home. She would never have them again.

★　★　★

396

Everything happened quickly after that. After spending five minutes with her, the doctor sent for an ambulance.

'I've no idea what it is,' he said to Angela, 'so I'm not going to take any chances. She needs to have some blood tests taken and some other tests done.' He shrugged. 'It could be a number of things – possibly a small stroke – but only the hospital can establish that.'

The day went by, with Angela and Mary Ellen going back to the house at midday. At that point there were still no results on the tests.

'She's in the best place,' Mary Ellen said.

Before the evening visiting in the hospital, Angela insisted that they both go for their evening meal to the restaurant in Hayes Hotel. 'You're not cooking for us tonight. You haven't had a break all day.'

'Sure, what else would I be doing?'

She made a few noises of refusal, but Angela knew she was delighted to be taken out and treated. Their father had always taken Mrs Mooney and Patrick out for a meal with the family at Christmas, and Angela knew the housekeeper had always enjoyed it.

She ordered them both a sherry before the meal, and then Mrs Mooney had a glass of stout with her meal while Angela had a glass of white wine. As they ate their roast pork and stuffing, they both began to relax and chat.

'Thank God Fiona's not here,' Angela said. 'She's

had enough to deal with – too much. I'm glad I was here and not her. That I was able to spare her the worry of this at least.'

'She's had a lot on her plate since your father died,' Mary Ellen said. 'She's too young to have all that on her shoulders. If things were right, your mother should have been up and about and back to running things at the shop and the house.' She shook her head. 'She's been like a different woman since she took that damned shingles. She was just getting back on her feet after your father died and then she went down like a deck of cards, and she's never been right since.'

'She went down like a deck of cards this morning,' Angela said. 'She really hurt her ankle.'

'That will heal – and the doctor said it isn't broken so we can be thankful for that at least. It's whatever is causing all the tiredness and the confusion is the big problem.'

Afterwards, Angela ordered a coffee for herself and an apple crumble and custard for Mary Ellen.

They began to talk about Fiona again.

'I hope she's having a great time down in Connemara,' Angela said. 'I believe it's lovely down there.'

'Kind of wild,' Mary Ellen said. 'Some English people we had for bed and breakfast once told me that it was like the highlands in Scotland. They would know, they were the kind that had travelled all over.' She thought for a few minutes. 'He's a lovely fella, the American . . .'

Angela's head jerked up. She looked across the table. 'You've met him?'

'I did, a few times over last weekend. He stayed around to see her every chance they got. And you don't need to worry, she told me that you knew about her going to meet him.'

Angela smiled now. 'Oh, thank God! I was afraid of putting my foot in it, because she said my mother doesn't know.'

'Sure the vague way your mother was recently, God help her, she wouldn't have known if it was Christmas Eve or rice pudding – no disrespect to her or anything. Fiona could have gone off with Bluebeard himself and she wouldn't have known.'

Angela looked at her and tried not to laugh. She knew it was awful finding something funny in the midst of such a serious situation, but there were times when Mrs Mooney came out with the most outrageous things without realising. How such a saying could be anything but disrespectful she did not know.

When they went for the evening visit in the hospital, her mother was sleeping. Angela left Mary Ellen at her bedside and went down the ward to see if she could speak to one of the nurses.

A young, efficient sister checked a few details with her first, asking her who lived at home with their mother and who would be there when she went home.

Angela felt the nurse was watching her carefully and listening to everything she said, as though weighing her up. Eventually, she seemed satisfied, and she then brought Angela into the office.

'I don't want anyone hearing us,' she said, closing the door behind them. 'I just wanted a private word with you.'

Angela felt a pang of alarm. 'Is it something serious?' she asked. 'Has she had a stroke or a heart attack?'

'No, no – nothing like that,' the nurse said. 'But it is serious enough in a different way.' She went over to the desk and lifted some notes on a clipboard. 'I was just looking at her file earlier.' She looked up at Angela. 'I'm afraid we had to pump your mother's stomach out this afternoon.'

'Why?' Angela said. She had never heard of this happening, and had no idea why it would be done.

'Because she had taken an overdose of her medication.'

Angela's hands flew to cover her mouth. 'Oh, my God!'

'The doctor said if she had taken just a small amount more it could have been very serious. She might not be here with us tonight.'

'Is she going to be okay?'

'We're still waiting on tests coming back from the lab, but it looks like she had been taking sleeping tablets, Valium and Codeine, and a mixture of other painkillers. When she came in earlier today it was obvious that she had been taking a much higher dose than she should have been of everything.'

'Oh, my God,' Angela said again. 'I know she got mixed up now and again, and was forgetting to take them but . . .'

'Well, it looks like this morning she took them all at once,' the ward sister said. 'Do you mind me asking, had nobody at home noticed a change in her moods or behaviour?'

Angela's mind was turning over, trying to remember all the things that Fiona had been telling her over the past months. 'Yes, we had,' she said. 'Especially my sister who lives with her. She said my mother was very tired all the time – extremely tired. But she had a bad case of shingles which started back around February, and she never really recovered from it. She was in bed for weeks with the painful rash, and she never came back to herself. In fact, she was getting worse.'

'That is a terrible thing,' the nurse agreed. 'I had an uncle who had it on his face, and he ended up losing the sight in his eye.'

'Thankfully, it wasn't on her face, it was around her back.' Angela sighed. 'The other thing is that my father died just after Christmas – not even six months ago. She was very low after that, and then she took the shingles.'

The nurse nodded sympathetically. 'I'm sorry to hear about your father.' She paused. 'Your mother has obviously been going through a very difficult period both physically and with depression, and it looks as though she has become dependent on some of the medication.' She looked down at her notes. 'According to her GP, she has been on Valium and sleeping tablets for the last year.'

Angela's eyebrows shot up. 'A year?' she said. 'But that was before Daddy died. That was when everything was okay.'

'Well, I'm sorry to tell you, dear,' the nurse said, 'but your mother was obviously not well even before that. She was having trouble sleeping and suffering from anxiety.'

'We had no idea,' Angela said. 'We all thought it was the shingles – all the tiredness and everything.'

The nurse went back to the notes. 'She was also very confused, and it may well be she was also suffering side-effects from the medication.' She looked up and shook her head. 'Some of the side-effects are worse than the initial illness. The sleeping tablets can change people's personalities, make them argumentative – even violent.'

'She's not been as bad as that,' Angela said. 'My sister would have told us – it was mainly the tiredness. And I suppose looking back, she was very depressed.' She thought back to the way Mam had been with them during the funeral, the rows about Aunt Catherine. The edgy, awkward way she had been for a long time.

'Well, that's maybe the thing we need to get to the bottom of,' said the nurse. 'Sometimes people repress things, keep them in for years and then it suddenly comes back and overwhelms them.'

Angela nodded, trying to digest it all. 'How long will she be in hospital?'

'Certainly over the weekend, possibly longer. The doctor will see her again in the morning, and we'll see how she is then. Hopefully, the worst of the medication will be out of her system and you might see a difference in her. She's off everything at the moment, so we'll see how she goes.'

Angela looked at the ward sister now and nodded her head. 'Thank you,' she said, quietly. 'I appreciate you taking the trouble to explain all this to me – because we would never have known. It helps us to understand what has happened to my mother, to help her – and I'll make sure to explain it to my sisters and aunt.'

'It's not that unusual, you know,' the nurse said. 'And believe it or not, with Valium, in a lot of the cases it's women your mother's age.'

As she walked along the corridor back to the room, Angela suddenly had a feeling of deflation. As if all the energy was draining out of her. She had only spent one day back at home and all this had happened.

But then she thought of Fiona, the day in Bewley's when she broke down and cried, feeling the strain of looking after her mother. No wonder she had cried. Angela didn't know how she had managed all these months on her own, with Mam like a complete stranger, and never knowing what kind of mood she was going to be in. She realised now that Fiona had probably only told her half of what had gone on.

Weighing it all up – even the way things were

between her and her mother – Angela was still glad she had been there when this happened, instead of her sister. She realised now that had it gone on for much longer, as the nurse had said, something much more serious could have happened to her mother. And that, after all that Fiona had done for her mother, it was the last thing she needed.

CHAPTER 34

On Monday morning Patrick drove Angela to the hospital to collect her mother.

Before she went to the ward with the bag containing her mother's clothes, she spoke to the ward sister again, who told her that they were delighted with the improvement in Mrs Tracey.

'We have a very good doctor who has spoken to her several times over the weekend and she now understands what has happened to her. To be honest,' the nurse said, 'it has given her a real fright. When the worst of the last medication had worn off, and she'd had a good sleep, the doctor sat with her for nearly an hour, and explained what had happened to her.'

'And how did she take it?'

'She has asked to be taken off all medication,' the nurse said. She pursed her lips together. 'It won't be easy, because her system is used to them, but it's probably the best way for someone like her. I would imagine that underneath all this, she's actually quite a strong lady.'

'Oh, she is,' Angela said. 'She certainly is.'

Angela went down the corridor to the ward,

405

apprehensive as to what she might find, and she was surprised when she saw her mother, sitting on the edge of the bed, chatting to a woman who had a dry mop and was cleaning the floor. Although her face was drawn and pale, Angela thought her mother looked and sounded brighter than she had in a long, long time.

She turned and when she saw Angela her face lit up. 'This is my daughter, Angela,' she said to the cleaner. 'The middle girl – the one I was telling you about who is working in Dublin.'

When the cleaner left, Angela said, 'I've brought the suit and things that you asked for. I've been talking to the nurse and she said we can go now as soon as you are ready. Everything has been sorted. Patrick is parked outside, waiting for us. He said not to worry – he brought the newspaper with him if it takes a while. His sister is in the shop and his brother-in-law is keeping an eye on the bar, but there shouldn't be too many in on a Monday morning.'

Nance came over to her and put her arms around her. 'Thank you, Angela. I know this has been a terrible weekend for you and I'm so sorry.' Her voice wavered. 'And I'm very grateful for all you've done.'

Angela was taken aback, as her mother rarely showed any signs of emotion. 'It's okay,' she said. 'I'm just glad you seem to be a lot better.'

Her mother moved to sit back down on the end of the bed. 'I've had an awful fright,' she said. 'The doctor told me about the medication, and how I'd taken an overdose.' She looked up at Angela. 'I want you to know it wasn't deliberate – I don't remember any of it.' She shook her head and sighed. 'And it's not just this weekend. To be honest, there are weeks and months that I can't remember.' Tears came into her eyes. 'I don't know what has happened to me . . .'

Angela felt a wave of pity for her. This woman who had never shown her any real care or understanding. But she looked so frail and so vulnerable – so unsure of herself. 'You just need to take your time, Mam. Give yourself a chance to get back to normal.'

Nance looked up at her. 'The doctor has told me that I need to stop looking back to the way things used to be with your father. I have to accept that the old life has gone, and start living in the present now, and to start planning for the future.' She shook her head. 'I don't even know where to start . . .'

'Just take it a day at a time, Mam,' Angela said. 'Give yourself a chance to recover from this and see how you feel when all the medication has gone out of your system.'

'You're right,' her mother said. She stood up now and lifted the bag of clothes. 'I'll just go down the corridor to the bathroom, and get myself washed and dressed and we'll go home. We don't want to keep Patrick waiting.'

A short while later she came back along the

corridor and into the room, and Angela noticed that she was walking more slowly than normal.

'Are you okay, Mam?' she asked.

'I think I did something to my ankle the other night,' she said. 'It's still feels a bit sore.'

'Are you allowed to take anything for the pain?' Angela asked.

'No, no,' she said, waving her hand. 'I can have aspirin or Paracetamol, the doctor said. But it's not that bad, I'm not going down that route again. Not after what's happened.' Then she stopped and looked at Angela. 'I should be ashamed of myself complaining about a twinge in my ankle to you.'

Angela looked back at her.

'All the operations you've had, even when you were a little girl . . . when I think of the pain you must have been in at times. I was lying last night, thinking about it all. All those years when . . .'

Angela's heart suddenly started to pound, and she felt a rage starting to build up inside of her. She put her hand up and shook her head. 'Don't, Mam,' she said, in a quiet voice. 'Don't say anything else. This is not the time or the place to talk about this. What happened in the past can't be sorted now.'

Her mother looked at her. 'Is it that bad, Angela?' she said.

Angela looked at her mother then she turned away. 'We'd better go,' she said. 'Patrick is waiting for us.'

*   *   *

When they got back to the house Mary Ellen had the fires lit and had some steak and onions in a dish in the oven. She made them tea while the potatoes and vegetables were finishing off and told them to go and sit at the fire in the sitting-room.

Angela noticed that, as she drank her tea, her mother's hand was shaking. She knew she was anxious about what had happened, and probably felt even more anxious having to explain it all to Fiona when she returned this evening. Then, it occurred to her that the shaking might be caused by withdrawal from some of the medication, as the ward sister had explained that this was one of the possible side-effects that could last for a few days.

When she finished the tea, Nance stood up and walked over to the mirror above the fire.

'Would you look at the state of my hair?' she said. 'The grey roots – they must be two inches long.' She turned to look at Angela. 'I'm mortified. I can't believe I was going around like that.'

'Well, you were only in the house,' Angela told her. 'It's not as if anybody really saw you. You can get them done in the next few days.'

Nance looked back at her reflection again. 'The hairdresser's closes on a Monday, but sometimes Maggie O'Connell goes out to houses – to people who can't make it into the salon.' She went over to the small table where the phone was. 'I'm going to ring her now.'

She dialled the number and spoke for a few

minutes, then she hung up. She turned back to Angela. 'I'm in luck. She says she can be over for three o'clock.' Her face moved into a small, uncertain smile. 'At least I'll look decent for Fiona coming home. It might give her a nice surprise.'

CHAPTER 35

On the appointed Monday morning, the blue van went slowly down the row of houses then came to a halt outside one of them. 'I think this is the right place,' the driver said, looking at the name engraved on the red brick wall. 'There can't be two by the name Moorhill House.'

'No,' Angela said, looking around, 'I suppose not.'

As he turned the van into the driveway, Angela felt her heart quicken. Everything was much bigger than she had expected. She had lain awake in bed the previous night, wondering what her new home and workplace would look like, but she had not imagined this.

The van came to a halt at the front door. The driver turned the engine off and then looked at her. 'Some place, isn't it?' he said, pushing his cap back further on his head to scratch it. 'And you say you're going to be working here?'

'Yes,' she said, in a distracted voice, waiting for him to get out and go to the door. She was feeling anxious now and slightly overawed.

'I'll get your boxes and bags,' he said, getting out now. He went around to the back of the van

411

and opened the doors, then he started lifting her two suitcases and the boxes tied with stout string which contained her belongings out onto the gravel path.

She got out of the vehicle and came to join him, keeping one eye on the door of the house. Presumably, Major Harrington or one of the staff had heard the van coming in and would come to greet her. She waited until the driver had emptied the van of all the bags and boxes and then she picked up the smaller of her suitcases. She stood until he was finished, waiting for him to go to the door.

The driver closed the van doors with a bang. He lifted one of the boxes and went to the door. 'I'll leave them here on the doorstep for you,' he said. 'It'll be handier for bringing them in.'

She realised then that he wasn't going to ring the bell and explain to whoever answered who they were, and that he wasn't taking in her belongings. Surely he didn't expect her to do it herself? She put her hand in her coat pocket and felt for the two shillings she had ready to give him as a tip. She felt so annoyed at him leaving her stranded that she now didn't think he deserved it.

Then, she heard the door of the house opening and she turned to see Major Harrington standing there.

'Ah, Miss Tracey!' he greeted her, a warm smile on his face. 'I'm so glad you arrived safely.' He came towards her now, his arm outstretched.

He shook her hand and then turned to the driver and shook his as well. 'Be a good man,' he said, 'and bring those items inside for us. I'll get my right-hand man, Jim Girvin, to lend you a hand taking them down to Miss Tracey's room.'

'No problem now, sir,' the driver said, suddenly stirred into action.

'Bring the boxes first. It would probably make sense to stack them in Miss Tracey's office until she's ready to go through them, and that will leave more room for unpacking her cases.'

Angela felt a wave of relief as she listened to the major taking charge of the situation. She thought he handled things so very easily. He was nice to people and, in return, they seemed more than happy to help him.

Major Harrington turned back to Angela. 'If you want to come with me, we'll find Jim to lend a hand, and then I'll show you where your rooms are.'

Angela followed the major into the large, open hallway, taking in her surroundings as they moved across the tiled floor towards the marble split staircase. She caught a smell of cinnamon and deduced that someone was baking scones or some sort of cake. Then, she was distracted when a door opened on the corridor to the right of the staircase and a tall, fair-haired man, possibly in his early forties, dressed in overalls, came out.

'Ah, Jim!' Major Harrington said. 'I'd like you to meet Miss Tracey, our new secretary.'

Jim smiled at her. 'I hope you find everything to your liking. If there's anything else you need, just let me know.'

Angela thought his accent sounded as though he was from Northern Ireland or one of the counties up that way. She went towards him with her hand outstretched. 'That's very good of you,' she said, 'but everything looks fine to me.' They shook hands.

'Jim Girvin works in the garden and on general maintenance of the place,' the major explained. 'His wife, Alison, oversees the cooking and the housekeeping, and we have a younger woman, Eileen Sweeney, who helps with laundry and suchlike too. I'll take you down to the kitchen to meet them shortly.' He turned back to the gardener. 'Miss Tracey has just arrived and there's a fellow outside with her belongings. Would you be a good chap and give him a hand bringing them in?'

'No problem,' he said, striding towards the door.

'Oh, and Jim,' the major went after him, 'I meant to tell you we had a phone call about the panels for the back fence. They hope to deliver them in the afternoon.'

'I knew well they wouldn't come this morning,' Jim said. 'That crowd are the most undependable you could meet. They never deliver when they're supposed to. Do you remember we had trouble with them before when they brought the wrong size of wood for the garage door?'

'Really?' Major Harrington said, looking surprised, as though it was the first time he had heard it. 'Doesn't sound a good recommendation – we shall have to keep an eye on them for future reference.'

'We'll see how they go this afternoon,' Jim said. 'And if they're no better, we might think of taking our business somewhere else.'

'Absolutely, Jim. No argument there.'

It struck Angela how easily the two men spoke to each other and she thought it was obviously the major who set the tone for the working relationships. He had been just as friendly and nice to the waiter in the hotel, she remembered. He was, she thought, someone who enjoyed other people's company regardless of their background.

Whilst the men walked back towards the front door discussing the unreliable company, Angela took the chance to have a discreet look around the hallway. Her gaze moved to the red-patterned inlaid carpet in the middle of the hallway, the consul table decorated with two matching vases of cream and pink lilies, the paintings on the wall. Then she looked at the red carpet going up the stairs to the turn in the landing where another smaller table stood holding framed photographs alongside a golden statue of a Grecian-type lady. The staircase split into two more sets of stairs to the right and left, which led to the upper floor.

Whilst Angela thought the house was beautiful, her overriding thought was how she would tackle these stairs every day.

The major came back towards her now. Then, as if reading her thoughts, he said, 'Did I mention that your accommodation is downstairs?' He shook his head and smiled. 'I can't remember everything we discussed that evening in the hotel . . . old memory isn't what it should be at times.' He raised his eyes to the ceiling and shook his head. 'Of course the wine didn't help . . . I thought it was best for you, save your leg going up and down those damned stairs.'

He had drunk so much that evening in The Gresham that she wasn't surprised he had forgotten all the details of their conversation. But she was surprised he had mentioned about drinking too much, and it made her feel that he wasn't a totally lost cause. Most drinkers she knew did everything to avoid mentioning the problem. She was also glad to note he was completely sober this morning.

She smiled at him now and said, 'Thank you.' She should have known. He had been so understanding about her leg that she should have known he would have thought about this, and not leave her in the embarrassing position of having to bring it up.

'Practicalities, my dear,' he said, slowly walking along the hallway again. 'Practicalities. We all have to adjust things to suit our needs. I'll have to consider moving downstairs in the future myself. The damn stairs play havoc with the old back and knees at times, especially in the winter when it's much colder. Could do with an elevator in the place, but there's no likelihood of that happening. We'd have to tear the place apart and it would cost a king's ransom.' He shrugged. 'Who knows, I may have to consider selling the place when that time comes. When I'm old and totally decrepit.'

'I wouldn't think that's something to worry about for a long time,' Angela said.

He gave a little chuckle. 'Very kind of you to say so, my dear.'

They walked further down the left-hand side of the staircase, and down three steps.

She noticed the major glance at her to see how she was managing but, when she did so easily enough, he said nothing.

He stopped at the first door and opened it wide so she could have a clear view of the room. 'This is your private sitting room and office.'

Angela caught her breath at the thought of having her own private accommodation. It was much more than she had imagined. Much more than the small, dark room she had been used to in the city. The major stood back to let her move to the door to look in.

'It's lovely!' she said.

It was a good-sized, bright room with two tall windows which faced the front of the house, and it was further brightened with white-painted panelled walls, which were decorated with gold-embossed wallpaper and pale green silk curtains. Surrounding the white marble fireplace there was a comfortable-looking green velvet sofa and two matching armchairs, and a glass-topped coffee table.

A large desk with a tooled-leather top stood over by one of the windows, with a typist's swivel-chair. On top of the desk was a grey Olivetti typewriter, which Angela noted was a newer model than the one she had been using in the Polio Fellowship office. There were other more decorative items around the room such as polished wooden tables and plant-stands, and a large, glass-fronted bookcase which looked as though it had been emptied for her.

'This is perfect,' she said. She had three boxes of books which would fill the top shelves, and a box with her typing files which could go in the shelves below.

'I'm glad you're happy with it.'

'I do, it's lovely and bright.' She looked around, feeling slightly overwhelmed and not knowing quite what to say. 'I love the colours . . .'

'Most of the rooms are bright,' he said. 'It was one of the few things I insisted on when I bought the place. I can't stand dark and dreariness in a house. We have enough of it in our lives without creating it for ourselves – especially when winter comes.' He looked at her, his face solemn now. 'I dread November, when we have only months of dark mornings and dark evenings to look forward to. I can't work in the garden as it's too cold and the ground is too hard. Everything is on hold until the spring comes and lightens things up again.'

'There's always Christmas,' Angela said. 'That brightens the winter up.'

He nodded. 'Of course, and for young people like yourself there are all the parties and the celebrations.'

She paused. 'Things will be different at home this year with my father's first anniversary coming so quickly afterwards. There won't be much in the way of celebrating.'

'Of course,' he said, 'that's very understandable. The first year of loss is always hard, but hopefully each year will get a little easier.'

The conversation came to a halt as Jim and the driver of the van came down the hallway towards them carrying the boxes with Angela's things.

The major waved them into the sitting room. 'You can leave them here – over by the window.'

After they left, they moved back out into the hall. 'Your bedroom is next door,' Major Harrington said, gesturing towards it, 'and the bathroom for your use is just down the corridor on the opposite side.'

Her bedroom was as bright and nice as the sitting room, with similar décor and curtains, and much better than the one she had in Dublin or even back home in Tullamore. Her mother would love this house, she thought, and wondered if there was a possibility of her mother visiting here. According to Fiona, she was gradually getting back to her old self, and was now back working a few hours every day in the shop.

'This is all perfect,' Angela said, 'and much more than I expected.'

'Good, good,' he said, 'we want to make sure you are comfortable here.' He held a finger up now as he thought of something. 'We have a television set in the main sitting room at the front. I've become quite addicted to it – never imagined I would at all. I held out from having one installed for a while, but now I can see what they were all raving about. You're welcome to watch it any time. There's a listing in the newspapers every day.'

'That's very kind of you,' Angela said, trying not to smile at the thought of him just discovering television.

'You will have to make the house your own home now,' he told her. 'And we have enough room to ensure you have your privacy. Don't want you to think that we live in each other's pockets. Out of your working hours, you can, of course, come and go as you please.'

She was suddenly conscious of it being Monday, when she would be working her way through a pile of filing back in her old office. She looked at her watch and saw it was half past eleven.

'When would you like me to start?' she asked. 'I'm ready whenever you are. I can unpack later.'

'There's no rush,' he said. 'Take some time to settle in – we can discuss where things are up to with the research in a while.'

The men came back with the last box and her cases, and Angela, feeling delighted with everything, had a change of heart and gave the driver the tip she had kept for him.

'I'll leave you to unpack,' Major Harrington said, 'and you can come down to the kitchen when you're ready and I'll introduce you to Mrs Girvin and Miss Sweeney.' He smiled. 'We have to keep on the right side of the housekeeping staff as I would never manage to hold this old place together without them.'

Major Harrington went out with the two men, and Angela closed the sitting-room door behind them and then turned to look at her room once again. She smiled and clasped her hands together. She had a good feeling about Moorhill House. This was a new start for her and nothing, she decided, was going to spoil it for her.

She was unpacking the last box of books when Major Harrington came back, his face quite serious. 'I hope you don't mind, Miss Tracey, but I have an important question for you.'

She looked at him, wondering what could be wrong. 'Would you prefer tea or coffee? Mrs Girvin asked me to check.'

She smiled in relief. Hopefully, she would get used to his odd manner. 'Tea would be lovely.'

They went down the corridor on the other side of the staircase to the kitchen and Angela was introduced to the two women, who she found to be nice and friendly. Eileen Sweeney, she thought, was around the same age as herself, and had a room upstairs in the house. In the office, most of the women were older so it would be nice to have younger company to go to Mass with.

She thought she wouldn't mention Mass to the Girvins as she wasn't sure whether they were Catholic or not, because the name wasn't one she was familiar with. Being from the North and working for an Englishman, they could easily be Protestant.

The kitchen reminded her of the one at the family house in Tullamore, only much bigger. It had green-painted dressers lining the wall filled with crockery and glassware, and a long scrubbed pine table which she reckoned could easily seat over a dozen people.

'It would be preferable if you bring the tea up to the library,' the major said to Mrs Girvin. He smiled. 'Did I detect the smell of freshly baked scones earlier?'

'You did,' she said. 'I thought Miss Tracey might be ready for something after her move out to the house. I'll bring you some with the tea.'

In the library there were three shelves of books which Major Harrington told Angela had information about his family in, going back to the seventeenth century. The problem was, he said, that although each of the books contained similar details, some of the information was contradictory. There were also other books which contained references to people or land that he had never heard of, and that needed to be followed up.

Angela, he hoped, would go through each book and note down the information contained in each. She suggested that she then type it up making a carbon copy so they could both go through the notes together. He thought this was splendid and said it would save them constantly lifting the heavy books. Some of his family had lived in Cheshire and some had lived in London, and there were more books, documents and deeds pertaining to the Harringtons and other related families over in England.

Eileen Sweeney came in with the tea and scones and, whilst they ate and drank, the major continued to talk Angela through the project. He explained about his intention to leave behind a comprehensive history of his family that could be easily understood for future generations of the family.

'A lot of the information to date is dry and dusty,' he told her, 'relating more to buildings and events as opposed to real people – which is where my interest lies. I know there are some damn good stories about interesting characters in our families. The ones we hear most about are the great and the good – the clergy, the army men and the like. But we also have gamblers, thieves and vagabonds – and that's the sort of thing I am going to include.' He suddenly stopped. 'It won't be unnecessarily salacious of course. I'll handle any sensitive information about illegitimacy and legal wrangles with discretion, but I do want it to be about real people. Far more interesting than the carefully edited stuff in most books – don't you think?' He stopped now to take a bite of his buttered scone.

Angela thought there was no point in pretending to know what he was talking about. She knew she would eventually be found out if she did. 'I don't have any experience of family histories,' she told him, 'but it certainly sounds interesting.'

'I'm delighted you think so,' he said, then went on to tell her about a Victorian ancestor who had gambled his way through a stately home and two fortunes and then went on the run to France, fleeing debtors. As he talked he grew more animated about his subject, and Angela noticed that something about him – the look in his eyes, she thought – made him look younger than she had previously thought. He was certainly much older than her, but probably not as old as her mother. As her mind flitted back to her mother and home, she thought how shocked the family would be to hear Major Harrington talking in such a casual manner about his family and the indiscretions of his ancestors. Most families, she knew, would never bring up topics of discussion which would include anything scandalous or which might show their backgrounds in a dim light.

They finished off their tea and scones and Angela put the crockery they had used on the tray and put it on a table by the door.

'I thought if we made a start on the documents

we have to hand,' the major said, 'then we can file it and compare it with whatever we find when we visit Manchester and London next month.'

Angela caught her breath. 'Next month?'

'Yes, I have a function over in London at the end of the month, so I thought we could take the ferry to Wales and carry on over to Thornley Manor in Cheshire for a week and then go down to London for a further week.' He paused. 'Have you any plans for the end of next month?'

Angela thought quickly. 'I was planning to go home for a weekend, but I can easily do that before we go.'

'Splendid,' the major said. He went over to the shelf and came out with a heavy tome, which he told her gave details of all the settlements in Cheshire at the time of the Domesday survey. 'We'll make a start now, because I would like to have covered most of the information I have here before our trip.' He put the book down on the table with a dusty thud and then opened the pages. 'I think this particular book has the earliest entries about some of the families we're descended from.'

Angela thought the book, full of small print, looked like the sort of thing a university professor would study – much more complicated than anything she had imagined. She hoped now that she hadn't bitten off more than she could chew with the work involved in Major Harrington's project. He talked her through some of the pages

425

he had already studied and marked with stickers, explaining how some of the family lines disappeared in previous centuries through lack of a male successor and how houses relating to certain families were sold up through economic pressure. The way he explained it to her made it seem more understandable and more interesting. An hour flew by whilst they examined the information in the book about the major's family and some of the other families he was related to.

By the time Mrs Girvin came down to tell them that lunch would be ready in the dining room shortly, Angela felt that she had some grasp on what she was doing, and she knew she would keep at it until she fully understood it. She liked the major's human attitude to things, and something told her that this work was already beginning to open up a side of life she didn't even know existed. For years she had felt excluded from the family life she should have had with her parents and sisters, and her bout of polio had left her excluded from many things that girls of her age had been part of. But, for some reason, fate had decided that she was now going to move into a world that was different from anything she knew.

Of course she knew the major was odd and eccentric – she had known that from the first few minutes of meeting him – but there was something about his unpredictability that she warmed to. She also knew that travelling with him over to England would probably not be as straightforward as she might want it to be. She was aware that his relations were unlikely to be as open and friendly with ordinary people as he was, and she might not find them as welcoming. For some reason it did not worry her. She already liked the work, and she knew as time went on she would grow more confident with it. The idea of tracking down houses and tracing the stories of people back in time – in Ireland and England and maybe even further afield – was exciting.

She wondered what her family would make of it when she explained it to them. And then, it struck her that this feeling of an exciting, new future opening in front of her – like a jet soaring up into a clear blue sky – was exactly what Fiona had been feeling when she had dreamed of moving to New York. She now realised how much Fiona had given up for their mother – all her hopes and dreams. She now realised how much Fiona had lost.

But, she thought, if their mother was getting better, maybe things could go back to how they were before their father died, with her working in the shop and Patrick running the bar.

Fiona was in regular touch with Michael O'Sullivan, letters were flying several times a week across the Atlantic between them. He was hoping to come back to Ireland again in July to see how work was going with the old cottage in Connemara. Fiona said he was hoping to stay for a few weeks to get the cottage decorated and furnished before his mother came over in August.

Although Fiona's plans hadn't worked out the first time around, Angela had a feeling that things might begin to change again.

CHAPTER 36

There was a tap on the office door.

'Angela?' Major Harrington said. 'If you don't mind me disturbing you . . .'

'Not at all, come in.' Angela sat back in her typing chair, thinking how very different things had turned out to be in her new job. She had started off as Miss Tracey, and had imagined that her formal title was how it would remain, but gradually it had changed and she had now been referred to by the major and the house staff as 'Angela' for the last two weeks.

He came into the centre of the room, waving a sheet of paper. 'I have the itinerary for our trip worked out now,' he told her, 'and if it is all right with you, we'll be spending three weeks in England.' He raised his eyebrows in question.

'That's perfectly fine with me, Major,' she said, smiling. It was much more than fine – she was actually excited at the thought of this trip. She was looking forward to the boat trip and to the drive through Wales and across into England.

He came into the room and pulled a chair over to sit down beside her desk. 'I did a quick handwritten copy which I thought you might type out for us, and make a few carbon copies. We'll need one for each of us, and one to leave with the staff.' He paused. 'I told you I had a function in London, didn't I?'

'Yes, you mentioned it.'

'Well, it's the middle week we're over, which would mean staying in Cheshire for a week, going down to London the middle week, and then finishing off with the last week in Cheshire again.' He held his chin in his hand. 'I have some friends and family I should catch up with while I'm over, but I'm conscious that you might find the evenings very boring on your own in the hotel. So, if you don't mind, I thought we might incorporate some shift-work, where you might have some time off during the day and then do your work in the evenings.'

She felt unsure as to what exactly the major was suggesting but, in the time she had been working with him, she had learned that things usually worked out, albeit in a roundabout way.

'I'm happy to work whatever hours suit you,' she said, 'and I actually have a cousin working in London – Harrow – so it would be nice if I could see him while were are there.' She had promised her Aunt Catherine that if it worked out, she would try to meet up with Joseph and see how he was getting on.

'I thought, since you've never been to London before, that it would also be a perfect opportunity for us to do a little sightseeing.' He smiled at her. 'I haven't been around places like the Tower of London or the Natural History Museum for a number of years, and I think you would particularly like the Victoria and Albert Museum. How would you feel about that?'

Angela stared at him, not sure what to say. It was not the first time her employer had taken her by surprise. But, she had learned that the best way to deal with these sorts of situations was to be straight and honest with him. 'I'm very happy to carry on with my work while you are meeting up with people. I can continue with my notes whether it's in the house in Manchester or in a hotel in London. I don't mind working during the day or in the evenings.' She took a deep breath. 'And really, you don't need to feel concerned about me at all. My role is to be a help to you, not a drawback. I'm quite able to fill my own time. I've lived on my own for some time and it's no problem to me. I will have my books with me and I'm happy to take little walks out by myself.'

'I don't think I've explained myself very well,' he said. 'It's not a matter of you being an inconvenience, Angela. Quite the contrary. I would not be bringing you over to England with me if you weren't a major help. And it would be a great pleasure to me to have your company whilst I'm in London.'

'In that case,' she said, 'I'd be very happy to go

along with your plans. I would love to have a look around London.'

His face lit up. 'And you needn't worry about it being a strain on your leg. We can drive around from place to place and we'll make sure any walks aren't too strenuous for either of us.'

'Thank you,' she said.

As she sat typing out the itinerary, it occurred to Angela how lucky she had been with her employers since she had entered the world of work. They had all one way or another, due to the involvement of the Polio Fellowship or other groups for people with physical handicaps, made it as easy as possible for her to work in the same way as any other secretary. She had thought the move to a more independent office working for the major might not have the same support but, in fact, it had turned out to be the opposite. He seemed to anticipate any physical difficulties she might encounter and planned ahead for them, and there were times when Angela thought he was even more conscientious about it than she was herself.

The only drawback about the job was that it couldn't last forever. His memoirs and family history research she thought might stretch to two years – three at most. After that, she would not be needed. She had a sense of disappointment about this, because it was way and above the most interesting work she had ever done. She had discovered an interest in old buildings she never knew she had, and she found all the stuff about

Major Harrington's family fascinating. The stories of the eccentric individuals were not only interesting but at times entertaining. And whilst she and the major were vastly different in backgrounds and in age, she had discovered in the short time she had worked for him that they had a similar sense of humour.

The night before they set off for England, Angela checked through her suitcase again.

Considering it was now summer, the weather was not at all what it should be or what she had anticipated when she started packing the previous week. She had filled her case with summer dresses and blouses and skirts. Gradually, she had taken some of the lighter things out, and had replaced them with sweaters and cardigans.

She had also had several shopping trips with Maureen and Jeanette into Grafton Street and had bought the slacks everyone had suggested, and was delighted to find that they covered her calliper very well. She had also bought several bright tunics which worked well with slacks or skirts, and something she never imagined she would fall in love with – a cornflower blue and cream sleeveless, polyester jumpsuit. It had wide legs, and large patch pockets on the front which were piped in cream, and it had a deep V-neck with a crossover fastening that emphasised her tiny waist.

The minute she tried it on, she knew she would buy it. The girls loved it on her and the colour, the style, everything was perfect. Just looking at it made her heart lift. Whether she would have the opportunity to wear it or not, she didn't know, but she bought it anyway.

'Well, who said she wasn't modern or daring?' Maureen laughed.

'I've surprised myself,' Angela had told her. 'And do you know something? I've enjoyed it so much, I might just start surprising myself more!'

A day or two later Angela paid a visit to her specialist shoemaker in Dublin and ordered two pairs of the Mary Jane shoes she liked in cream and blue to match her new jumpsuit. She had also packed her black patent shoes, so she reckoned the three pairs would match more or less every-thing. The calliper she would wear for the journey over and use when she felt it necessary.

As she closed her suitcase for the final time, she decided that anything that she had missed she would buy over in England. She thought she'd probably treat herself to a few new items over there anyway, as she might find herself at a loose end if the major was busy with visiting relatives or meeting friends. The shops, she knew, would be much bigger with more choice, so she thought she might find something different or more fash-ionable that was not available in Dublin. She was not short of money, as she had no rent or food expenses living in Moorhill House, and she still had her savings account.

It was a breezy morning as they set off from the

house in a taxi to the port in Dublin for the ten o'clock ferry which would arrive in Holyhead that evening. Mrs Girvin and Eileen came to see them off at the front door, and the housekeeper had given Angela a small box with cake and biscuits she had baked for the journey over.

'Very kind,' the major had said as they pulled off, 'but unnecessary as we will have all our meals on the boat.'

When they reached the port they went into a waiting room and then they were met by staff who carried their cases for the journey upstairs into one of the lounges.

Angela had to climb up stairs behind the staff, which the major apologised for, but she took them slowly and managed okay without too much difficulty. She was surprised at the luxury of the lounge – deep carpets, low music playing, lots of uniformed waiters – and how spacious it was. She had also expected the lounges to be much busier, as she had seen all the cars and coaches that were queued at the docks, waiting to board the ship.

From what she had heard from friends who had travelled by boat to England – and from listening to her aunt and Joseph – the boats were fairly basic and usually overcrowded. Maureen had warned her to find seats straight away and never leave them, as someone else would take their place and they might be left standing for the rest of the journey.

Angela thought maybe they had all been on a

different boat from the one she was on, or that they had travelled to Liverpool instead of Holyhead, and with a different company with lower standards. It was only when she went to look for the ladies' toilets that she discovered she was in fact on the first-class deck, and she concluded that everyone else she knew had travelled second-class on the deck below.

They had croissants and scones served with coffee around eleven o'clock, and then Angela read her book while the major read the complimentary newspapers and then sat back in his chair and dozed. Every so often she lifted her eyes to glance at him, and smiled to herself. He was such an odd, very individual man, she thought. Very much 'himself' as they would say back in Tullamore, meaning that he went about things in his own way, without feeling he had to subscribe to what others might deem the more normal way.

He seemed without any self-consciousness, which she had found odd at the beginning. The way he would suddenly start reminiscing about a drunken uncle who had died in a fire in a rundown mansion in Edinburgh. The result of falling asleep whilst smoking in bed, he informed her. How he would describe the countries where the fresh fruit they were eating had travelled from, and wonder about the lives of the people who had picked them. How he would suddenly start talking about a character in a book he had read, describing them in such great and interesting detail that Angela almost felt she had read the book herself.

How he would strike up a conversation with the man who was sorting out the luggage room on the boat for the foot passengers, and ask him how he came to be working there.

Waiters, she had already discovered, gave him great mileage for conversation, and he had already engaged a few on board, asking them about their daily routine and where they originally hailed from. She noticed that he treated all of them with great courtesy, unlike some of the other first-class passengers who clicked their fingers to get their attention, and spoke to them in a condescending and dismissive manner.

Some of his ways of thinking were actually beginning to rub off on her. Especially with regards to his attitude to her damaged leg, which he referred to in the most matter-of-fact way. This, in turn, had begun to make her feel less concerned about what other people thought. She no longer felt she had to hurry when there were people behind her as she was walking to the shops, in case she held them up and they noticed she was lame. If she was walking upstairs, she took her time and let people pass her by.

When they were having a tea break in the morning in her office, she found herself chatting about things more randomly, as she would with her friends or family. She no longer felt she had to guard every word she said to the major, or be conscious of making a good impression, as she had with her previous employers. Occasionally she even found herself telling him stories about her father and the characters who came into the pub in Tullamore, and they would laugh over the things she recounted.

When she recounted the conversations in her mind later in the day – checking she hadn't been too forwards or presumptuous – she usually realised that Major Harrington had started off the light-hearted conversation in the first place.

They had lunch in the restaurant at half past one – soup and then chicken with dauphinoise potatoes and broccoli, and then they had lemon meringue pie to follow. The major had ordered a bottle of white wine to go with it. After the meal and the wine, Angela felt very relaxed when they went back to the lounge, and when the major went off to talk to a man he recognised from Dublin, she closed her eyes and slept for almost an hour. When she woke, she found him sitting at the table quietly doing the crossword in the *Irish Times*.

She sat up and straightened her suit jacket, and checked that her hair was still tidy.

A waiter came around with tea and coffee and slices of fruit cake and, as they ate, the major presented the unfinished crossword to her, seeking her help in finding the missing words.

Afterwards, when they had finally completed it, he clapped his hands together in delight.

'Now,' he said, looking at her, 'would you like

to take a walk around the deck? I had a look outside while you were asleep, and the weather is reasonable. The sea breeze might just help to blow all the cobwebs away.'

'I think that would be a great idea,' she said, smiling at him.

As they stood together, leaning on the rail, a couple – who Angela guessed to be a bit older than the major – came past with two little boys aged around two and four. The man commented on the weather and how calm the sea was, which then led into a short conversation about the couple going over to England for their youngest son's wedding. They were travelling, they explained, with their daughter and husband, and their two grandsons.

'Lovely family,' the major said, when they had gone. 'Lucky man. He won't be lonely in his old age with those lively little fellows.'

Then, as they turned back to look out over the Irish Sea, Angela suddenly heard herself ask, 'Do you ever regret not marrying, Major?'

He looked thoughtful. 'I think we really only regret the things we made the wrong choice over. I never really had that choice. I never came close to marrying anyone, unfortunately. None of the women I had any acquaintance with were the right type for me.' He laughed and gave a little shrug. 'And probably more correctly – nor was I the right type for them.' He turned to look at her now. 'Occasionally, when I see nice families – like the one we just met – I think how different my life would have been if I had met the right person and got married and had a family. I think it would have been nice to even have had nephews or nieces, but of course you know my only brother died young . . .'

Angela saw a sadness come into his eyes that she had never seen before, and she wished she had not brought the subject up. It was such a pity, she thought, that such a kind, nice man had not met anyone over all the years. She thought of her parents, and how they had met in their twenties, around the age most people meet their husbands and wives. Their life, she knew, had been happy in the main. Her mother wasn't an easy woman, but married life had suited her and kept her as happy as she could ever be. She was a totally different woman now without their father. Her life had just fallen apart.

The major, she thought, was in a very different situation. He had more or less always been on his own, but he'd had his army career and all the other things he did. He wasn't an unhappy person, she thought, but she did think at times that he was lonely.

As they made their way back to the lounge, she wondered whether she herself would meet someone. So far, none of the boys she had gone out with had been the type she would have married. She presumed that at some stage she would meet someone and they would just click together – that she would somehow know that it was the right person. What, she wondered, if that never happened? How would her life turn out? Would she end up lonely and on her own like him?

They found their seats again and, as he helped her take her coat off, it suddenly occurred to her that, in spite of the fact he was probably more than double her age, she felt more comfortable and relaxed with him than she had ever felt with any other male. She found him interesting and entertaining, and all the things she would have written in a list, had she been asked to describe the sort of man she thought she could spend her life with. But, unfortunately, all his good qualities came in the wrong package – along with three unsurmountable obstacles.

The first was the biggest one – his age. Then, of course there was the difference in social class and financial backgrounds. The third obstacle – she was nearly ashamed to admit to herself – was the major's looks. There was no nice way around it, she thought, he was just not the handsomest of men. Even in his younger days, at his best, she probably would not have looked twice at him. Then, she suddenly caught herself. Who was she to think such things of anyone else? She who had felt judged about her appearance all her life?

She glanced over at him now, watched him as he searched for his gold pocket watch to check the time. The heavy brows, the nose that was just too large for his face, the thinning hairline, the wrinkles around his eyes. But, she thought, his eyes were kind. And when he laughed, his face became more alive and somehow younger.

He wasn't that bad, she thought, and of course he had money which provided security. Surely there were some nice, older women in Dublin, who would appreciate a man like that?

She looked at him now and wondered.

CHAPTER 37

A hired car had been arranged, and was waiting for them when they disembarked from the boat. Angela had been in the car with him back in Dublin on several occasions, so she knew that he was a confident and capable driver. As they drove out of Holyhead and made the long journey through Wales, she discovered during one of their chats that in his younger days he had actually been involved in racing driving.

'It was only a hobby really,' he told her. 'A bit of fun. I wasn't talented enough to do it professionally, but I enjoyed it very much. I gave it up years ago.' He laughed. 'The old knee again, but I still go to the Grand Prix and that sort of thing, when I'm over in England.'

'You have a busy life,' Angela said. 'You do a lot of interesting things.'

'And I intend to keep it that way. It's all too easy to get into a rut, go into yourself. Better to keep an active mind with travelling and meeting people.' He smiled. 'And that's good advice at any age, Angela, but more important as you get older.'

They stopped en route at a hotel the major knew.

'Something quick,' he told Angela, 'that will keep us going until we arrive at Thornley Manor. Mrs Young will have something waiting for us there.'

The young waitress at the restaurant door told them that it was a full dinner menu, so the major asked her if he could possibly have a quick word with the manager.

When the manager arrived, the major explained their situation – that they only wanted a quick sandwich or bowl of soup, and wondered if the chef would be good enough to oblige, and to mention that it was Major Harrington from Dublin.

Angela stood quietly behind him, and was not a bit surprised when they were shown to a quiet corner table and served soup and fresh crusty rolls.

'They're very decent here,' he told her. 'I've stopped off here on a number of occasions, and I recently discovered that the chef was from Leitrim. We had a great chat when I had dinner here last time, and I explained that I'm usually anxious to get to Cheshire and don't have time to stop off. He said any time I was rushing he could sort something quickly for me. I don't like to take advantage, so we'll make time on the way back to have the full dinner.'

Later that night they drove through Thornley Village, just as it was starting to get dark. At the edge of the village they took a laneway which went uphill for about half a mile, and then they went through tall gates which took them down a driveway to the house.

Angela had seen photographs and drawings of Thornley Manor, which was much bigger than the house back in Dublin, so she wasn't surprised by the imposing old building, although she was rather taken aback that the grounds were neglected, with dilapidated stables and outhouses. She also noticed that one of the gable ends was particularly rundown looking with cracks in several of the leaded windows where ivy was creeping through into the house.

The major had explained as they drove along that he wasn't the sole owner of the house.

'An uncle left it jointly to me and two cousins, Philip and Jeremy, when he died five years ago, as he thought it stood a better chance of being kept in the family if we shared the running costs. It has worked out fairly well so far, although it's a money pit. Always something needing done, and trying to heat it in the winter is nigh impossible. We don't have any regular full-time staff, to keep the costs down. Whoever is using it contacts a local man, Gerry, who does basic maintenance on the house, and he organises someone to come in to cook or clean or whatever is necessary. My cousin Jeremy spends quite a lot of his time here – his brother Philip is based in Edinburgh with his family.'

'Will Jeremy be at the house when we arrive?'

She hadn't imagined that there would be other people there.

'No, I expect to see him at some point later in the week, although that could easily change. He's not the sort that's given to planning too far ahead. He's up in Scotland at the moment, I believe. He fancies himself as an artist – does a bit of painting and sculpting and he uses some of the upstairs rooms as studios. Bit of a shambolic affair in my opinion.' He laughed. 'Not that my opinion counts for much where Jeremy is concerned. He organises painting weekends and so forth at the house, but I tend to avoid them at all costs. You never know who could appear without notice and it can be rather disconcerting to have people wandering in and out, when you have planned a quiet week.'

'I can imagine,' Angela said.

He looked at her and smiled. 'I checked with him about this weekend well in advance, so our research shouldn't be disrupted by any roving artists. I'm rather depending on him coming down this week, as he said he would organise to have the deeds and documents for Thornley Manor available for us to work on.'

As soon as they pulled up, a young man with fair hair and wearing a casual sweater came out of the house to greet them and bring their bags in.

'This is Gerry,' he said to Angela. 'The chap who tries to keep everything in order here. Gerry, this is Angela Tracey, my personal secretary and research assistant.'

'*Tries* being the operative word,' Gerry said, grinning at her. 'It's not a place that's kept easily in order.'

Angela tried not to smile at her convoluted title as they shook hands, and was grateful that the major had introduced her by her name and not 'Miss Tracey' which had made her feel old and spinsterish.

In the large hallway, she looked around her at the old stone-flagged floors, the worn Turkish carpets, the hallstand overflowing with waxed jackets, raincoats and tweed caps. Beside it stood a rack with wellingtons and muddy hiking boots, which Angela imagined should have been in the kitchen area or back entrance, and an umbrella-stand filled with golf clubs and cricket bats.

The house had an air about it, she thought, which was distinctly male. There were few of the feminine touches that Mrs Girvin had lent to Moorhill House, bar a tall vase on the table in the middle of the hall filled with flowering branches cut from one of the bushes outside.

Gerry carried their cases in and the major told him to put Angela's in the first bedroom at the top of the first flight of stairs.

'I'm sorry we don't have any suitable rooms downstairs for sleeping as we do back in Dublin,' Major Harrington said, looking faintly anxious. 'And it would have been difficult to have a bed brought downstairs – the beds are rather ancient and not suitable for moving around . . .'

'It's perfectly fine,' she said. She wouldn't like to have to tackle the stairs every day, but it was only for the short while she was here. 'We have stairs to the bedrooms back in Tullamore. I can manage them as long as I take my time, and I do need to have some exercise.'

'Excellent,' he said. 'We will use one of the rooms downstairs for an office, and the library is down here as well, so we should be fairly comfortable for working.' He rolled his eyes. 'That's presuming that Jeremy hasn't commandeered them for some crazy art project since my last visit.'

Angela laughed. 'He sounds a bit of a character.'

'Oh, he is. He's certainly that.'

When Angela woke the next morning, it was only eight o'clock and too early for breakfast. She hung her clothes up in the big Victorian wardrobe, and placed folded items like her underwear and pyjamas on the shelves.

The room assigned to her was one of the biggest bedrooms she had ever seen, and when she'd first laid eyes on the old four-poster bed in it, she immediately knew what the major had meant when he said the beds were not suitable for moving around. It was, she reckoned, around a hundred years old, and she wondered about all the people who might have slept in it before her. She walked around it now, looking at the mahogany furniture – the wardrobe, the chest of drawers, the ornate dressing-table with three circular mirrors and numerous tiny, velvet-lined drawers. Some of the pieces were not unlike the furniture they had back in the house in Tullamore – but the ones in this room were duller from lack of regular polish and use.

There was a door leading off her room which she discovered led to a smaller bedroom. This, she deduced, must have been a room used for nursing a child or something along those lines. The major's room was across the corridor, and she reckoned that there were two or three other bedrooms on that floor.

She went down the corridor to the nearest bathroom – a big room with tall windows, a black-and-white tiled floor, and an old roll-top bath standing in the centre – and had a quick, shallow bath in the lukewarm water. Back in her room, she quickly dressed. The house, she felt, was generally chilly, so she had decided that one of her new long jumpers, in blue, and a pair of navy slacks would probably be warm and casually smart for work.

Downstairs, she found Gerry had arrived in to stoke the Aga in the huge old kitchen and light fires in all the rooms they were using. The major then appeared and explained they would spend most of their time in the kitchen when not working, as it was the warmest room in the house thanks to the old Aga.

Lynn Dolan, the lady who looked after the domestic side of things, had left them all the basics like fresh bread and milk and eggs, and the pantry was well stocked with boxes of porridge oats and tins of soup, sardines and custard. She had left a large homemade shepherd's pie and cooked chicken with salad which would get them through the first couple of days.

'I'm afraid we have to cook for ourselves,' the major said. 'It's actually one of the things I enjoy about being here. I tend not to look at the clock, and just eat whatever is available when I'm hungry.'

'I don't mind doing the cooking,' Angela said. 'I was used to doing it every evening at the house in Leeson Street, so it's no trouble.'

'Ah, but that would be taking advantage – your remit is secretarial rather than domestic.' He paused. 'We'll work it together. I'm quite accomplished with the frying pan when necessary.'

He was in fact, as she had expected, fairly ham-fisted, but she managed to work around him and enjoyed the informality of their working together on something practical for a change.

Used to seeing him in suits and semi-formal wear, Angela was taken by surprise when he arrived in the kitchen on the second morning, wearing a nice black cashmere sweater with a subtle diamond pattern in grey, black corduroy trousers and grey suede boots. The outfit made him look a little younger and more up to date, but she made no comment about it in case it seemed forward or too personal. He said nothing about his change of clothing either, but she felt both of them looked more relaxed and casual which befitted their country surroundings.

The days began with a light breakfast, usually eggs, then work until mid-morning, another little break, more work, then an hour for a sandwich lunch. Afterwards, Angela would take a walk around the grounds and the buildings outside. It gave her a little exercise and it helped with her research about Thornley House, as she could physically see the remains of the buildings and stable blocks that were in old photographs.

In one of the better-preserved sheds she found a broken-down Victorian carriage that would have been pulled by horses, and the shell of an old car from the 1920's. There were also boxes and metal containers on a shelf, filled with old car number plates and badges and an old pair of binoculars in a tattered leather case that had a military crest on it from the First World War. When she told the major what she had found, he came down straight away and started sorting through the containers, delighted with the memorabilia.

He told her to feel free to explore inside the house, to look around the library and any of the empty rooms on all three floors.

'It's a beautiful place,' Angela said.

'Not as formal or as smart as Moorhill House, but of course it's a country house after all.'

'Yes, but it has old grandeur and great character,' she said. 'It's a place you can really relax in.'

'I'm glad you feel that way,' he said. 'Because

I'm aware we're of different generations, that you're such a young woman . . . I thought you might find it rather boring or old-fashioned.'

'But it's nice old-fashioned,' she said. *Interesting* old-fashioned.'

He looked at her, smiling. 'I'm grateful to Stephen Hall, you know, for recommending you. He was spot on. He knew about the work involved in the research – what I hoped to achieve with the book. I told him it was going to be a challenge to find someone who would tick all the right boxes, so to speak – have all the office skills necessary and the social skills. He said you would be ideal – "a clever, skilled, independent young lady" is how he described you.'

Angela felt a glow rising from her chest to her face. 'Well, I'm grateful to him as well. This is the most interesting job I've ever had, and one I never even imagined existed.'

He started to laugh. 'It's nice to be two very grateful people!'

When she went upstairs to have a look around, the major warned her. 'The top floor,' he said, 'is not in great condition, and neither is the west wing of the house. Jeremy was supposed to take charge of the repairs, but he has only done them to a standard suitable for working in – his never-ending experimental art projects – as opposed to a decent standard for living in. He sorted the windows and the roof to make the rooms water-tight, and has made repairs to the floors and had some sort of damp-proofing done with the walls, but that's it. He has bright murals everywhere, and God knows what hanging from the walls, but I suppose he does own the house, and is entitled to use part of it as he pleases. He's always promising that he'll find a studio elsewhere, so we can finish the renovations, but he doesn't seem in any rush.' He shrugged and smiled. 'I shouldn't complain, he's a nice enough chap in his own individual way . . . and I'm not over here often enough to help with the work.'

Angela thought that being individual must run in the major's family and this cousin must be fairly unusual for the major to comment. She was suddenly curious about Jeremy, trying to build up a picture of him in her mind before he arrived. 'Do you mind me asking if he is older or younger than you?'

'A few years younger.' He actually chuckled. 'That's speaking chronologically, of course. With regards to our personalities and lifestyles – I'd say we are probably decades apart.'

The top floor was worse than the major had described. When Angela walked into the first studio she could hardly believe her eyes. Huge rooms with ornate ceilings and coving – rooms which had once been beautiful – were now covered in gaudy orange and purple paint, and the weirdest art work hanging from them that she had ever seen. The first thing that caught her eye on one of the walls was a fish made from flattened out salmon and sardine tins. Then there was a sculpture of a man's head made out of squashed spectacle frames. Another wall had a blue sky with clouds painted on it, and bird cages suspended from the ceiling in front of it with stuffed parrots inside. There were dozens of paintings – many of which made no sense to her, just squiggles and blotches of colour – the sort of thing she imagined a child would do.

The second studio was similar, but the main exhibit which caught her eye was a group of a dozen or so tailor's dummies which were dressed in a variety of material such as old torn-up books, music manuscripts and feather dusters. Above her head was a massive bird made from papier-mâché and several kites, pieces of driftwood with anti-war symbols burned into them and a suit of armour made from egg boxes. A row of four rifles – made from books in varying sizes – pointed towards the tall high windows.

Angela spent half an hour slowly walking around the rooms, stopping every now and again to look at certain things in detail. By the time she had finished, she thought, in fairness, some of the work was actually very good and she was impressed by the imagination of some of the artists. She particularly liked a collage of poppies which was constructed with painted metal and a sculpture of a naked lady made from broken pieces of jewellery.

On her way back downstairs, she looked into

another room and found it filled with old bunk-beds that looked as though they had come from a boarding-school dormitory and a pile of crumpled sleeping bags and pillows.

Later, when she mentioned the room to the major, he told her that when any artists came to work, they slept in that room, and often dragged mattresses into the studio.

'Bohemian is the only word to describe them,' he said, 'or perhaps mad!'

Angela shrugged and laughed, saying, 'Well, I suppose the world would be boring if we were all the same.'

Each day, after her walks around the grounds, she went back to work long into the afternoon. Most of the time she worked alone in the dining-room, while Major Harrington worked in the library. He spent his time reading through boxes and files of family letters and documents, searching for stories and anecdotes of his more errant forebears to add levity and humour to his work. More occupied with his project than before, he was drinking less alcohol than he did back in Dublin, Angela noticed. He didn't drink wine with his lunch every day now, nor did he disappear off for afternoons and come back smelling of whisky. His high colouring – which she reckoned was from drinking too much – had toned down, and he was somehow quieter too, and less needy of other people's chat and company.

There was no official finishing time for work as Angela carried on reading or typing, taking notes and carefully filing things away, until it was time for the evening meal. They spent most of the evening over dinner and a glass of wine, talking about the information both of them had come up with, and how it might best be used.

On the third evening Angela noticed the major looked concerned. 'I hope you don't feel you're working too hard,' he said. 'If you were in a conventional office, the lights would be off and the door locked and everyone would have gone home long ago.'

'The research doesn't feel like work,' she replied. 'I find it fascinating. I'm really enjoying finding things out about the building, which parts were built during which period, and any renovations that were carried out later, and I particularly enjoy reading about the families who lived in the house over the last few hundreds of years, and trying to work out where they all went, and who married who etcetera.'

'Your enthusiasm is making a huge project much easier,' he said. 'I thought I would have to explain things more, but you're off working on maps and family trees on your own as if you've done it for years.'

In the middle of the week, Lynn Dolan arrived again, bearing a piece of beef and some fish and fresh vegetables, and washed around the kitchen and mopped floors, and gave the rooms they were using a good brush out and polish. She was pleasant, but unobtrusive, and was in and out of the rooms before they even noticed. Angela was relieved to find there was someone taking care of the domestic things so she could concentrate on her work.

On the Friday afternoon she was busy typing when she heard a car engine. She glanced out of the window and saw a red-and-black Volkswagen campervan rolling up the driveway of Thornley Mansion. It parked close to the door, and she watched from the edge of the heavy curtain as a girl around her own age, with a short Twiggy-type hairstyle, got out of the passenger side. She was wearing a pink trouser suit and a purple hat with a flowery scarf tied around it, and a pair of multi-coloured sunglasses. A few moments later, a man with a handsome face emerged – probably late thirties, she thought. His dark hair was cut into a short pageboy style, and he was wearing a blue velvet jacket piped with a flowery edging, jeans and a flowery cravat.

Angela smiled to herself when she saw them, as she had never seen anyone wearing such extreme clothes. She had seen people like the Beatles or other pop bands wearing them on television, but she had never seen real people dressed like this. She wondered with amusement whether Maureen would approve of their outfits for being modern and daring or whether she would describe them as outlandish and ridiculous. As she watched them laughing and chatting together outside, she couldn't decide exactly what she thought of them herself.

She wondered who the couple were and what they wanted at the house. As they came towards the main door, she suddenly thought that if the major wasn't around – she hadn't seen him for several hours – she might have to answer the door to them. She listened for a few moments, waiting on the bell to ring, and then she heard footsteps and loud voices in the hallway, and she realised that they had let themselves in.

She went over to the door, unsure now whether to go out or what to do. Just as she had her hand on the doorknob, she heard her employer's voice coming from upstairs and then there was loud laughter. The couple were obviously people he knew. And then it dawned on her that the man might be Jeremy, the cousin he had mentioned who was one of the owners of the house.

Before she could speculate any further, the voices started moving in the direction of the dining-room. As quickly as she could, she moved back towards the top of the room, to the end of the table where her typewriter and her chair was. She did not want her limp to be the first thing this glamorous, confident couple noticed about her.

She sat down to compose herself, and when the knock came on her door and then it opened, she took a deep breath.

458

'I hope you don't mind me disturbing you, Angela,' the major said, coming in, 'but I'd like to introduce you to my cousin, Jeremy, and his friend Marjola. They've just travelled down from Scotland today, and they've dropped in for a flying visit.'

They came in behind him, Marjola openly gazing around the room. 'It's fab, Jeremy! Absolutely fab!'

Angela stood up, feigning a vague, preoccupied manner, as though she had been deeply engrossed in her work, as she didn't want them to know she had seen them.

Jeremy came towards her, an amazed grin on his face. 'Wow, Edward – you old dark horse. This secretary is not what I was expecting at all!' His eyes opened wider. 'Not at all . . .'

Angela felt herself shrinking back, and just caught herself in time as he took her hand and shook it briskly. 'I'm pleased to meet you,' she said.

'When Edward told me he had a personal secretary working with him,' Jeremy said, 'I thought I would be meeting some old spinsterish battle-axe . . . never did I imagine I would meet such a goddess of beauty!'

Angela felt herself squirming now. He was so over the top, she thought, one could not take anything he said seriously. He was like someone in a play – and a particularly bad actor. How on earth, she thought, could he be related to the major?

'Jeremy, Jeremy!' the major said. 'Enough! You're embarrassing the poor girl!'

It also crossed Angela's mind that, on closer inspection, Jeremy looked older than she had earlier presumed – probably in his forties. The girl, she thought, looked not much older than her, probably mid-twenties at most.

'A compliment is like a flower, Edward,' Jeremy said. 'And this angel of yours deserves a bouquet. I'm so glad we called in, otherwise I would never have guessed you were hiding such a young beauty here in Thornley Mansion.'

It was all so ridiculous that Angela found herself wanting to laugh, but she realised that it might well offend the cousin or the major. Instead she turned her attention to Marjola, who was standing silently, leaning against one of the dining chairs. 'It's very nice to meet you, Marjola,' she said and the girl came over to shake her hand. Angela noticed she did not smile or say anything, but she thought it was more to do with Jeremy and his over-effusive compliments than anything to do with her.

'We'll leave you to your work now, Angela,' the major said, taking his cousin by the elbow to guide him towards the door. 'I want my dear cousin to show me the deeds to this house before he disappears on his travels again.'

'Do not let this old devil work you too hard,' Jeremy called as they went.

They went off down to the library and Angela went back to her work. An hour or so later she was standing at the table checking a map when a knock came on the door again and it opened and in came Jeremy.

He put his finger to his lips as though asking her not to speak and then he closed the door.

'Did you want something?' Angela said then, not quite sure what he was going to do. She started walking back to her chair.

'Have you hurt your leg?' he said, noticing her limp.

She sat down in the chair. 'No,' she said, looking straight at him. 'I haven't. It was affected by polio.' She was surprised that she did not feel embarrassed or awkward telling him this. In a way, she thought, by introducing this more serious note she could cut through all the silly nonsense from earlier on.

His mouth formed an O of surprise. 'Polio?' he repeated. His face became serious. 'Oh, God – sorry for asking you such a crass question . . . what bad luck . . .'

Angela shrugged and smiled. 'Don't worry about it, I'm used to it.'

'Tony Armstrong Jones – Lord Snowdon, you know, Princess Margaret's husband? The British royal family? I know the Irish aren't quite as familiar with them as the English.'

'Of course I know about Princess Margaret,'

she said. 'She's the Queen's younger sister.' She had often read about her in newspapers and magazines.

'He has the very same trouble with his leg. Apparently he caught polio as a boy.'

Angela nodded. She had actually read something about it a few years back. 'Do you mind me asking what you wanted?'

'I believe you saw the studios upstairs?'

'Yes,' she said. 'Major Harrington said it would be okay. It was very interesting. I hope you didn't mind?'

Jeremy waved his hands. 'Don't mind in the slightest.'

She felt awkward now. She would have to say something. 'I really liked some of the sculptures and paintings. Particularly the metal poppies.'

His eyes lit up. 'That's one of mine. Did you like any of the other ones?'

She tried to remember. She moved her head up and down. 'The lady sculpted from jewellery.'

'Really?'

'Yes,' she confirmed. 'I thought it was lovely.'

'Excellent! So the nudity didn't offend or anything like that?'

Angela felt her face flush. She felt he was really studying her now – first her face – and then his eyes moved down to her neck and the top part of her body. 'No, not really . . .' She could not think of anything else to say. Why, she wondered, had she picked that particular one to mention? It hadn't really struck her as being a naked woman. It was simply the outline of a female filled in with old brooches and earrings and suchlike. It was just a shape with no identifiable body parts.

'I'm glad to hear you're a forward-thinking young lady,' Jeremy said now. 'It's a pity I'm here on a flying visit, leaving in the next few minutes for an exhibition over in Liverpool.' He paused. 'But I wondered . . . you have such a striking face and, well . . . everything else is beautifully proportioned.'

Angela felt a little stab of alarm.

'I wondered if you might be interested in posing for one of my paintings? If you would be a life model for me? Unclothed preferably.'

'What?' She started to laugh. 'Are you joking?'

'Your leg wouldn't be a problem, we could have you positioned so it wouldn't be noticed in the painting.'

Just then there was a quick tap on the door and the major came in.

'Ah, Jeremy, Marjola was wondering where you had disappeared to . . .' He looked at Angela now, then back to Jeremy, sensing something. 'Is everything all right?'

Angela quickly decided that she had no allegiance to Jeremy, and it would be best to let him know how the land lay if she was to come across him again. Also, should his pestering continue she would have to tell her employer about his cousin's proposition.

'Jeremy was just asking if I would like to pose for a nude painting for him,' she said, her voice light. 'I'm sure he was joking.'

'My motives are purely artistic,' Jeremy cut in. 'I think Angela has much more to offer in life than her typing skills.'

He moved across the floor to stand nearer the window and the way the light hit his face, Angela suddenly noticed the wrinkles around his eyes and mouth, and then it struck her as she saw a thin tell-tale line of grey at his parting that Jeremy's shiny black hair was indeed dyed.

'Angela has brains, Jeremy,' the major said, raising his eyebrows, 'something you're not too well acquainted with.'

Angela caught her breath, wondering if the major had gone too far.

Jeremy grinned, obviously enjoying the banter. 'She's a grown woman, Edward, and I thought she might like to explore her artistic side. I was merely giving her the chance to do so.' He turned to Angela. 'You're a rare beauty, my dear, and I would have been honoured to have you as the subject of one of my paintings.'

Angela started to laugh. 'I'll take that as a compliment, but my answer is "no".'

'Jeremy,' the major said, going over to open the door, 'I think you said this was a flying visit and you had to rush to Liverpool for a boutique opening?'

Jeremy held his hands up and grinned. 'Okay, I

get it – my presence is no longer required since I came up with the deeds and documents.'

'Spot on,' the major said. 'We would like to get on with our work.' He made a sweeping, bowing motion with his arm to indicate to his cousin that he should leave.

Jeremy came across to Angela and took her hand and kissed it. 'Give me a ring should you change your mind about the painting,' he said, looking into her face, 'and it needn't be nude. There's a famous American painting of a girl with polio – *Christina's World* – and I'm sure we could come up with a modern twist on it.'

'Out!' the major said, moving towards his cousin. 'Time to go, Jeremy.'

'I'm going.' He gave a theatrical sigh as he went towards the door. He paused. 'You say you're in London next week and here again the week after?'

The major looked at him with raised eyebrows, but said nothing.

'Pity, I'm in Paris then over to Malaga for a Picasso convention . . . Ah well, maybe another time.' He suddenly grinned. 'Oh, and Edward, a word of advice, which I'm sure Angela would agree with – I think you should drop the "Major" tag, it's not very avant garde to use military ranking these days.'

The major sighed and shook his head.

After the camper van rolled down the driveway, the major came back into the dining-room.

'What can I say? He's incorrigible and getting worse as he grows older.'

'Did you get all the documents you needed?' Angela asked.

'Yes, thank goodness.'

'Well, that's the main thing.' She started to laugh. 'I can't imagine how people back in Tullamore would react if I told them about his suggestion to paint me.'

The major slapped the palm of his hand to his head. 'I am truly embarrassed by him, and sorry for that poor girl who is trailing around after him. She is one of dozens, you know.'

'I'm not surprised.'

He paused. 'I think he might have raised one worthwhile point. How would you feel about calling me Edward – while we're here? Would it make things easier?'

She gave it a few moments' thought. It would feel strange being so familiar with him, but she supposed she would get used to it. 'I don't mind either way.'

'It's something I got used to in the army, and afterwards in Ireland I just continued with it without any real thought.' He leaned against the jamb of the door. 'I was just thinking when we go to London . . .'

She looked at him and for the first time, saw uncertainty and perhaps even vulnerability. It occurred to her that he might not have anyone else to discuss such a personal thing with. 'You have got to make that decision,' she said. 'Don't be pushed into anything because of what Jeremy says. He's hardly a sensible person to take much heed of. It's your name after all.'

He nodded and then turned away. 'I'll give it some thought.'

CHAPTER 38

The hotel the major had booked was a small one with only ten rooms, and a short walk from Victoria Train station. Angela had a room along the corridor from her employer, and he had insisted on giving her the bigger room as it had a table and chairs which would let her work more comfortably. He pointed out that it also had a bathroom next door which would be more convenient for her.

The first few days in London were busy with visits to a record office to check out family birth and death certificates, and to visit an elderly uncle of the major's in Kensington. He had a large townhouse where he lived with his wife, who Angela found pleasant and welcoming, but strangely vague and forgetful. Within minutes, she had asked Angela her name and where she came from at least half a dozen times.

'If you could just humour her that would be kind,' the major's uncle said at one point, 'as she has recently developed a problem with her memory.'

In the middle of the week, the major spent a day on his own, visiting an aunt who was in a nursing home in Buckinghamshire, so Angela stayed alone in the hotel writing up her notes. Her aunt had given her Joseph's number, so she rang the hotel he worked in and the girl on reception went through to the restaurant to get him. They chatted for a while and Angela was pleased that he sounded well and seemed to be enjoying his work. They made arrangements to meet the following evening in an old pub across from the station called *The Shakespeare*.

The major was delighted she had her own plans, and he organised to catch up with some of his army friends while she was with Joseph.

The following day they worked, had lunch in the hotel, and then, since it was a nice afternoon, the major suggested they go to The Tower of London. Angela enjoyed it, and he was delighted to explain any of the English history she didn't know.

She set off to meet Joseph for half past seven, and he was there as arranged, waiting outside the bar. The bar was busy – and with a good number of women in it, which made her feel relieved. It had a good, friendly atmosphere, and they went in and were lucky to find a table over in the corner. Joseph ordered drinks for them – a lager for himself and a gin and tonic for Angela – and then they sat chatting and listening to the juke box. The place he was working in, he told her, was great for experience, but not a long-term prospect.

'I miss Ireland,' he said, 'but I know the longer I stay here, the more experience I'll have for finding work in a decent place. I'd really like a place where we can have a bit of live music as well.'

'Wouldn't you miss your girlfriend?' Angela asked. 'Your mother was telling me you had met someone really nice.'

His face took on a serious look. 'It's finished,' he said. 'She broke off with me two weeks ago.' He leaned forward and put his elbows on the table. He looked around and then spoke in a low voice. 'Her family weren't happy when she told them I was Irish and a Catholic.'

'You're joking!' Angela said.

He shook his head. 'I wish I was. They hadn't even met me, so it wasn't because I'd said or done anything wrong. But she didn't put up any kind of fight, so I think she might have been having doubts herself. She didn't like me working shifts, so . . .' He held his hands out.

'Maybe it's for the best,' she said. 'Are you okay?'

'Yeah, I'm grand,' he said, giving a sidelong grin. 'I liked her well enough, but what can you do? It wasn't going to go anywhere if her family are that prejudiced.'

'And have you come across any other people like that? People who don't like the Irish?'

'No, not really. Most are nice.'

'I'm glad. You'll meet someone else.'

'Ah, girls come and go in London, and there are nice ones working in the hotel, so I won't be at a

470

loose end if I need company.' He lifted his glass of beer and took a drink.

Angela smiled back, relieved he seemed okay. 'I wouldn't think you would ever be stuck for company, a fine-looking lad like you.'

He sat forward now and put his glass down on the table. 'Talking of company, Angela, I hope you don't mind, but I've just noticed my father coming in. He's over at the bar.' He shook his head. 'I was stupid – I phoned him last night and I told him you were coming to London and he asked me where we were meeting. I never thought he would turn up . . . I know my mother won't be too happy about him coming to see you.' He craned his neck to look. 'And, to make matters worse,' he said, nodding across to the bar, 'it looks like he's been in another pub before he came here. He looks more than a bit jarred.'

Angela felt uncomfortable at the thought of seeing her uncle again, knowing that he had deserted her aunt, but she knew she would have to make an effort for her cousin's sake.

A half an hour passed, and there was no sign of him.

'Maybe he didn't notice us,' Joseph said. 'With the help of God, he's gone out to another pub.' He tightened his mouth. 'He's become an awful heavy drinker since he came back over here. I know he liked a drink before, but he didn't drink the way he's doing now. I don't want to mention it to my mother because she seems to be managing now without him. I don't want to bring it all up again, because, believe it or not, she will worry about him.'

Angela was just about to say something, when a shadow loomed over the table and when she looked up her Uncle Ken was standing there, swaying backwards and forwards while precariously holding drinks for them. When Joseph saw him, he quickly stood up and took the glasses from him.

'The Babycham is for Angela,' Ken said, pointing to her. 'All the girls love a Babycham! Isn't that what the adverts say?' He sat down in the chair with a thud. 'Yes, *I'd loooooove a Babycham!* Isn't that what they say?'

Joseph put the drink in front of Angela and she smiled and thanked her uncle.

'Well,' Ken said, 'you're looking very well, Angela. You look like a new girl since I last saw you. I hear you have a new highfalutin' job that's brought you to London.'

'It's just for the week,' Angela said. 'It's for research.'

Ken reached forward and took Angela's hand and squeezed it. 'I'm proud of you,' he said. 'You've done well – in fact you've done fantastic. You've shown that uppity mother of yours that you didn't need her. That you've managed to do well for yourself in spite of her.'

Angela felt her throat run dry. She lifted her Babycham and took a drink as though he had never spoken.

'Dad,' Joseph said, 'there's no need for talk like that. We're meeting up for a nice drink and a chat. We don't want any ill-feeling.'

'I'm only speaking the truth . . . but of course there's no room for that.' He let go of her hand and sat back in his chair, a sullen look on his face. 'There's no room for the truth.'

Angela felt her stomach churning. She had never seen this side of her uncle before. She looked at Joseph. 'So, the new job is going well? I hear you did some interesting courses on wine and what food to serve it with.'

'Yeah,' Joseph said, 'I've really enjoyed it. There's a lot more to it than you would imagine.'

His father suddenly laughed. 'That's the story of life, son – there's always a lot more to things than any of us would imagine.'

'Dad,' Joseph hissed, 'you're talking crap here – will you just stop? You're embarrassing yourself.'

Ken halted for a few seconds, thinking, then his face looked contrite. 'Well, I'm sorry, son, I wouldn't ever want to embarrass you.' He leaned over now and clapped a hand on Joseph's shoulder. 'You know how much I think of you, don't you? No matter what ever happens, I'm your father. I'm the one who brought you up. Never forget that.'

Joseph looked at him, incredulous now. He glanced around him, concerned others might hear. 'Are you talking about me being adopted?'

'Maybe . . .'

'But why would you bring that up tonight? I know all about it, Angela knows about it – and it doesn't bother me. It never has. Why are you making it sound like a problem?'

Angela could see people at the next table looking at them, so she touched her uncle on the arm. 'I'm only in London for a few days,' she said, 'and Joseph and I came out to have a quiet drink together and catch up. We don't want anyone arguing.'

Ken started waving his finger around. 'There's nobody arguing – I'm just saying there are bigger problems that have never been talked about.'

Joseph prodded his finger on the table. 'The big problem was you leaving my mother, but we've managed to get over that too.' He held his hands out. 'We've all survived.'

Ken reached out again and put his hand on his son's shoulder. 'We have survived, son, haven't we?'

Joseph nodded. 'And you and I are doing okay, Dad – so let's leave it at that. There's no point in looking back.'

'But I'm not looking back – I'm not talking about back then. I'm talking about now.'

'For God's sake, what's got into you?' Joseph said. 'What the hell are you rambling on about?'

'I'll tell you what it is,' he said. 'There's something been bothering me for a while, something I don't understand. Something I want to know. And, I've decided that I'm going to put my cards on the table tonight. I'm going to ask Angela about it.'

Angela's head jerked up 'What is it?' she said. 'What is it you want to know?'

'I want to know why your mother wouldn't give Joseph a job in the bar. She needs somebody to help her out – a man to replace your father – but she wouldn't have him near the place. Can somebody tell me why that is?'

Angela gave a huge sigh and was ready to snap at him when she suddenly saw he had tears in his eyes. 'How can I answer that?' she said in a quiet voice. 'I don't know why. It doesn't make sense to me either. You know I'm not that close to my mother. You know I would be the last one to know the answer to that.'

'Dad, leave it,' Joseph said. 'Just drop it. It's not fair to Angela. I'm fed up with you and my mother both going on about this. I know you wanted to get me away from Dublin because of that trouble with the band, and losing my job. I understand all that.' He shrugged. 'I'm having a break away from all that scene – whether it's London or Tullamore it doesn't matter. I'm here now for the time being, and the job is going fine and that's all that matters.'

'That's not the point,' his father argued. 'She should have helped you. She's your family. I always thought that when push came to shove, she would be on your side. I'm surprised at her.'

'Well, I'm not a bit surprised,' Joseph said. 'I

knew she wouldn't want me down in Tullamore – she never has. For some weird reason, known only to herself, Aunt Nance doesn't like me or my mother. But, at the end of the day, she is entitled to have whoever she wants working for her. If she prefers local people, then that's fine – I don't care. Good luck to her.'

'But that's not the answer,' Ken said. 'That's not the answer at all.'

'I've had enough,' Joseph said. He took a gulp of his lager, then swung round to put his jacket on. 'Come on, Angela, we don't need all this crap. We're going somewhere else.'

Angela started to put her coat on.

'Don't go,' Ken said. 'You don't understand.'

'No,' Joseph said, 'It's *you* who doesn't understand. Will you just get it through your thick head that she doesn't owe me anything? She's only my aunt!'

'But she's not . . . she's not your aunt. She's your mother.'

Joseph and Angela both froze.

'What did you say?' said Joseph.

There was a silence while Ken tried to focus his eyes. 'I said your Aunt Nance is your real mother. She gave you to us, and we adopted you.'

CHAPTER 39

The waiter brought two cups of tea and set them down on the table in front of them. 'Would you like biscuits with them, madam?'

Angela glanced at Joseph, who was sitting back in the deep, winged, leather armchair, lost in his thoughts again. There was no point in asking him anything so trivial.

'No, thank you,' she said. 'The tea will be fine.' The waiter went out of the otherwise empty sitting-room, quietly drawing the door closed behind him.

Angela leaned forward and picked up his cup and saucer. 'Talk to me, Joseph,' she said, handing it to him.

'Oh, I'm sorry, Angela,' he said, taking it from her. 'I'm just not sure what to say. What do I do, now I know all this? It changes absolutely everything.'

'You mean, what do *we* do?' she said. 'You're not alone in this, it affects us all.' She suddenly smiled. 'There is good news in all this, Joseph. It means we're not just cousins, we're brother and sister.' He looked up at her, and she could see confusion and vulnerability stamped on his face. 'We'll face it together.'

'What are we going to do?' he said, putting the tea back down on the table. 'Should I get on the phone to my mother now . . . my aunt . . . whatever she is? My first instinct is to do that, because I need to know one hundred per cent if what my father told me is the truth.' He sighed. 'And yet, I know in my heart it is the truth. I know the way my father was when I was growing up. He's an idiot at times, and I find it hard to forgive him for all he's put my mother through – but I know he cares about me. He wouldn't do that.'

'I believe him too,' she said quietly. 'It makes total sense what he said. When he explained about them discovering they couldn't have children, and then my mother going over to live with them in England when she was pregnant with you . . . I suppose it was the obvious answer.'

'That's the easy part to understand, Angela.' He looked down at the floor now, his gaze directed on the patterned carpet. 'We all know what people are like about unmarried mothers in Ireland even now, and it must have been harder back then – twenty-five years ago. I've always wondered if I was illegitimate . . . being adopted . . . so I suppose I was half-prepared for that. But what I don't understand is why my real mother has always seemed to hate me so much.'

He looked up at her now. 'I need to find out the truth, so, do I just throw everything up here now and fly back to Ireland to confront them both?'

'Well, I suppose it's the only way to find out the real truth,' Angela said. 'But I'd advise you to plan it. Think carefully how you're going to go about it.'

'I don't want to throw a bomb into everyone's lives – my mother especially – I mean Catherine. I don't care about Nance, I don't care how she reacts. My mother and father are to blame for keeping the truth from me – letting me think they just randomly adopted me from an orphanage – but the real villain of the piece in this is Nance. But I need to think of people that it affects, like Fiona and Bridget – Bridget especially. Can you imagine how she will feel when she hears this, and her preparing to be a nun? And it's so soon after Uncle Seán – they're not over that yet.'

'They'll be fine, eventually,' Angela said. 'When they hear the truth, they will understand. You're the last person they will blame.' She thought back to the rows at the funeral with her mother about the way she had been treating Aunt Catherine and Joseph, she thought back to the huge row between her parents the night before her father died. She now realised that it had all been about Joseph. About Joseph being her son, and about her being terrified that the truth would come out.

'And, of course, I still don't know anything about my real father,' he said. 'I need to find out about that as well.' Tears glinted at the corners of his dark brown eyes. 'What should I do?'

'I was thinking as we walked back over here, and, after talking now, I think for the time being you should do nothing with regards to your mother. I think you should go and see your father tomorrow – when he's stone-cold sober – and get him to tell you everything he knows.'

Joseph sighed and looked up to the ceiling. 'He's a bloody idiot!'

'But he does love you, and I think he will want to help you,' she told him. 'When you know more of the facts, you'll be able to plan what is the best thing to do next. You don't need to make any decisions tonight. Drink your tea. It will make you feel better.' She reached into her handbag and found a hanky. Then, she got to her feet and went over to give it to him.

She perched on the arm of his chair, put her arm around him and kissed him on the side of the head. He leaned in against her, his head resting on her shoulder. They sat in silence for a few minutes, then, just as she thought to move back to her own chair, the door opened and Major Harrington came in.

He looked at the young couple in front of him, cuddled up on one chair together, then he took a step backwards. 'Oh, I do beg your pardon, Angela – I'm so sorry. I didn't realise you had company . . .'

Angela moved off the chair as quickly as she could, and went towards the door, but before she had a chance he had closed the door behind him. 'I won't be a minute,' she said to Joseph. 'That's my boss, and I just need to talk to him.'

She went out into the hallway, and could see the major striding off in front of her to the bar. She stopped for a minute, to catch her breath, to steady herself before she spoke to him. It was then that she realised her leg was aching badly. It was no wonder it was sore, she thought. She had been on her feet for a good part of the day, and then she had walked all the way from the hotel to the pub and back. If she was at home, she would have immediately gone and put her calliper on, but tonight she would push through. She had more important things to sort out first.

She straightened her back now, and walked across the hallway and into the half-empty bar. Her eyes moved straight to where she knew he would be, standing at the end of the bar, waiting while the young man serving poured him a large whiskey. As she slowly went towards him, she noticed for once that he was not talking to the barman. He was just standing quietly.

She went over and touched him on the elbow and he turned around.

'Angela . . .' he said. 'I'm sorry I disturbed you. You needn't have left your friend. You're not working tonight.'

481

'It's my cousin,' she said. 'I just wanted to explain.'

'My dear,' he said, 'you don't have to explain anything to me. You're entitled to your privacy. I don't expect you to spend your time off with me, or justify what you're doing during it.'

She suddenly felt she needed reassurance from this storm that had erupted around her. And for some reason, this older, eccentric employer suddenly seemed like a safe raft in the middle of it all.

'My cousin has just had a terrible shock tonight. He's adopted, which he has always known, but he has just discovered that his real mother is a family member. His aunt.'

'The poor chap,' he said. He sucked his breath in, thinking. 'That must be an awful thing to happen . . . the feeling of betrayal. I can't imagine . . .' He shook his head. 'I know it's small comfort, but these things are not uncommon – secret adoption within the family.'

Her lip suddenly trembled. 'It's more complicated than that. It affects our family too. It appears that my mother is actually his real mother . . . she had him before she met my father. Her sister, my Aunt Catherine, and her husband adopted him. Joseph's father turned up tonight, rather the worst for drink, and it all came out. None of us had the slightest idea.'

'Oh, my dear Angela!' he said. 'What a terrible

shock for him – for you both. Is there anything I can do?'

She shook her head. 'I honestly don't know what to do myself. It's the most awful situation.'

The barman put the major's whiskey down in front of him now.

'Would you bring me two brandies please?' the major asked. He turned to Angela. 'Brandy is good for shock. A small drink might possibly help the two of you. Since there's nothing else I can do.' He paused. 'If you want to go back to him now, I'll send the waiter into the sitting room with the drinks. I don't want to come myself – I wouldn't like to intrude or embarrass the chap. But I will be waiting here when you need me. Take as long as you both need.'

'I don't think Joseph will stay much longer as he has work in the morning, and he will probably need some time on his own to think all this through. To decide what he's going to do about it.'

'Of course, of course . . .'

Angela glanced towards the door, thinking of Joseph sitting on his own. 'I should go now.' She turned back to the major and put her hand on his, and looked up at him. 'Thank you for being so understanding. I feel a little better after speaking to you.'

His hand moved to cover hers. 'I wish there was more I could do to help.'

'Knowing you are here is the biggest help,' she said

quietly. Then as she looked at him, something inside her seemed to shift. She didn't know what it was, but something had changed. 'Thank you,' she said, drawing her hand away. 'Thank you, Edward.'

CHAPTER 40

The next morning, Angela lay in the comforting warmth of a deep bath, her mind going over the events of the night before, scene by scene. She was surprised, in a way, by how little the revelations about her mother and Joseph had affected her. She felt quite happy now knowing that Joseph was her half-brother. He was the best person she could imagine to be her brother.

How she felt about her mother, knowing what she did now, she was still unsure. Not having been close to her physically or emotionally for years, she had no real idea of the sort of person her mother was, deep down. She knew her only as a meticulous, practical woman who had to have everything done just the right way. To have the shop run in a certain manner, to dress in a certain manner, to behave in a certain manner – a manner that was as correct and perfect as possible. A manner that was above criticism or reproach.

For Angela, to picture her now as a young girl giving birth to an illegitimate baby over in England all those years ago, seemed almost incomprehensible. And yet, she knew in her heart every word her drunken uncle had said was true.

At the time – in the mid-forties – it would have been the ultimate shame. To many in Ireland, she knew it still was. Times had moved on in the world now, and people were more relaxed about sex before marriage in big cities like London and even amongst certain types in Dublin – but nothing had really changed in small towns like Tullamore. The church still had the same rules and most people still subscribed to them.

Whatever now followed was not going to be easy for everyone involved – especially her mother. She was surprised her Aunt Catherine had managed to hide this huge secret all these years, considering how awful her mother had been to her and Joseph. Especially of late. She wondered about it all now, and concluded that there would be more things to come out – more pieces of the jigsaw to be put together, before the whole picture became clear.

Over breakfast, the major asked her if she wanted to go home. 'I understand if you do,' he said. 'And we can organise it quite easily. You don't need to worry in the least about me. I come over to England often – we can easily shelve things until another time.' He smiled. 'It's one of the glories of being an independent employer. We have no one else to answer to.'

She shook her head. 'No, I would rather we continue with the plans we made. Finish off what has to be done here, and then go back to Thornley

Manor and get the notes and the typing up to date while it's all fresh in both our minds.' She looked at her watch. 'I will probably hear from Joseph at some point this morning. He said he would ring the hotel when he had a spare minute.'

'We're in no rush,' the major said. 'And we're fairly ahead with things down here. I thought, since it's wet outside today, it might be a good day to visit the Victoria and Albert Museum. I think you will enjoy it, and it might help to take your mind off other things.'

'That sounds ideal,' she said. 'I might try to get some work done while I'm waiting to hear from Joseph. I could go through the papers you brought back from your uncle's and from the record office?'

Angela was busy typing when Joseph rang at eleven o'clock. He had thought about things, and decided not to do anything rash.

'I'm not going to phone my mother,' he told her, 'because she is all on her own. She doesn't even have you there to talk to. I would rather talk to her face to face. I know it is going to kill her, and I'd rather be beside her and reassure her that nothing will change.'

Angela listened, saying very little, letting him make all the decisions.

'I spoke to my father,' he said. 'He came out to the hotel early this morning. He was well-dressed and sober, and full of apologies. I got half an hour off to go and sit somewhere quiet and we had a good talk. It seems he and my mother argued for years about telling me about how my adoption came about. My father thought I should know the truth, but my mother had promised Nance never to tell me. And I think she was also terrified that if I found out who my real mother was, I might want to go and live with her. She kept telling Dad that she wanted to wait until I was older and could make my own choices. Well, of course, they split up and my father went to England before that ever happened.' His voice sounded a little choked now. 'It's sad really, because I think this secret was always a bone of contention between them.'

'It must have been very difficult. I suppose an ordinary adoption is more straightforward than an adoption in the family. All the people involved are strangers, and presumably all the arrangements are made by nuns or the people running orphanages.'

'My mother and father were living in Dublin and so was Nance. Apparently Nance was overwhelmed when I was born, and somehow between them it was decided that Catherine and Ken would adopt me. Nance was living nearby so she could still see me on a regular basis.'

'It's all so hard to believe,' Angela said. 'We're not the closest mother and daughter, but it makes me feel as if I don't know anything about my mother at all . . . Imagine all that happening to her and none of us knowing . . .'

'I don't know all the details either,' Joseph said. 'It seems it all worked for a while after I was born, and then Dad said there was a big falling-out because Nance was becoming too involved. Apparently she was calling in after work every night and wanting to have me at the weekends. I couldn't take in everything that Dad was saying, it was too overwhelming, but the gist of it was my mother and father went over to England for a few years so she couldn't interfere. In the meantime, your mother met your father and they got married and started their own family. Then a few years later, my mother and father brought me back to live in Dublin. That's as much as I know.'

Angela shook her head. 'It seems like an awful lot of coming and going when you were little.'

He shrugged. 'I suppose with Dad being English, they were used to going backwards and forwards between Ireland and England.'

'Can I ask you something?' she said. 'Did my father know early on about the adoption? I was wondering that this morning.'

'Yes, he did. Your mother told him a short while before they got married. To give him the chance to back out if he wanted. They must have worked it out, because they went ahead with the wedding.'

'I'm glad to hear that,' Angela said, filling up with tears. 'My father was a decent man.'

'All the business about me losing my job and my mother asking if I could come down to Tullamore – Uncle Seán was in agreement with that. Ken explained it all this morning. What I didn't know was that he and my mother were in

489

constant touch about me. Odd really, since they were separated, but it seems he was the only one she could talk to about things. The only person who knew all the facts.'

'I can understand that,' Angela said. 'It must be hard when you're bottling everything up and have no one to share it with.'

'Well, my father admitted he was the one who was pushing for them to tell me the truth. He felt it was time I knew, and that your family knew I was your half-brother. He warned my mother that if she didn't tell me soon about the adoption, then he would have no choice but to tell me. She asked him to wait, and she said she would talk to Nance and Seán and give them time to think about it – to prepare.'

Angela rolled her eyes to the ceiling. 'And of course my mother just shut down – evaded the whole thing.'

'My mother told them all this when they went to visit her house after Christmas.' He halted. 'Just before your father died . . . she told them that Ken was planning to tell me, and your father said he agreed that I should know. Then, my mother told them about me being out of work and the trouble in the band. So, Seán being the decent man that he is, said the best thing would be if I came to Tullamore to work in the bar and live with them for a while, then they could both break it to me about the adoption, at the right time. And that, of course, is when the big row happened between your parents, as your mother didn't agree with any of it. She didn't want to hear of me coming to live with them, and didn't want me to know about the adoption.'

'Yes,' Angela said, nodding to herself. 'It all fits into place. It's exactly as Fiona described.' She thought now of her sister, and wondered how she would react to this news, after all the months of pressure of looking after Mam. Selfish, uncaring Mam– who had brought everything on herself.

'So,' Joseph said, 'I'm going to leave it for now. I'm going to see if I can get time off work to go home for a few days, and see if we can sort all this out.' He gave a wry laugh. 'With both my mothers.' He thought for a moment. 'It could take a few weeks before I can arrange the time off, but I suppose it doesn't matter, it's not going to change things that much. It will give me time to work out what I'm going to say to my mother. She's the one I'm concerned about.'

'I'll be home the week after next,' Angela told him. 'In the meantime, I'm in London for the next couple of days, and then I'm back to Cheshire for a week before going back to Ireland.' Then, she gave him the number of Thornley Manor in case he needed to speak to her at any time.

She rang the major's room to say she had spoken to Joseph, and that she would be ready shortly to go to the museum. He came down the corridor to tap on her door minutes later.

'Are you all right?' he asked, when she let him in.

491

'I think so,' she said. 'Nothing is going to happen before I return to Ireland. Joseph is going to take some time off in a few weeks and come back home and try to sort things out.'

She went over to stand by the table, while he stood just inside the door, as though uncertain of invading her privacy.

'Not easy,' he said. 'Families can be the best of things and the worst of things. And of course, they're all riddled with secrets.' He thought for a moment. 'You know Jeremy, whom you met?'

'Yes,' she said. As if, she thought, she could ever forget him.

'His younger brother, Philip – the chap in Scotland. It emerged a few years ago that they have different fathers. Apparently his mother went off abroad for a few months – Switzerland, if I remember correctly. Supposedly, he was the result of a summer dalliance with a relative of the exiled Italian royal family.' He shrugged. 'It was an open secret in our family for years, but it didn't appear to cause more than a minor hiccup. Philip is a lovely chap, and I'm glad to say that his father has always treated both boys exactly the same. In fact, Philip would lead a similar quiet lifestyle to his father, as opposed to Jeremy's more artistic bent.'

He gave one of his quiet chuckles, which warmed Angela further to him, and lifted her spirits. She thought his open attitude – free from judgement – was so much better than the one she would eventually have to face, when all the secrets came out in Tullamore. But that, she decided, would wait. In the meantime, she would enjoy the rest of her trip to London, and the last week back in Thornley Manor.

'I'll get ready now,' she said. 'And I'll meet you downstairs in five minutes.'

'I'll have a taxi waiting for us at the front of the hotel.' He went towards the door, then he turned back. 'I think I might change into a casual shirt and dispense with the tie, since we're having a day as tourists.'

She smiled at him. 'I think that's a good idea,' she said. 'I might do the same.' She put her hand to her mouth laughing. 'Obviously I don't mean I was planning to wear shirt and tie!'

'I'm sure you'd look very nice in it, Angela,' he said. 'You always look nice.' He halted. 'If I could give you a little fashion advice?'

She looked at him quizzically.

'Wear the calliper. We'll have a bit of walking around the museum, and you'll enjoy it so much more if your leg is supported.'

She came downstairs a short while later wearing one of her new pairs of trousers and one of the daisy-printed tunics she had bought the day she went shopping with her friends. She carried a yellow, swing-style raincoat over her arm. She had also pinned her hair up in the looser style that Maureen had shown her.

The small foyer of the hotel was busy with a queue of a half a dozen guests with bags and cases waiting to check out, and a similar, parallel one waiting to check in. People were dotted about at tables, some in groups and some in couples or on their own. A group of Japanese tourists were having a loud discussion in their own language, and jabbing fingers at maps of the city.

The major was standing over by the window, away from the tables, watching for the taxi, unaware she was there. He was wearing a black-and-grey Paisley-patterned long-sleeved shirt, with a button-down collar, and black soft moleskin trousers. He had a dark trench coat over his arm. She was pleased he looked so nice, and surprisingly modern in a classy, subtle way. It was certainly not in the louche way that Jeremy's dressed, she thought, but he was dressed with a style that suited both him and her.

As she walked towards him, she gave a little cough.

'Ah, Angela . . .' he said. Then he stopped and looked at her. 'May I say how particularly lovely you look?'

'Thank you,' she said. 'And I have to return the compliment. Your shirt is very nice – very nice indeed.'

They stood smiling at each other.

'This feels like a day off school,' he said, a slight self-consciousness about him. 'Playing truant. I haven't done anything like this for a long time. I've never had the right company, someone who would get the same enjoyment from it.' Then, he caught himself. 'At least, I hope you will find it enjoyable. I know you haven't been there before, but I'm basing it on the things I know about you already.'

Angela felt her heart quicken. She didn't know if she was reading things correctly or not, but she was going to take a chance on it. He would, she knew, be kind if she had read the situation wrongly.

She moved towards him. 'I don't think it feels like having a day off school, Edward,' she said, sliding her arm through his. 'I think it feels more like a date.'

'A date?' He repeated, a bemused smile on his face. 'You surely don't mean you and me?'

'Would that be so terrible?' she asked.

His eyes widened in disbelief. He looked around the room, checking to see if anyone was observing them. But it seemed as if the foyer had just emptied itself of most of the people. The noisy Japanese group had gone, most of the queues had gone, leaving only a few people at the desk and one or two tables quietly occupied over in the far corner, well away from them.

'Angela,' he said in a low voice, 'I'm not sure if you know what you're saying . . . but do you realise that I am almost fifty-one years old?'

Her confidence faltered. She nodded, momentarily unable to find any further words. Eventually, she said, 'I presumed you were around that age, maybe even older . . .'

They stood looking at each other.

'Have I made a mistake in speaking out?' she asked, her arm starting to slip away from his.

'Not at all.' He caught it with his hand, and gently eased it back in place. 'I never let myself imagine that this could happen. Never for a moment. And it's not just because of the age difference. It would not have mattered if you were much older than me. It's the fact that someone so lovely – such a clever, capable woman would consider such a . . . well, such a socially clumsy and . . . well, the generally inept person that I am.'

'Edward Harrington,' she said, her voice almost stern, 'you are not in any way as you have just described yourself. You are the kindest, most interesting man I have ever met.'

His hand came to his mouth. 'I'm struggling to understand this unbelievable change of circumstance,' he said. 'The best I had hoped for was to have your company, to share a meal with you, to talk about the project with someone who understands and appreciates it. Anything more, I wouldn't let myself even imagine.'

'Well, you have all that,' she said, 'and you also have a good friend who you can always trust.' She moved her hand now, to trace her fingers along the back of his hand. 'But you also have someone who admires you, who cares deeply about you, and who could perhaps even grow to love you.'

She looked up at him now and saw him smiling at her. Yes, she thought, he was older than her – but not as old as she had thought. People, she knew, would stare at them and wonder – perhaps even think he was her father.

None of it mattered. She did not care – she had been stared at for most of her life. And although he was by no means handsome in the conventional way, neither was he unattractive. And as his deep brown eyes held hers, she felt the same little shift deep inside her, which she now recognised as a physical longing to be closer to him.

'I am overwhelmed,' he said. 'And since you have been so brave and honest, I am going to be equally so with you.' He lifted her hand to his lips. 'All the things I have thought about you – the many fine qualities that I have admired since the first day we met in the Gresham Hotel in Dublin – have all suddenly culminated into one single fact. I, Angela, am already very much in love with you.'

The shrieking sound of a car horn suddenly startled them apart. Then, without saying another word, they moved together, his hand tightly gripping hers, out of the hotel and into the depths of the London taxi cab.

CHAPTER 41

Bridget came out of the main building with a group of three other girls – dressed in tennis skirts, sports shirts and carrying racquets – and stepped into the warm sunshine and the damp scent of the newly watered wall-flowers, Sweet William and roses. There was a relaxed, almost lazy feel about the early summer evening as everything was heading towards the end of the school year in just a few days' time.

The exam results had come out, and while she could have done better in certain areas such as Maths and Geography, Bridget was happy enough with the overall pass in all her subjects.

In a few days' time she would go back home for the summer to work in the shop with her mother and Fiona. Most years she had looked forward to having the time back in Tullamore, but things had somehow changed this year and she wasn't quite sure how she felt about going home. She still felt the loss of her father very deeply, and missed his cheery, comforting presence in the house, and she knew everyone in the family felt the same.

She was always happy to see Fiona, and Angela,

and she now felt fine about seeing her mother. She had not been so keen to go home whilst her mother was ill. It made her feel uncomfortable to see her so sleepy and lethargic and rambling in her conversations. She knew from the recent letters she had received from her that there was a big improvement in her mother's health and her general demeanour, and Fiona and Angela had confirmed when they wrote that she was much better too. While she was thankful about the news, she still had a certain reluctance to return to Tullamore.

She had given the situation some thought, and talked about it with Sister Bernadette, and she had come to the conclusion that she had become so used to the routine of the convent school that this now felt like her home. The Masses, the prayers, religious books, the comfortable silences, the predictable routines – the whole ethos. She realised she was reluctant to give it all up for two months. Entering back into the hustle and bustle of normality at home and in the shop and in the streets of the town, no longer felt like her real life.

But Sister Bernadette had said it was important for the girls to go back to their families at the end of every term. It would be some years until they made their final vows, and they had to be one hundred per cent sure that their vocation was for life – that this cloistered world was one they could not just tolerate, but flourish in.

Bridget said she understood all that, but she had

no doubts whatsoever that she wanted to become a nun. She was happy with the religious life. It was as simple as that.

Sister Bernadette had given examples of other girls who had started at the school with Bridget's class – girls who had decided not to return after previous summers. 'And,' she said, with a grave look on her face, 'I have a feeling that certain girls in your class this year may not return.'

Bridget had looked up at her with surprised eyes, but the nun had just shaken her head.

'I can't say anything more about it.'

After the chat with Sister Bernadette was over, Bridget stood up and went towards the door, and then she halted for a few moments, thinking.

'Did Mother Superior ever ask you anything about . . . the thing I overheard my father saying?'

There was a small silence then Sister Bernadette smiled at her. 'No,' she said. 'I wasn't asked to report back on any family issues.'

Bridget had felt a wave of gratitude. 'Thank you,' she said. 'I felt much better about that after I told you, and I haven't dreamt about it since.'

'I'm glad,' Sister Bernadette had replied. 'Families all have difficulties, and there are times when it's best not to dwell on them. Any time you feel anxious, pray to Our Lady and she will help you to let go of it.'

The four girls stopped at the side of the tennis court now, and then split into twos for a doubles' game. Some of the other girls from their class sat on the benches at the side to watch them, while others went to the netball area.

As they played, Bridget wondered which of her classmates Sister Bernadette had been referring to when she mentioned about girls not coming back after the summer. A few weeks ago she would have thought the obvious ones were Veronica and Carmel, but recently the girls had gone much quieter and didn't seem quite so friendly with each other. Maybe, she thought, the recent trouble they had got themselves into had taught them a lesson, and made them think in a more mature way.

The girl playing diagonally from her on the tennis court, Lynn Dolan, hit a particularly high serve and the ball came flying towards Bridget. She quickly moved backwards to get a better swipe at it, but even though she jumped as high as she could with the racquet fully stretched, the ball flew a few feet above her head and off into the high hedges by the wall.

Bridget straightened up to get her balance and then she stood, hands on hips, laughing.

'That was a good one!' Lynn called. 'It's just a pity I'm not another two feet tall!'

The other girls came to a halt at the middle of the court, all laughing now.

'I'll just get the ball,' Bridget said.

She went strolling over to the hedges while the others stood chatting. She took a minute or two to locate the white ball, and then she spotted it in the side of one of the hedges, up quite a height.

She stood on her tip-toes swishing her racquet backwards and forwards in the branches, to dislodge it. The ball fell down about six inches and got stuck again.

As Bridget stopped to catch her breath, she noticed four nuns she didn't recognise coming out of the side door of the main building and walking towards cars parked just outside the door. Then she saw Mother Superior walking behind them with the priest who said Mass in the convent. The car with the nuns drove off and, as Bridget went to turn back to the ball, she noticed Mother Superior shaking her head at the priest and then moving her hands up to press both sides of her head. It struck her that it was a gesture her mother had often used when she wasn't feeling well, or was overwhelmed if anyone suggested she should do something she didn't want to do. It didn't make sense to her that the head of the convent would feel like that.

'Bridget!' Lynn yelled. 'What about the ball?'

'Coming!' she called back. She threw the racquet up into the hedge and after the third attempt, the tennis ball came bouncing down onto the path.

After breakfast on the day before they broke up for the summer, the girls in Bridget's class were told to leave their cleaning duties and go straight down to one of the classrooms. When they went in, Mother Superior was already there with several of the other nuns, including Sister Bernadette.

Silently, the girls all slid into seats and waited to hear why they had been summoned.

Mother Superior came to stand before them, her hands clasped together in front of her. 'Girls,' she said, 'I know you're all preparing to return home to your families, but I have to advise you of a difficult situation that we are trying to settle before the end of term. You are all aware that we had a problem with certain behaviour amongst this particular class over the last number of weeks and maybe even months.'

Bridget felt her stomach clench. She gave a carefully guarded glance around the room and noticed that Veronica and Carmel were not there.

'More investigations have been carried out,' Mother Superior said, 'and it seems the situation is much more serious than we thought. We have had to advise the parents of those involved about what has taken place.' She paused. 'I'm not at liberty to give anyone any details – it's strictly private and only the related families' business, and must remain that way. What I have to tell you now is that both the behaviour and the covering up of serious incidents by certain other girls in this year has left us facing a situation we have never had to deal with before. And it has left the order feeling that all the good work we have done with this class over the year has been somehow tainted. That all the secrets and lies that we have had to drag out of some of you, has left us very concerned about the class as a whole.'

Bridget's heart was pounding as she listened. She was quite sure that the two girls had now been expelled. She had a mixture of feelings about this. There was a kind of relief that the girls were going as they had never seemed the right sort to become nuns, but there was also a sense of guilt about having helped the nuns arrive at their decision by telling about the letter that had been hidden.

'We have been in serious discussions with the hierarchy in our order,' Mother Superior said, 'and later today, a major decision will be made about the situation.'

She then asked everyone to join their hands and led the girls in a prayer, and then she told the girls they could go and do the last fifteen minutes of their cleaning duties.

CHAPTER 42

Fiona looked up as her mother came into the kitchen. She was just finishing off her breakfast and then she would get ready to head down to the shop.

'Two airmail letters from America for you,' Nance said, handing them over to her. 'And a typed brown letter for me.' She went to sit in the armchair by the fire. Her dark hair was neatly pinned up, and she was wearing a new brown trouser suit.

Fiona looked at the front of the blue airmails, checking the handwriting. She guessed one at least would be from Michael. It wouldn't be the first time two of his letters came together on the same day. On this occasion, one was from him, with a Boston postmark, and the other, with the familiar New York postmark, was from Elizabeth.

Since her mother was sitting just across the kitchen from her, she decided to read Elizabeth's letter first. She slid her thumb under the envelope seal and took it out. It was a fairly short letter, just the back and front of one page. Fiona's eyes quickly scanned down one side of the pale blue paper, then turned it over to read the back.

'You're not going to believe it,' she said, looking up at her mother. 'Elizabeth is coming home for a wedding in October. A cousin from Wicklow. She's coming for a fortnight's holiday. The people she is working for are paying her air fare.'

'That's great news altogether,' her mother said. 'You'll look forward to that. It shows you how easy travel is getting. I heard one of the women in the hairdresser's talking about going out to see her son in Chicago.' She smiled at Fiona. 'But you know more about travelling back and forward to America from Michael.' She nodded to the letter on the table. 'It won't be long until he's here again. July, isn't it?'

'Yes, it's only five or six more weeks.'

'Did Elizabeth have any other news?'

Fiona looked down at the page in her hand. She wasn't going to say anything, but since her mother had asked, and was looking at her she said, 'She just added a little note at the end to say that Mrs Davis asked her to let me know that the other girl who took my job is leaving at Christmas. She said that if I'm still interested to get in touch at the end of the summer, before they advertise the job.'

Nance looked directly at her. 'And, are you still interested? Would you still like to go?'

Fiona's gaze moved back to the letter. 'I don't know,' she said. 'I'm not sure. I hadn't expected the job to come up again, and I don't know how things will be here with you, or between me and Michael . . .'

'Well,' her mother said, 'you don't have to make that decision right now, do you? Give yourself a bit of time and see how things go over the summer.'

Fiona nodded and looked out of the window, trying to think it through. Her mother was undoubtedly much improved. She was now back at work every day in the shop, doing what she had done before their father had died. She looked much better, and she was fitter than she had been in a long time. The doctor had advised her to start walking every day, and to take up some interests in the evenings.

Fiona had not imagined that her mother would do either of those things but, surprisingly, she and Mrs Mooney had started walking for an hour together every morning, after breakfast. They did a circle around the town and out the Charleville Road.

And even more surprisingly, her mother had joined a local amateur drama group. Her friend Nora helped to produce the shows, and she had asked Nance if she would help out as a prompter. At first she had been unsure, but after reading the script over and enjoying it, she decided that it would be something that wouldn't require too much pressure and would get her out in the evenings.

Her mother was so busy with rehearsals now

that Fiona was in the house in the evenings more often on her own than not. On the whole, things were much improved, but not enough, she thought, to consider leaving her on her own in the house and shop.

Her mother suddenly cut through her thoughts. 'This is a strange letter from the convent,' she said, 'and it's from the Mother Superior. She is asking if the parents can come early on Friday morning to collect the girls in Bridget's class for the summer. She says that if possible it has to be the parents or guardians as it's of the utmost importance.' She put the letter down and looked at Fiona. 'What do you make of that?'

Fiona raised her eyebrows. 'I was going to drive over and collect her myself, but I think we better go together.' She picked up her letter from Michael, which she planned to read in the privacy of her bedroom, then she stood up. 'I'll go upstairs to finish getting ready for work now.'

'I'll be down as soon as I've had my walk,' her mother said, looking at her watch. 'Mary Ellen should be finished the breakfast down at the pub now. She only had one fellow to cook for. I'll put my coat on now and meet her down there. It will save her the walk up.'

'She's done well,' Fiona said. 'She told me she's lost nearly a stone already.'

'It's the walking,' her mother said, smiling at her. 'I think it's helping us both.'

⋆　　⋆　　⋆

On Friday afternoon, Fiona and her mother and Bridget walked up the path to the house and came in. The two girls went straight into the sitting-room, while their mother went to put the kettle on to make them all tea.

'Are you okay?' Fiona asked her sister again.

Bridget nodded, her face white and strained. 'It's just the shock,' she said, tucking her blonde hair behind one ear. 'Our whole year being dismissed. Fifteen girls being sent home and told there's no place for us next year. I've never heard of it happening before.'

Their mother came in now, and went over to put her arms around Bridget. 'You'll just have to try not to worry about it. You're off now for the summer, whatever happens. Try to put it out of your head.'

'But the nuns didn't tell us anything. I don't understand it – I never even got a chance to talk to the other girls.'

'They didn't tell the parents much either,' her mother said. 'I told you that in the car coming home.'

'What was it they said again?' Bridget asked. 'I couldn't take it all in when you were talking in the car. Can you tell me again?'

'Mother Superior just said that several serious incidents had occurred over the year between some of the girls – both in the convent, and at home – and they felt it had affected the quality of the training of all the aspirants in that year. She said that some the girls' vocations were now in question, and they had taken advice from the main convent. They were advised to just dissolve the whole class.' Nance's brow wrinkled, as she tried to remember. 'She said while the main problem was caused by only two girls, the bigger problem was that a number of the girls in your class knew that something was going on, and helped keep it a secret.' Nance shrugged. 'She kept going on about the secrecy thing, which the convent felt had completely broken the trust.'

Bridget threw her hands up in frustration. 'But they questioned us all a few weeks ago, when Mother Superior brought us all in one by one, and I told them anything I knew.' She thought about how she had told the nuns about the letter in the wall and how she had seen the farmhand taking it. 'It wasn't much, but I told them.'

Nance patted her daughter's shoulder. 'I have a feeling it was something more serious than anyone knows. But they said it was confidential, and that it was between the two girls and their parents. I suppose they have to respect that.'

'What am I going to do?' Bridget asked. 'I don't want to give up my vocation. I still want to be a nun.'

'There's nothing we can do about it,' her mother said. 'We can't argue with the nuns – especially that Mother Superior. Their minds are made up on it. They've said it's up to the girls who feel they still have a vocation to apply to other orders now, so we can look at different ones over the summer, and see if you can find a place somewhere else. It's not as if you were involved with the two girls, I don't see why you should suffer because of them. We can talk to Father McEvoy. I'm sure he will advise us.'

'Or Father Fahy,' Fiona said. 'I think he's more open in his thinking.'

Bridget looked from one to the other and gave a great sigh. 'I can't believe it. My whole future is up in the air now – all my plans. I don't know where I'm going to be or what order I'm going to be in – if any order will take me.'

'Bridget,' Fiona said, 'don't worry about it. It will work out. You're exactly the right sort of person that is suited to be a nun, and I'm sure one of the other convents will be delighted to have you.'

'Do you think so?' Then she put her hands up to her mouth. 'Oh, I'm sorry, Fiona! Going on about my future when all your own plans to go to New York had to be cancelled.'

'It doesn't matter,' Fiona said. 'Things have a way of working out, and some things just take a bit longer than others.'

Their mother stood up. 'The kettle will be boiling – I'll go and get us all a nice cup of tea and a slice of cake.'

After she left the room, Bridget turned to Fiona. 'There's something else. I need to speak to you and Angela together.'

'What is it?' Fiona said. 'Is it something to do with those girls at the convent?'

'No, it's nothing about that.' She could see Fiona was worried now. 'Look, it's something I just need to sort out and get some advice about. It's complicated . . . and I'd rather wait until I can talk to the both of you.'

'Okay,' Fiona said. 'As long as it's not something very serious?'

'It's nothing that can't wait a few more days.'

'I can ring Angela this evening and maybe we could drive up to see her on Sunday. I haven't seen her since she came back from England, and I know she wants us to go up to see the new place she is living in out in Ballsbridge. Mam is out in the afternoon at a drama rehearsal, so she won't mind us being out. Isn't it great she's out and about herself now?'

'Mam is the best I've seen her in a long time,' Bridget said. 'Thank God she's back to her old self. When I saw her at Easter I'd almost given up hope of that happening. She was really bad with the shingles, wasn't she?'

'She was,' Fiona said. 'Hopefully, it's all in the past.'

The sound of their mother's heels came tapping along the hallway.

'We'll get a chance to talk about it on Sunday when we're all together,' Fiona said.

Nance came in and put the tray down on the table. She gave a cup of tea to Fiona. 'So, you're in the bar tomorrow afternoon and evening while Patrick is at his cousin's wedding in Athlone?'

Fiona nodded. 'Yes, I offered to do it. There's nothing particular on tomorrow night, and if you can give me a hand we should manage it between us.' She took a sip of her tea. 'Isn't he an awful man that he wasn't going to go? I only found out about it when Mrs Mooney mentioned it to me. She was saying that all Patrick's family were going but him.'

'He didn't say anything about it to me either.' Nance handed a cup and saucer to Bridget now, and a side plate with a slice of chocolate cake. 'I wonder if he thought we couldn't manage without him?'

'No,' Fiona said. 'Mrs Mooney said she thought it was because he had no one to take to it, and the others all had partners.'

'Well, he won't be on his own – all his family will be there.' Nance sat down with her own tea now. 'At least the day out will do him good.'

CHAPTER 43

On Saturday morning, Fiona waited until her mother went to her hair appointment at eleven o'clock to ring Angela from the shop. Angela was delighted to hear from her, and glad that her mother was continuing to make a good recovery and was back at work.

'She's been very good ringing me more often,' Angela said. 'In fact, she's made more effort since that weekend she was in hospital than she's ever made.' She paused. 'And how is the romance going?'

'Great,' Fiona said, 'apart from the fact he's on one side of the Atlantic, and I'm on the other.'

'Hopefully, it won't be for too long.'

'He's definitely coming in July, so I'm looking forward to that. And we'll see how we get on.' She stopped for a second, seeing someone passing the shop window, wondering if they were coming in, but they passed on by. 'The reason I rang is to see if Bridget and I could come up to visit you tomorrow? I'm sorry it's short notice, but we wanted to come on our own, and Mam is out at a drama rehearsal.'

'I think that's fine for me. What time were you thinking of?'

'Would around three o'clock suit? We'll have our lunch at one, so we can leave after that.'

'Could you hold on for two minutes?' Angela asked. She came back, sounding a little breathless. 'Yes, that will be absolutely perfect for me. We'll have a nice afternoon tea, and catch up on all the news.'

'Before we do, just to let you know that Bridget's class have all been dismissed at the convent school.' She quickly filled Angela in on the bones of the story. 'Mam is planning to ring you later to tell you all about it, so I'll leave it to her to tell you the details. And no doubt Bridget will tell you more about it tomorrow. Apparently Bridget has something else she wants to talk to you and me about, so she'll be delighted we're seeing you tomorrow.'

'I'm really looking forward to seeing you both,' Angela said. 'I think you'll really like Moorhill House. I hope you do, because I absolutely love it.'

As Fiona put the receiver back in its cradle, she thought how well Angela sounded. She was the most relaxed she'd heard in a long time. And it occurred to her that she had been much better about Mam since that awful weekend, it was almost as though it had brought them a little bit closer. And the new job certainly sounded as if it suited Angela very well. She had been full of stories about the old house in Cheshire and then the trip down to London.

Her mother arrived back from the hairdresser's sooner than usual.

She stood at the door. 'What do you think?' she said, turning around.

'I don't believe it!' Fiona said. 'You've had it all cut off!' She stared in silence for a few moments, taking it in. 'It's absolutely gorgeous – a short bob really, really suits you. It takes years off you.'

'Maggie and the girls in the salon said the same.' She came into the shop now, patting the back of it. 'I'm delighted with it, and it will be easier to manage myself. I'm getting too old to have it long now, and I was fed up pinning it up.'

'It's lovely. I didn't know you were thinking of having it cut.'

'I was sitting waiting to have it done,' Nance said, 'and I was just looking through a hairdressing magazine when I saw a picture of this style, and I just took a notion to have it done. Maggie was in an awful rush this morning, so one of the other girls did it. Maggie was actually under the dryer herself – one of the other girls had put rollers in her hair. As I was leaving, she came out to the door to tell me how well the bob looked on me, and to give me a little bit of news.'

'Oh,' Fiona said, 'what was that?'

'You'll never guess – she's going to the wedding with Patrick.'

'What?' Fiona said. 'Oh, my God . . . how did that come about?'

'Seemingly, Maggie went down to the bar last

night – to the snug – to get a bottle of peppermint cordial. Don't ask me why she wanted that, but they got chatting and then he asked her. She looked delighted with herself.'

Fiona remembered the night in the bar, the night she met Michael for the first time. 'I'm delighted for them, too. I think they would make a nice couple.'

'Well, it will be interesting to see where it leads, if anywhere.' Nance went over to the little mirror on one of the shelves. 'I didn't need my hair coloured today, but I said I'd have a tint in it next week as well as the wash and blow-dry.'

'Good for you,' Fiona said.

'I'm not letting myself go again.' Her mother lifted her eyes to the ceiling and sighed. 'I'll never get over the state my hair was in when I was in hospital last month. The length of the grey roots – I looked like an old witch. That will never happen again. My hair will be blown dry twice a week from now on and coloured every month.'

Fiona smiled. Her mother was definitely getting back to her old self.

CHAPTER 44

Sunday was cool for June, and a generally dull day. As they pulled into the driveway of Moorhill House, Fiona could see Angela watching for them by the window.

By the time they got out of the car, she was at the front door waiting to greet them.

'What a place!' Fiona said, as she came towards her. 'It's beautiful.'

'Huge,' Bridget said, looking around her. 'I didn't realise it was so big.'

'Come inside,' Angela said. 'I have a nice fire in the sitting-room.'

'I've a box of groceries that Mam sent for you,' Fiona told her. 'They're in the boot.'

'Oh, that was good of her. We'll get them in later.'

The girls had a quick look around the hall and then Angela brought them down to her private quarters. They sat down on the deep sofa and chairs in front of the marble fireplace, and then she went along to the kitchen to let Eileen know that the girls had arrived. She went back to join them, and then a short while later there was a knock on the door and the major came in.

'I hope you don't mind my intruding?' he said, smiling over at Angela. 'I thought I might just come and introduce myself to the ladies before you have your tea.'

'Not at all,' Angela said, getting to her feet. 'Girls, this is Major Harrington, who I work for.'

'Edward, please,' he said. 'We don't need the formalities.'

'This is my older sister, Fiona, who I've told you lives at home in Tullamore and works in the shop.'

The major came to shake hands with Fiona and then when Bridget was introduced he did the same.

He stood chatting to them for a few minutes, telling them about his friend who lived outside Birr, and how he hoped to come down to Tullamore at some point to see the exact area where the hot air balloon had crashed. Fiona told him that one of her friends lived in the same street, although the houses were different as the original ones had burned down.

When Eileen came to put the tea tray on the coffee table in front of the girls, he said he would leave them to enjoy their tea and chat and he went off to listen to a radio play.

'What a lovely man,' Bridget said, when they were on their own.

'He really is,' Fiona said. 'How do you find him to work for?'

'Excellent,' Angela said. 'I've never been happier or more settled in my life.'

'Well, you look it,' Fiona said. 'You always look good, but you look even better.'

By the time the girls had poured their tea, Eileen was back with a cake stand filled with finger-sized sandwiches, scones and a variety of cakes.

'Tell us about your trip to England,' Fiona said after Eileen left. 'That definitely sounded interesting.'

'I will soon,' Angela said, 'but I'm anxious to hear what happened to Bridget. I can't believe that the school dismissed a whole year.'

They spent the next while going over the story again, and Angela was as mystified as her sisters as to why it had happened. Gradually, the story moved on to Angela's trip and Fiona and Bridget drank their tea and ate the sandwiches and cakes as they listened while she told them about The Tower of London and Madame Tussaud's and the Victoria and Albert Museum.

They did not discuss Fiona's trip to Clifden, as she had asked Angela not to bring the subject up. She didn't want to say she was with Michael – but neither did she want to tell a big story about being there, pretending she was with girlfriends. It wasn't fair on Bridget, who spent a lot of her days praying and thinking about doing everything according to the church. There was no point in upsetting her over things that did not concern her.

They were on their second cup of tea when Fiona said, 'Bridget, I think you wanted to talk to us about something when we were all together?'

'I do,' Bridget said, 'although I'm not sure where to start.'

'Take your time, Bridget,' Angela said. 'And don't be worrying. There's nothing you can't tell us that we won't understand.'

Bridget suddenly felt nervous, and her throat felt dry. She took another drink of her tea. 'The thing is,' she started, 'I'm worried that I've been keeping a secret about Daddy. A secret that could come out in years to come.'

Fiona caught her breath. She shot a concerned look across at Angela.

Angela's face tightened. 'Go on,' she said.

'It was something I overheard before Christmas, and I thought I was doing right by not telling anyone. Especially after he died. But it's been on my mind, and I talked to one of the nuns about it, and she said I should tell you.'

'On you go,' Fiona urged. 'We're listening.'

Bridget took a deep breath. 'Basically,' she said, 'I overheard Daddy talking to Aunt Catherine, and from what I can make out we have a brother we know nothing about.'

Angela's hands flew to her throat. 'Oh, God!' she said. 'I didn't think anyone else knew . . . I said nothing because I was waiting until Joseph came over, to talk to you then.'

Fiona looked from one to the other. Had Bridget really said they had a brother? And did Angela know about it too? She wondered had she misunderstood something? Her brain seemed to have slowed down – almost frozen. Something was undoubtedly wrong, but she could make no sense of what they had said.

'What are you talking about?' she finally said.

Bridget joined her hands together, as though praying. 'Daddy said it was time we were told there was a fourth child in the family, whether Mam liked it or not. He said it had gone on far too long. To me, it seems he's had an affair with someone, and they've had a child. What else could it mean?'

Fiona looked at Angela now.

'No, Bridget, you've got it wrong.' Angela's face was grave. 'It's Joseph. He is our brother. And Mam is his real mother. This has got nothing at all to do with Daddy.'

'Oh, Sweet Heart of Jesus!' Fiona said. 'This is something I can't even begin to understand!'

'She had Joseph before she married Daddy,' Angela explained, 'and she gave him up for adoption to Aunt Catherine and Uncle Ken.'

'Are you sure?' Bridget whispered. 'Are you saying that Mam had Joseph illegitimately?' Her voice was appalled, astonished, her usual calm temperament jolted with the news.

Angela slowly moved her head up and down. 'Yes,' she said. 'I found out when I met up with Joseph over in London. Uncle Ken turned up drunk and blurted the whole thing out to me and Joseph.'

Fiona's eyes were dull with shock. 'Does anyone else know?' she asked.

'Nobody,' Angela said. 'Joseph is hoping to come home in the next week or two, and he's going to talk to Aunt Catherine about it. He doesn't want to speak to her on the phone as he's afraid it will be too much for her to deal with, when she's on her own.'

'How could Mam have done this?' Fiona said, her tone bitter now. 'How could she have lied all these years to us – to everyone? She must have made Daddy lie about it too. How could she have seen her own son growing up, not knowing who she was? What kind of woman is she?'

'This is obviously what all the rows and coolness between her and Aunt Catherine have been about,' Angela said. 'It seems that she wasn't coping after Joseph was born, and that's when the idea of the adoption came up. But later, when Aunt Catherine and Uncle Ken were all settled with Joseph, she changed her mind and wanted to spend more and more time with him. From what Uncle Ken told Joseph, it got so bad that Aunt Catherine and Uncle Ken moved away to England with Joseph for a few years to get away from her.'

'From what I've just discovered this afternoon,' Fiona said, 'it seems my mother is capable of anything.' She let out a low sigh. 'I can't believe that she could be so critical of other people – other women – and there she was, with a secret illegitimate child.'

'We have to be careful not to judge her too harshly,' Bridget said, her calmer demeanour now settled back into place. 'We don't know all the reasons behind this.' She thought how Sister Bernadette would deal with this. 'She was a young woman, and probably terrified with the situation she found herself in. We don't know why she did what she did.'

'You're a saint, Bridget,' Angela told her. 'I wish I had such kind thoughts about Mam.'

'The one thing we all know,' Fiona said, 'is that she's been terrible to Joseph for the last number of years. She showed no interest in him as a nephew – she wouldn't give him a job in the bar when he was unemployed.' She let her breath out in a long, low sigh. 'God knows how he is feeling – knowing she is actually his mother. He must feel sick about it. I know I do . . .' She suddenly thought. 'What are we going to do? I don't think I can face her now I know all this.'

Angela looked at them. 'I don't have any answers,' she said. 'I've been thinking about it since I came back from England, and I still haven't come up with anything.'

Something suddenly struck Fiona. 'The only person who knows all the answers here is Aunt Catherine. I think we should drive out this afternoon and see her.'

Angela thought for a few moments. 'But Joseph isn't here, and he's the one who's most affected by this.'

'It affects us all,' Fiona said, 'and I think if we get some of this sorted out, we'll be doing him a favour.'

'I think I agree,' Bridget said. 'And it's different from her finding things out through a phone call. Joseph was worried about her being on her own when this was discussed, but we'll all be there.'

'What about Mam?' Fiona said. 'She's the one person who won't be at Aunt Catherine's.'

Angela felt a sudden ache in her leg and stood up to stretch it out. 'It's for the best Mam's not here,' she said, walking towards the window. 'It will give us time to talk to Aunt Catherine and decide how we are going to work all this out.' She stared out into the landscaped garden for a while, then she turned back to her sisters. 'There's one good thing that's come out of all this: Joseph is our brother. If I had to pick a brother, he's the one I would choose.'

The two girls looked at her.

'You're right,' Bridget said, smiling. 'I hadn't thought of it like that. He's a lovely person.'

'That is the one good thing,' Fiona agreed.

A knock came on the door.

'What time is it?' Angela said.

Fiona looked down at her watch. 'Half past four.'

'Oh, God,' Angela said, going over to the door, 'with everything, I forgot . . .'

Before she got to the door, it opened and Eileen Sweeney came in carrying a tray with five champagne glasses. Behind her followed Major Harrington carrying a bottle of Moet and Chandon champagne.

'Oh, Edward,' Angela said, sitting back down in

her chair. 'I'm not sure if this is actually the right time . . .'

He looked around, sensing something was going on, while Eileen quietly slipped out of the room. He came around them to put the bottle down on the coffee table beside the glasses. 'It's *good* news, my dear,' he said, 'and I think it is always the right time for that.'

She pressed her hand to her mouth, then she suddenly smiled. 'You're right,' she said. 'Of course we should tell them.' She looked first at Bridget and then at Angela. 'I wanted you to be the first to know. Edward and I have got engaged, and we're to be married next month.'

There was a stunned silence as her sisters tried to take the unexpected news in.

'When did it all happen?' Fiona asked.

'London,' Angela said, beaming at them. 'Although, really, we hit it off from the first time we met, didn't we, Edward?'

'We did indeed,' the major confirmed. 'I'm the luckiest man – makes you think that miracles do indeed happen – still can't believe she would take an old codger like me.'

Bridget's eyes lit up, but she managed to stop herself from laughing at the major's turn of phrase.

Angela noticed Bridget's laughter and she smiled at her and rolled her eyes. 'Oh, Edward, stop saying that,' she told him, shaking her head. 'Isn't he awful, running himself down like that? It's me who's lucky, finding someone who's so absolutely kind and thoughtful, and who enjoys the same things as I do.'

Edward felt in his jacket pocket, then he felt in the other. 'The ring?' he said, looking slightly anxiously at Angela.

'Inside pocket, dear,' she said, smiling at him.

He fumbled about and then produced a small box, and handed it to her.

'It was Edward's mother's ring,' she said, opening the box. 'It's an antique . . . it came from Paris.' She lifted out the triple-diamond ring and slipped it on her finger, and held it out to show them.

Both girls got to their feet to examine it, while Edward began filling the glasses.

'It's beautiful,' Fiona said. And then, after all the things that had flown through her mind about the differences between them – his age, the class difference and no doubt religious difference – she could think of nothing else to say except, 'I'm so happy for you, Angela, and I think you're the perfect match for each other.'

'Hear, hear!' the major said, handing the filled champagne glasses to the girls. Then, he lifted his glass. 'To my dear Angela,' he said. 'The light of my life.'

'And to Edward,' she said, smiling, and lifting her glass. 'And lots of happy, future surprises for us all.'

They all took a sip of the dry, bubbly drink and then the major suddenly said, 'Where's Eileen?' he said, 'I brought a glass for her.'

He went over to the door and looked out into the hallway. He came back in, shrugging. 'She's gone,' he said. 'Disappeared back to the kitchen.'

'We can take it down to her later,' Angela said.

Later, when the major went off in search of Eileen, Angela went out into the hallway and rang to check that her aunt was home, and to tell her that they would be out to her in the next half an hour. Then she came back into the sitting-room where the girls were finishing off their celebratory drink.

'How will we arrange the transport?' she said to Fiona. 'It's a nuisance I don't drive. Edward has suggested I take driving lessons, but I haven't had time to sort it out as yet.'

'Come with us,' Fiona said, 'and I'll drop you back later.'

She thought for a few moments. 'Yes, that would probably be best, but I'm sorry to drag you back through the city.'

Fiona raised her eyebrows and gave a sidelong smile. 'After all that's gone on this afternoon, I don't think it's a problem.' She suddenly stopped, then smiled warmly at her sister. 'I don't mean your brilliant news, of course. Bridget and I are delighted for you both.'

'He is the loveliest man,' Bridget said. 'I can see exactly how you like him.'

A pink colour came to Angela's face. 'I have never been so happy, or even imagined I could feel this happy. I know it was quick but, when you know something is right, why waste time?' She bit her lip. 'Although I should imagine that Mam will have plenty to say. Well, it's all sorted now, whatever she thinks. We'll be married up here in Dublin – Edward is not a Catholic, but he immediately offered to marry me in the church, so she should be happy about that.'

Bridget bit her lip, thinking, then she looked at Angela. 'Does the difference in religion worry you at all?'

Angela shook her head. 'Not a bit. He is a better and kinder man than most Catholic men I have ever met. Besides, I can still continue going to church and he has said he'll come with me any time I ask.' She smiled at her sister. 'I know religion is particularly important to you, Bridget, but please don't worry about it.'

'I won't worry,' Bridget said, looking relieved. 'The fact that Edward is so understanding and not against you going to church will make things easier for you both. I'm sure you will work it out.'

'We will,' Angela reassured her.

They set out and Angela told them all her plans about the wedding as they drove along. How it would be a small affair, the ceremony in a church off Grafton Street followed by a meal for twenty or thirty in the Shelbourne Hotel in Stephen's Green. Nothing big, she said, nothing showy in any way. They planned to do a month-long tour of some of the European cities as their honeymoon.

'Edward is busy planning a driving route as we speak,' Angela laughed.

As they turned into Lucan, the light-heartedness left the car, and they all fell silent.

'I don't think I've ever dreaded anything so much in my life,' Fiona said as they walked up the path. She turned halfway up, to give Angela time to catch up on them.

'It's where to start,' Angela said. 'I don't know how I'm going to find the right words.'

'We'll start with the truth,' Bridget said, 'and then we can't go wrong.'

Catherine was watching a Sunday evening film on television, unaware that her nieces' visit was anything other than an unexpected pleasure.

She brought them into the sitting-room, where she had the small table to the side set with four places for tea, and told them the kettle was just boiled and she would go and fill the teapot.

'If you could leave it for the minute,' Angela said. 'We've just finished tea an hour ago, and we want to talk to you.' She looked at her sisters and then gestured to the table. 'I think it's best if we all sit down.'

'This all looks very serious,' her aunt said, smiling anxiously at them.

'I'm afraid it is,' Fiona said.

'It's not your mother, is it?' Her face looked stricken. 'Has something happened to her?'

'No, she's absolutely fine. Better than she's been in a long time.'

'Well, that's good. I was so worried about her.'

'I'm not sure if she deserves your concern,' Angela said. She looked at Fiona and Bridget, and then she began.

An hour later, they were still sitting around the table, each looking drained from the intensity of the sensitive, difficult conversation.

Aunt Catherine's eyes were ringed with red. 'I'll make us that cup of tea,' she said, getting up from the table. 'And then I think we all need to go down to Tullamore. Down to finish this off with your mother there.'

'No,' Fiona said. 'Forget the tea.' She lifted her bag. 'We need to get this over, let's go now.' She turned to Angela. 'You have clothes and everything there if you need to stay the night, and you can borrow anything from me.'

'That's fine,' Angela said. 'Edward will understand.'

Fiona then looked at her aunt. 'If you don't want to stay in the house afterwards, you can stay in one of the rooms above the bar.'

Her aunt nodded. 'I'll just go and put a few things together in a bag.'

CHAPTER 45

Fiona put her key in the door and they all came inside. They hung up coats and jackets on the stand inside the door, and dropped their bags.

'Mam?' Fiona called.

Her mother was in the kitchen when she heard them, and she came down the hallway. Her astonished gaze took in her three daughters, and then her sister at the back.

'What is it?' she said, the colour draining from her face. 'What's this all about?'

They all sat down in the lounge. The fire was not lit, so Fiona plugged in an electric heater they kept hidden behind the sofa for such occasions.

Catherine started first. 'It's all happened, just as I told you it would,' she said in a flat, strained voice. 'Kenneth told Joseph and Angela when she was over in London. They all know about Joseph being their brother.'

Fiona watched her mother closely – watched as her mouth opened and but heard no words coming out. Then she watched as Nance's hand came up to cover her mouth, watched as she then just sat there in total silence.

'I kept my promise,' Catherine said, 'I didn't tell them. I kept waiting until you were ready, until after the funeral, and then I waited while you were sick. I was still waiting and then they came to me today. And now it's all out. In the open – and my poor son is stuck over in London, trying to work this out on his own.' Her body was shaking now and her voice was rising with all the pent-up anger and emotion of the last few years. 'I warned you that something like this would happen and so did Seán!'

Whether it was the mention of her husband or that something had just occurred to her, Nance suddenly sat up straight in her chair. She looked at the girls. 'Can you leave us in privacy for a few minutes?' When no one moved, she raised her eyebrows and said, 'Please?'

The three girls looked at their aunt.

'I don't know what good it will do us talking on our own now,' Catherine said. 'Because I don't know if I've anything to say to you. I've kept quiet for a long time, afraid Joseph would get hurt. But the damage is done – he's already hurt.'

Bridget sat forward now. 'Mam, there's been secrets for too long. We're all grown up now. You might as well just get it all out in the open, and then we will all know what we are dealing with.'

Nance looked at her youngest daughter, as though unable to believe what she had just heard.

She seemed to be digesting it, then she said, 'Maybe you're right, Bridget.' She looked around the girls with solemn eyes. 'I don't know what you already know, but it doesn't matter. I know what you've found out is enough to change what you think of me. And I don't blame you.' She looked over at Catherine. 'You might as well say all you have to say, because it looks like I have absolutely nothing more to lose. You've got what you wanted. They're never going to think the same of me again.'

'You forget it was you who asked me and Kenneth to take Joseph and bring him up as our own. You forget you were in such a state after you had him that you were nearly suicidal.'

Angela and Fiona looked across the room at each other, not knowing what was coming next.

'I was in a state of shock at the time,' Nance said. 'I had to have a Caesarean and it took ages to heal. I had a bad infection. I was panicking and didn't know where to turn.'

'How did you let yourself get into the situation?' Fiona asked. 'You're always warning us about men, and checking up on us – and very critical about others who make that sort of mistake.'

'I know.' Her mother was shrugging now, holding her hands up. 'I suppose it's because I know how easily it can happen. I was a silly, naïve young woman who was taken advantage of by a married man. He told me he was single.' She looked over at the girls, big tears sliding down her face now. 'I didn't know the first thing about sex, and I didn't even know I was expecting until I was over five months.'

'But you made a choice,' Catherine said. 'You said you couldn't look after Joseph, it was all too much for you, and it was your choice to give him away.'

'I know that. But I can see, looking back, I can see I wasn't well. I didn't know what I was doing . . .' Nance's voice was cracking now. 'Our father had just died the year before – and we'd had no mother since we were teenagers. I had no one but you to turn to.'

'Don't forget you were afraid that the authorities were going to take him away,' Catherine said, her voice lower and more gentle. 'You said you didn't want him to end up with strangers.'

Nance nodded. 'I know . . . I thought it was the best solution for us both and Joseph. Since you and Ken wanted a child – and I was in no position to look after him on my own.'

'I'm not denying that,' Catherine said. 'And we were talking about adoption down the line, after the doctors told me there was little chance of me having one of my own. It would have been terrible for you to have a child taken away when we wanted one. It made sense for us to bring Joseph up.'

'It all started out so well between us in the beginning,' Nance said. 'I was so grateful when you gave him a good home – especially when I wasn't able to do that. And then when I felt better, I loved coming out to visit you and Joseph. It was all I could think of – the first thing on my mind when I woke every single morning. I used to look forward to it all day, but then,' she shrugged, 'it all went wrong.'

'And that's exactly what caused the problem,' Catherine said quietly. 'After suggesting that we could adopt him and promising that he would be brought up as our child, you changed your mind. You said you would just be like a special auntie to him. You got a room the other side of Dublin, so we weren't on top of each other and you were supposed to visit him at the weekends. At the beginning it was all right, you calling out a Saturday or a Sunday, just like an auntie would do, but then you started calling out more regularly until it was nearly every night.'

'I couldn't help it – I just wanted to see him . . .'

'But, Nance, Joseph was over a year old and Ken and I loved him like our very own child. We'd just got used to being our own little family and then next thing you were at our house every spare minute you had. Bringing him presents, taking him for walks, bathing him and putting him to bed – constantly reminding us that he was *your* son.'

There was a silence now and then Nance looked over at her sister. 'But he *was* my son, Catherine. And I couldn't help my feelings about him.'

'We felt the same, we loved Joseph and believed he was ours. But as the time went on, we knew you would never let us be like a normal family.

That's why we took the chance to go to England when Ken was offered the job there. It was to make a new start on our own.'

'But you didn't write for ages. I had no idea where you were. I nearly went out of my mind not seeing him.'

'That's not true,' Catherine said. 'I left you a letter explaining everything. I just didn't give you my address for a while until we were all settled in.'

'It was cruel, you should have given me the address to visit you. It was ages before I heard from you again.'

There was a long silence then Catherine closed her eyes and sighed. 'We were both naïve thinking that it would all work out easily.'

'After you went to England, I fell apart. And it took me months to pick myself up again. If it hadn't been for meeting Seán, I don't know what would have happened.' She looked at the girls. 'Your father was so good, so understanding when I told him.'

'And you built a good life, Nance,' her sister said, her voice quieter now. 'And you went on to marry Seán and have your lovely girls. And then, after you had Fiona and Angela, when Joseph was starting school, Ken and I came back to Dublin. I thought that we could start over again with you and Joseph – that you could see him on a regular basis as you would any normal nephew – but you went the opposite way – you didn't want *anything* to do with him. You completely rejected him.'

'It was too late, I had changed,' Nance said. 'Something had happened to me – I don't know what. I had to block out all the feelings I had for Joseph and all the bad memories or I knew I would go back to the same way. I would start wanting to have him back again, and I knew that would never happen. I could never be his mother again.'

'It was years ago. You need to let go of the past, Nance,' Catherine said. 'We're here now and we need to sort this mess out one way or another. Joseph is coming home next weekend, and we both need to speak to him and hope he can forgive the two of us.'

'But you lost nothing, Catherine – did you? I've lost all those years with him.'

'We should have sorted it out somehow, and I know I wasn't always the easiest. We've both made mistakes. It's done now and what has happened over the years can't be undone.'

Angela suddenly stood up. 'I'm sorry,' she said, her voice low and strained, 'but I think I've heard enough and I don't want to listen to any more arguing. You both need to sort this out – Joseph is twenty-seven and you've been arguing about it since he was born. What a waste of all that time.' She sighed. 'My leg is cramped and I need to walk around a bit.'

'Are you all right?' her mother said, her voice anxious.

Catherine stood up now and moved towards Angela. 'Can I get you anything?'

Nance's eyes widened. 'Leave her – leave her alone!'

Angela and Catherine froze in shock.

Nance stood up and went over to Angela, almost pushing Catherine out of the way. 'She's my daughter, I'll look after her. If she needs anything, I'll get it for her.'

'So, you're looking after Angela now?' Catherine's eyes blazed. 'You didn't look after her when she was up in Dublin lying in a hospital all on her own!'

'How dare you!' Nance's voice was thick and hoarse. 'You weren't content with keeping my son, you tried to take my daughter as well. I couldn't always leave the house and the shop and the girls to go up to Dublin! I was trying my best to keep everything going. And I did go up on a few occasions. One of the times I went up to Dublin, one of the first times when we were allowed to actually hold and touch Angela, you were already there in the ward, Joseph on one side of Angela, you on the other.'

'But I lived in Dublin, Nance. It was easier for me to get to the hospital.'

'I know . . . but it always felt as though you were trying to get between us. You would ring me after the visits to tell me how she was, as if you were her mother and not me.'

Angela turned to her mother. 'Aunt Catherine

couldn't have come between us – we were never close enough for anyone to come between us.' She shook her head. 'You were never like a real mother to me. You were never there when I needed you.'

Nance looked at her with wide eyes, as if she was going to argue back – then her shoulders suddenly sagged. 'I'm so sorry you think that, Angela. I loved you from the bottom of my heart, but I obviously didn't do things right.'

'It would have been right if you tried to show it,' Angela said. 'Even as I got older, it would have made all the difference.'

'Well, like in everything else, I was a failure there too,' Nance said. 'No doubt your Aunt Catherine would have made a better job of it.'

'Don't blame me for everything!' Catherine said, her voice rising. 'I've had enough of being made the scapegoat for all your mistakes!'

'This needs to calm down,' Bridget said. 'It all needs to stop.' She went to Angela and took her arm. 'Come on, we'll leave them to it. Are you coming, Fiona?'

Fiona stood up. 'You're going to have to sort this out between you,' she said, looking at her aunt and her mother. 'You've already wasted twenty-five years of your life arguing, and if you don't stop now, you're going to be at it for the next twenty-five.'

She went out into the hallway and down to the kitchen where her sisters were. She went over and gave them both a hug. 'Come on,' she said to them, 'Get your coats on. We're going into Tullamore for a couple of hours, and we'll let them sort this whole mess out.'

The house was silent when they came in after ten o'clock and the sitting room was in darkness. They stood in the hallway looking at each other and listening for any sounds.

'I think I can hear the radio in the kitchen,' Bridget said, pulling an anxious face.

'But there are no voices,' Angela said. 'I hope they haven't killed each other . . .'

Normally the comment would have been made to bring in a light-hearted element, but nobody laughed.

Fiona moved first. 'We'll go down and see what's happening.'

When she opened the kitchen door, Aunt Catherine looked up from the book she was reading. Fiona noticed she was wearing a dressing-gown.

'You're back,' she said, taking off her reading glasses. She tried to smile, but her pale face seemed unable to form the right shapes.

'Where's Mam?' Fiona asked. She halted. 'Is she okay?' Part of her did not care, but the other part could not help but slip back into concern.

'She's up in bed,' Aunt Catherine said. 'She's worn out. I told her to go to bed, and a half an hour ago I brought her up a cup of tea and a piece of toast.'

'Well, that sounds an improvement on earlier,' Fiona said.

Angela came in and sat down in the armchair opposite her aunt. 'What's happened? Have you sorted anything out?'

'I think so,' her aunt said. She sounded weary. 'Well, let's put it this way, we've talked more in the last few hours than we've talked in the last number of years. I won't say it's been easy, and we've both had to listen to things we didn't want to hear, but I think we've listened to each other.'

'What's going to happen now?' Bridget asked.

'Well, the biggest thing is that your mother is going to come up to Dublin next week when Joseph comes home, and we're going to talk to him together. He needs to hear what happened from both points of view, and we have to listen to how he feels about it all.' She sighed. 'It's not going to be easy or solved overnight, but it's a start. It's better than the way it was.'

Angela woke early the next morning, thinking of Edward, and hoping he wasn't too worried about her. He had been understanding about her suddenly taking off with her sisters, and had assured her on the phone last night to take as much time as she needed to sort things out.

She went downstairs and found her mother sitting alone at the kitchen table. She was dressed in a checked skirt and a short-sleeved black sweater, as if she was going somewhere. Her hair

542

was perfect and, although her face was pinched and drawn, she had put make-up and lipstick on to try to look normal.

'Oh Angela,' she said, 'you're up earlier than I thought. Did you sleep all right?'

'No,' Angela said, 'not really.' She knew her mother would love her to talk as if nothing had happened. As if last night had never happened. To act the way she had done all her life. But the floodgates to all the hidden family truths had now been opened, and she was not going to pretend any more. 'I don't think anybody will have slept well last night – do you?'

There was a silence then her mother looked at her with sorrowful eyes and said, 'This is all such a terrible mess. I'm so sorry, Angela. If I could only turn the clock back, I would do it all differently.'

Angela said nothing. She went over and sat down at the table. Then, after a few moments, she looked across at her mother.

'Why did you leave me all those years up in Dublin? You made no effort to see me. How could you do that to your own child?'

'It wasn't like that . . . it wasn't like that at all.' Nance started twisting her hands together in her lap. 'I was lying awake last night trying to work it all out. The truth is, I suppose I couldn't face seeing you like that, because I blamed myself for what happened to you. I felt your catching polio was all my fault.'

Angela's brow furrowed. 'But why would you think that? It's just a germ anyone can catch.'

'But that's not the way people looked at it,' her mother said. 'Two things always stayed in my mind. The evening you fell off your bike, I was standing chatting to someone outside the house. Afterwards, you were crying and saying your legs hurt, and I thought you were just being silly and making a fuss.' Nance closed her eyes for a moment, shuddering at the memory. 'When you had a sore head later that night, I didn't think it was anything serious and put you to bed as normal. Then, the next morning, you had a high temperature and couldn't move, and your father and I realised you were seriously ill. When we found out – days later – that it was polio, I blamed myself for not believing you. I always thought if I'd got you to the doctor then, we might have been able to save your leg.'

'Did the doctors say that?'

'No, they said it would have happened anyway.' She looked over at Angela. 'It wasn't just the accident with the bike – there was this whole big thing about polio and cleanliness and germs. I always did my best to keep up to date with washing and that sort of thing. But . . . oh, I don't know. I thought that if I'd been more careful you might not have caught it.'

Angela got up now and went over to the kettle.

'There's a fresh pot of tea made not five minutes ago,' her mother said. 'Do you want some brown bread and butter with it?'

'I'll have a slice with marmalade if there's any.'

Her mother moved to sort it for her, so Angela sat back down.

Her mother talked, with her back to her, as she stood at the worktop, sorting the tea and the bread. She talked quickly, to say what she needed to, while they were on their own.

'I want you to believe how sorry I am about not going up to the hospital more often. The main reason was that I was working in the shop while Daddy went to Dublin, and then somebody was needed at home with your sisters.' She paused, catching her breath. 'And, of course, Catherine and Ken were back living in Dublin with Joseph, and well . . . I just found it hard to see him there with her. So it was doubly hard when you were in hospital and they were coming up to visit you.'

Angela did not make any comment. Her mother brought her breakfast over to the table, and set it down in front of her. Angela lifted the mug and started to drink the tea without speaking.

'I know none of it sounds right to you, and you just feel I let you down,' Nance continued, 'and I'm so sorry for that. When I look back, there should have been no excuses, I should have just sorted things out with your Aunt Catherine, and done the right thing by you. But, believe me, Angela, none of this was planned, it just happened that way. I kept hoping you would just be let home and things would go back to the way they were.'

'For the first few years,' Angela said, 'I kept hoping that I would go back home too. But then, I got used to hospital and the nurses and the other children, and gradually it turned around, and I began to dread going home. I felt you were all strangers.'

'Oh, God . . .' Her mother just sat for a few minutes then she looked up at her. 'I always knew there was something not right between us, but as you got older I thought – I hoped – it was a normal change as you were growing up – a difference in our personalities. I thought things were a bit strained between us. I had no idea you felt like a stranger amongst your own family – a stranger to your parents. I thought you were happy enough in Dublin, that you were coping. I convinced myself that you were just a very independent child, stronger than the other girls – stronger than me. How absolutely stupid – ignorant of me!'

'Daddy did his best,' Angela said. 'He tried.'

'I thought I tried too, Angela . . . I really did.' She put her head in her hands. 'I've made more and bigger mistakes than I ever realised. The mess I made of the handling everything with Joseph . . . and now finding out how much I've hurt you over all these years. It's as bad if not worse. You will never, ever know how sorry I am that I've done this to you.' Her voice broke into a sob. 'I've been an absolute failure as a mother. My whole life feels like a failure . . .'

As Angela listened to her mother and saw how utterly wretched she was, the realisation dawned that she was, in fact, telling the truth. Her mother really seemed to have been wholly ignorant of how bad things were between them. Somewhere in the midst of all the anger and the hurt and resentment, a small flicker of compassion started to grow. She even found herself wishing she could say things were not really as bad as they sounded, but she knew that would be rewriting the past and pretending – and she could not do it.

She knew that if there was any hope for their relationship as a mother and daughter that the past had to be examined and acknowledged. And most importantly – things had to be learned from it, in order to move forward with a new understanding. How long that would take Angela did not know.

But there was one thing she instinctively did know – that new ground rules and boundaries for their relationship would have to be set. And they would be set by Angela. Her mother would have to understand that any role she would have in her life from now on would be at Angela's say-so.

Angela lifted her mug and took a sip. She looked over at her mother. 'Are you having another drop of tea?'

Her mother looked confused at the sudden change in conversation. She looked over at the teapot on top of the range. 'Yes,' she said, getting up now. 'I think I will. I meant to have one earlier but I never got around to it.' She took a mug down from the shelf and started to pour. She turned to Angela. 'Will I top yours up?'

'Yes, please,' Angela said, holding the mug out.

They sat in silence for a few minutes while Angela ate her bread and marmalade, and her mother sipped at her tea.

Then, Angela said, 'I know it's not the best time to tell you, but there's no point in leaving it any longer – I have some important news.'

Her mother put her mug down on the table, and clasped her hands, her fingers knitted tightly together. 'What is it?'

'I got engaged after I came back from England, and I'm getting married in July.'

Her mother stared at her as though she hadn't heard it clearly.

'It's Edward – Major Harrington. And before you waste your time saying anything, your opinion won't change my mind. It's all arranged and it's going ahead.'

Her mother slowly nodded her head.

'I know you haven't even met him yet, and I know that he's much older than me, and we haven't known each other long. But it's long enough for us both to know we're doing the right thing. He's not a Catholic, but he has offered to marry me in the church, so it doesn't affect my own religious beliefs.'

Her mother looked over at her. 'And do you truly love him, Angela?'

'I do,' Angela said. 'I actually love him very much.'

'And is he kind to you?'

'He is the kindest, most caring person I have ever met.'

Nance closed her eyes, and when she opened them a few minutes later, tears started streaming down her face. 'Then I'm happy for you, Angela. I'm happy you have found someone who loves you and is so good. After all you've been through, you deserve it.'

Angela looked back at her mother, her eyes filling up now. 'I would have married him whether you liked it or not – but it makes me feel better to know that you are not against it.'

'I know I have no right to ask you anything . . . but can I ask you to think about letting me pay for the wedding breakfast?' She took a deep breath. 'I know you might not even want me there, but that doesn't matter. I would like to pay for it anyway, because it's what your father would have wanted to do, if he was still with us.'

'Edward was going to pay for everything,' Angela told her. 'But I'll talk to him about it, and we will let you know.'

CHAPTER 46

Manchester

February 1970

Bridget came rushing down the hallway, holding up the hem of her long mauve dress so she didn't trip up. 'That's the coach just gone down to the pub.'

Fiona came to the door of her bedroom, wearing an identical bridesmaid dress to her sister. 'We're grand,' she said. 'It's not due to leave for another half an hour, and they won't expect us to be first on.' She stood back to get a better look. 'That colour is beautiful on you. It suits your blonde hair. Are you sure it's okay on me?'

'You look gorgeous.' Bridget started to laugh and then went over and took her hands, and guided her into a waltz around the floor. 'We *both* look gorgeous!'

Fiona went back into her bedroom to check again in front of the full-length mirror on her wardrobe. She studied the flowing mauve short-sleeved dress, with the tiny rosebuds in the same colour sewn in under the bustline. It was flattering, she thought. Angela had a good eye and picked dresses that suited both her and Bridget. She turned now to check her hair. It was caught up at the back, with the same little roses which Maggie O'Connell had pinned into the chignon earlier in the morning. Bridget's hair was too short to wear up, so Angela had got a satin hairband made for her decorated with the same rosebuds.

Fiona was delighted that Angela had eventually agreed to a traditional white wedding. Initially, she had argued, saying she wanted no fuss. She had planned to get married in a dress and matching coat – until Fiona and Bridget sat her down and told her that most brides would kill for her tiny little figure and gorgeous dark looks, and what a waste it was to hide it all away. She hadn't been convinced until Fiona told her that Edward's heart would just burst with pride when he saw her walking up the aisle.

Angela said she would give it some thought.

A week or so later, when Maureen and Jeanette came out to Moorhill House to be introduced to Edward – and to see where their old housemate was now living – both girls emphatically agreed with her sisters.

'Angela,' Maureen said, 'what have we told you about being more daring?'

'Do you not think Edward is a bit too old for the whole white wedding thing?' Angela said.

'So what if he's older than you?' Jeanette said.

'Don't forget there's been many a good tune been played on an oul' fiddle.'

Angela's eyes widened, and then she sighed in mock exasperation. 'I don't believe you've just said that!'

Then all three girls started to giggle.

'No, seriously, Angela,' Maureen said, 'do you not think he deserves to see his gorgeous bride wafting down the aisle the same as a younger man?' She waved her hand about the room. 'Look at what he's giving you, Angela – this mansion of a place. The man is besotted with you – and I think he would just love to see you in a traditional white dress.'

Angela wondered what they would say if she told them about Thornley Manor, but she thought there was no point in emphasising the difference in the lifestyle she had shared with the girls in Leeson Street, and the new one she was going to have with Edward. She would remain friends with them, whatever her circumstances.

Mrs Mooney arrived at the house dressed up in a wine-coloured costume and pink hat to see the bridesmaids' dresses and Nance's outfit.

'Beautiful, beautiful altogether,' she told the girls, as they all congregated in the sitting-room. She studied the little rosebuds on the dresses. 'They must have been the devil to sew on. I'd say it took as long to hand-stitch them on as it did to make the rest of the dress.'

Nance's blue satin coat and matching dress with the pillbox hat drew the most praise. 'No doubt about it,' the housekeeper said, 'you're the double of Jacqueline Kennedy.'

Nance smiled and thanked her, but pointed out that Jackie Kennedy was a good ten years younger than her.

Fiona smiled. 'I hate to remind you both, but she's been Jackie Onassis for a good while now.'

'Don't talk to me about it.' Mary Ellen gave a great sigh. 'Imagine marrying that oul' Greek fella after being married to such a fine-looking man as President Kennedy. Sure, he must be more than double her age.'

Bridget's eyebrows shot up, and she tried not to laugh. 'Mary Ellen, you better not mention age at the wedding – don't forget that Edward is a good bit older than Angela.'

The housekeeper looked at her. 'That's different altogether. And as I said to Angela myself, better to be an oul' man's darling than a young man's slave.'

They all started to laugh.

'Where do you get the sayings?' Nance smiled at her.

'It's a true one – Angela will be well looked after. When I met them last week, you could see he worships the ground she walks on.' She looked thoughtful for a few moments. 'You would wonder all the same about Jackie Kennedy, when she could have had the pick of all the men in America and she goes for oul' Onassis.' She shrugged. 'And it can't be about the money, because they say she had plenty of her own.'

'Well, maybe he's a nice man,' Bridget said, shrugging. 'Maybe they just get on well together.'

'Maybe,' Mrs Mooney said, 'but it would make you wonder all the same.'

The doorbell went and Nance went down the hallway, past the table where the bridesmaids' bouquets were standing in a basket.

When she opened the door, Michael O'Sullivan was there on the step.

'Good morning,' he said, giving her a small salute.

'Good morning. Come in, Michael,' she said. 'We're all more or less ready.' She paused before closing the door. 'Thank God it's a lovely morning. Let's hope it keeps dry.'

'You're looking very lovely,' he said.

Nance touched the back of her hat and then her hair, checking everything was in place. 'Thank you,' she said. 'This will be your first Irish wedding, won't it?'

He confirmed this with a nod

'It's not a typical one though, since Angela wanted it small, but it will be nice. The Shelbourne Hotel is lovely.'

'I'm sure it will be – it's getting busy down at the bar,' he told her. 'A number of people are already on the coach, and apparently a few of your neighbours have arrived to view the bridesmaids' dresses.'

'That's the custom around here,' Nance said. 'They'll be disappointed not to see Angela, but she doesn't like the limelight.' She shrugged and smiled. 'It's her big day, and she's happy going from Dublin, so that's all that matters.'

'So, where are these lovely bridesmaids?' Michael said, clapping his hands together.

She led him into the sitting room and he went around Bridget and Mrs Mooney and Fiona, kissing their cheeks and saying how beautiful everybody looked.

'Fiona tells me that the cottage is coming on great,' Nance said, smiling across at her daughter.

'Yes,' he said, 'it's almost finished now. I just have to buy some basic furniture and get someone to do some work on the garden, and then it should all be ready for my mom arriving in a few weeks.'

'I'm going down to Galway next week to help him pick some things out,' Fiona said. 'I can't wait to see it all finished.'

Bridget went over to look out of the window. 'Maggie O'Connell has just come out, and looks as though she's heading down for the coach. She has the loveliest pale green dress and jacket on.'

'Isn't it gas about her and Patrick?' Mrs Mooney said. 'They're a great match, aren't they?'

'They are,' Nance said. 'I think she's bringing him out of his shell a bit.'

'And I think you officially making him the bar manager has given him more confidence.'

'I should have thought of it earlier, but I suppose I wasn't thinking of anything straight.'

She looked at the clock now. 'We better go, the coach leaves in ten minutes.'

The sky was still blue when the coach pulled up in Grafton Street in Dublin. The group of around forty guests – a mixture of neighbours, family and friends – walked the short distance to St Teresa's Church in Clarendon Street.

Fiona took Michael's arm as they walked along, leaving the other hand free to carry her bouquet.

'I am so glad the timing worked out so you could come over for the wedding,' Fiona told him.

He squeezed her arm. 'And so am I.'

She indicated her mother who was in front with Bridget. 'I can't believe the change in Mam since you were last here. She's a different woman altogether. If you had met her before and then saw her now, you would think it was a totally different person. If it hadn't been for Angela catching her that night, and getting her into hospital, she might not be here today.'

'It's surprising what drugs can do to people,' he said quietly. 'Prescribed or illegal.' He squeezed her arm. 'It's all worked out in your mom's case. Have you said anything to her yet about your plans to come out to New York at the end of the year?'

Fiona shook her head. 'I haven't said anything definite to her. I thought I would let the wedding come and go and then I'll bring it up. She's getting stronger every day, and with Bridget helping in the shop things are much easier all round.'

Over the weeks since finishing school, Bridget had given her vocation a great deal of thought. She had prayed about it and spent time talking to both the local priests. Father Fahy had been particularly helpful, and he had asked her to be involved with the organisation of retreats in the parish and to help set up a new prayer group in the evenings. He had also told Bridget and her mother, in the strictest confidence, that he had heard through the religious grapevine that one of the girls involved in the school incident had been in some kind of relationship with a married man. Apparently, she had enlisted some of the other girls and a farm-worker to send letters to him and to cover up for her. There had also been incidents when she was supposed to be collected by a relative to attend the dentist, when it was actually the married man who had collected her outside the school.

Bridget's throat had run dry as she took in the information. It had been more serious and more sordid than she had imagined. She had somehow thought Veronica had been involved with the farm-hand or one of his friends. An older, married man sounded very frightening to her.

'What happened to her and the man after all this came out?' Nance had asked.

Father Fahy had held his hands up. 'I heard something about her being sent to live with an aunt in England for the coming months. That's all I know.'

Nance had shaken her head. 'The poor girl. Her life will never be the same again . . .'

When the shock of being dismissed from school had started to fade, Bridget did a lot of thinking and a lot of praying. She had come to the conclusion that her desire to be a nun was still as strong as ever and, after checking out various orders, had decided to apply to join the Benedictine Nuns in Kylemore Abbey as a postulant nun. She would do her best to explain the situation that had happened in her old convent, and hope they would understand she had done nothing wrong. If it didn't work out, she would find somewhere else. But whatever happened, she wouldn't give up.

When they arrived at the door of the church, the majority of the guests from the coach went straight inside to take their seats. There were groups of people already seated, mainly from Dublin – friends of Angela from work and from the house in Leeson Street, and there was a girl and a man in wheelchairs, friends from her time in hospital. The staff from Moorhill House, Mrs Girvin and Eileen and Jim, and other friends and a few army colleagues of Edward's were also inside waiting.

Aunt Catherine, looking elegant in a peach outfit, was sitting in a pew on her own near the front. Mrs Mooney went down the aisle with Patrick and

Maggie. She guided them towards Catherine's pew, to ensure she was in a prime position to view the service. After a while, Michael left Fiona and went inside to join them.

Nance stood at the back, waiting with Fiona and Bridget. 'Are you okay?' she asked the girls. 'You're not too nervous about walking up the aisle?' She looked from one to the other. 'Just take it slow and easy, and remind Angela to do the same.'

'Somehow,' Fiona said, 'I don't think Angela needs any advice from us. She has organised every-thing down to the last "t".'

'Of course, of course,' her mother said. 'I was only saying.'

Edward arrived at church with his best man, Jeremy – both dressed in formal morning suits and wearing white roses in their lapels. Edward, Fiona thought, was slightly jittery and was talking a little louder and quicker than normal, as Angela had said he would be. The rakish-looking Jeremy, she noticed, was the opposite. He had kissed both her hand and Bridget's and told them they were visions of beauty, and had been equally effusive when introduced to their mother, insisting that she looked like their sister.

Fiona checked her watch then looked at her future brother-in-law. 'Angela will be here any minute, so I think it might be a good idea if you are inside and waiting for her.'

Edward straightened up like a soldier who was

heading for the frontline, and then he and Jeremy went down the aisle together.

A short while later the iron church gate creaked and all three turned to look as Joseph came into the small yard, his longish hair neatly trimmed for the occasion, with Angela on his arm.

The sight of Angela in her classic-style white lace dress and veil had Nance searching for her hanky. Fiona watched as her mother went to greet her son and daughter at the door. She couldn't hear what she said to them, but both Joseph and Angela nodded at her and smiled. Then, Nance whispered 'Good luck' to the girls again, and went off with a quiet dignity, down the carpeted aisle to join her sister at the front of the church.

Fiona was grateful for the way events had worked out over the last number of weeks. Things had settled back down at home with her mother working full time in the shop and helping in the bar a few evenings during the week. With Bridget in the shop too, Fiona had more time for herself, and was free to travel up and down to Clifden now that Michael had returned to finish off the cottage. Somewhere, she had found the courage to tell Mam that she was staying a few nights in Galway with him while they were choosing furniture. Her mother had sighed and said it was her own decision, but to be very careful.

'I will,' Fiona had said, 'but I need to be sure.

I need to spend as much time with him to know if the relationship is going to work out in the long-term.'

So far, she had no doubts. Michael O'Sullivan was everything she had looked for in a man – attractive, interesting and romantic – but more importantly, like Edward, he was kind and considerate. His blue airmail letters had come regularly and with each one she felt she was getting to know and understand him better. It was not the same as seeing him every day, but it was the best they could do. But even if they both were living in Ireland, Fiona would have felt she needed to take things slowly.

After hearing of Angela's sudden marriage plans, Michael had recently written to say that at some point in the future they might want to formalise their own relationship and look at plans for the future. She had been thrilled when she read it, and it confirmed to her that he had taken the physical closeness in their relationship as the same serious commitment that she had.

But, it had occurred to her recently that while she hoped they would work out a future together in Ireland or America, there was a part of her still wanted to experience the adventure she had originally planned. The same adventure she had dreamed of before her father died.

After giving it careful thought, she had written to Michael about it, explaining as best she could, and suggesting that she take the nanny position with the Davis family in Park Avenue for a year. Since he was based a lot of the time in New York, it would mean they would see each other regularly, and they could explore all the places she had planned to see in New York together. They could even go to the dances with Elizabeth and her boyfriend.

Michael had sent a letter back saying anything that started the process of them being closer together was great by him, and he would introduce her to Boston and his family as well. His mother she would meet for the first time in a few weeks when she came to stay in the renovated cottage in Clifden.

The only problem was telling her mother she was going. But she would find a way to reassure her that she wasn't disappearing forever, and that she would travel home as often as she could afford.

If she was accepted into the convent as a postulant, Bridget would still come back home on occasions, and Mam was busier now with her drama and the golf lessons she had recently started. And, she was travelling up to Dublin more often, and had recently stayed a weekend with her sister. Aunt Catherine was also spending time down in Tullamore, and had offered to help in the shop any time they were short of staff.

The situation with Joseph had been quietly dealt with and, after a long talk, it had been agreed that Catherine would continue to be called his mother, and Nance would still be his aunt. In his eyes, he said, nothing had really changed apart from the fact he now had three lovely sisters instead of three lovely cousins.

Mam had broached the subject of him coming to work in the bar in Tullamore, but he said he was happy enough in London. Maybe, in the future, he might come back, but for the time being he wanted to get more experience in the hotel, and continue working with his friend on their music. They had sent demo tapes off to a record label, and things were looking hopeful for a contract. That sort of opportunity, he explained, was much harder to come by in a smaller city like Dublin.

Fiona smiled now as Joseph went first towards Bridget, and then came to her to give her a hug and a kiss. He then turned back to Angela, to make a whispered, inane joke about it being her last chance to back out and make a quick getaway. They all laughed and then, as the taped bridal music started to play *Pachelbel's Canon*, everything suddenly became serious and they moved quickly to get into position for walking down the aisle, Angela on Joseph's arm, with her two bridesmaids in attendance close behind.

As they moved through the doors, Fiona noticed that Angela did not seem in the slightest bit nervous.

She had already told Fiona that she and Edward planned to start a family immediately – hopefully on their European tour honeymoon. With Edward's age, she explained, they had no time to waste. Fiona could already imagine Edward as a father, with his open enthusiasm about the most trivial of things. Angela knew – with great certainty – exactly what she was doing, and what she hoped for the future.

As they took the first steps in the short journey down the aisle – the journey which would lead to Angela becoming Mrs Edward Harrington – Fiona wished she had the same certainty about her own life. Then, as she got closer to the crowd who were waiting with great anticipation, her eyes flickered along the rows of people and her gaze came to settle on the back of Michael's head.

Seeing him sitting there, beside Patrick and Mrs Mooney and Maggie, made him look more familiar and closer to her than ever. And she realised she would probably never find anyone else who she would feel this way about, and be so attracted to. He caught her eye as she passed by the pew and he winked at her and she had to stop herself from smiling.

As the altar and the waiting Edward loomed into view, a quiet assurance seemed to settle over her. Whatever they decided – however they worked things out – Fiona somehow knew that all would be well.